BURNING DOWN THE HOUSE

BURNING DOWN THE HOUSE

A NICK HOFFMAN NOVEL

Lev Raphael

Walker & Company ✸ *New York*

First published in the United States of America in 2001 by
Walker Publishing Company, Inc.

Published simultaneously in Canada by Fitzhenry and Whiteside,
Markham, Ontario L3R 4T8

Library of Congress Cataloging-in-Publication Data

Raphael, Lev.
  Burning down the house : a Nick Hoffman novel/Lev Raphael.
    p. cm.
  ISBN 0-8027-3365-4 (alk. paper)
    1. Hoffman, Nick (Fictitious character)--Fiction. 2. College teachers--
Fiction. 3. Michigan--Fiction. I. Title.

PS   3568.A5988 B8 2001
813'.54--dc21

                                                            2001026250

Series design by M. J. DiMassi

Printed in the United States of America

2   4   6   8   10   9   7   5   3   1

for my posse

Special thanks to Dr. Patti Nakfoor, FACEP, for her clear explanations of emergency medical treatment and procedure; Officer Scott Stratton of the Meridian Township Police Department for details about police procedure at accident scenes; Dan Jinks of Dreamworks for information about screenplay deals; Martha Lawrence for intro gun talk that headed me in the right direction; and, of course, G. K. Consulting, Inc., whose indefatigable staff worked overtime—and under unexpected pressure—in assisting me with this book, more than earning its bonuses and vacations.

Only part of us is sane: only part of us loves pleasure and the longer day of happiness, wants to live to our nineties and die in peace, in a house we built, that shall shelter those who come after us. The other half of us is nearly mad. It prefers the disagreeable to the agreeable, loves pain and its darker night despair, and wants to die in a catastrophe that will set back life to its beginning and leave nothing of our house save its blackened foundations.

—REBECCA WEST, *BLACK LAMB AND GREY FALCON*

1

Y OU bought a *gun?*"

My department at the State University of Michigan at Michiganapolis was not a place where they made mountains out of molehills—they made volcanoes, and you never knew when the next eruption was due.

But despite that combustibility, I was shocked by Juno Dromgoole's announcement when she had me over for dinner on a mild early December night. And so I asked her again, twice.

"You bought a gun? You really bought a gun?"

Juno nodded and set down her wineglass. "Of course I did. Teaching here is too dangerous. How else can I protect myself?"

Having shared this news, Juno calmly took another sip of Kenwood zinfandel.

While I may have been shocked, I wasn't going to stop eating when the food was so good. I finished the last of an outrageous salad of watercress, Belgian endive, toasted walnuts, Gorgonzola, and roasted pears in port with a touch of balsamic vinegar. The vinaigrette was first-press olive oil, Dijon mustard, and red wine.

"That was terrific," I said, for the third or possibly fourth time. Juno shrugged as if it were merely Lean Cuisine. Finished, I couldn't help but return to her surprising confession. "Juno, don't you think getting a gun is—"

"What?" she snapped. "Extreme? No, it isn't. Not when they mow down professors left and right here."

Of course she was exaggerating, but even though the State University of Michigan at Michiganapolis wasn't quite Bosnia or even the Alamo, Juno definitely had a point. The faculty at SUM had suffered heavier-than-usual attrition in the past few years through murder, and there really was no way of knowing who was going to become the next dead academic.

How bad was it? Well, if SUM were the Dow Jones index, brokers would be talking about a "market correction."

"Why not take a self-defense class?"

"I've done those, I train at the gym, I swim, I'm in perfect shape, and I'm a mean bitch, but I'm no match for a killer."

That silenced me, especially since I had been attacked here at SUM myself a few years before, and might have been killed. Flashing on the incident made me suddenly feel ashamed that I had taken no steps in response to being endangered, while Juno had. Was I jealous, I wondered, of Juno's strength and determination?

With the Kenwood done, we moved on to a Montbazillac as luscious as the curves of Juno's thighs and breasts, which I was trying not to stare at while she cleared the table. I wasn't entirely successful, but then I don't think anyone—straight, gay, or Republican—could avoid staring at Juno. She was just too magnetic.

Boisterous and sexy, fortyish Juno combined Tina Turner's hair, legs, and attitude with Frank Sinatra's temper and foul mouth. A powerful swimmer, she was muscular and ripe, with the kind of coolly brutal voluptuousness you find in some of the nudes Tamara de Lempicka painted in the 1920s and 1930s.

Her body was molded that night by black leggings and a hip-length turtleneck cinched by a 1950s-style superwide leopard-print belt. In that phrase waiters like, her outfit was "finished with" Audrey Hepburn flats. She looked good enough to eat, and there would be plenty of leftovers. But would she leave me with heartburn? That was the question.

I wondered if she really noticed my attention and perhaps liked posing for it, or did she simply, beautifully take it for granted that all men, even those who lived with other men, admired her or at least took a second look?

"Stay where you are," she insisted when I offered to help. "You're my guest." Juno reset the kitchen table and continued cleaning up, moving around the kitchen with exaggerated nonchalance—James Bond rather than James Beard—as if the meal were potentially dangerous. I suppose it was, calorically, though in all my travels to France with my partner Stefan, even in the Dordogne (home of foie gras), I'd never seen the kind of fat people you ran into all the time in Michiganapolis, especially if you shopped for food late at night. I guess in France, overweight citizens are under a Ministry of Tourism curfew so as not to alarm visitors.

Like the rest of Juno's small house, the kitchen was a perfect backdrop for her extravagance of manner and style. Juno's home actually reminded me of Carmen Sherwood's boudoir in *The Big Sleep*—a seductively chilly layering of ivory on white on chrome. The living room, in fact, was "self-striped": glossy ivory stripes over the same tone in flat paint. When I saw it, I couldn't help thinking of one of those puzzling, almost blank canvases at MoMA I'd assumed as a kid growing up in New York had to be a joke. Juno herself was an updated version of a Raymond Chandler bombshell, the kind of woman who could "make a bishop kick a hole in a stained glass window."

I suppose there must have been some lingering skepticism as well as surprise on my face, because when she sat back opposite me, she asked a bit truculently, "Shall I show you my Glock?"

Despite my curiosity, I demurred. "Michigan's my home," I said, thinking briefly of our getaway cottage up north, "but I was born in New York, remember? I'm not really comfortable with handguns—or the idea of hunting for anything more than a parking space." As I said it, I had the uneasy sensation of being a character in a Woody Allen film.

"But Nick, really, you can't imagine," Juno said, with lambent eyes, "how powerful it would make you feel just to touch it."

Though I remembered John Lennon singing about happiness being a warm gun, I was pretty sure I didn't want Juno handling even an unloaded firearm around me (it would be unloaded, wouldn't it?). After all, pistol-whipping didn't involve bullets, and Juno was the kind of woman who would be combustible even in a coma. I'd seen her enraged before, and it was like a sequence from *Twister*.

Anyway, it wasn't her gun I wanted to touch.

The phone rang, and Juno checked her watch and cursed. "Same time every time," she said, moving to the counter. She picked up the receiver, listened, and slammed the phone down.

"What's going on?"

"Crank calls. Somebody muffled, a man, I think, saying, 'Get out!' "

"Get out of what?"

Juno shrugged.

"Can the police trace the calls?"

"They have. It's no help. Public phones—all in town."

"So that's why you bought a gun," I said.

"That—and everything else."

We sat there in silence for a while, I suppose both contemplating the bizarreness of being a professor and fearing for your life on a college campus.

"Are you being stalked?"

"Not exactly. Not yet."

"Wow."

Having been the recipient of crank phone calls and other harassment, I felt more than empathy. I dreaded what might be in store for Juno. Before I could ask who she thought might be angry at her, she said, "Excuse me," and slipped from the room. I wondered if she were going to check on her gun—a natural enough response to a threat. Who could be hassling her on the phone? An ex-lover? A rival of some kind? Juno was so over-the-top, I could imagine her igniting cinematic-size passions like Sophia Loren or Gina Lollobrigida.

I didn't mind her being gone for a moment; I welcomed the interruption. Being this close to Juno for so long was as overwhelming as I had guessed it might be, but I hadn't refused her invitation to dinner. I was torn: attracted to her, and puzzled.

My trouble about Juno had begun a few months earlier when she and I wound up swimming together near campus at Michiganapolis's premiere health club—daringly called The Club—and she had seemed to flirt with me in the pool when we stopped to stand and talk at the shallow end. Juno had looked incredibly sexy squeezed into a gold mesh one-piece with matching swim cap, her deep cleavage glowing with promise in the shattered light of the pool.

Surveying her physical bounty, I had responded with my own surprising mutiny, feeling a hot burst of excited shame as if I were a teenager again, trembling and tumescent. Whether she had inflamed me deliberately or not by teasing, I was exhilarated and scared by being attracted to a woman for the first time in my life since I'd come out to my cousin Sharon at fifteen. It had never really happened before, and I was shocked by the intensity, the suddenness, and my sense of vulnerability and exposure there in the pool.

Sharon, my ultimate confidante, had met Juno on a visit from New York earlier that fall, and when I told her what happened, she said she thought Juno would be a bit daunting for a first-timer. "Work your way up to Juno," she had joked. But she'd also quizzed me seriously more than once. "Are you *sure* you want to have sex with her? It's not just idle curiosity? Are you sure this isn't happening because I've been sick?"

I couldn't at that point absolutely rule out Sharon's upcoming surgery for an acoustic neuroma being at the root of my confusion, but I told her I didn't think it was.

"Well, sweetie," she'd said after a pause, "you don't have to do anything about Juno, really. Maybe you can even enjoy it a little. You know, accept that your sexuality is fluid right now?"

"Fluid? It's always been solid as a rock." I had suddenly felt possessed by the Spirit of Bad Puns. And "fluid sexuality" was as dismal a prospect as overturning the cliché of straight men suddenly realizing they were gay in midlife. I did not want to be a trendsetter. I was a bibliographer, for God's sake. My job was to be humble and helpful, not create scandal.

But whatever I felt for Juno and whatever it meant, there was the whole question of whether Juno was really flirting with me, or just playing some strange private game. Because what had passed between us was more than idle dishing—at least I thought so. Unless I was totally off base.

"Yes," Juno said, striding back into the kitchen, "I have a gun, and I know how to use it. I didn't come all the way from Winnipeg to become a fucking American crime statistic. You should see me at the firing range. I'm a natural. Nobody's taking *me* out!" Juno rattled on about her shooting skills.

I tried to shake the image of her in the pool and stay with the conversation. It wasn't easy. I had not exactly been alone with her before—the pool didn't count—and up close, she was even more remarkable, her heart-shaped face incredibly alluring.

"Maybe you're on the right track," I said. "But it's probably not enough for professors to start carrying weapons. What we really need at SUM is a squadron of armed guards. To protect the faculty."

"Bad idea. It would never work, because anybody could turn them," she said, as if Cold War spies were being discussed. She joined me at the table and took up her wineglass.

"Well, you know how Michigan's full of militia and conspiracy theory types? People are saying the murders over the last few years are part of some insane plan."

Juno frowned. "A plan?"

"Yes—the administration's trying to speed up what's happening at universities across the country: replacing tenured faculty with lower-paid temporaries. You know, kill some professors, terrorize the rest into early retirement."

"That *is* insane. The idea that it's real, I mean."

I nodded. "But at least nobody's saying the dead faculty are being kept alive in crypts under the Administration Building—with Amelia Earhart and Bobby Kennedy. Personally, I don't think SUM's upper administrators are organized and efficient enough to mount a terror campaign against the faculty. Even sub rosa. And what's the point? They don't need to kill anyone off. They're fully capable of tormenting and alienating us without any stratagems. It's second nature. The lunacy here is atmospheric and institutional, not agenda-driven."

"True enough."

"But even if *we* don't believe it, Juno, lots of people do. They're insisting there has to be some kind of design to the killings. Even my mailman is obsessed. He's turned into one of those crusty peasants in horror movies, you know, the kind who limps along and makes all these dark observations just before the monster bursts loose."

She grinned, intrigued. "What does he say?"

"Oh, his favorite dire warning is, 'There's bad blood over there.' "

Juno laughed. "I think septicemia would be the clinical term."

She was right.

"I don't know why people mock academia and say it's an ivory tower, that it's not like the real world. It's as real as any other closed environment, isn't it? Boiling over with jealousy, spite, cruelty, coldness, and hypocrisy. Passions here can become as crazed as any Mediterranean vendetta. And that's over minor issues—so it's no wonder that major contention can lead to murder."

"Given all that," she said, "I don't see why you haven't bought yourself a gun and learned how to shoot it. With your track record, I'm sure you'll have plenty of cause to use one." She rose and started laying out the ingredients for our main course: foie gras seared in butter.

I had unfortunately been involved in each of the recent murders, all of which had some connection to our Department of English, American Studies, and Rhetoric (EAR). This made me popular with thrill-seeking students who expected my composition classes to turn into crime scenes, and unpopular with administrators, who blamed me for the university's bad PR. If there's anything a university hates more than a losing season or its football players getting involved in a gambling or date rape scandal, it's murder.

While nobody was calling me the Perilous Professor or saying I had a doctorate in death, I suspected that wasn't far off, along with a cheesy Lifetime channel movie version of my story—*SUM: State University of Murder*—and a position on the advisory board of the Jack Kevorkian Institute.

"Honestly, Nick, I really am surprised that you of all people don't have a gun," Juno observed, turning from the sink, French-manicured hands on her hips as if she were about to berate me. "After all the trouble you've gotten into over the last few years."

"A gun wouldn't have helped me stay out of trouble."

"How do you know?"

"Well, maybe." I sighed. "But a gun sure won't get me tenure." Perhaps nothing could now, despite my good student evaluations and two forthcoming books that I had edited. Not only was I underpublished and disliked by many of my colleagues and by the administration, but my tenure committee was in need of major re-constitution, thanks to a campus murder just at the beginning of the semester. If I wasn't exactly doomed or even suffering under an intermediate-level curse, too much had gone wrong over the past few years for it all to work out in my favor. I sometimes felt so cynical about the academic environment that I wondered if I would want tenure after I got it, anyway. Wasn't that the dilemma in *Remembrance of Things Past*? When Marcel finally gets to kiss Albertine, it's a letdown.

Juno was one of the few women I knew who could moue without looking childish, and she did a great job of it just then in response to my gloom. "Nick, your chances of tenure can only be enhanced if they know you're armed and dangerous. And think how good it would make you feel—how satisfied and complete!"

I'd heard lots of self-help advice in my time—but this had to be the most original: Get thee to a rifle range!

"Are you going to tell everyone at EAR you have a Glock?"

She frowned. "Why not? It's legal, and what's the point if people *don't* know? How would that be a deterrent? How would that make me safer?"

Did guns make people safer?

"Nick, really, think about getting a gun. It'll change your life."

That wasn't the best argument for anything at the moment. I wasn't looking for change. I wanted stability. Fat chance. Here I was, lusting after a woman who might be interested in lusting back, after I'd been living with a man I loved for fifteen years. It did not make sense.

What was going on with me? Was it Juno being so unlike the rest of the geeks, freaks, and ghouls who were my colleagues? Though Juno was a professor of Canadian literature, there wasn't much that was professorial about her, aside from her dedication to teaching. Moving in a perpetual nimbus of chic perfume, she was devoted to leopard-print clothes and accessories (before they became popular), and completely unafraid of expressing her opinion. All of that was profoundly anomalous in our generally craven EAR department, where the average look was a sort of tag-sale cross between incoherent and bland.

Trying to change the subject from her gun, I said, "I've never had foie gras as a main course." I watched her at the counter.

"I thought you'd appreciate something more refined than spaghetti and meatballs. Though I guess it would depend on the balls, wouldn't it?"

"Doesn't it always?"

She grinned. "Some balls depend, some don't, or not much, anyway."

I confess it took me a few seconds to get the pun on "depend."

Until that moment, our talk hadn't been remotely personal or risqué, just about classes and general end-of-semester complaining (and the gun, of course).

Don't get me wrong, I love teaching and always have. Especially since I teach composition, I can almost always see tremendous, heartening changes in my students over the course of a semester—that is, if they come to class and do the work. It's one of the most important courses taught at the university, because in other classes, professors don't pay enough attention to how students write.

Devotion aside, however, you can't just teach your classes and keep your head down; no matter how you try to avoid it, the quicksand of academic politics and administrative idiocy is always ready to suck you under. Shop talk quickly turns to war stories in that kind of environment.

Like me, Juno was dedicated to helping her students, which was refreshing. Too many of our EAR colleagues acted as if office hours were an imposition and simple politeness to their students a crime. And after five years at SUM, it was clear to me that the university was a small-potatoes version of Russia's current kleptocracy; it existed solely to enrich a small group of people: upper-level administrators, the president, and the sports staff. SUM's athletic director, for example, not only earned $750,000 a year, but the university had bought him a Lexus and a BMW, a thirty-foot boat, and a vacation home on Beaver Island. And that's just the largesse that had been made public. SUM may also have been supplying him with Rogaine, Viagra, and any other drugs he craved.

But all those musings burned off like morning fog as I watched Juno at the stove, and I drifted back to the vision of her in the pool, shocked and excited to imagine myself standing up, slipping behind her to stroke her breasts and kiss the back of her neck. I pictured slipping a hand down from behind to spread her legs, rubbing against . . .

I crossed my own legs, trying to act cool. I had never fixated on a woman like this before, and each time the vision hit me, I shook my head to clear it, but unsuccessfully. The disorienting sensation of fantasizing about her was almost like entering the love scenes I'd been seeing my whole life on film and reading about in books. Could that be what drew me to her? Some kind of crazed midlife longing to be like the majority? Great! Next I'd be seeking baptism and reading Stephen King.

King made me think of Juno's Glock again. Now that she'd mentioned it, would I ever be able to think of anything else? Maybe I should accept her offer to see it, I thought. I'd never been close to a gun before. And wouldn't it help me teach my mystery class next semester to be at least mildly familiar with a Glock?

I asked, "Who else in our department do you think has a gun?"

Juno shrugged, unconcerned.

"Because maybe you're not the only one. The next department meeting could turn into a shoot-out. I suppose if I hit the floor in time, there wouldn't be much of a downside."

Juno grinned, and I wondered if she saw herself as Sigourney Weaver laying waste to a host of aliens. No, too messy. Perhaps it would be Queen Elizabeth I calmly sending opponents to the block.

I asked, "Why did you choose a Glock?"

Juno rejoined me at the table, suggesting we wait a bit before she actually started the foie gras, and I refilled her wineglass.

"The Sig Sauer has the smoothest action around, but I wanted the Glock nine-millimeter because of its stopping power, and because it's light. You can throw it against the wall, and it won't go off. You can dunk it in a bucket of water, and it still fires. Sixteen gorgeous rounds without reloading. "

"You can take it swimming?"

"Funny man. Have you ever heard of either of those? The Glock and the Sig Sauer?"

"Of course. Both of them tend to be the big guns in mystery novels these days." And before I could apologize for "big guns," Juno said, "God—speaking of big guns—I had a lover from Vancouver, and God, Nick, he was just too damned big. Like what they say about that Matt Damon."

"They do?" I hadn't heard that rumor, or noticed. But then I did fall asleep halfway through *Good Will Hunting*.

"Or maybe it's Ben Affleck. One of those boys. But anyway, Nick, it was awful. Take a photograph of it, fine. Or a plaster cast and use it as a towel rack. But fuck him? Please! I'd rather run a marathon. Or compare jewelry with some nitwit doctor's wife at a day spa. Or read one of those dead-on-arrival Robert Ludlum books."

Embarrassed, intrigued, I asked the obvious question: "How big?"

Juno rolled her kohl-rimmed eyes, and her voice deepened as if she were a husky-voiced cabaret singer declaiming about *chagrin d'amour* through a pall of disillusionment and cigarette smoke. "A freak of nature," she summed up. "But even when they're not quite *that* big, it's just dreadful."

"Why?" I would have guessed that Juno was a size queen, so her complaint surprised me.

Juno carefully considered my question. "Because it's like having a ménage à trois when you don't expect or want to: there's you, him, and *it*. Those men are always so damned pleased with themselves for being inhumanly well hung, as if it's an achievement, a talent, a skill. Hel-lo? How about luck? And they either show off or give it a name or expect you to ooh and aah. Or they do the opposite, which is rather slimy. They elaborately pretend as if they think it's nothing special when they're just dying for you to sink to your knees in awe."

I drank more wine, turned on by hearing her talk about sex, but unsure what to say. Was this all a kind of come-on, or was she just enjoying her own outrageousness? I could tell with no problem when a man was flirting with me, but I felt rudderless with Juno, adrift.

"Nick, I was at the mall last week and I ran into the boy who used to cut my hair. Big, beefy, a soccer player type. With that edge of stupidity in the eyes that makes you know he can go all night, not that it was ever an issue, of course. We had coffee, I asked him what he was up to. He told me he was married, was studying law now, and that he and his wife were looking for 'the third person'—as he put it."

"He wasn't talking about grammar," I said, feeling that I'd been hijacked into an episode of *Sex and the City*.

"Not hardly. I told him I wasn't interested, and I suppose to win me over he said just the wrong thing. He told me he had ten inches."

"So you said—?"

"I said, 'Get yourself some cheerleaders! I'm not dancing around any maypole.' "

I set my wine down, laughing.

She drained her wine and said, "Back in a flash," heading to the bathroom, I assumed. Vivaldi was playing softly out in the living room, where Juno stopped this time to coo at Turandot, her sleepy West Highland white terrier. Turandot had been to the vet for a shot that morning, Juno explained when I'd arrived, and was quite logy. The cute Westie puppy had barely acknowledged me when I leaned down to where she lolled on a tiny puppy-size damask leopard-print sofa next to the real sofa.

I'd wanted to pick her up and pet her, but Juno said another time would be better—"The *principessa divina* will be happy to grant you an audience when she's herself again." I was not an opera buff, so Juno had to explain the reference to Puccini's opera *Turandot*. Once she did, I figured, what else would Juno call her dog? It was dramatic and ironic at one and the same time—a little white puppy with a regal name. Watching her with the dog, I saw a flash of something kinder, gentler—but I wasn't sure if it was an act or not.

I sipped some more Montbazillac. Ever since meeting Juno last year when she was a visiting professor, before she got a permanent position, I had been admiring her iconoclasm, her brio, her freedom to say whatever she wanted to without apparent consequences, and certainly without fear. Perhaps that was because I was untenured in a department where I'd actually been threatened for having made a joke. People were so sensitive and hostile in EAR you could think you were in Serbia or Austria-Hungary on the brink of World War I.

But it wasn't just the pettiness of academic life that had people baring their fangs, it was a deep split in the department that had originally been called English and American Studies. Over a decade ago, in a paroxysm of cost-cutting, the university had forced the independent Rhetoric Department to join it. The twin faculties were as likely to get along as cold fusion would be the power source of the future, and calling this mixed bag dysfunctional was an insult to neurotics everywhere.

The craziness hadn't ended there. Just that past semester, the shrunken and beleaguered Humanities Department had been finally, brutally dismantled, and its faculty ordered to join EAR or retire. Rather than join a unit that didn't want them, most of the handful of professors left. But the bellicose and belligerent former Humanities chair, Byron Summerscale, had chosen to stay, creating a new source of tension. It didn't help his mood that he'd been given a basement office that was formerly a supplies closet, and his tirades didn't endear him to the department.

Juno, however, wasn't remotely intimidated by departmental pressures. "What a bunch of whiners and weasels," she'd once snorted during a departmental meeting, loud enough for most people to hear. And while she wasn't entirely right—there were a few hyenas in the department, too—it was satisfying to hear someone label EAR fairly honestly instead of repeating the clichés about dedication to learning, scholarly fellowship, caring about our students' intellectual growth, and all that other high-toned propaganda that disguises the university's venality and lackluster performance.

I completely understood her simmering at departmental meetings. They're one of the worst sides of the academic life, combining the effervescence of a serial killer's family reunion with the intellectual depth and maturity you see on display in a U.S. Senate subcommittee's inquisition of a governmental flunky. Juno would sit through these meetings like the precociously talented bad girl in high school called to the principal's office, as defiant as if she has seen her future clearly revealed and knows she's headed for success. She muttered, she jibed, she rolled her eyes, and if she'd been younger and blonder, she might even have contemptuously tossed her hair, hissing a flat "Whatever" or "As if!" Instead, she let out a rolling, guttural "Balls!"

And me, I was the National Honor Society nerd determined not to get in trouble myself, but enjoying her subversion.

But of course that wasn't all I'd been enjoying. Beyond being attracted to her loose tongue, I had found myself more and more admiring her looks. No, not just admiring, ogling. When we'd first met a year before, I was impressed by the *son et lumière* she put on just by strutting down the stained old linoleum-floored hallways of decrepit, bat-infested Parker Hall, her Manolo Blahniks an indictment of the shabbiness around her.

But ever since that episode in the pool, I had stopped feeling as if I were watching a glossy one-woman musical from a front-row-center seat. She'd broken the fourth wall, as theater folks say.

Now, if I were writing an advice book for academics, I'd certainly suggest that untenured professors should avoid midlife sexual identity crises if they want to advance their careers. Too distracting. But hey, given that I'd been involved in a handful of murder cases in my five years at SUM, I suppose you could argue that by comparison, this wasn't a big deal. Or was it?

And how had I come to this surprising place in my life after almost fifteen years with my partner Stefan, SUM's writer-in-residence, and another ten or so years before that in which I'd responded deeply only to men? As yet, I had not mentioned my unnerving thoughts about Juno to Stefan.

Juno strode back in and headed to the stove, where in a few moments she began searing the slabs of foie gras in butter.

"Tell me about your puppy."

Juno grinned. "I adore her! She's smart, loving, feisty. It's a wonderful breed, Westies. Are you thinking of getting one?"

"Stefan and I talk about a dog. It's just talk. A neighbor of ours has a bichon frise—"

"Oh, those are just poodle wannabes. Westies are much heartier dogs than both of those breeds, and tougher, but still manageable. You should come by some time and play with Turandot, see what she's like. I warn you, though, having a dog is a tremendous amount of work! Hours every day."

"I wouldn't mind that. It would be a relief from SUM and everything else."

"Exactly—because they don't send you memos, they don't talk. It's wonderful. What's stopping you?" She peered at me. "Oh. Two men? A small white dog? Stereotype alert?"

"It's not that. I just don't know if I'm ready for the responsibility."

She nodded, and then I asked her why she didn't have a Christmas tree, even a little one.

"You're kidding, Nick, aren't you? You think I'd be caught dead near anything that tacky and vulgar? Christmas in this country is awful, it's obscene, not that Canada lags far behind these days, I can tell you."

"How about when you were back home, growing up?"

"I was a good Catholic girl," she began, smacking her bosom with her free hand as if sounding a battle cry of mockery. "Yes, it's true. Until the day my mother asked me to cut some flowers in the garden to decorate a statue of the Virgin in our church, and I said I didn't see the point of giving something that was alive to a statue that was dead. She smacked me, and that was it."

"The smack that launched a thousand quips."

Juno frowned and drew herself up. I know the term "heaving bosom" belongs to a romance novel, but her breasts were doing something very close to that. "I don't make quips. I don't take shit. And I don't take prisoners."

"Jeez—you sound like Faye Dunaway in *Mommie Dearest.*"

Juno laughed. "Too bad they made Crawford so mellow."

If I'd assumed we were well and truly done with the subject of penis size, I was wrong. Juno suddenly felt the urge to sum up what she thought about the issue: "You know, Nick, what it all comes down to with a man's equipment is that I really like a manly man, but nothing bizarre." I wondered if that was because, she herself was so colorful, she didn't appreciate competition. In which case, did that mean her previous flirting with me meant I was ordinary? No, that couldn't be true, because she'd said she admired my body, which she'd seen a lot of in the pool. "A man like you. Or Cash Jurevicius."

The comparison with EAR's angriest adjunct professor startled me.

"Well, you do look a bit alike, actually," she said. "You and Cash. More than a bit. Haven't you seen the resemblance? Your hair's almost as long as his, too, though not as curly. I'm not sure which I prefer. . . ."

I was flattered and flustered. Cash was a lean, handsome surfer type, ten years younger than I was. Had swimming this past year made that much a difference for me? Perhaps I was so used to my old body image, dating back to junior high, that I had lost all objectivity.

Juno was grinning, and suddenly it hit me. "You're sleeping with him," I said.

"Am I? Why are you interested?"

"But he's an adjunct! I mean—"

Juno laughed. "Nick—do you honestly think it makes a difference? Are you a snob?"

I couldn't figure what the hell I had been trying to say. Cash was a good ten years younger than Juno, but that wasn't what made him seem unsuitable.

"If you think there's such a status difference, just chalk it up to what Huxley wrote about intellectuals in *Point Counter Point,* "High minds—low loins.""

"Okay, okay, sorry." I felt embarrassed and jealous and confused.

Juno lifted out the now-browned foie gras, deglazed the pan with Calabrian fig molasses and what she informed me was eighty-year-old Italian balsamic vinegar, reduced that, added some more butter, then poured the sauce over the foie gras on glass plates, topping it all with kumquat slices. At least she said that's what they were; not having ever seen one, I couldn't have testified either way. But the aroma was extraordinary, and the Montbazillac was the perfect choice to accompany the foie gras.

We ate at her round white kitchen table, as quietly intimate as if we were lovers taking comfort in food after having devoured each other. It was all somewhat tense for me, especially with the image of Cash and Juno drifting through my thoughts, but deeply, mysteriously enjoyable.

"This—is—phenomenal," I said, savoring every little bite of the foie gras, determined to make the same meal at home, soon. Then I decided it might feel like a bit of culinary-based adultery to enjoy the same food with Stefan that Juno had made for me. Though would Stefan even notice or care? He'd gone from depression over his dead-end writing career to exaltation over Keanu Reeves's production company optioning his long-out-of-print first novel for a movie. The deal was still in the works, but it looked like it was going to be very juicy, and Stefan spent most of his free time reading *Variety* and recontacting old writer friends to share his good news, aka brag. He expected to be in *People* any day now.

Juno brought out Belgian chocolates and Belgian cherry ale for dessert. "In honor of your heritage. The Belgian part, anyway." I was Jewish, so I suppose she could have produced rugelach or New York cheesecake for dessert if that had been her chosen theme.

As Juno brewed coffee, we chatted about our plans for the winter break and Stefan's recent good luck. When the coffee was done, Juno's mood turned somber. "Nick, we have to talk about the department. After all the scandal this semester, it needs firm leadership. You know that."

What it needed was an exorcism, in my opinion, or possibly napalm. And it would only get worse: Juno was planning to run against the current acting chair, Serena Fisch. Former friends, both of them were unpopular in EAR for different reasons. And either one of them could screw up my chances for tenure, since the chair's approval was the second step in getting tenure after the tenure committee made its report.

"Don't you think I'm the one to take charge in a time of flux?"

I drank some coffee. Then I temporized. "You're a very strong woman." It didn't work.

"Don't bullshit me, Nick. Serena Fisch is a strong woman. Me, I'm a bitch. And that's what EAR needs. An alpha bitch. A top dog."

"I've always thought of you more as the czarina type."

Juno laughed. "You're quick with your tongue. But someday it might get bitten off if you're not careful."

I winced, but tried to make a joke out of it. "A killer salad, foie gras and Montbazillac, chocolates, Belgian ale and coffee, threats. Nice menu."

She grinned wolfishly. "With your sense of humor, maybe you should run for chair."

"I should just run."

But Juno was serious again. "I know what you're thinking, Nick. You owe Serena because she helped you organize the Edith Wharton conference. Not that it was a raving success with all those murders."

"Two murders—just two!"

"Fine. But you don't like Serena, not really."

Even though Serena was something of a friend of mine and Stefan's, or at least friendly to us, there was truth in that. But then you couldn't say I actually liked Juno, either. I enjoyed her. I was fascinated by her. I seemed to have the hots for her. Not exactly the same thing.

"And I don't believe you trust Serena. Maybe you don't trust me, either."

I kept silent.

"But I'd be a better chair, Nick, and a worse enemy."

"What do you mean?" It couldn't be that she had a gun and Serena didn't.

Juno leaned back in her chair and surveyed me *de haut en bas*.

"Serena's too self-obsessed to cause anyone real trouble. But nobody should ever fuck with me, Nick. Serena would have nothing on me when it came to getting revenge. And I'll get it, on everyone who won't support me. I want to be chair of EAR. Nothing's going to stop me. Nothing—and no one."

Though she didn't speak about herself as "Juno Dromgoole," she sounded as confident and quietly crazed as some twenty-something Web tycoon who's never known failure. And that struck me as bizarre—here was someone who justly criticized EAR, saw how shallow its rhetoric was, how meaningless its gestures were. Yet she wanted to be in charge of this low-rent circus sideshow. What was the point?

The evening's free-floating eroticism had completely dissipated, and the air around Juno had a distinctly lunar chill. I was ready to go, and invoked Stefan as my excuse: "Stefan's waiting for me."

"So am I," Juno said menacingly, as I rose, headed for the coat rack at the front door, and bundled into my down parka to escape.

2

I walked down Juno's driveway to my car, parallel to a giant, over-grown row of yew hedges that ran from down near the curb back past Juno's house, blocking most of the neighboring ranch house and its lawn from view. Looming over me, the hedge was easily twice my height, and I heard what must have been birds skittering around inside it, encouraged by the relatively warm weather. And something louder, either inside or behind it. A cat stalking winged snacks? It would have to be a very big cat.

I stopped, and there was a rush as if something (someone?) had moved deeper into the shrub, or away from it entirely. I didn't feel as if eyes were staring at the back of my head, the hair on my neck didn't tingle—none of those novelistic clichés. But by the time I got into my car, I was mildly spooked, convinced someone had been lurking inside or behind the hedge, and I drove off quickly. The person who had called Juno before?

As soon as I was a block away, though, the specter of someone watching me—or more likely Juno and her house—had vanished. My brain reverberated with the chorus of some reggae song where the chorus was, "I'm like a cutting razor, I'm dangerous, I'm dangerous." That was Juno, all right: rhythmic, sensuous, and volatile. To get the song out of my head, I slipped a Nona Hendryx CD into the car stereo, finding some relief in the fiery voice and surging music of the first track, "Busting Out." I might be stuck, but it was heartening to hear someone sing about freedom.

I had not wanted to think too much about the consequences of being caught between Serena and Juno in an EAR election campaign. It seemed that the only way out of such a dilemma was a hostile takeover of EAR by another department and a subsequent rash of layoffs, or a sinkhole opening up under Parker Hall. Of course, Parker was built of sandstone and visibly crumbling, but its collapse wouldn't come fast enough to save me.

The scenario played out in my head like some tangled episode from a medieval chronicle: factions, charges, oaths and imprecations, alliances and threats, and slaughter—of a kind.

At the first stoplight, I pounded the wheel. It wasn't enough that I had no tenure and wasn't even sure if I wanted to stay at SUM anyway, and that my tenure committee was all screwed up, and that whoever I chose to vote against for chair would undoubtedly ferret out my betrayal and try to punish me somehow.

No, it was worse than all that. I hadn't even touched Juno—or her Glock—and already I was having castration anxieties! Why the hell else had I even thought about that reggae song?

I kept coming back to Juno's Glock. Was it real? God, Juno with a gun—it was a terrible prospect. We had moved as a nation past men going berserk in post offices or public places; now teenagers were shooting up their high schools. So there was nothing at all unlikely about college professors using each other for target practice. The revenge of the powerless.

So what was Juno planning? An announcement at a departmental meeting? Flyers in faculty mailboxes? A memo on the EAR e-mail listserv? Leaflets dropped from the Goodyear blimp? Or would she try to get the *Michiganapolis Tribune* to profile her and go for citywide publicity? I could see the photo: Juno looking fierce and bursting out of a Diana Rigg *Avengers*-type jumpsuit, a gun to her lips. Local readers who hated the university (or the "college," as they called it) would eat it up. Here at last was a professor who knew what was really important in life: not books but bullets. Juno would even be able to parlay the publicity into a radio talk show or run for state office if she became an American citizen.

It could spark even more craziness on campus. The return of ROTC. Gun clubs. Firearms Studies. A Wild, Wild West halftime show at home football games. Marksmanship awards at graduation. An NRA-sponsored endowed chair complete with gun rack.

Anything ridiculous was possible at SUM, a place that made *Alice in Wonderland* seem like a documentary. If parents only knew the kind of lunacy and corruption their tuition dollars were supporting, they'd be less impressed by the university's PR.

Brooding about Juno and her gun, I drove through town, which had undergone its Christmas makeover, trying to screen it all out. The holiday season is always uncomfortable for me as a Jew. It starts with the endless wishes of "Merry Christmas." It intensifies with the culturewide ubiquity of Christmas advertisements, whether on TV or people's hand-knit sweaters. And it explodes in a blizzard of wreaths, garlands, bows, Santas, trees, angels, and green and red ornaments and ribbons on every possible surface in every conceivable space: supermarkets, the post office, banks, light poles, mailboxes, car antennas, backpacks, garbage trucks, dogs.

Then there's the Christmas music on every radio station, and even when you're put on hold; the Christmas specials on every TV channel; and the blizzard of cards from people you barely know. Here in Michiganapolis, it was worse than back in New York, because the decorating was totally unironic. Growing up in New York, I had found the fuss somewhat entertaining. There, it was proof of how extraordinary we were in the city: the whole world wanted to see the tree get lit at Rockefeller Center; reporters from across the country extolled the crowds on Fifth Avenue and particularly at FAO Schwarz. New York was big, brash, excessive—and tough. Shopping amid the Christmas hordes was a rite of passage.

But here in Michiganapolis it was all for real.

I especially disliked socializing at so-called holiday parties, which were the same old Christmas parties politically corrected with some halfhearted decorative attempts to please Jews and Muslims and Native Americans and anyone else who might conceivably take offense and start a lawsuit. EAR had renamed its Christmas parties "end-of-term parties," which was fine by me, not that I particularly wanted to attend any gathering of my colleagues.

Overexposure probably altered your DNA as much as it did your mood.

I drove around town a bit aimlessly, musing once again over my tenure dilemma. I was in a tenure-track position, I had a home here, Stefan was EAR's writer-in-residence, so of course I had to get tenure. Tenure was the ineluctable goal once you had your Ph.D. and your job. Yet the more I struggled for it, worried about it, and feared I wouldn't get it, the less desirable it seemed. I wonder if the great explorers felt this way, reached a point where nothing they discovered could be worth the emotional treasure they'd squandered to find it.

But it felt crazy to be questioning a lifelong goal, the capstone of my love for teaching. My head was starting to feel as full as if I had sinusitis. God, this was like the David Bowie character singing that his brain "felt like a warehouse with no room to spare." I wished I could talk to Sharon, but since her surgery, she had found it hard to hear anything on the phone or to even concentrate long enough to have a conversation. E-mail wasn't any easier because the glowing screen bothered her eyes and the letters blurred. I kept track of her recovery through her parents and mine, but that wasn't a real connection.

Home, I found Stefan sprawled by the fire, immersed in reading Michael Connelly's *Blood Work*. Sade's *Diamond Life* was playing, and Stefan wore dark blue sweats and heavy black wool socks. Stefan looks a lot like a stockier, shorter version of Ben Cross, the Jewish runner in *Chariots of Fire*. Watching him, I thought this was a Norman Rockwell scene reinterpreted by Bruce Weber, the wholesomeness overlaid by beefcake, with a soupçon of the Eddie Bauer catalog.

Was that my problem? Had I been with Stefan so long I had stopped experiencing him, and instead saw him as a picture? Was that why I was drawn to Juno—a hunger for a more visceral connection? It didn't make sense to me. The longer you lived with someone, I thought, the deeper the intimacy.

Without asking about my dinner with Juno, Stefan launched right into a complaint about Connelly's book. "Don't you think the clue about the killer's identity is too obvious?"

"Which one?"

He leafed back through the book, found it, and told me. I agreed.

Stefan shook his head. "I liked *Pulse* better. Better atmosphere, and the story moved faster." Both books featured heart transplants, which was why Stefan was reading them back-to-back—at my recommendation, of course.

"Really? So you think Edna Buchanan can write, huh?"

He looked abashed. A literary novelist, Stefan had long been critical of mysteries and thrillers, and the fact that crime and murder had entered our lives in bucolic Michiganapolis had not eased his prejudice. He complained that besides being indifferently written, most of the mysteries he came across were formulaic, the same old genre song-and-dance in book after book, with few surprises. I agreed, to a certain extent.

"Listen," Stefan said. "I've been thinking about something."

"Always a dangerous sign in people over forty."

"The mysteries that are usually the worst are the ones with murders right away. Why not create tension differently and have the murder come late—or maybe not at all?"

"But people expect a murder," I insisted. "Readers and reviewers."

"That's my point—play with expectation, tension, menace. The *threat* of a crime. It's like the difference between horror and terror. Horror blasts you, grosses you out; terror scares you because you're not sure what's next, or even if there *is* something to be afraid of."

"You can guest-lecture in my mystery class."

He smiled.

Of course Stefan's dislike of the predictable wasn't helped by the fact that he was the kind of writer who would pick up a mystery or thriller, leaf through it, and somehow stumble across the most ridiculous line in the whole book, like the one he'd found last year in a romantic thriller: "Marla heaved a gusty sigh that sent the breasts in her silk shirt atremble."

We both had cracked up at that one, and Stefan said he wondered if the breasts were sent FedEx or UPS. Then he added gloomily that, given the general decline of literacy in the United

States, most people would think there was nothing wrong with that description, and many would consider it vivid and strong. The slide was irreversible; the quality of freshman writing I worked with had declined every single year that I'd been teaching. And there were always students who didn't understand—in a composition class, yet—why they were graded down if their ideas were good and their writing wasn't.

Despite all the bad writing, over the past six months Stefan had been seriously sampling books I'd been considering for my next semester's mystery course, and now that he had a potential film deal in the works, he seemed even more relaxed, freer of his old prejudices. Stefan was not at all averse to reading best-selling authors like Connelly now, whereas before, he had always seen that kind of status as a counterrecommendation. If too many people read a book, he assumed, it couldn't be good, though somehow his bias excluded *Midnight in the Garden of Good and Evil* and *Angela's Ashes*.

Of course, literary writers aren't the only snobs. I've read some interviews with mystery writers who sneer at what they consider literature: books "where not very much happens to people who aren't very interesting." And they dubiously trot out Joyce or Proust or Virginia Woolf as examples. I hate that anti-intellectualism. Give me a writer like Scott Turow who enjoys both mysteries and classics, and is proud to say so.

"Back to *Pulse*," Stefan was saying, sitting cross-legged now. I joined him on the hearth rug. "Don't you think Buchanan's book is better?"

I nodded. "It's shorter, too. I don't mind spending over five hundred pages with an author I know has something significant to say. Like Balzac. But I like shorter mysteries unless we're trapped at an airport—then it's Nelson DeMille time."

"I'll take Ken Follett. His prose is juicier. At least in *The Man from St. Petersburg* and *Lie Down with Lions*."

I laughed, since writers like Follett would never have entered Stefan's conversational orbit before, and it always gave me a charge now to hear evidence of his turnaround. After all, I was a big mystery fan, and Stefan's former contempt for the genre had always irked me. Now he was reading and enjoying Robert Barnard, David Handler, Ngaio Marsh.

"So you still think you'd never want to try writing a mystery?" I said.

Stefan frowned. "What kind? I don't know anything about police work, and those are the ones that seem most realistic. Amateur sleuth books are a joke—how many real people stumble across bodies?"

"Hel-*lo*. What about the last five years of my life?"

He shrugged. "Okay—you're an exception. No—if I ever did branch out, the only thing I could imagine writing would be like Diane Johnson's books. You know—a literary novel but with a killing, some light terrorism. Crime, but no heavy mystery plot."

This was new. Until the last year, his contemporary idols had been Gina Berriault and Andre Dubus, "writers' writers" who'd only become mildly popular recently; both were as far from crime fiction as you could get. Stefan had even seemed a bit disappointed when they gained wider audiences, as if somehow they were fine goods being handled by the hoi polloi.

On a pedantic note, I should say that Stefan often reminds me not to say "the hoi polloi," since *hoi* means "the" in Greek. He also corrects my French, which is a sore point, since my parents tried raising me bilingual in English and French, but it wasn't quite a success. And sometimes Stefan even points out that I don't use "whom" consistently. Well, I feel like Henry James's Isabel Archer about matters like that: I always want to know the difference between what's correct and incorrect—not to do the former, but to have a choice.

"Stefan, did you ever think you'd be reading so many mysteries and enjoying them?"

He shook his head. "But you know, there are mystery elements in books I've always loved, like Hawthorne, and Poe's one of the first mystery writers, too. And Henry James—there are mysteries his characters have to figure out. Strether doesn't know about Madame de Vionnet, remember? And there's the conspiracy in *The Wings of the Dove* . . . ."

"Do you think I look at all like Cash Jurevicius?"

"What?" Stefan frowned, clearly surprised by the switch from mysteries. "Cash?" He surveyed me through half-lidded eyes, as if conjuring up Cash's image next to me. "In a general way, sure. Same height—build—coloring. Yes, I can see a resemblance."

"But he's so skinny—don't you think he looks like Ryan Phillippe in *Cruel Intentions*—with darker hair?"

"Nick, you're much leaner now that you're swimming. Haven't you noticed? But if there's a resemblance, it's superficial. You're not at all like each other down deep. He's so arrogant, and he's never cheerful—there's something missing with him."

"What he's missing is a tenure-stream appointment. Teaching as an adjunct year after year would turn anyone into a creep, even Princess Di."

"Why are you interested in Cash all of a sudden?"

"I'm not, it's just that Juno said we looked alike."

"She did? So how was your dinner? You haven't mentioned it."

I described the evening lavishly, all the while conscious that I was leaving out the most important fact: I was drawn to her and wondered if it was mutual. The slightly mocking details of my account built up a wall between us behind which I could hide my confusion. Uncomfortably, I thought of Stockard Channing in *Six Degrees of Separation* complaining about turning life into a series of anecdotes and herself into a jukebox, spitting them out.

And how much had Stefan picked up on my discomfort and my weird attraction? Was that why he hadn't mentioned Juno until I spoke her name? Was Stefan quietly letting me follow this strange path without interfering?

Stefan sat up and closed his book. "Juno threatened you if you don't vote for her as chair? What's she going to do? Toilet-paper our trees with leopard-print scarves? Rent a plane and bomb our house with all her shoes? Park a van outside and blast us with audiotapes of Robertson Davies books?"

I remembered Manuel Noriega under stereo siege in Panama.

"Wait a minute—you used to think she was crazy and dangerous. You used to think she was capable of murder."

He gave me a quiet "That was then, this is now" shrug. "Nick, Juno's all talk and titillation."

I squirmed a little, like a grade-school kid hearing that last word for the first time and trying not to giggle. And I wondered if I should tell Stefan about Juno's gun. But then I thought, What if she doesn't have one? What if it was some kind of joke, and she'd just been testing me somehow?

Stefan went on: "Juno is just like Merry Glinka. *She* talks tough, but she's just fond of her own sound bites."

That last bit about our new provost seemed true.

SUM's last provost had decamped the previous month after an administrative scandal. As her replacement, SUM's board of trustees—in a closed meeting—had quickly hired Glinka, who was in-state and supposedly scandal-proof, at a salary of $250,000. The big bucks were necessary to steal her away from wealthy, ul- traconservative Neptune College in southern Michigan, where she'd been provost for a full decade. Glinka was given to Pat Bu- chanan–ish pronunciamentos, and despite the occasional mala- propisms, they had gone down a treat at Neptune College. In the past, though, I had dismissed her fronting as an attempt to balance the silliness of her name: Merry Glinka sounded like an operetta, not a person.

"Of course Glinka likes her own rhetoric. Who doesn't? But it's not just talk. She's truly hard-core," I said. "She probably thinks the NRA is full of pussies and that Charlton Heston is gay."

Mentioning the NRA reminded me of Juno's gun, and I told Stefan.

"Juno's got a gun?" he asked, incredulous, and then started laughing. "It sounds like a musical."

"It's for real."

"That's completely nuts," he said.

"Why? What's so crazy about wanting to protect yourself? How many people have been killed since we got here? Five? six?"

He shrugged, as if counting were obscene. "We do live in a city," he said.

"Stefan, Michiganapolis will never be Detroit or Atlanta or Miami. This is an overgrown town that *thinks* it's a city. But that's not what I'm talking about. The murders have been at SUM—they're not muggings or robberies or drug deals gone bad."

"So what are you saying? You want to be Mel Gibson? Arnold?"

"I'm not saying I would ever buy a gun, but I do think it makes a lot of sense."

"Come on, Nick. You've never been pro-gun."

"I've never known anyone who was murdered either, right?"

Stefan nodded. But the deaths we had witnessed or become involved in at SUM had not touched Stefan the way they had affected me. Over the past few years he had become obsessed with his fading career as a novelist—the declining sales, diminishing reviews, publishers uninterested in buying the paperback rights for his work. These conditions were industrywide for literary fiction, but being part of a trend didn't take the edge off his suffering, and he saw what happened at SUM through a haze. More profoundly, though, as the child of Holocaust survivors, Stefan had a much darker vision of life than I did, and this worldview hadn't been so much shaken as confirmed by events at SUM. "Et in Arcadia ego," he had quoted to me once. Even in our bucolic college town, there was death.

"We've never known any murder victims before," I repeated. "And even though we grew up in New York before it was all safe and Disney-fied, neither one of us was ever threatened or attacked."

Stefan's eyes dimmed at my reference to very painful incidents at SUM, one of which might have ended with my being killed if he hadn't rescued me.

"I've been wondering if I should take a self-defense class."

Stefan nodded. "Fine. There's nothing wrong with that."

"But there's something wrong with Juno's gun?"

Stefan laughed. "Nick—I think she was goofing on you. I bet she doesn't have a gun."

I might have originally suspected the same thing, but without knowing why, I felt slightly oppositional. Stefan's certainty sometimes brought that out in me. "Why do you say that?"

"Because Juno doesn't need one. She's the least frightened,

least fragile woman in the department. She's a ball-buster."

"She said she had one—she offered to show it to me."

"But did you see it? No? Well, then—"

"She got a threatening phone call when I was there."

"Sure."

"Why would she lie about the call or the gun?"

"Juno's given to self-dramatizing."

"Bullshit. Juno's her own Cirque de Soleil. She doesn't need to invent any drama. And what's so surprising about her being harassed? Look what happened to us last month."

But Stefan was not persuaded by my bringing up the alarming incidents of the semester, which had made me consider giving up my job at SUM and getting the hell out of Michigan. He rolled his eyes as if nothing that happened to Juno could ever compare to what we'd been through.

"Why are you so suspicious of her?" I asked. "Why don't you take her seriously? Why does she push your buttons?"

"She's too outrageous, like a bad drag queen."

"Oh, come on!"

"No—the hair, the clothes, the attitude."

"She's a free spirit," I argued.

"She's a banshee," he countered. "A shrew. A virago."

"Thank you, Mr. Roget."

"Well, why are you defending her so much? Why do you believe her?"

"Stefan, I was there when she got the call—I saw her face. She wasn't acting. Somebody's harassing her, and you know that's usually just the first step. So of course she bought a gun. And I don't have to see it to believe it."

"Listen, if Juno has a gun, then Merry Glinka has a howitzer. *And* a humvee."

I couldn't help but grin. SUM's administration building looked like a cross between a temple and a fortress, and I had a sudden image of troops swarming up its steps.

From Stefan's lighthearted reference to our new provost, I knew he was still in a really good mood. He hadn't even brought up the campuswide resentment about Glinka's salary or the lavish buyout of SUM's previous provost. Our university had a tradition of flinging cash like confetti at departing mugwumps, so if you were high up enough, being kicked out in disgrace could be very lucrative.

"Glinka's probably going to move on as soon as possible," Stefan had reasoned. "Run for senator, governor. SUM's just a quick step up."

That made perfect sense to me. A larger school would give her even more notoriety. To date, Glinka's media fame in large part resided in having authored a smarmy book on her life in the Reagan administration as an undersomething, which earned her guest shots on MSNBC where she could bash Alan Dershowitz. Her political connections had guaranteed constant visits to Neptune by the likes of Gary Bauer, Pat Robertson, Orrin Hatch, William Bennett, and other freethinkers. Her name and photo often popped up on the local news and in the *Michiganapolis Tribune* in connection with one of those dim luminaries. I'd always cringed as much at Glinka's photos as her declarations: she had the hard, flat beauty of an android in *Blade Runner*. And now that she was entrenched at SUM, was it time to run screaming onto the highway, warning everyone about the pods?

We had a glass of Vouvray and watched *Shakespeare in Love* on DVD. Once again, we relished the satire, which works on two levels, like Shakespeare's plays, and ogled Joseph Fiennes, though I thought Stefan had more piercing eyes. But early on, I was disturbed by Gwyneth Paltrow's rhapsodic desire for a love "that overthrows life. Unbiddable, ungovernable, like a riot in the heart, and nothing to be done, come ruin or rapture."

Was that what I was unconsciously seeking after years of sanity with Stefan—immolation? What the hell for? Wasn't my life at SUM tumultuous and unpredictable enough?

Despite all the wine and scotch I'd had that evening, I wasn't too sleepy, so after the movie, I headed to my study to check my e-mail before bed.

Now, sometimes I can resist that particular nightcap, but most evenings I'm curious to know who in the widespread but insular world of Wharton scholarship might be contacting me with a question, request, invitation to a conference, or sometimes even a compliment—though I don't get many of those. Most academics are as free with praise as they are with money for decent clothes.

Stefan says I obsess about my e-mail and check it too often. But since I'm the world's foremost Wharton bibliographer (and the only *living* one)—a status that carries weight everywhere but at SUM—I like logging on to feel important, if only in cyberspace.

Of course Stefan admits that he's obsessive about snail mail, as finely tuned to the sound of the USPS truck as a dog to a trainer's high-pitched whistle, ready to race down to the curb if he's at home when the mail arrives, so we're both ensnared by our expectations. Stefan still talks about the transformation one little letter made in his life, the first time he had a story accepted after years of submissions that came back with form rejection slips.

My study is a deeply calming room, and I needed it after the disturbing conversation with Juno. Sharon likes to gently mock it as overdone, but maybe that's what I need to shut the world out. Soundproofed by heavy maroon drapes and oriental rug, the small room is filled with floor-to-ceiling bookcases. The furniture is substantial, too—an Empire-style desk and chair, plus an overstuffed armchair and ottoman upholstered in a tapestry print of Watteau shepherds and shepherdesses. I feel comforted there, cocooned.

I slipped Maurizio Pollini's *Chopin Ballades* into the CD port and dialed up the university to access my e-mail. A quick glance revealed it was currently all SUM or EAR related. Much of what comes on e-mail from the university or the department isn't remotely dramatic or interesting: announcements of lectures, policy changes, beheadings, that sort of thing. Like most departments at SUM, EAR has its own listserv so that you can send a message to everyone in the department, staff included, which means endless trivialities endlessly repeated, commented on, disputed.

Usually I wade through all that inattentively, deleting messages without scanning too much past the subject lines because there's so damned much of it.

But I didn't get far at all that night because Stefan followed me, came up behind me at the computer, and ran a finger along the nape of my neck, easing my fatigue and tension as if he were a shaman drawing evil spirits from someone possessed.

"Boom, boom, boom," he said softly. "Let's go back to my room."

I turned, grinning. "Jeez, I haven't heard *that* song in years. What was the guy's name?"

Stefan said, "Doesn't matter. Come on."

I exited Netscape, shut down the computer, and followed him upstairs, where he'd filled our bedroom with musk-scented candles. He showed me the CD of golden dance oldies he'd put together as the evening's soundtrack: Sylvester, Grace Jones, Heaven 17, ABC.

"Wow. This music takes me back years, back to when *we* were gay." I laughed, remembering our hot youth, as Byron called it. Stefan set the CD to play. There were enough candles burning so that with the lights off we could still see everything we were doing.

And with the large mirror opposite the bed, it was quite a show.

An hour later, I thought through a haze of satisfaction that it had been like the perfect swim: the plunge, the power, the surge, the wonderful exhaustion. And lying next to Stefan, I felt that sense of glowing protection you'd find in some guided imagery trip or meditation. I stroked his chest, which in the candlelight seemed as serenely burnished as a Roman legionnaire's breastplate.

This was my reality—my center—my home. We were soul mates. How could I even question that?

The CD was playing over again, and Grace Jones was singing ominously about not being perfect. Was the song a warning, a plea?

Stefan asked, "Do you miss those years when we first met?"

"Well, we were both in grad school, so I'd never go back to that. Never. Graduate school is an exercise in being a worm. That's why I try to be nice to grad students when I get the chance, because I've been through it." But Stefan knew how I felt; there was no need to tell him. I was just surprised by his question.

"No, not grad school—the rest of it, I mean. Being out and young in New York."

"Dancing all night? Recreational drugs? Recreational sex?"

"Any of that. All of that."

I nodded, my head filled with visions of a life Andrew Holleran captured in *Dancer from the Dance*, his reworking of *The Great Gatsby*. Even though we had entered the gay club scene after the book came out, to Stefan and me, Holleran's gorgeous, sad book had at times seemed more like a memoir or chronicle than a novel. We could have written some of those pages, some of those scenes. Stefan had always been good-looking and popular, but I'd probably slept with as many men because I had what was almost as good as beauty then—I was young, and eager, and easily impressed.

Given our histories, it was a miracle we were healthy.

"So?" Stefan asked.

The wild years before AIDS really exploded were not a time Stefan and I talked about much anymore, and I never brought them up with other people, even when pressed. I wasn't denying it to myself, only to them, because I didn't want to confirm stereotypes about gay men as promiscuous and drug-crazed. That time was like an ancient city lost to a flood, its color and life vanished beneath smooth and tranquil water. Stefan and I had settled down a very long time ago. Was that my problem, then; was I *too* settled? Had I ended up like D. H. Lawrence's repulsive vision in *Women in Love* of couples "each in its own little house, watching its own little interests, and stewing in its own little privacy"?

I said, "Don't people always miss the time in their lives when things seemed more open?"

Stefan waited for more.

"Like Adam and Eve in *Paradise Lost*," I said. "The world was all before them. We didn't know where we'd end up, what our lives would be like. All those possibilities are gone. Come on, Michigan? As improbable as moving to Jersey when you grow up in New York. But it worked. It's working—most of the time." I mentally brushed aside the violence we'd witnessed. "There was no way of knowing. I don't know."

Stefan eyed me thoughtfully because I was babbling.

I tried to slow down. "Thinking back makes me—"

"Nostalgic?"

"Not at all. Nauseous. I get this sense of vertigo, like I'm looking over a cliff, down into my old life."

"So you don't ever wish you were younger?" He softly wiped sweat from my forehead, absentmindedly licked his hand.

"No way. That's not it. What I really wish is that I had tenure. And that Sharon was completely recovered—*now*. And that nobody we know would ever get threatened or harmed or killed ever again." I didn't say that I also wished that my uncertainty about Juno would disappear. "And I want your film deal worked out and the movie to get made and be nominated for a Golden Globe so we can fly out there and chat up Daniel Baldwin at the awards."

"You think he'll be in the movie?"

"I'd take him or any of the cuter Baldwins."

"Me, I'm a Steinway man," Stefan said, and it was so corny, even from someone who used to play the piano, that I couldn't pretend not to get it.

"What do you *wish* for?" I asked. "Or regret? Like, do you ever miss that woman you slept with? Madeleine?"

"Marilyn. It was more than sex. It was—" He sought the words. "Discovery. Freedom. Opening up. I didn't know how to talk about anything that was inside of me before I met her. She taught me that labels didn't matter. She'd slept with women, I had sex with a guy, so it felt safe. Nobody was going to get judged. It didn't matter what we were, except together."

Now that was a lesson I wish I had learned. I asked, "But do you miss her?"

"Never. She was in my life, she changed it, and then she wasn't."

"Don't you wonder what happened to her?"

He smiled reflectively. "Sometimes. I imagine the kind of life she has. Is she married? Did she move to a women's collective? Is she a political consultant or a stockbroker? Did she join the Peace Corps and stay abroad? Does she have kids?" He smiled tentatively. "Once or twice I thought it would be interesting to write a book like that, about the different possibilities, the paths her life could have taken. But when I read Carol Anshaw's *Aquamarine*—remember, where the woman has three completely different futures—I thought it was so good, why bother? People would just say I was copying her."

"But it wouldn't be plagiarism—"

"No. Not exactly," Stefan said sleepily, starting to drift off. "Just inferior."

So his relationship with a woman came down to a question of material for Stefan. What had I hoped in asking him? That he'd admit thinking about women, or about Marilyn, a lot, and I'd have an opening to talk about Juno? It hadn't worked, and even if it had, I just didn't think I could do it. Telling him I thought I might have the hots for Juno—especially when he had a low opinion of her most of the time—seemed too raw, too humiliating.

"Do you ever regret becoming a teacher?" Stefan asked, sounding even less alert. I knew this was a loaded question because he had no natural love for his trade, but had learned it. "You could have worked for your father."

"And been a drone. Well paid, but a drone. I never wanted to go into publishing. Never. So I guess the answer is, *Non, je ne regrette rien.*" I tried singing the defiant French assertion made famous by Edith Piaf. Stefan smiled benevolently, already half asleep, and he was completely there well before I was.

He left me with some questions. What was behind all his probing about the past? Was he like Obi-Wan Kenobi picking up "a disturbance in the force"? Registering on some level what had been roiling inside of me?

I felt like a coward. We had been through so much together, and yet I wasn't confiding in him.

It was as I fell asleep myself that I realized with faint relief that at least I'd stopped thinking about Juno's gun.

3

BY the time I woke up Thursday morning, Stefan had already headed for campus, leaving me a welcome pot of Sumatran Mandehling down in the kitchen and a very unwelcome note: "See you at the reception this afternoon."

I'd been so obsessed about having dinner with Juno, I'd forgotten the SUM reception honoring faculty who had published books in the last five years.

Not the last year, mind you, but five years. That turned what could be considered a mildly dignified event into a cattle call. At a university SUM's size, there would be hundreds of faculty who'd come, determined to squeeze some joy out of their miserable academic lives. There would be a reception—plaques—and probably lip service about how important their contributions were, when in fact everyone knew that it was really the football, basketball, and hockey teams that the university cared about because their success was directly proportional to alumni donations.

I made myself breakfast, trying not to think about the reception, trying to slow down, focus on my surroundings, make the moment last. Maybe someone should market Zenflakes. I know I'd give them a try if they offered some calm.

I mixed chopped shallots and herbs de Provence into egg whites to start an omelet and sipped some grapefruit juice, thinking about Juno's fear, and whether someone had actually been spying on her last night. I made a mental note to call her about what I'd seen—or thought I'd seen. I didn't think she'd accuse me of being Chicken Little, since the sky had fallen for me and Stefan. My office had been broken into, we'd suffered arson—

So why didn't I own a gun? Knee-jerk New York liberalism that brands gun owning as savagery? Or just plain stupidity on my part?

After breakfast I cleaned up in the kitchen, enjoying the smooth, cool feel of the new gray-blue granite countertops and thinking about the reception. SUM had never had one of these faculty receptions before, but was always throwing blowouts for winning teams.

I imagined it would be grim: a horde of shabbily dressed geezers and geeks whose uninviting-looking and unreadable books would be on display. Deathless tomes on soil science; the evisceration *topos* in Bulgarian medieval epic; and various disquisitions on macro-, micro-, and velcro-economics. Spicing that visually and textually dull stew would be several handfuls of books that were both attractive and interesting to more than a small audience.

I confess, my Edith Wharton bibliography could certainly be classed with all those publishing wallflowers. But that didn't have to make me like the category. I'd published the book before coming to SUM, so I was actually going along as Stefan's partner, and that had involved some murkiness, since Stefan's call to the provost's office to find out whether I could come with him had been very inconclusive. No, partners and spouses were specifically not invited, to keep numbers down. But they would not be excluded if they showed up.

Lovely. Let's honor the faculty and not invite their loved ones.

It wasn't as if Stefan was eager to go himself. His plaque would mention two novels, both of which had tanked, and on a bad day, the plaque would no doubt be a kind of visible reminder of their failure. Would he even hang the plaque up in his study?

But given his excitement about the impending film deal, he felt armored enough. The money wasn't in billions of dollars, the way everything seemed to be measured these days, but it was a lot: a $50,000 option payment against a purchase price of $300,000. And all that for a book that had just barely earned back its advance of $3,500.

Nothing this wonderful and life-changing had ever happened in Stefan's career before, which made it even more extraordinary.

God, being a writer was like being some kind of invalid—you always needed protection, cushioning from anything that might depress you: reviews, another writer's conspicuous interview, and just the plain sight of thousands of books at any of the book barns masquerading as stores, each one more than just a challenge but a punch in the stomach, reminding you that you were no one, nothing, just another piddling author.

The only thing worse than not being published, Stefan was fond of quoting, was *being* published, and it was true enough for him.

I suppose Stefan was also going to the reception because of a touch of morbid curiosity, and a vague search for material. *Humani nil a me alienum puto*, in Terence's words. Rough translation: I've seen some pretty weird shit in my life.

If EAR events were depressing, these large assemblages of SUM faculty were a special kind of grotesquerie. Perhaps because few faculty members knew professors in other colleges, people tended to eye each other with suspicion and hostility, as if they were rival claimants to a fortune and anyone else's presence dimmed the luster of their future. It was perhaps a bit like everyone crowding Count Bezhukov's reception room in *War and Peace*, only nowhere near as colorful.

Yet the smoldering envy was ridiculous, because other faculty members weren't the enemy: the administrators were. They were the untalented smiling thugs pulling down enormous salaries while SUM faculty were among the lowest paid in the Midwest. With huge travel budgets, SUM administrators trolled around the country on fund-raising junkets or attended meaningless conferences in plush resorts, while most faculty had to beg their department chairs for travel money to legitimate conferences at distinctly unglamorous locales like Lincoln, Nebraska, as opposed to Montreal.

And no doubt people would also be grousing about SUM's latest lunacy: a task force to study the institution of a Whiteness Studies Program, housed in the College of Arts and Letters. Whiteness Studies was the newest fad in academia, including everything from disquisitions on Elvis to the fiction of Erskine

Caldwell. Some people thought it was post-cutting-edge, others that it was a sick joke, and many branded it racism with a pretty face.

Bringing Whiteness Studies to SUM was the brainstorm of our mooncalf president Littleterry, SUM's former football coach. He had mistakenly dubbed the initiative "White Studies" when he lost the notes for the little speech announcing his intention and had to extemporize. Littleterry's handlers usually managed to keep him from making such gaffes; as Winston Churchill had once said about a rival, "Each time he speaks, he subtracts from the sum total of human knowledge."

There had been one or two protest demonstrations on campus so far, and isolated outbursts from faculty, but no concerted opposition, since the task force hadn't even had its first meeting yet. There was a general feeling that like most so-called innovations at SUM, this one would be responsible for a monsoon of memos and meetings, after which—in typical university fashion—little or nothing would happen. Paperwork was to SUM what incense was to the Byzantine Empire. And of course, given the ideological time lag at SUM, if a program was created, it would already be passé, and there would be pressure to create a Great Books track for all freshmen or something equally revanchist.

I thought about all this on and off that morning and afternoon as I graded sets of papers that were generally very good. My notoriety on campus had swollen my enrollments, but the students weren't all potato-heads. I was actually drawing a more insightful, mature set of students whose writing was above average.

Though "average" was relative, of course. In the decade-plus that I'd been teaching, I'd seen command of the language slip and slide. Whether it was due to MTV, the Web, or global warming's impact on neurological functioning, I couldn't tell. Stefan said that even his graduate students seemed to be writing more pallidly, more imprecisely, and he was frequently shaking his head in disapproval and quietly pained surprise those rare times we graded papers together. Of course his classes were small, and his piles of papers matched, so his complaints didn't last long, especially when I reminded him, "This is why we're here. To help our students. That's our *job*."

The reception was being held at SUM's Campus Center/hotel, a featureless redbrick and concrete building that had grown since the 1950s rather like Michiganapolis itself: haphazardly. It was a building easy to get lost in, with its winding wide corridors and frequent cul-de-sacs camouflaged by hulking planters and chairs and couches made for lurking. Despite the glaring overhead lights and the recent remodeling, it gave you the murky feel of *Blade Runner*.

The plus side was that, like many of SUM's uglier buildings, it was well landscaped and set among enough old trees not to be a complete eyesore. Nevertheless, as I parked nearby and headed inside to meet Stefan, I cringed; not because of my aversion to the building's decoration but because I'd avoided it ever since my Edith Wharton conference two years before—a conference that, foisted on me, had lost me as much sleep as Lady Macbeth (with only half as much fun) and had led to, as Juno said, "all those murders." Just outside the wide chrome-framed glass doors, I hesitated, catching a glimpse of the dark blue, orange-flecked twelve-by-twelve granite tiles decorating the bottom half of each wall. Pretty in situ, but ugly when wielded by a vengeful hand, as someone had done a few years ago, when the center was being remodeled during my conference.

Standing there poised to walk in, I felt the pull of noise and commotion—and memory. This building had been the scene of very ugly moments in my career. It was tempting at that moment to imagine saying to Stefan, "I want to leave Michiganapolis—I want to start over again. Somewhere, anywhere."

Perhaps, then, my attraction to Juno was nothing more than a warning, or an ache. My life had grown too restrictive, and I needed to break free.

As I opened the closest door, no ominous thunderclap greeted me or warned me off; no frenzied birds whirled up into a Gothic sky. Nothing so corny. I heard a silky voice behind me: "Yo, Nick. Wassup?"

It wasn't a hip-hopper but Rusty Dominguez–St. John, one of EAR's flashiest and most elusive faculty members, who dressed like Clint Black, except for the hat. Rusty followed me in, and we stopped at the edge of the center's main hallway, with students eddying by in shoals or streams or whatever the technical word is for bunches of undergraduates. There was so much bustle and noise we could have been standing at one end of an airport people mover.

"Looking sharp, my man," Rusty said, surveying me with fake good spirits. Everything about him struck me as fake, especially his supernova smile: it was too broad, too welcoming, too indiscriminate, too much of a sales pitch. Perpetually tanned and built like a heavyweight wrestler, Rusty was graced with the furry brush cut, sharp jawline, and raspy voice of a TV sportscaster. He had the sportscaster's overempathic body language, too, that made you feel he wasn't just invading your space, he was colonizing it.

Rusty was a professor of popular culture who had earned his master's and Ph.D. while serving twelve years for aggravated assault somewhere in Minnesota. He rarely attended department meetings or lingered at Parker Hall because he spent most of his time flying around the country doing Recovering Criminal seminars that plugged his book, videotape, CD-Rom, and cassette series, *Breaking the Bars That Imprison You.*

Though only half Hispanic, he'd been hired as an affirmative action candidate and for the PR value he would supposedly bring with him, but he had been a disappointment; he was never visible enough on campus to be bragged about or exhibited as a Person of Color and Recovered Criminal. *People* magazine had profiled him once, but there hadn't been any photographs of the university, and some alumni even protested his hiring and canceled regular donations. Another hiring success for the department, which could have done just as well contacting Monster.com.

"I never see you!" he said, as if we were old pals.

I nodded. Rusty and I rarely crossed paths, but that was fine with me, because he always left me with a twisting feeling in the pit of my stomach. He was as bright and loud and phony as one of those late-night ads for exercise machines that promise amazing results in only five minutes a day, a perfect example of a phenomenon Stefan and I loathe equally because it's become so common in the United States: a man making a fortune off crappy books that do little more than repackage other people's research and theories.

"You headed to that reception thing?" Rusty asked, as if delighted at the prospect. Then he added with far too much cheerfulness, obviously masking dubiety, "You published a book lately?"

"No," I said, "but I have two in press." They were edited books, so the statement was partially true, but it bugged me to be interrogated. "I'm waiting for Stefan."

"Oh, right. He's published a couple of books in the last five years."

Whether it was meant that way or not, it felt like a zinger.

Rusty wasn't done. "But I thought this reception was just for—I didn't know you could come if you're just someone's—ah—"

"Partner?"

He grinned and held out his arms in an I-love-the-world-it's-so-crazy shrug. "Hey, man, I can't say that word. Makes me think of business."

"What would you prefer me to call myself, Stefan's bitch? I mean, since you've been in prison."

"Whoa! Chill!" He reached forward to tap my cheek as if I were a sulky little boy who needed calming down.

I backed away, but didn't leave; this was where I'd said I'd meet Stefan. And I could imagine my highly civilized parents eyeing me with disapproval for being so rude. As if they were there admonishing me, I resentfully eked out a question. "What are you writing now?"

Rusty cracked his knuckles and rocked back on the heels of his cowboy boots. "Just published a new one—it's on the best-seller charts with a bullet: *Healing Your Inner Crook.*"

"That's a joke, right?"

You know that weird moment when you're driving on the highway late at night, and you check your rearview mirror, and it's blank—all the cars have suddenly fallen away behind you? That's how I felt looking into Rusty's eyes at that moment—entering a darkness that stretched way, way back.

"Funny guy," he said, with the hint of a threat. He checked his twenty-pound Rolex and said he'd see me at the reception.

Relieved, I sat down in one of the square, blocky chairs, which was as uncomfortable as it looked, and peeled off my leather car coat. Because the center's main hallway bisected the building and was so wide, the building was used by many students as a thoroughfare between different parts of campus. I was amazed at the sheer number of them, most hunched forward under the weight of their backpacks and listening to CDs on headphones.

Stefan had asked if I missed the time when we met and were just coming out for real. Watching the undergraduates, I think I probably missed my college years, when everything I read and saw and felt in the realm of the mind seemed new and exciting. Graduate school had none of that magic for me—it was more like an obstacle course. Only when working for five years on my Wharton bibliography had I felt a sense of renewed intellectual excitement. And as much as I loved teaching writing, I had to admit that it wasn't challenging enough anymore. Hopefully the mystery course next semester would provide what was missing.

Two similar-looking girls in black leggings and minidresses strutted by, chewing gum, eyes hooded, one saying, "I really want to be, like, a talk show host. One of those chicks on *The View*. Not for the fan mail or anything. I would kill to have someone do my makeup and hair every day."

"And then you could be interviewed on *Larry King Live*."

I was for some reason thinking of Sharon when Serena Fisch strode by, apparently en route to the reception, with a hurried "How are you?" Sharon's surgery had made me unexpectedly mawkish and confessional, and I told Serena I was worried about Sharon and why, but she kept moving, turning on her heels in annoyance and snapping out, "Oh, who *cares* about your cousin's brain tumor?"

Shocked into silence, I watched her stalk off. Dressing in 1940s retro and looking like one of the Andrews Sisters, Serena

Fisch had always been given to catty or cutting remarks, but this unwarranted harshness was new. Perhaps it was connected to her running for EAR chair. Or perhaps it was simply that her elevation to acting chair had coarsened and hardened her. Either way, it still hurt. She could have just nodded and said, "That must be tough."

I was proud of myself for not feeling cowed or worrying at that moment about tenure. "Fuck you," I muttered, thinking about Juno's gun, wishing I had one. They might not make you safer, but I could already see how they made you feel more powerful.

Faculty were streaming in by the bushels, many of them looking as if they needed industrial-strength makeovers. There were lumbering, fat men in sweaters that barely covered their bellies; others in worn and shabby tweed jackets, chinos, and loafers; and a large sprinkling of what I thought of as Senators: men with horrible combovers. I had told Stefan that if anytime in the next few decades he found me trying to disguise my balding hair like that, he should just slap me. "I may slap you even if you don't," he said.

So where was Stefan? He was fifteen minutes late, and I didn't have my cell phone to call him. If I got up to find a phone, I might miss him.

Cash Jurevicius strutted in, wearing a long black leather coat like a Keanu Reeves *Matrix* clone—not that there was anything wrong with that, of course. He even had a black leather knapsack over his shoulder, with a Quality Paperback Book Club copy of *The Name of the Rose* sticking out of it; I had a similar copy at home. He was probably deconstructing it for some essay. But why was he here? Had he published a book I didn't know about? Then I caught myself—wasn't I being as obnoxious as Rusty had been, questioning his right to be there?

It had to be jealousy of Cash and Juno. He was very handsome, and his feral good looks made for some hot pictures when I imagined him and Juno in bed. No—it wouldn't be bed. They'd do a *Fatal Attraction* kitchen hump.

Uncomfortable with this trend of thinking, I spotted Stefan rushing through the doors right toward me, cashmere coat over his arm. He'd bought the coat the day after hearing about his film deal. "Sorry, sorry, sorry. I was meeting with Peter de Jonge, and it got heavy—" He shook his head, then plumped down into the chair at right angles to mine, looking reluctant to leave its dubious shelter. He looked good in his black Armani, but his face was flushed and tight. What had that graduate student said, or done?

"We'll be late for the reception," I said carefully, not sure what was going on.

"So?" he said wearily. He stared down at his watch as if it were something alien. "What?" he asked, even though I hadn't said anything. Then he seemed to snap to attention. "I'll tell you after the reception—it's too complicated." His face was so set there was clearly no point in insisting he let me know now. He rose, and we headed off into the throngs.

It wasn't noble of me, but I wondered if the handsome graduate student had made a pass at Stefan. Peter de Jonge was my age and married, but maybe he was having a midlife crisis of his own.

As we neared the turbine-like thrum of status-hungry professors, all I could think of was escape, but we had taken so many turns to the room where the reception would be held that I could never have found my way back to an exit in an emergency. Standing at the door, I thought that the spectacle before me wasn't quite ignorant armies clashing by night, but close enough. The heat bursting from inside was so intense it made me loosen my tie.

The room was actually a series of bland, badly soundproofed, high-ceilinged lecture rooms whose shabby dividers had been opened to fit rank upon rank of back-knifing chairs. Hundreds of people milled around these cruel chairs, awkwardly holding paper plates and plastic cups, while dozens more clustered at the back of the grim mauve-walled room, near a bank of tables draped in cheap-looking paper tablecloths that were already ripping under faculty attack.

Along the wall opposite the open door were two Formica-topped tables with rank after dispiriting rank of books. Rather than celebratory, this display struck me as funereal. The ugly steel-blue-and-black curtains, which appeared to be sewn by prisoners, didn't help.

Just inside the door where we lingered stood a square table piled high with thick beige pamphlets, apparently the program for today's event. I leafed through one, which listed "remarks" by the president and the provost and then Presentation of Awards, followed by an infernally long list of faculty members and their book titles.

I saw Rusty chatting up Serena, who looked imperious but charmed, as if he were giving her an amusing report of what he'd been up to while avoiding EAR. Cash Jurevicius loitered nearby, apparently eager to join the conversation but uncertain when to intrude.

"Why's Cash here?" I asked Stefan, despite having remonstrated with myself earlier for wondering.

"He edited a book of his grandmother's essays, remember? SUM Press did it a few years ago."

I drew a complete blank on the book, even though I knew Cash's grandmother had been a highly respected chair of EAR in the 1950s.

"Doesn't matter," Stefan said, watching me struggle. "I doubt more than a few people bought it anyway—for sentimental reasons. That is, if they heard about it. The SUM Press does a lousy job of promotion. Are you thirsty?" he asked.

We started to push through the crowd to see what kind of reception goodies waited for us. I could make out urns, pitchers, and something uninspiring-looking on trays.

"Don't bother," Juno said, appearing at my side in an eye-catching black pantsuit, high-heeled leopard-print boots, and matching toque, with a black Chanel bag slung over one shoulder. "The coffee is cold, and the punch is warm. Oh, yes, there are some miserable brownies." Her perfume wafted over us as heavily as bus exhaust on a city street. I felt momentarily dizzied.

"That's it?" Stefan asked, mouth twitching on the edge of a smile as if he were expecting a punch line. "That's the reception?"

"Sadly, yes."

Stefan plunged toward the table to verify Juno's report, and I eyed Juno a bit warily. After all, she'd threatened me the night before. But she looked so ripe.

Juno glanced around her with a lot less compassion than Princess Di visiting AIDS patients. That's when I decided to tell her about what had happened when I left her house the previous night. "Someone might have been lurking in your shrubbery." Despite myself, I almost choked at the phrase.

"Excuse me?" she asked, cutting her eyes at me.

"It's like something out of a P. G. Wodehouse novel."

"As long as it doesn't turn into *The Shining*, fine."

"I didn't mean to—"

"I know, I know. It's all so ludicrous, what's happened to you, to everyone at this godforsaken hole of a place, that hysteria seems the only appropriate response. Threats, stalking, arson, murder—at a university? Unheard of!"

"But do you honestly think someone's after you?"

Juno gave me a sultry grin. "Someone is always after me."

"No jokes."

She switched moods as quickly as someone coming out of hypnosis with a finger snap. Very soberly, she said, "I do, yes."

"Get out of the race for chairman? Get out of town? What? What's it about? What are you being warned to do? Why is someone telling you to get out?"

"You're the detective, aren't you?"

"Not by choice. And there aren't any clues, anyway."

"There are always clues if you look for them."

I was pondering that when Stefan rejoined us. "The brownies are gross," he said. "Pure sugar, gooey, you can hardly get one down."

"It's a plan," I said, "to keep the faculty from saying anything. Gum up our mouths while Littleterry and Glinka blather on and on." I'm not sure the brownies were making a difference, though, because the high-ceilinged room echoed like a mall during a post–Memorial Day Sale.

My mention of the coming speeches made us all turn to glance toward the front of the vast, churning room, where an oak podium stood on a low black riser. We were supposed to be addressed by the provost and the president, but neither was in sight, and it was already after four-thirty.

"Didn't the invitation say 'Reception, 4–6 P.M.'?" Juno asked pointedly.

Stefan and I nodded.

"This isn't a reception," I said, and both of them waited for me to explain. "A reception, that's wine, cheese, fruit, something substantial."

"What would you call it, then?" Juno asked. "A *de*ception?"

"That's good," Stefan said. "That's really good."

"This is *refreshments*," I said. "Crappy refreshments. Nothing more than that, and the invitation should have said it."

" 'Crappy refreshments,' " Juno repeated. "Enticing."

Talking louder than usual to make ourselves heard, we had gathered a number of listeners, who were muttering similar complaints about the food, the speakers' lateness, and the venue. None of them looked especially familiar, yet they all had the weary, beaten-down air of so many faculty at SUM, the ones who weren't bringing in huge grants or making big names for themselves or were simply worn out by teaching in a crazy-making environment where what they did and who they were was not valued, no matter how hard they worked.

The Kinderhoeks, Avis and Auburn, waved and headed over to join us. I'd heard that after some sort of spiritual awakening, she had recently changed her name from Mavis to Avis, which had prompted departmentwide snickering. Even Stefan had said, "How's that a name change? She just dropped a letter. It's more like reversing a typo." I had told him to think of it as an orthographic circumcision, but neither of us tried making any puns on *rara avis*.

Juno growled now, "Give me a fucking break. Here comes Bore and Dumb." She strode away, and I saw her heading back toward Rusty Dominquez–St. John, who held out his arms to her. They didn't hug but kissed cheeks *à la Belge*: three times. It turned me on to see her in another man's arms. Wait, not another man. She hadn't been in my arms. God, was I jealous of other men with her already? That was completely crazy.

The Kinderhoeks made hello noises and comments. Ostensibly part of the writing program, they'd managed to secure temporary berths away from SUM so often they seemed like visiting professors rather than permanent faculty. She was the poet, he was the essayist, and both were despised by students for cruel hectoring in the classroom.

"Terrible," Avis said. In her mid-fifties, so short and fat she seemed to have been squashed into her Capezios, she always wore clinging satiny-looking dresses that seemed like nightgowns.

"Disgraceful," Auburn agreed. He was just as short, but whippet thin and with the sleek, vacuous good looks of Dan Quayle. Both had vague southern accents that might have been acquired at Office Max—I was sure I'd once heard Auburn talk about a play that he pronounced as something like "Ee-Antony and Cleopaterer." Pure Brooklynese.

"Littleterry and Glinka keeping us waiting, you mean?" Stefan asked.

"Gracious, no!" Auburn said, eyeing Avis with amusement.

"The heat," she said, fat cheeks flushed. Despite her age, she had a young-looking face ("Women like that always have good complexions—it's all the fat cells," Sharon had once explained to me).

"The heat in this room," Auburn explained, as if we thought his wife might have been talking about the weather in Somalia.

Stefan and I nodded our understanding, and I could tell he wanted to escape, so I grabbed his arm and said, "There's Margo—you wanted to ask her about the show."

He gratefully moved off with me, and when the Kinderhoeks sloped away, he said, "What show? And who's Margo?"

"Margo Channing—who else? And if you don't know the name of the show, you'll never be able to play Gay Trivial Pursuit."

Stefan smiled, and then asked, "What's on that table?"

We headed up the center aisle, nodding at those few faces we recognized. Up at the front and off to the side was a standard-issue long metal table stacked high with padded, labeled envelopes. It was guarded by a couple of sharkskin-suited, anxious-looking flunkies who stared at the door with wild eyes when they weren't consulting their watches and muttering. I think they were trying for the aplomb of headsetted FBI agents, but they seemed more like testy supplicants at a shrine who had been promised a miracle. They glared at us and moved forward, so much alike that if not for their height difference, they might have been clones.

"The plaques," Stefan muttered.

"You can't take yours until your name is called," one of the toadies shot at Stefan. "The reception hasn't started."

"It started over half an hour ago," I observed, silently adding, "Bitch." But the adjuration surely meant that nothing truly began until SUM's ersatz royalty arrived. And wasn't he right?

"What's that about the plaques?" someone called, and the two suits drew together and back toward the table as if ready to defend its contents. Their well-manicured hands clenched.

"Who do you work for?" I asked them.

"The president," they said. "And the provost."

"Not really. You work for the people of Michigan. This is a land-grant university, remember?"

They sneered mildly at each other as if I were a harmless fanatic of some kind.

"This is an outrage!" a voice boomed from the middle of the crowd. "This is a travesty!" It was rumbustious Byron Summerscale, the burly and Hemingwayesque former chair of Humanities, whose department had been hacked to pieces over the years until he alone was left to tell the tale. No doubt determined to crush his inveterate complaining about SUM's hypocrisy and ill treatment of faculty and students or drive him off, the administration had reassigned him to EAR and given him an unrenovated, windowless basement supply cupboard as his office in Parker Hall.

But Summerscale was more Liberty on the Barricades than shrinking violet, and his handling had not tamed him in the slightest: last month he had drunkenly and dramatically insulted the president at a faculty party held by my dean. Towering over the professors around him now, he looked like a wizard about to unleash a terrible spell on his enemies or a thundering prophet, eyes glowing, long white hair as wild as if it had been plucked at by the Furies.

"Who does his hair?" Juno purred, rejoining us.

Professors fell back from Summerscale as if fearing he was

flammable. "They've kept us waiting for almost an hour!" Summerscale roared. "It's intolerable, unforgivable."

Voices in the crowd shouted back his words, egging him on and adding more abuse, though in less elegant language: "This sucks!" "I hate SUM!"

"The president and provost should be ashamed of themselves," Summerscale shouted. "They should be shot! Don't they think we have lives, that we have something to do besides waiting around for them like servants expecting a Christmas turkey?"

It wasn't the most poetic image of humiliation, but it seemed enough for this crowd. "Fuck 'em all," someone cried, and vociferous yelling in favor of Summerscale was countered by shouts of "Shut up!" and "Hooligans!"

A wide-shouldered, bearded professor I didn't recognize, who looked like a Marlboro man in his jeans and plaid shirt, stomped up to the plaque table, announced his name, "Grassley!" and said, "This is bullshit. I have a class to teach and I'm going to be late. I'm not waiting anymore. Give me my plaque."

The two functionaries stared at him as if he were speaking gibberish. When they didn't reply but moved toward him as if to block his access to the table, he shouldered between them, knocking them off balance, roughly sorted through the envelopes, which I assumed were alphabetically arranged, grabbed one, and left, cursing under his breath.

The room, even hotter now, seemed about to burst into real violence—looting, sacking, general brigandage—when a shocking wave of quiet spread from the door. As it moved my way, I was transported back to a noisy assembly in sixth grade one Friday when our Frankenstein look-alike principal (with a clubfoot) had silenced an unexpectedly rowdy auditorium merely by clomping down the center aisle to the stage.

President Littleterry blustered into the crowd, which parted theatrically. He didn't say hello or even apologize, but he seemed harassed and unhappy to be there.

Suddenly docile and quelled, people oozed into their seats, even Summerscale. Stefan and I took seats at the end of a row near the door, where it was moderately cooler, while Juno found a seat near the back. Littleterry's stooges at the plaque table looked so relieved I wouldn't have been shocked if they kissed his feet—or each other.

Ill dressed and maladroit as usual, Littleterry tried adjusting the microphone at the podium when we were all sitting down, his forehead sweaty. It screeched with feedback for a moment, and he jerked back as if electrocuted while people complained from their seats as if growling at a broken play in the football stadium.

"This is a great universe," he finally began, then shook his head as if he had water in his ears after a swim. "A great university."

His handlers eyed him with Nancy Reagan beatitude.

"Our sports teams are nationally ranked year after year—"

Mocking groans rose up across the room, as oddly hilarious as if walruses had been let loose at a tea party. But Littleterry, oblivious, blundered on. "And our faculty achievements have meaning, too. This is a great school with great professors who write great books. The words in these books are important, and that's why we're here to honor them." He paused and blinked. "The professors, not the words." Then he laughed. "Hell, it's both, isn't it?" he asked a bit desperately, like a comic dying in front of a late-night crowd. Then he beamed. "And here's the provost to do the honors."

"That was all he had to say?" Stefan whispered to me.

"Wasn't it enough?"

"Too much," someone behind us said.

Merry Glinka glided from the doorway up to the podium, shook Littleterry's hand, and waved at us as cheerily as if we were her kindergarten class and she were about to hand out finger paints.

Littleterry scuttled from the room as if pursued. Watching his retreat, you wouldn't have guessed he'd been SUM's aggressive, rude football coach. But ever since his assumption of power, he had seemed progressively more uneasy with groups of people who spoke English in complete sentences. All those years as coach had not prepared him for the challenge.

Merry Glinka looked eerily like Sue Ann Nivens on the *Mary Tyler Moore Show*, though her smile had even less warmth because her eyes were always angry and cold. She was dressed that day like a 1980s businesswoman, that is, in bad male drag: charcoal gray pin-striped suit with a fussy bow at her neck. Its softness fit her oval face but not her glazed-looking, blond-streaked pageboy, whose tips seemed lethal.

"Hello, everyone," she sang. "I'm sorry I'm late! Busy, busy, busy!"

"For a whole hour?" I said, leaning toward Stefan. "What a crock." I couldn't believe Glinka had the nerve to say it. What business couldn't have waited?

"I am so glad, so *very* glad, that I'm at a school that has been recognizing faculty with these receptions for—how many years?" She turned to the two minions, one of whom stage-whispered, "This is the first time." Then he blushed.

Unfazed, Glinka surged on. "What a wonderful university to honor its faculty in this splendid way—"

"Some honor," Summerscale heckled. "Cold coffee. Warm punch."

Glinka froze as people across the room murmured and laughed, turning to Summerscale, who was sitting tall and censorious but enjoying the attention. Then she said, "The publishing record at SUM is extraordinary," looking down at an index card she'd slipped from a pocket.

"And faculty salaries are the lowest in the Midwest!" Summerscale challenged.

Glinka turned a bit to beckon over one of the two goons, whispered something to him away from the microphone, and he sped from the room.

4

BEFORE Glinka could continue, a very dignified-looking sixtyish woman in a long black wool skirt and cowl-neck sweater rose from the front row with a loud, disgusted sigh. "I'm fed up—this is impossible," she said, and strode to the door. She turned there and called back to the provost, "Send me the plaque by campus mail."

She was saluted by spotty cheers. The steely-eyed Glinka clapped her hands together as if trying to quell unruly puppies. It didn't help when she said, "People—people," in the obnoxious tone of a junior high school teacher. "Now, I'm going to read out your names. Please come to the front and—"

Glinka stopped when the missing lackey returned with a campus security guard, wearing the stupidly overbraided new uniforms Littleterry had instituted just that past week. Though a sober dark blue, they were almost as bad as the ones Nixon had tried foisting on the White House guards, to national ridicule. Glinka nodded her head, and the guard slowly but efficiently followed her goon around the back of the room to the center aisle and down to the row where Summerscale sat glowering, seven or eight seats in. The guard looked quietly ready for anything.

"She's going to eject him," someone said with horror, as if witnessing the Defenestration of Prague. Hissing broke out in the crowd, along with catcalls. "Leave him alone! "What about free speech?" "Nazis!" "Go back to Neptune College—we don't want you here!" There were also a few cries of "Shame!" from people who had probably spent too much time watching British parliamentary debates on cable.

It was ugly—it was thrilling.

As the beefy, middle-aged guard approached Summerscale's aisle, I experienced the kind of moment you read about in clichéd books: a hush actually fell over the room, and the air was filled with hundreds of professors' bated breath.

"Sir," the guard told Summerscale from the aisle, "I'll have to ask you to leave." It was said with remarkable kindness, as if the guard were a bouncer at a chic club trying not to embarrass or enrage a celebrity patron.

"Go ahead," Summerscale replied. "Who's stopping you? Ask away."

A childish riposte from anyone else, perhaps, but Summerscale's baritone carried it off beautifully, making the guard's statement sound ludicrous. Hoots and more applause rallied Summerscale, who rose now to his very impressive height. He looked so belligerent that his battered tweed jacket might have been armor. For a moment I thought he was going to leave gracefully and turn his exit into a dignified demonstration of typical SUM injustice, but he faced the provost and stabbed a huge gnarled finger at her.

"Madame Provost, you are unconscionably rude. You kept us waiting for an hour, for no better reason than your pride. It thrills you to make a room full of people wait. Even the president arrived before you did."

Glinka waved furiously at the guard to suppress Summerscale, to *do* something, but he didn't move, as astounded as everyone else by Summerscale's denunciation.

Stefan grabbed my arm as if we were watching a John Woo action scene. This kind of confrontation, this display of truth being spoken to power, was a fantasy for most faculty on campus, and who knew how many staffers and students: the revenge of the subservient. It was so public it was amazing, and a little embarrassing, too, I thought. Then I realized that was the unconscious censoriousness of my parents working on me, the voices that had always urged fitting in, being dignified, never making a fuss. My parents were the epitome of the lines Edith Wharton had penned in *The*

Age of Innocence about people who believed that "nothing was more ill-bred than 'scenes,' except the behavior of those who gave rise to them."

Summerscale rolled on: "And better still, Madame Provost, you get to remind the faculty of their lowly position. The plaques are worthless. The real message is your having come an hour late. Short of fire or flood, there's no reason on earth to have kept us waiting. All it would have taken is saying to whomever you were busy with, 'I have to address the faculty now.' Seven simple words!" Summerscale crossed his burly arms. "Even if you were only making yourself busy," he added, the sarcasm weighted with just enough opprobrium to feel not petty, but devastating.

Glinka stared at him, her face curdled with rage.

I had thought Summerscale a well-meaning blowhard earlier in the semester, when he had tried to recruit me in some sort of vague liberation movement aimed at changing things in EAR. Sure, I thought, count me in any time for SUM's Taliban. But now I was impressed, and whether he was drunk or crazy didn't matter. The result was brilliant, in the British sense of the word.

Rusty Dominguez-St. John stood, a few rows behind him, and said in a smarmy bantering tone to Summerscale, "Hey, man, why don't you cool your jets?"

Summerscale roared, "Don't talk to me like that, you punk! I'm not a simpering idiot attending one of your phony workshops. Peddle your snake oil somewhere else."

The gloves were off. Rusty shot back, "Fuck you, limpdick! You think anyone cares about that tired old politeness crap—who are you kidding? This place is a business, and if you can't handle it, you should move on. You should have retired years ago. It's geezers like you who hold this university back."

Eyes as wide as if they could flash thunder at Rusty, Summerscale retorted, "I love this school, I love what it used to be. You're a cheap crook, even if they've put you on PBS."

Rusty seemed ready to thrash Summerscale, but easily half a dozen faculty held him back, and just as many across the room jumped up to shout at Rusty that he was a thug. One even called him a "Visigoth." It made me wonder why the Ostrogoths had never gotten a bad rep—were they really that much nicer?

Rusty sank back into his chair amid a growing frenzy of howls. I had no idea that he was so unpopular—as unpopular as Merry Glinka, it seemed.

But this exchange was just a sideshow. At the front of the room, a cluster of faculty members from the first few rows was swarming around the table, bent on retrieving their plaques, however dubious the honor. It was the perfect picture of what the administration had reduced us to: bald men fighting over a comb.

The second underling tried holding the faculty back and was soon tussling with one or two of them, seeming almost to be doing a funky kind of two-step. While he was occupied, a dozen more faculty members advanced on the table.

"Stop it!" Glinka shouted from the podium, her face red.

One of those dreadful brownies I hadn't bothered to even taste went flying up from the audience to sail right past Glinka's head. She ducked as if she'd been shot at. Others followed, like spitballs assaulting a substitute teacher.

As the struggle intensified at the table, padded envelopes slid from it, and other faculty members rushed to rescue their plaques from possible damage. People were on their feet in the room, shouting, pointing, holding their faces in stagy postures of disbelief. Some were appalled, some were enjoying the show, some just stared in horror at the growing chaos that was beginning to fill the room with as much noise as a train roaring into a tunnel.

Stefan and I were rubbernecking just like motorists passing a crash.

"How badly do you want your plaque?" I asked.

"We should get out of here." But even though the door was less than ten feet away, we couldn't move. I had witnessed a deadly riot last spring on campus, and had felt the same mix of shock and fascination. Both times were like the afternoon a few years back when there'd been a tornado in town. Just before the sirens went off, Stefan and I had stood in our backyard watching the greenish black sky start to twist and boil like a giant python curling in and around itself to suffocate its prey.

"Order! Order!" Glinka called, pounding the podium, her voice turning shrill. Who did she think she was, Judge Judy?

"Down with Whiteness Studies!" a woman shouted, and it might have been a good rallying cry, but it was somewhat premature, since the idea was only in the task force stage.

Now people were barging up to the plaque table by the dozens and barreling into the crowd with the avidity of claim jumpers in a gold rush. Summerscale was shouting something I couldn't make out, but it sounded like a mix of abuse and encouragement. He surged toward the back of the room, brushing past the security guard, who seemed utterly adrift.

Summerscale advanced on the buffet tables with their measly refreshments, surveyed them, then reached down, grabbed the edge, and upended one, then the other. Coffee urns crashed to the floor, rolling, clanking, disgorging grinds and what was left of that cold coffee. Pitchers of inadequately iced punch shattered, and the blood-red liquid shot onto the pallid floor tiles.

Then the lights went out across the room as people jostled and struggled near the wall switches, and the room was dimly lit from the hallway.

"This is crazy," Stefan said, and though we were holding our coats, still we didn't move from our spot until chairs started falling over as panic sparked in the darkest half of the room and professors surged forward. Stefan grabbed me by the shoulder and pulled me to the door just as the plaque table crashed onto its side in the midst of struggling, desperate professors. The crash sounded like an explosion as loud as the boom of the only earthquake I'd ever heard. And there was something else. I turned and saw that the books tables had been overturned onto each other, books pouring onto the floor. A woman shrieked.

Stefan shoved me through the door, and we tore down one hallway after another, jammed with curious students who were pushing in the opposite direction to see what was happening.

"That was a gun in there!" I said outside, catching my breath, amazed that Stefan had been able to retrace our path. "Some maniac fired a gun. The security guard? Why? Unless it went off by accident. But why would he even draw his gun?"

"It's not possible," Stefan said. "It was one of the tables. Or somebody broke a window."

"No, the tables came first. And I think I smelled smoke, too.

What else could it have been? Glinka may be a windbag, but I don't think she was in danger of exploding."

"Oh, God—like that fat man in the Monty Python movie," Stefan said, and we both started laughing in hysteria. Suddenly two campus security cars came screeching into the curved driveway in front of the center, disgorging half a dozen campus cops, who entered the building as grimly determined as if they were the muscle-bound heroes in *Predator*.

"I'm telling you, Stefan, somebody fired a gun in there."

"You've got guns on the brain—it's all those mysteries you're reading for your course, and Juno's Glock."

We looked at each other, and Stefan was obviously thinking what I was: "Juno. Juno shot someone in the melee." That meant Stefan had decided Juno *did* have a gun. I did not point out that he was reading mysteries and thrillers, too.

"Do you think anybody was hurt?" I asked.

"We're not going back there."

Word of the riot inside had apparently spread by cell phone; backpacked students were streaming to the glass-and-chrome doors nearest us from every direction. Stefan shook his head as if wanting to clear it of the entire afternoon. "Where's your car?"

I pointed. Stefan had walked over from his office at Parker Hall, so we took my car back to his.

"I need a drink," he said as we pulled into the treeless lot behind Parker, and I felt so cold and spaced-out it was a great idea. I thought his jaw might be trembling a bit.

"Are you okay?"

He shuddered a little. I wondered if the riot had triggered his secondhand memories of what his parents and Uncle Sasha had suffered during World War II when their city had been seized by the Nazis and they'd been forced into a ghetto. Sometimes a frantic crowd scene in a film disturbs him so much he can't watch it, and has to leave the room. Stefan had refused to see *Schindler's List* after reading a description of the terrifying half-hour sequence showing the liquidation of the ghetto. That was what impelled me to see the movie, but I hadn't pushed him. It was not for me to say anything about how Stefan dealt with his family's terrible past—at least not directly. With the help of his stepmother, I had tried to bring some Jewish observance into our lives to help heal his past, but sometimes I thought it was like trying to fix the *Titanic* with a wad of chewing gum.

"I don't think I could actually sit in a bar or anything right now," he said, "and I don't want to go home yet. There's a bottle of Seagram's in my office—and since we're right here . . ."

"Fine. Let's go upstairs."

Ah, Parker Hall. Resplendent in its decay and desuetude, the shabby nineteenth-century building was all the proof anyone needed that the university had a low opinion of EAR, which camped out there. The building was grimy and ramshackle enough to be the setting for a second-rate slasher film: *I Know What Class You Flunked Last Summer.* Other departments had newer buildings or had been retrofitted with carpeting and air conditioners. Other departments had their offices painted more frequently. Other departments did not have to be regularly visited by exterminators and campus animal control. Other departments didn't hear rumors that Parker might be torn down—even though it was one of SUM's original buildings—because it was beyond renovation.

But as writer-in-residence, Stefan had a gracious, large and airy corner office on the second floor, not far from EAR's main office, with fairly new sturdy oak bookcases, file cabinets, and desk. Stefan had supplied the ocher-and-beige southwestern-style rug that filled most of the open floor space. The glossy beige walls were covered with matted and framed Sargent, Caillebotte, and Caravaggio posters from exhibits we'd seen around the country, but the real pictures were through the two giant windows that framed exquisite views of the oldest part of campus, a pleasing blend of quirky sandstone buildings, curving walks, mammoth oaks and maples, and dense, low yew hedges. It wasn't remotely as picturesque as the kind of cloister you find at Oxford or even Harvard, given that the university was only 150 years old, but it was beautiful and contemplative enough any time of the year. A place to hide in.

We closed the door and hung up our coats, and I sat on the well-padded rust-and-beige-striped love seat while Stefan put the first CD of Handel's *Julius Caesar* on the portable CD player, turned it down low, and brought the bottle and two shot glasses out of his desk's capacious bottom drawer. The Baroque music was very soothing. Across from us were framed some of Stefan's favorite press pieces, features and reviews.

"Here's to chaos," I toasted, abashed now that I had been enjoying the spectacle at the Campus Center, and trying to exorcize it with a joke.

Stefan grimaced, but he toasted back. "This place is cursed. SUM. It has to be. It's like some Greek tragedy."

"You need a tragic hero for a tragedy."

"Okay, then, it's like the Peloponnesian Wars, where nobody wins."

"Listen, I bet there's violence on other campuses, it's just that we don't read about it, we're not there."

"How many other schools need their own emergency room?"

Stefan was referring to a recent multimillion-dollar addition to SUM's medical school, donated by a business school graduate who had made hundreds of dot-com millions. Remembering his days of drunken revelry at SUM—and a few broken bones—he wanted SUM students from now on to be as close to an ER as possible. It was a glamorous, embarrassing gift, showing off SUM at its best and its worst.

"And we both go to conferences," Stefan continued. "Do you ever trade forensic notes with people in your field? I don't! Come on, Nick, have Edith Wharton scholars ever attacked each other physically? Of course not. But when the Wharton scholars meet *here* for a conference, it's a disaster."

Sharon had recently said something similar about SUM, comparing it to that horrible doomed subdivision in *Poltergeist* that's secretly built over a graveyard.

"What's the place in Arizona—Sedona, right? Where there's supposed to be good energy? SUM is the opposite." Stefan looked disgusted and drained. I couldn't blame him.

"Then somebody should study it, right? Maybe turn it into a weapon."

Stefan grudgingly smiled, but the word *weapon* made me think of the din at the center, in which I could have sworn I'd heard a gun.

"Did it remind you of that spring—at the bridge?" Stefan asked with concern, stroking my hair.

I nodded. I had been having lunch near the Administration Building bridge when a brawl turned lethal, and a former student of mine was killed.

If I ever wanted to switch careers, I could probably lead a guided tour of SUM murder scenes, given my involvement in so many of them. Call it Playing the Zero SUM Game, perhaps.

The image faded. "You're right—this campus is like a fucking minefield. I should just never go anywhere," I said. "Stay home and become one of those obese shut-ins Maury Povich or some other daytime idiot coaxes back to life."

"Why not skip all three stages of that fantasy and just leave things the way they are? Your students would miss you. I'd miss you."

"Why? I'd be safe—and I'd be home."

"Right, lost under three hundred pounds of self-pity."

"Sharon's always said I have a comic vision of life. But it may be wearing thin. It's hard to see the humor in all this. I mean, what's going to happen next? An asteroid hits my car when I park at the mall? A herd of buffalo from northern Michigan breaks loose and stampedes through our house?"

"They'd have a long trip."

"So would the asteroid!"

Stefan laughed.

"You put up with a lot," I said.

"We both do. Neither one of us is especially low-maintenance."

"That's for sure." I kissed him, and then suddenly recalled his flurried entrance to the Campus Center. "So, what was up with Peter de Jonge? What couldn't you tell me before?"

"You're not going to believe this. He's the son of Holocaust survivors."

I waited a moment for Stefan to amplify what was so upsetting about that, but he seemed lost in the conversation he'd had with Peter, whom I'd only met once.

"I'm not tracking," I said, trying to prompt him. "What's the problem—?"

Stefan said, "He came up here to do Ph.D. course work in EAR partly because of me, because of what happened to me and how I've written about it."

"Wait. He wants to write fiction?"

"No. Maybe. It's confusing. He's also interested in the library, in one of their special collections. The hate groups."

"That's right." My cousin Sharon, who was an archivist at Columbia, had told me once that SUM was nationally known for its collection covering the Klan, the John Birch Society, and every other radical hate group, whether on the right or the left, dating back to the nineteenth century, when Christian Identity thinking took root in this state, a transplant from England. It was the lunacy that saw the British (or the people of your choice) as the true Jews descended from the Lost Ten Tribes, and the current Jews as poisonous frauds. Militias hadn't taken off in Michigan in the twentieth century in a vacuum.

The archives seemed an unsavory kind of fame, but there it was.

"Neptune College is pretty racist, isn't it? Down there they must think SUM is Babylon or worse, so what the hell is Peter de Jonge doing at Neptune College anyway?"

"His wife was born there—her family owns the town, almost. Peter told me he met her at Columbia when he was doing a psychology degree, and they moved back because she wouldn't live anywhere else."

"Wait a minute—Peter de Jonge was at Columbia?"

"Around the same time we were. Pretty strange."

"So Peter de Jonge is our age, right? And he's Jewish in a place like Neptune. That must be tough."

"I'm sure it is."

But Stefan wasn't done, I could tell that, and I asked, "There's something else, isn't there? Is he gay? Bi?"

"No, not at all. I didn't pick that up at all."

"What did you pick up?"

Stefan poured us another set of shots and then leaned back, eyes half-closed, as if he'd been asked by the police to describe an assailant and was trying as hard as possible to capture every detail.

"He was hiding something else."

"God, what else could he have to hide? He's a pyromaniac? A CIA agent? A registered Democrat?"

"It was something. I could sense him coming around to it, avoiding it, coming back. He seems tormented. Like he wanted to tell me, tell someone."

"A tormented psychologist. That's new."

"He's definitely anxious, and paranoid. He didn't want to go near the windows."

"What's the big deal?"

"It's like that thing you quoted to me about Sherlock Holmes, about the dog that didn't bark. Everyone who comes to my office comments on the view, sooner or later. But it was almost as if he didn't want to be seen."

"By whom?"

Stefan shrugged. "Like someone was following him."

"Great, Juno's being harassed, and a grad student is being stalked. What's next?" I tried picturing Peter de Jonge. "Tell me something—does he look Jewish to you?"

Stefan shrugged. "What's Jewish look like? We've both been to Israel. All those Jews from around the world, and they look like everybody."

"Yeah, but there are Jewish types." My parents had always noted who among my friends and acquaintances looked or didn't look Jewish with the same kind of attention that some black people focus on "good hair" and "bad hair." Growing up, I had come to think that not looking Jewish—or like what people generally thought was Jewish—was a definite advantage.

"Peter looks sort of like you, actually."

"Well, that settles it, because my folks always said I didn't look Jewish."

"Wait a minute—"

Before we could pursue Peter de Jonge's looks or mine, there was an impatient knock on the tall, solid-core door, and when Stefan opened it, we were both surprised to see Detective Valley there, surveying us with his typical sour expression.

The campus police had complete legal authority at SUM, which in effect was like a small town, though in emergencies like postgame riots they could call in cops from local jurisdictions for backup. The campus cops were recruited from Michigan's state police and various municipal police forces, and it was a plum job, but you wouldn't know that from Valley's perpetual dissatisfaction. He viewed the students and faculty as nothing more than potential or actual miscreants, and he definitely didn't like me or Stefan, based on five years of acquaintance and several criminal investigations we had unavoidably been involved in. I strongly suspected homophobia and anti-Semitism as well.

"Where's your bullwhip, detective?"

Valley glowered in the doorway, lamppost-thin and dressed in the kind of suit you saw on Mormon missionaries.

As always, Stefan spoke with far more cool. "Can we help you?"

Valley took that as an invitation and walked in, drifting over to one of the windows. "Nice view," he said suspiciously, as if Stefan had acquired it in some underhanded way.

"Is that the small talk before you zap us with tough questions?"

He rounded on me. "You think you're pretty clever, don't you?"

"I *am* clever. I come from a long line of clever people."

Valley breathed in, and seemed to be counting. He came out with, "What do you know about the incident that took place this afternoon at the Campus Center?" He leaned back against the thick old window frame and sat down. The ledge was almost as deep as a window seat would have been.

"We were there for a faculty reception," Stefan said. "It got weird, so we left."

Valley nodded. "Weird."

"Weird," Stefan repeated, and I burst out, "If you two are going to repeat everything, this'll take forever."

"Okay," Valley said. "What happened? What did you see?"

"Was someone hurt? Why are you asking us?" Valley almost always made me antagonistic.

He frowned. "I was assigned to EAR because I know what you people are like." He couldn't have been more disdainful if he were scraping dead bugs off his windshield. I wasn't ready to declare EAR a haven of sanity, but I sure didn't care for his outsider's contempt.

Stefan tried placating Valley by offering him some Seagram's, but Valley declined, so Stefan offered a brief narrative instead. "What happened? The provost gave a speech. Lots of people objected because she was an hour late and didn't even make a legitimate excuse. There was shouting. The table that had plaques honoring the faculty members for their published books was overturned. That's when we left."

I noticed that Stefan avoided mentioning Summerscale's vandalism at the back of the room. I would have done the same, feeling oddly protective of him. Besides, so many people had been there, including the one guard; why would we be needed as witnesses?

"That campus cop who was trying to eject Byron Summerscale," I said. "Was he the one who—"

"That professor is a troublemaker," Valley said with conviction. "He tried disrupting a party last month at Dean Bullerschmidt's house, and now this."

"All he did last month was get drunk and tell the truth. If that's a disruption—" I shrugged. Dean Bullerschmidt was a petty autocrat who could stand some disruption. He was currently off on a junket (aka "conference") in Beijing with other American university administrators, no doubt learning the finer points of handling unruly crowds.

"But was it the cop?" I asked.

"Was what the cop?"

"Did he fire the gun—and who was he aiming at—and did anyone get hurt?"

"What gun? Nobody fired a gun. What the hell are you

talking about? There wasn't any report of a gun at the scene," Valley assured me with all the charm of Lily Tomlin's Phone Lady. He asked Stefan, "Did you hear a gun?"

Stefan shook his head but, obviously embarrassed for me, said, "I didn't hear any gun—we were getting the hell out of there before it turned into a riot."

"You wouldn't call what was going on *already* a riot?" Valley asked, squinting at Stefan. "You're a writer, aren't you? Don't you pick words carefully?"

Stefan squirmed. "Okay, it was a riot, but—"

"You called it an incident before," I pointed out to Valley.

"That's true. I did. I'm not a writer. So you think someone brought a gun? You know faculty members who are in the habit of bringing weapons onto campus?" He looked as if he was on the edge of exploding. This was clearly beyond the pale even for him, a man who loathed the faculty.

"No," I said, "absolutely not." It wasn't exactly the truth, and it wasn't exactly a lie, either. It was convincing enough, anyway, because Valley nodded and seemed to dismiss my story. He turned back to Stefan. "Did you know things were going to escalate the way they did?"

Now Stefan was angry. "How could we know? Are you nuts? You think that chaos was *planned*? It was a conspiracy? The faculty on this campus couldn't even get themselves together enough to join a union, and they've tried three times. The only thing the average professor at SUM can pull off is himself."

"Huh," Valley said, reluctantly agreeing. Before he could go on with his peculiar interrogation, I heard loud footsteps down the hall, and Juno suddenly came to a halt outside Stefan's office door.

"You!" she bawled, entering the office like a trireme at ramming speed and heading right for Valley. She jabbed him in the chest, and he reared back. "Someone tried to kill me at the Campus Center, and not a single one of your shit-for-brains dimwitted lickspittle morons with their toy badges believed me!" Juno pulled down the zipper of her black top to reveal red marks at her throat, incidentally exposing the northern reaches of her cleavage. "Someone tried to strangle me when the lights went out. They pushed me down and got on top of me."

Valley might have gulped a little at the image.

"Get your mind out of the gutter!" Juno bellowed at him.

"Did you see the perpetrator?'

"In the dark?" she snapped. "With people pushing and shoving like *The Day of the Locust?* Of course not! I don't have X-ray eyes. Now, what are you going to do to find who was responsible?"

Valley surprised me by apologizing for any campus policemen who hadn't taken her seriously. "The situation was very confused."

So now it was a "situation."

"I'll be happy to take your statement when I'm done here," Valley told her.

Juno nodded fiercely. "Good. My office is at the end of the hall—you can't miss it. And don't keep me waiting long, or I'll sue your ass till there's nothing left but your butthole gasping for breath."

It may have been a strangely mixed metaphor, but it sure had force. Juno whirled around, adjuring Valley not to be late, and marched herself out the door, but she popped back in and said to Stefan, "Put some window shades up in here—it's like a fucking fish bowl," and then she tromped out and down the hall.

Valley watched her go, cleared his throat, then renewed questioning us with even less bonhomie than before. This time he was more direct.

"Do you know anyone who brought a gun to the Campus Center?"

Trying not to hesitate, I must have paused too long, and Valley pounced: "Well, do you?"

"So there *was* a gun," I said to Stefan, stalling. "See? Isn't that what you're saying, detective?"

"I don't believe it," Stefan said. "All that noise—it could have been anything. Car backfire, I don't know—"

Valley studied both of us, not revealing a thing.

"I don't know of anyone bringing a gun to the Campus Center," I said briskly, as if the question was stupid and I hadn't raised the whole subject myself. Of course this was technically true. Juno may have had a gun, but she hadn't mentioned bringing it to Parker Hall or anywhere else, though I supposed she must, since what good would it do protecting her if it stayed at home?

Stefan nodded, and neither one of us looked at the door that Juno had recently stalked through.

Clearly dissatisfied, Valley said he would want to talk to us again and started to leave. But he clearly had something more to say—to me. "This investigation isn't a joke, you know."

"We do."

"You're always around when there's trouble," Valley observed, as if trying to goad me.

"There were three hundred other people in that room."

"Three hundred and twenty-six. But none of them have your record."

"I have a *record?* I've never been arrested, how can I have a record?"

Valley left, having scored his points, and Stefan closed the door after him. I noted that the room was still redolent of Juno's perfume, and so did Stefan as he breathed it in. "Hurricane Juno strikes again." He laughed almost appreciatively.

"Don't laugh at her," I said. "Didn't you hear what she said? Someone tried to kill her."

"Nick—it was a mob scene, that's all. People get hurt without anyone intending to do it."

"What about those bruises?"

"They don't prove anything. She fell, she could have been stepped on."

"She said she was pushed—there's a difference."

"The room was dark—"

"But there was some light coming in from the hall," I said.

"Then why didn't she see who did it? Is she hiding his identity? I don't think so. It's all bullshit." Case closed, Stefan's expression said.

"Come on, why would she make up a story like that? And don't tell me it's because she wants attention. Juno gets attention just by walking into a room. You know that. Hell, she can be down the hall, and you'd hear the heels and smell the perfume. She doesn't have to invent crank phone calls or a stalker."

Stefan was thinking hard. "Juno claims she has a gun, right? What if she used it at the reception, or it went off by accident, and the attack is a cover story?"

"You're joking, right?"

"And what was she doing at the reception anyway? Her book was published under another name—she's only told a few people it was her." Juno had written an unlikely pseudonymous best-seller, part Western, part Egyptian epic, and all trash (which she freely admitted): *The Pharaoh's Last Stand*. "So if it wasn't because she was getting a plaque, why was she there? To cause trouble? Or get into it?"

"Come on, Stefan."

"Juno gives loose cannons a bad name," he said, his recurring suspicion of her welling up even stronger. "I wouldn't put anything past her."

Well, he had me there. We'd just seen her abuse Detective Valley. And though it was less fiery, how about flirting with a gay man in a pool, having him over to dinner, and talking about well-hung men? She was the poster girl for over-the-top.

But Stefan wasn't thinking about Juno anymore, because he said, "Did you notice how Valley never answered your question—about whether anyone was hurt? Maybe no one was, maybe there wasn't a gun, and he was trying to trick us somehow. There's no reason to trust him either."

"Come on, he's not smart enough to be Columbo."

"But he is shabby enough."

"Granted. And how do we know he actually works for the campus police? He's never shown us an ID, not that we asked. But seriously, he just showed up and said who he was, and we've always taken it on faith."

"So have the other cops on campus."

"Good point."

"You know what we need?" I said. "Let's forget about all this. Let's go home and open a really good bottle of wine tonight and make a blowout meal. Like that oregano-crusted roast leg of lamb with lemon, the one we made for your dad and Minnie last year, the one with potatoes and onions? We could pick up the lamb on the way. And we still have two bottles of that amazing Australian Grand Shiraz. Let's drink them both up. I'll even wear my tux for you."

We went right home and ended up ordering a large pepperoni pizza from our favorite place, drank a bottle of Valpolicella, and fell on each other afterward in bed like Byron's Assyrian army that "came down like the wolf on the fold."

I woke up in the middle of the night, my mind drifting through the afternoon's carnival. SUM was more and more starting to stand for State University of Maniacs. I grinned, remembering Juno's outrageousness, even though I was worried about her safety, and gloomily imagined tomorrow's headlines in the *Michiganapolis Tribune*.

I didn't want to read in case that woke Stefan up, so I headed down to my study and booted up to check my e-mail. I expected to see some with subject headings about the reception-turned-Guernica, but there were none.

The first e-mail I saw was from Dulcie Halligan, EAR's grim office manager, who was a lot like Barbara Bush without the pearls and the smile (and the smirking sons). Dulcie carried herself with a wounded, disappointed air that alone would have made it clear she felt superior to everyone in EAR, if she never spoke a word. But in case you were too dim to read her signals, she was ever quick to announce that she had graduated from SUM cum laude when she felt she was being dissed by the faculty, which was basically all the time.

Her defensiveness and sense of entitlement meant she was perfectly in tune with the quiet hysteria in our department, where professors knew all too well that the university didn't value what they did because they were so badly underpaid compared to other departments.

Perhaps Dulcie took EAR's low status personally, and that's why she was rude to faculty, though I had emerged from the crowd

of people she quietly loathed. Besides my being faculty, untenured, Jewish, gay, and from New York, Dulcie had an extra reason
not to like me: I had made the mistake of talking back to her that
semester. It had popped out even though I had always known the
worst thing you could do was alienate support staff, since they
were usually overworked and treated poorly.

So when I saw Dulcie's e-mail in the middle of the night, I was
predisposed to scowl—at her, and at myself.

The subject line read "Diversity Tree," and I had no idea what
that meant (was it like a phone tree?), so I had to find out:

> You'll notice that there's going to be a darling artificial
> tree on the counter in our main office. I've brought it in
> as a Diversity Tree for the holiday season and I wel-
> come everyone to adorn it with ornaments reflecting
> their faith persuasions so that we can celebrate the di-
> versity that is at the heart of us all.

I reread her post, imagining Dana Carvey's Church Lady
saying, "Well, isn't that special?" and wincing again at "faith per-
suasions," but I still didn't understand what was going on. The department policy was no official recognition of the holidays—that
is, Christmas—so wasn't this a violation of some kind? Or didn't
the policy apply to the secretarial staff? If it did, why was Dulcie
taking this initiative now?

I checked the time the message was sent: after five. I wondered what other people in the department thought about her
post, and just then I heard the ping of incoming mail and the
Netscape envelope icon appeared at the bottom right of my
screen. The new message also had the subject "Diversity Tree,"
and it was from Cash Jurevicius.

It read: "I feel so incredibly assaulted by Dulcie's e-mail that I
have to come out." That line threw me until I read on: "One of my
grandparents was Jewish, and I have always felt a kinship with the
Jewish people. But while I feel it's important to recognize difference, I don't think the office is a place to do that. I believe my
grandmother would have agreed."

Cash's late grandmother Grace had been chair of the old Department of English and American Studies at a time when the university was expanding and SUM had been a less contentious place to teach. Invoking her name wasn't just rhetoric, I had learned in my years at SUM: she was respected and even loved and often held up as an example of what academics should be like, but had ceased to be. Since her day, the field had been infested with criticism, which had become, as the essayist Fred Busch put it, "a living blanket of flies on the body of literature."

But did Cash mean Grace Jurevicius had been Jewish? Or was it a different grandparent he was talking about?

From the doorway, Stefan said, "Aren't you tired after everything you've been through? Don't you want to come back to bed?"

I waved him over, punched up Dulcie's e-mail. He leaned down to the screen, read it, glanced at me. "Is there more?"

I pulled up Cash's e-mail.

"Huh," was Stefan's response. "I wonder which grandparent he means."

"Yeah. Me, too. And why he's never mentioned it to us."

"Well, it's not like we're the Jewish welcome wagon or we're recruiting people for one of those home prayer groups," Stefan said.

"A *chavurah*."

"Right. It's none of our business."

"It is now."

Stefan settled onto the edge of my desk, looking as dreamily casual and handsome in blue silk pajama bottoms, with the books and files around him, as a guy in an Abercrombie and Fitch ad. See—I was doing it again, perceiving him as a figure, not a person. But maybe that was unavoidable in such an image-conscious culture? I sighed at his beautiful dark high-arched feet.

"Does it bother you?" he asked. "The tree."

"It's against departmental policy, isn't it? There haven't been any Christmas decorations the last few years."

He waved that away. "Since when have you been so rigid? EAR policies drive you nuts."

"I guess it does bother me, then. Christmas gets on my nerves. It's everywhere. Shoved down your throat. Walk around the neighborhood—people don't just have Christmas lights, they have flags and banners and gnomes and metalwork reindeer, and you can't escape it."

"Why should you have to?"

"Look. I can't screen things out the way you do. I'm not an introvert."

He frowned at the sharpness of my tone, and I apologized. I knew that was too simplistic a response, and I think I was snapping at him because I felt guilty about my attraction to Juno. Great. My confusion about her was already leaking into our relationship.

Stefan asked, "Are you worried about Juno?"

"No! Why should I be worried about Juno?"

He paused. "You believe her story about being attacked, so—"

"Oh. Yeah."

He frowned. "What did you think I meant?"

"You're right. It was the attack, and what's happened to me, and— Hey, is there any pizza left? I'm starving."

5

J UNO arrived unexpectedly Friday morning with a box of
doughnuts. She trooped up the driveway just after 7:00 A.M.
when I was picking up the morning paper from our front
steps. She waved with her free hand. She hadn't called first, but I
suppose that was a blessing, since it would have woken up Stefan,
who would not have been pleased with the news of her imminent
visitation.

I confess I thought my face might be turning a little red while
she approached, and to disguise that, I looked down as I unrolled
the newspaper for a quick check of the headline: "SUM PRO-
VOST ASSAULTED AT VIOLENT RALLY."

Violent, yes, but assaulted? By brownies? And why call it a
rally? It was a reception. Didn't the *Michiganapolis Tribune*'s
writers and copy editors know the difference? Perhaps not, since
the *Tribune* had run a headline a few years back announcing that
"Gandhi Ancestor Visits Governor." Not that you could fault
them, I suppose; Stefan complained that he was finding sub-
ject/verb agreement errors and incorrect vocabulary choices (like
"aside" instead of "beside" or "dignities" instead of "dignitaries") in
the *New York Times*.

Juno shoved the doughnut box at me and strode through the
open doorway down the hall into the kitchen, heels clacking like
maracas. I was glad to see her—there were some questions I
needed to ask. I closed the door and followed to find her peeling
off her calf-length raincoat, revealing a shiny black dress with
thick leopard-print cuffs that looked almost like a sculpture.

"Is that dress vinyl?" I set the box of doughnuts down on the kitchen island, ditto the newspaper, saving that for later.

Juno whirled for me. "No, darling. Rubber."

"Does it bounce?"

"That depends on who's playing with it. I bought it the last time I was in London, at the Sam Jones boutique. I'm sure your cousin Sharon's been there. You told me she adored London. How is she doing?"

"Recovering. It's going to be very slow."

Juno nodded sympathetically. "Honestly, Nick, it'll be worse than you think. It was for my sister. I don't mean to depress you, but you should be realistic. If she'd like my sister's phone number or e-mail, let me know."

Well, score one for Juno. Serena had insulted me when I mentioned Sharon yesterday afternoon, but Juno had brought her up unprompted. I suppose that was as good as any other reason to vote for Juno as EAR chair—perhaps a better reason, maybe even the best. Stefan would probably maintain that she was only pretending to be concerned, but even faked concern showed a kinder heart than Serena's rude question. And maybe Juno was a strong enough personality not to be brutalized by power the way Serena had been so quickly.

Oh, hell, that was stupid. Look how Juno had threatened me when I had dinner at her house. As chair of EAR she would probably run amok like some depraved Roman empress. Of course, there was something to be said for that: at least the common folk would get bread and circuses.

While Juno opened the box and surveyed the doughnuts as if she hadn't picked them herself but was confronting a slightly suspect gift, I was glad that I was showered, shaved, and dressed, and that Stefan was still asleep. I felt alert and ready, and he would have definitely resented Juno's intrusion, which was more than physical. The strong aroma of roasted coffee was giving way to her perfume, which filled the kitchen.

I was also pleased that Juno was wearing that outrageous black rubber dress because it turned me off completely, despite looking very good on her. I associate rubber clothing with English kinkiness and pasty-faced, flat-chested, skinny-armed men with teeth like battered tombstones. If Juno always wore rubber, it might cure me of my confusing sexual attraction to her.

Brandishing what looked like a coconut creme, Juno sat on a stool at the island (her dress creaking a bit) and explained the box: "People are always eating doughnuts on American television when they're in trouble—like the Brits drink strong tea."

"It works for me, Juno. But are we in trouble?"

She glanced around. "I did wonder, though, if you might be whipping up a nightingale frittata or some such delight."

"You can't get good nightingales this time of year."

"Too true."

"And you're a bit of a gourmet chef yourself, aren't you, judging by that foie gras festival?"

"I can fake it," she said. "Now, pour some coffee so we can make our plans." She crossed her legs tightly, her posture as regal as if she were holding court, and I thought of the way Edith Wharton liked describing how impressive people sat: they "throned." It fit Juno as well as her rubber dress.

I brought her a mug of Jamaican Blue Mountain and after pouring one for myself, asked, "Plans for what? Are we throwing a party?"

"Nick—do you think that ridiculous melee yesterday was spontaneous? Of course not! It was planned—it was a cover."

This was really bizarre—Stefan had used the same word to describe Juno's report of being attacked. That's what SUM had done to us—made us see everything as a sham, a facade. And in the middle of that realization, with the fragrance of the coffee seeming to tease every molecule of sugar from the doughnut box, I couldn't help wondering what life would be like having breakfast with Juno more often.

Noisy, to start with. And exciting. Like a performance of *Carmina Burana.*

What was wrong with me? I'd been having great sex with Stefan lately, and still my mind was straying to a fantasy life with Juno. So much for the rubber dress as—shall we say—a psychological prophylactic.

"Nick, I'm sure it was a cover," she repeated.

I asked her what she meant.

"It had nothing to do with that miserable Merry Glinka—God, what a name!—or that mouthy Byron Summerswitch."

"Summerscale."

"If you say so. But here's how I see it: the whole fracas was set up to camouflage the attack on me. Merry Glinka wasn't the target—*I* was."

I chomped into a delicious frosted chocolate doughnut, chewed a bit, and considered my reply. With faculty so demoralized on campus, and Merry Glinka having been hired so swiftly and in a closed meeting of the board of trustees, there was certainly a lot of brush for a forest fire. Anyone wanting to cause trouble could have done so without much incitement. "But that's pretty elaborate, isn't it? Staging a riot to get at one person?"

"No, it's simple. It's bloody elegant. It's perfect. Even *you're* skeptical." She delicately brushed some crumbs from one slender French-manicured hand onto the island's gray-blue polished granite. She was fastidious and crude—I loved the mix.

"I didn't say that I don't believe it—it's possible."

"But unlikely? That's the reason why it has to be true."

I thought of Oscar Wilde's Jack saying to Ernest: "Now produce your explanation, and pray make it improbable."

"Then who did it?"

"If I knew that, I wouldn't be plying you with doughnuts, now, would I?"

"You didn't see anything? It wasn't pitch-dark. There was light out in the hallway, wasn't there, even if it was getting dark outside?"

I expected her to lash back and say she wasn't a bat, but instead she put her head down in a completely uncharacteristic posture of embarrassment. "I panicked. When I went down, when I was pushed, I closed my eyes. Squeezed them shut. Like a little girl," she said disgustedly. "Hoping it'll all go away." Chin high now, she said, "I was scared."

"Do you remember *anything*?" I felt frustrated; Juno was the last person I'd expect to lose her bearings, ball or otherwise.

"I'd make a terrible witness." She sighed and considered. "Noise. Shouting. Things crashing."

"Why didn't you use your gun?"

"Because I wasn't thinking fast enough—" She started, face turning red. "That was sneaky."

"So you did have your gun with you. In your purse?"

"Of course I had it in my purse," she snapped. "Do you think I strapped it to my thigh, hoping for a shoot-out?"

"Does Valley know you had a gun with you? Because he asked me about it."

"My gun?"

"No. He asked if anyone I knew had brought a gun to the reception, or something like that."

"And you said—"

"I said no—what else? I wasn't going to betray you, don't worry."

She sipped her coffee thoughtfully, accepting the tribute. "Why was he interested?"

"Well, I brought it up, actually, since I thought I heard a gun go off." A bit desperately, I asked, "Didn't you?"

Arched eyebrows up, Juno shook her head, looking perplexed. "Really?"

"Nick, there was a lot of noise, all that shouting, tables falling over, broken glass . . . Maybe that's what you heard."

"Stefan says the same thing. But then why was Valley so intrigued? It seemed like he'd been waiting for me to bring it up."

Juno uncrossed her legs and crossed them again, slowly, almost contemplatively, if legs can be contemplative. It wasn't as revealing a moment as Sharon Stone had made it on film, but it was close.

"Didn't he raise it with you?" I wondered.

Juno glared at me, looking as hostile and surprised as I'd once seen David Bowie look when Dick Cavett kept asking him during an interview what Mick Jagger was like.

"And why did you go to the reception? Your book's anonymous, the most recent one, isn't it? So how could you have been on the list for a plaque?" I couldn't recall having seen her name in

the program book, and I had left mine behind when we ske-
daddled.

"What if I was there to see someone?"

"Who?"

"It's *whom*, and it's none of your business."

"I want to know."

"Are you interrogating me?"

"Juno, you said we had to make plans, you asked me to help
you. Don't I need information? I really think there's something
going on that involves a gun at the reception, even if nobody else
does. Wait—"

I grabbed the *Tribune* and quickly scanned the article, which
was actually a fairly accurate description of the chaos, with colorful quotes from Summerscale, who accused the provost of incitement by "malign neglect," and prim quotes from Merry Glinka,
who expressed sorrow that "unsavory elements disrupted a beautiful tribute to SUM's best and brightest."

"Revolting," Juno said as she leaned forward to read over my
shoulder, her perfume embracing me like a fog. "That woman
should be shot." Then she looked a bit embarrassed. "You know
what I mean." She recovered her brio. "Fired. Rebuked. Tormented. Exiled."

She reminded me just then of Serena Fisch a few years ago,
quoting with creepy accuracy the lines from *Conan* where
Schwarzenegger as the title character defines happiness this way:
"To crush your enemies, drive them before you, and hear the lam-
entation of their women." And just as I had felt then about Serena,
I was sure that Juno was not a woman to cross.

I read on in the *Tribune*. There was no mention in the article
of any gunfire, just that the university was planning an investigation, and the board of trustees had issued a brief statement expressing alarm and disappointment. Amazingly, though, nobody
had been hurt.

"And no significant property damage," I concluded.

"Of course not. Those superannuated farts couldn't throw
dice, let alone each other across a room. Breaking pitchers and
knocking over books—it's pitiful, it's a disgrace. You'd have to

party with students to see some real destruction." She sounded ready to launch into a dithyramb about flaming couches heaved into the street, an SUM student specialty that had given the campus a national black eye, so I headed her off:

"Juno, okay, it sounds like someone is after you. Granted. But what if there was a lot more going on yesterday?"

She finished a mildly phallic-looking cruller and reached for a napkin to blot her full and glistening lips. Even without the baked item, she was a woman who made the smallest gestures like that look hot, moving with the indolent grace of an odalisque.

"What are you thinking?" she asked. "I can tell it's about me."

"That you would have made a wonderful *grande horizon-tale*"—the French term for the famous courtesans of the nineteenth century.

"True." She said nothing, and for a moment I thought we were on the verge of flirting again. "Except I like doing it standing up. The friction's so much better."

I laughed, and it broke the mood.

"Nick, tell me what you mean by 'a lot more.'"

"Let's work backward, sort of. Let's say someone started the riot—and let's forget about your being attacked—"

"I'll never forget it."

"—and look at the impact. It's bad publicity, right?"

She nodded. "For the university."

"Yes, but not just SUM. For the faculty. It makes the faculty look bad. What if the administration is planning something, like—" Then it hit me: "Like abolishing tenure. Other schools have done it, or want to. So, what if this is part of a plan to undermine the faculty, to get public support for taking steps against them? It could be Merry Glinka's big move."

"But isn't that just like the conspiracy theories we were talking about at dinner?"

A bit huffily, I said, "Well, it's not exactly crazy."

"Maybe so, but it's too complicated," Juno insisted. "Remember Occam's razor? We should make the least assumptions and take the simplest solution. The administration here isn't smart enough to plan anything beyond fund-raising or a parade. You've practically said so yourself."

"Then what if it's somebody outside of the university?"

"Why bother? This university is choking on its own mediocrity. The vultures can let it turn to carrion on its own."

"Yuck."

Juno held out her mug for more coffee, and I obliged. When I sat back down, I said, "You still haven't told me what Valley asked you."

"It was nonsense, a waste of time. I gave him my statement, and he asked for details. I don't have details. He's useless and won't get anything done, though he's up to something strange, I feel it, too. And he didn't believe me—I'm sure he was humoring me because he's afraid of a sexual discrimination suit. He's going through the motions. That's why you and I have to take this on. Campus police! All they're good for is handing out parking tickets and trying to intimidate hardworking faculty who are—"

Before she could launch into an aria of defensiveness and abuse, I asked her about the Diversity Tree.

"The what?"

"Haven't you read Dulcie Halligan's e-mail?"

"I usually don't bother with my e-mail, it's a waste of time—unless I get one of those invitations to visit a teen sex website."

"Really?"

She grimaced. "Of course not! I was just winding you up. But even if I did read e-mail, I'd delete anything that sniveling bitch had to say. She's a weasel, a worm, a—"

While she struggled to find another noun starting with the letter W, I gave Juno the gist of Dulcie's message, but Juno didn't seem to care, which was a surprise. Given Juno's distaste for garish Christmas displays, I had expected her to be outraged by the Diversity Tree, and I had wanted her to be my ally.

"Nick, that hardly seems important now, given everything else. Let that little wench have her tree. Maybe she'll electrocute herself on it, multiculturally, of course."

Well, that was a start.

"So," she said. "Where do we begin?"

"Begin what?" Stefan asked from the door, wearing a black robe over his pajama bottoms. Barefoot, tousled, he looked gorgeous. He shambled over, said, "Doughnuts, yum," and kissed the top of my head as if Juno weren't there. She was admiring his dark, high-arched feet and didn't seem to mind being ignored. Pouring himself a cup of coffee, he repeated his question.

"Juno wants me to help investigate."

"Investigate what?"

"The attack, whoever's calling her, the riot, what Valley is up to." I turned to her. "That's everything, right?"

"Basically."

Stefan leaned back against a countertop, nodding, taking it all in. "You don't need an investigator, you need a SWAT team."

"I can't *get* a SWAT team," Juno growled.

"Really? I would have thought you could get as many men as you want, whenever you want."

Juno took it as a compliment, but I knew Stefan. When his face had that bland, helpful expression, it meant trouble.

Abruptly, Juno said, "I won't keep you any longer," scooping up her raincoat. "Let's talk later this morning and decide where to start." I followed her to the door. "He's a bit grouchy in the morning," she threw off as I opened the door. "It's very sexy."

Stefan was sitting on the stool Juno had just vacated. "The seat's really warm," he observed. It didn't sound like a compliment.

I tried a joke: "She's a hot momma."

"She's nuts. She's invented a stalker, and now she wants you to confirm that. Does she want you to find the stalker, or whatever he is?"

I didn't answer.

"Does she?"

"Sort of."

"You really believe somebody is after her? Even though you haven't seen anything or heard anything yourself? Even though you have no proof?"

"She's not making any of this up. I can feel it." I couldn't say that I was convinced because I also felt something about Juno—

though I suppose if I'd admitted it, he would have had more reason to doubt my perceptions.

Stefan closed his eyes wearily. We were back to the same disagreement, his slumping posture seemed to say.

"It's one thing to read mysteries and even teach a course in them. But trying to solve one yourself—?"

"So you think there *is* something mysterious."

"No, I just mean that life is life and books are books."

"Bullshit, Stefan, you're a writer—what's the difference? Some books are more real than anything that could happen to a person—they change you and stay with you forever. What about that night in college when you stayed up until three in the morning reading *The Portrait of a Lady*, and how it blew you wide open and you knew you wanted to be a writer? You've read that book five times since then, haven't you?"

"Seven," he admitted.

I, myself, had read it three times. "That book *is* life; at least, it's part of your life."

"Okay, I made a poor argument. I'm just trying to tell you that you're not a sleuth, you're a professor."

"Tell that to the students lining up outside my office at office hours. Stefan, I'd clean up if I sold T-shirts and baseball cap souvenirs. They think I'm da bomb. So how can you say I don't have a chance of figuring out what's going on with Juno? I haven't done too badly so far, have I?"

Stefan met my challenging stare. "It's a folie à deux if you get involved. But you're not getting involved. You've been talking about how crazy life is here, and on and on about *Poltergeist* and Greek tragedy, throwing in everything from the sublime to sitcoms."

"Actually, you're the one who was talking about Greece this week. Ancient Greece."

"And I'm right! How much bad publicity have you been part of or even responsible for? How many scandals? The dean dislikes you because you accused him of murder—yes, with my help. The president probably thinks you're a paid agitator working for the University of Michigan to make SUM look bad. Your tenure committee collapsed—"

"It wasn't my fault!"

"But people don't keep lists and mark things down accurately, do they? You get the blame no matter who did what. And now you want to risk getting into *more* trouble? You're not a lawyer taking a pro bono case, you're an assistant professor who needs to get tenure. You think tearing around campus with Juno pretending you're the Hardy Boys is going to help you in the slightest?"

"That's not why I would do it."

"Why, then?"

"To help Juno, and because I'm curious. I know I heard some kind of gunshot."

"Did Juno hear one? No? She didn't? Okay, then what more proof do you need if even Our Lady of Hallucinations disagrees with you?"

"I'm sure someone fired a gun."

Stefan shook his head and chose a doughnut. "These are good," he mumbled, his mouth half full. "Does Juno deliver pizza, too?"

"You're trying to make me laugh, to get me unhooked." And he was probably a little embarrassed by his outburst.

"Is it working?"

"Not really. Juno's being stalked, or at least it's starting. I was stalked, so I know how it feels, and I want to help her."

"It's not the same thing."

"Why not?"

He shoved a doughnut into his mouth, chewing angrily, obviously unable to make a point that would make my night of ignorance as bright as the Fourth of July. I wondered if he suspected I was attracted to Juno and wanted me to stay away from her, but hadn't worked it out clearly enough, or even at all. It was just reverberating, the way the truth did quietly for the characters in a Henry James novel until it rushed in like a storm and nothing was ever the same again.

I felt compelled to help Juno, but I realized it could be dangerous in too many ways.

Stefan had some errands to run, and I went to my study to check my e-mail. On his way out he stopped in the doorway and said, "I hope you won't get into anything messy with Juno."

I turned from the computer, worried that he might uncharac-teristically ask me to *promise* not to, but all he added was, "See you later."

I didn't have the courage to stop him and say that my relation-ship with Juno was already a mess.

I dialed up the department's listserv and found that there had been an overnight cascade of e-mails for and against the so-called Diversity Tree. As I leaned back and sipped what must have been my fourth cup at the computer and followed their trail, I saw what I'd seen on other lists before: the rhetorical violence people felt free to commit when they weren't face-to-face.

Several faculty members crudely asserted that Cash Jurevicus had no right to bring his grandmother into the argument, but they professed to speak for her, since they had known and worked with her. Huh?

But did any of that mean Grace Jurevicius—who'd left her wonderful collection of Michigania to the department, which had turned her office into a memorial library—was Jewish? If so, it was funny that no one had ever mentioned it, unless it was a secret and Cash was outing her and himself.

Both Kinderhoeks slammed Cash separately for having an opinion at all (since he was only an adjunct professor) and for not being "truly part of the EAR community."

Community? Lynch mobs had more fellow feeling.

Byron Summerscale attacked critics of Jurevicius for squash-ing his right to free speech, accused them of anti-Semitism, but also charged Cash with insensitivity. Predictably, Rusty Domin-guez–St. John said that everybody should take a deep breath and try to get centered. He, in turn, was told by three professors to take a hike.

And so on, with easily two dozen more e-mails, replies, and counter e-mails on the subject, the vitriol bubbling over like the cauldron in *Macbeth*. There was also a slew of e-mails with the subject line of "Reception," but I thought I'd save those for later. Before I could even compose a reply to add my own voice to the cyber-caterwauling, the phone rang. It was Juno.

"I'm at Parker Hall, and there's been another threat. You have to see it."

"See it? See what? What happened—are you all right?"

Juno hung up. I was dressed already, Stefan was gone, and I didn't have classes that day, which meant no explanations or hassles. I grabbed a coat and my keys and made the short drive to campus, worried, but assuming from the steely note in her voice that Juno wasn't hurt, just angry.

At Parker, I dashed upstairs, not running into anyone, and hurried down the second-floor hallway to Juno's office. I had never been in it before, though I'd caught glimpses. It was small but amazing: black wall-to-wall rug, black leather desk chair and accessories, and black-and-gold-striped curtains and tiebacks. The file cabinets were black, too, of course, and perhaps predictably, the only artwork was a framed poster of a gleaming, erotic Gustav Klimt.

Juno sat at the glass-topped table she used as a desk, fine hands clasping a garish-looking note. She passed it to me without a word. It was like the ransom notes you see in movies, a white sheet of paper bearing a message composed of wildly disparate letters cut from newspapers and magazines, a disorienting mix of colors and type fonts. The message itself was quite simple, though:

WE DON'T WANT YOU HERE

I set the note back on her desk, remembering the threat I had received just last month, one that had talked about death. This didn't seem so bad.

"It's almost polite," I ventured.

"Polite? It's a fucking warning."

I sat in a small black club chair. "Right. Sorry. Good point." God, I was as fumbling as Hugh Grant in *Four Weddings and a Funeral* after he proposed to Andie McDowell.

"How did it come?"

She handed me the standard business-size envelope with a Michiganapolis postmark and, of course, no return address. The date stamp was two days old.

"Did you call Detective Valley?"

"Why? What's he going to tell me?"

"It's not what he's going to tell you—it's what he can do. They can test this, trace it, track down the freak who's hassling you."

"Oh, Nick, everyone knows about fingerprints and DNA, even crazy people. Especially crazy people. Nobody's bloody stupid enough to spend the time on this letter and give himself away."

"Himself?"

She shrugged. "Force of habit. It could be a woman, why not?"

"Somebody really wants you gone. But why? Is it the race for EAR chair? That seems so—"

She narrowed her eyes at me as if aiming. I'd been going to say "petty," but she and Serena both were passionate power seekers, that was clear. Neither thought the job was petty in the slightest.

"Why does it say 'we' ?"

She shrugged, looking as dispirited as I'd seen her recently. "I wish I'd bought *two* dozen doughnuts."

"Well, you know what Molière said, don't you? 'When in danger, when in doubt, run in circles, scream and shout.' "

She begrudged me a smile. "I'm sure the original alexandrine was a bit more stately."

"I gave it just a workmanlike translation," I nodded, wondering if I should ask why she called me to her office. "But seriously, don't you think you should talk to Valley? This is under his purview, since it's happened on campus."

"He's a scumbag, and he's going to think that I sent the note to myself," Juno said darkly, as if already planning her retort should the accusation get made.

Stefan would probably have made the same assumption, and I caught myself thinking, What if Juno was crying wolf for some reason as strange as whatever had made her flirt with me in the pool at the Club?

"Even you," she muttered.

"God—am I transparent?"

"You're not opaque, that's for sure."

"So what happens now?"

"We have to investigate."

"Okay. If you mean that, get your coat. We're going to the

Campus Center, unless you have a class to meet— No? Then come on."

Juno didn't ask why, which impressed me. She dressed and locked up her office, and we headed down the hall to the stairs but were waylaid by the Kinderhoeks, who started chattering antiphonally about the riot with as much noise as a flock of grubby pigeons.

"Shocking."

"Disgraceful."

"No respect."

"Outrageous."

And so on. Juno and I nodded and escaped. "There's something freakish about them," she snarled as we stomped down the stairs. "As if they've been locked up in a cellar by their saner relatives and just escaped, and all they've been doing is talking to each other for the last hundred years. Shall we walk? I could use the fresh air."

Stefan loathed them, too, because they didn't treat students well and by avoiding teaching over the past few years as much as they could, eviscerated EAR's writing program, which had to rely on temporaries.

The Kinderhoeks didn't seem quite so awful to me. In fact, they were rather typical SUM professors, with the almost lubricious avidity for disaster that the university seemed to breed as successfully as some of its genetically engineered crops, which were earning it huge sums in patent rights. Sometimes I thought SUM could stand for Schadenfreude University of Michigan as well as anything else. If you had it bad in your department, then there was always someone who had it worse in another, or some university scandal or idiocy to revel in. The administration made a big deal about customer satisfaction when it came to students, but if it ever opened a complaints hotline for the faculty (without caller ID, of course), it would have to be available 24/7.

In our own way, we were as balkanized and disputatious as the students, whose acrid calls for diversity over the years had led to Babel. Korean business students, for instance, had their own group totally separate from Japanese business students, and even the gay business students couldn't get it together: their graduates and undergraduates had different organizations that seldom met and always disagreed. The competition for attention and funding was intense.

Pushing through the streams of students, Juno and I headed along a series of brick paths past old and peeling buildings and enormous cottonwood trees that in the late spring would litter the grass underneath them and seem to be snowing when the wind was up. Off to our right, the traffic on Michigan Avenue sounded farther away than it was, thanks to the dense shrubs and walls of trees that dulled the noise somewhat, even without their leaves.

"This is a beautiful campus," I said, thinking about its glories in spring; the acres of forsythia and lilacs, the cherry trees and redbuds, and the masses of tulips—all of it lovingly tended to by a small army of groundskeepers and students.

"It can be."

"No, it is. It's always beautiful. Any season. It's the people who spoil it."

"There's a lot to be said for the neutron bomb," Juno observed without irony.

When we reached the Campus Center, both of us slowed down, and I almost expected Juno to turn back, though she couldn't have known what my mission was. She was hesitating, and so was I. After all, I'd seen a dead body here a few years back, and now a riot. If I stepped inside, would the ceiling collapse? Would there be a fire? And she had been attacked there—it couldn't be easy to reenter the scene.

But as if signaled, we both moved on. Just inside the glass doors was a sign listing the various conference rooms on the first floor. "Do you remember which rooms we were in yesterday?"

"Huron, and Erie. I think. Or Superior? Two of the Great Lakes, anyway."

Around us everyone seemed to know exactly where they were going, which made the next minute or so a bit unreal, especially since most of them were students and twenty years younger than we were. Their quiet confidence made me feel suddenly superannuated.

Remembering how confusing the path had been to the reception, and the blur of leaving in the midst of chaos, I was determined not to get lost, so I slowly followed the series of white arrows as one corridor fed into another. Sooner than I thought it would happen, we were standing outside the scene of the reception whose failure had probably made the university glad it had waited five years to hold one. I doubted there would ever be another like it, given the bad publicity. SUM's students had rioted after winning games and losing them, but the faculty had always been docile up to now.

"It's different," Juno said in the quiet hallway, which looked like a dead end, as we stood at the doorway, looking in.

The two rooms that had been joined were separate again, but the difference was also the strange quiet in this part of the Campus Center, where the granite tiles on the bottom half of the walls and the pale gray paint above them gleamed as if brand-new.

"Shall we?" Juno said, and we entered. Juno flicked on the neon lights, which made the quiet seem more unnerving. The chairs were folded up and stacked against the back wall, there were no tables, and the heavy curtains were drawn against the sunshine. Juno stood smack in the middle of the empty room, gazing around.

"What did you bring me here for?" she asked almost seductively. "Are we communing with spirits? Tapping into the energy that hasn't been dispersed? Dousing?"

"Show me where you were sitting."

Juno dutifully turned to the back of the room as if picturing the tables that had held the chintzy refreshments and estimating how far forward the rows of chairs were from that spot. She paced over to the far side of the room. "I was in the back row—enjoying the bedlam."

"Show me."

Juno strode over for one of the chairs, dragged it over to a spot a few feet out from the curtained windows, opened the chair, and sat. "Right about here."

"Don't move."

I wandered around her, not sure what I was hunting for, but

making myself look as intensely as if I'd been blind all my life and an operation had just given me sight. I tried drinking everything in as I walked in slow, widening circles around Juno.

"Are we going to play musical chairs? Musical *chair*?"

"Quiet."

"Don't you want me to try reconstructing what happened before I was attacked? It might be easier in situ."

As I neared the window, I brushed against the curtains, and my hand seemed to catch in something. I pulled the heavy, ugly fabric closer.

"What?" Juno asked sharply.

"It looks like a bullet hole."

"Is *that* why we're here?" Juno jumped up to inspect the cloth I held out to her. "Nonsense—it's a moth hole."

I thought of Whoopi Goldberg saying in *Jumpin' Jack Flash* that she had moths—giant, junkie, mutant moths.

"It can't be. It's too even, too regular. Moths don't use circular saws." I found the seam where the curtains met, and slipped behind them. The stale air was dusty and hot. I examined the wall below the window where I estimated the "moth hole" lined up.

"Juno—look at this."

She rushed behind the curtains to join me, and stared where I was pointing.

Juno and I looked at the cinder-block wall. There was a hole in it. It looked like a bullet hole.

6

I couldn't breathe back there and slipped out, but Juno stayed behind the curtain for a moment longer. When she emerged, dust motes glinting around her, she had drawn a pen from her coat pocket. She crouched in front of the curtain and poked the pen through. It made a scratching noise on the cinder block. Then she stood and vigorously yanked the curtains back with the ratty cord that had been hanging there almost invisibly.

"See?" she said with triumph.

Her pen had left a mark quite a few feet to the left of the bullet hole.

"Give me the pen." I took it from her. Finding the hole in the curtain, I made my own test, sticking the pen through, and there was a little give. I yanked the curtain away from the wall and did my own bit of crowing: "Take a look! The curtains were open yesterday."

The holes had lined up—there was an ink mark clearly visible inside the one in the wall.

"Jesus, Mary, and Joseph," Juno breathed, walking back to the lone chair and sitting down, though her eyes were fixed on the cinder block.

"Somebody took a shot at me," she said, softly outraged. "You were right."

I nodded. "That's more than phone calls or a threatening note. That could have been lethal."

"Which means we've been tampering with a crime scene," Juno observed tartly. "Wait! If that's an actual bullet hole—where's the fucking bullet?"

And now I felt as creeped out as if someone were listening in on us, or watching us. Because it seemed obvious that the bullet had been dug out. And it couldn't have been Detective Valley or any other campus cop, since he claimed there hadn't been a gun fired. I bent over to inspect the hole, and it did seem scored by something sharp like a knife. I turned back to Juno, who looked pale, but supernally alert.

"Whoever shot at you must have come back when there wasn't anything in the paper about a gun and removed the evidence."

"But how could I have missed it?" Juno wondered.

Now I was quoting her: "The noise—the confusion—"

"—the excitement." She grinned evilly. "What a fucking zoo it was."

Yes, indeed. It had been a dirty little thrill to see the provost brought low, if only rhetorically. She had so much power over all our lives and was so totally removed from oversight and accountability, whereas we professors were always on the spot, it seemed, though of course no one monitored us systematically. You could almost say we were totally unsupervised, since we were on campus only a small part of every week meeting classes and seeing students during office hours. Yet we felt as spied upon and harassed as employees whose firms monitor every keystroke they take and every phone call.

I pulled over a chair, opened it, and sat by Juno, thinking we had come a very long way from when we had dined à deux at her house. We had crossed another border, together.

"How could it miss me," Juno went on thoughtfully, "is the other question. Unless it wasn't meant to kill me or hurt me, just to scare me off."

"From what? Running for chair? That's nuts. Serena wouldn't do it or set someone else up to do it for her."

"Why not? Since she's become acting chair, she's been a horror. And I say that as someone who used to be her friend."

I couldn't disagree. Serena's formerly wacky charm had been eclipsed, or maybe mummified was a better term. She was now aloof and distant, as if acting remotely human would soil her in some way, and in fact had come to resemble Coral Greathouse, the former chair, in manner if not in style—Coral had dressed and acted like an ex-nun, while Serena still wore flashy retro clothes that made you expect her to burst into a Cole Porter song in the hallway, or jump on a desk and jitterbug at a meeting.

Serena had been helpful to me before in a rallying, sarcastic kind of way, but I had no idea anymore if she was a friend or an enemy. She had been the former chair of Rhetoric before that department had been disbanded and combined with the Department of English and American Studies, and she often complained about second-class status in EAR. Yet here she was, meting out the same kind of mistreatment. Clearly her years of oppression had not filled her with magnanimity. She was bent on revenge.

And perhaps she feared that Juno might stand in her way.

"Would Serena be that desperate to scare you off?" I asked.

Juno nodded fiercely. "She's crazy—she's been deprived of power for ten years, more. Isn't that right? And now's her chance. It doesn't have to be her, anyway. It could be one of her adherents."

"But people hate her." Because Serena was tainted by having been the chair of a department even less respected by SUM than the one she had joined.

"That would make her even more hateful herself."

People in EAR also hated Juno for being so outrageous. Though you could say, like caged and abused animals, they hated in general, out of boredom, and were always ready to lash out.

"But is that definitely a bullet hole?" Juno said, frowning. "How can we tell for sure? And more to the point, how do we know it's recent?"

"It looks recent. You think this room is a firing range?"

Juno's eyes were scorching. "How many bullet holes have you seen in your life? I'm not talking about *Law and Order*. I mean close up. We could be totally fucking wrong, and the wall and the curtain were damaged years ago, and no one noticed."

"No, that's not possible; they've renovated this building extensively since some pipes burst a few years ago."

She glanced around the room and shuddered. "This shithole has been renovated?"

"Trust me, it looked worse." Though no one had been murdered there before.

We had been alone with our speculations for so long that when my cell phone rang, it was as if someone I didn't know was in the room and had tapped me on the shoulder. I dropped the phone digging it out of my pocket.

"Nerves of steel," Juno noted dryly as I took the call. It was Stefan.

"Nick—I tried you at home—"

"Where are you?" I asked.

"At Parker. There's an emergency departmental meeting called for four. I tried you at home but you didn't pick up. Where are you?"

"I'm in the middle of something—I'll call you back later," I said, and hung up before he could ask me anything more. I didn't want to explain what I'd been doing with Juno, certainly not on the phone.

"Hubby checking up on you?" she asked coyly. "Doesn't trust you alone?"

I told Juno about the emergency meeting.

She leaped to her feet. "Good Christ, *another* fucking meeting? That's all anyone does around here is hold meetings, plan meetings, talk about meetings, analyze meetings. And breakfast meetings! Is there anything more obscene! As if I want to face any of those turds over greasy bacon and cardboardy scrambled eggs."

I put my chair back against the wall, but Juno looked like she was just gearing up for a rant, so I took her chair, too, folded it up, and stacked it against the others. That seemed to get her attention, or at least refocus her attention away from her gripes.

"If you beat Serena in the election," I said, "you'll have constant meetings with the department cochairs, committees, subcommittees, upper administrators, the dean, even students. You can't just issue pronunciamentos and hope everyone obeys."

"No? Maybe it's time someone tried." But the bravado seemed unconvincing even to Juno herself.

We headed out, and the return trip to Parker seemed much longer, not just because the air was chillier or because we faced some kind of departmental crisis—again. I think Juno was as weighed down by what we'd discovered as I was. Well, more, of course; after all, the bullet had been aimed at her in one way or another, to warn her or hurt her.

And perhaps she was also thinking about the maelstrom of meetings that would threaten to drag her under if she were chair of EAR. Like most people, she probably had imagined only the benefits of what she desired, ignoring the problems and commitments involved. Power, even the limited power of a department chair, would come with enormous hassles that could easily overshadow the joy of claiming the office. It was like moving into a new house and suffering the automatic crash and depression many people go through afterward, the sense of dread: "What have I gotten myself into?" Stefan and I had both suffered after moving to Michiganapolis from western Massachusetts, and that dislocation was more than the genetic suspicion New Yorkers have of the untamed lands to the west of the Hudson River.

Walking alongside Juno, I was thinking of our nascent investigation, and Stefan warning me to stay out of any involvement with Juno. For better or worse, I was committed, and not just because of my unprecedented attraction to Professor Dromgoole. In part, it was the same stubbornness that had fueled my five-year work on the Edith Wharton bibliography, a project far more complex and frustrating than you'd imagine if you were leafing through the finished book, which covered everything Wharton had ever written and everything ever written about her.

There were days I spent trying to track down journals or newspapers that had changed their names. Or obituaries that Wharton had written about people whose names meant nothing to me and were incredibly difficult to trace. Or articles written in Urdu or High Mandarin or Locust Valley Lockjaw that meant finding a reputable translator, always harder and more expensive than I expected.

Then there were the surprising mysteries: articles that had been cut out in library after library. At first I had thought it was just coincidence, but then I discovered that a number of contemporary Wharton critics had something to hide. They had been quoting much earlier reviews or articles without attribution, or claiming discoveries that they had never made—but only *I* knew the truth, since I had followed the documentation through every year, every decade. It was no joke to say I knew where the bodies were buried in Wharton studies, which was doubtless one reason everyone in the field was nice to me.

None of this activity was exactly fighting overpopulation, but it demanded doggedness, following clues, and piecing together evidence.

It was barely noon when Juno and I returned to crumbling Parker Hall, its nineteenth-century sandstone pillars and steps looking even duller than usual in the cloudy light. I felt depressed, as I often did facing that gloomy pile. It was the kind of characterless but mildly sinister menacing building that Vincent Price could have presided over in some tacky 1950s horror movie, brooding and cackling.

"We should have lunch," Juno proposed. "I brought enough for two."

I looked up the wide stairs to the incongruously modern front doors that reduced heat loss and increased ugliness.

"Maybe another time."

"But don't you want to see the miserable Diversity Tree?"

I told Juno I could wait and circled the building, found my car, and drove home, feeling as if something embarrassing had passed between me and Juno, and we needed distance from each other right away.

I felt tired even though I had the afternoon off—all of my students were supposed to be working in the library—so I took a nap, finally waking from a sleep that was so deep I not only felt disoriented but almost dematerialized, as if my dim consciousness were simply floating in the room with no connection to my body or anything around me. It was as if someone were trying to drag me back from an abyss. And when I did start to feel present in my body, I realized I was sweaty and suffering from cottonmouth.

I dragged myself to the kitchen to gulp down a few glasses of water, thinking that the darkness I'd emerged from, well, that must be like death. Except you didn't come back—unless you were on a Discovery Channel special and the reentrance was accompanied by flashing lights and eerie music.

I woozily cleaned up in the kitchen, the habitual motions at the island, the counter, and the dishwasher slowly bringing me back to full awareness of myself and my surroundings, though I still felt logy enough to pop some Tylenol. The clock on the double oven read 3:15, and that's when I remembered the meeting. I tore back upstairs to shower and change, since I felt as if I'd been sleeping in my clothes for days in a ditch somewhere.

Down in my study, feeling almost completely awake now, I checked my messages. There was one from Stefan: "I tried you again after my class, but you didn't answer. And your cell phone's off. Are you okay? I'll be in my office—call me, please."

I called him, and his relief at hearing my voice was the last piece I needed to complete my return to awareness.

"Nick—what's been going on—where have you been?"

I explained, briefly, and was glad he didn't criticize my expedition to the Campus Center. I left out the bullet hole.

"Is that all? God, I was imagining the worst—a car accident—a heart attack—"

"I'm too young for a heart attack."

"And Sharon's too young for a brain tumor," Stefan said grimly. "Why don't I wait for you at my office, and then we'll go to the meeting together, okay?"

"Fine."

The EAR secretaries must have sent up enough flares, because when I hit the second floor of EAR for the meeting, the sepulchral hallway was jammed with dozens of faculty members, everyone looking as surly and put-upon as Bourbon Street revelers who've just been told there's no more beer.

I pushed through to Stefan's office just as Peter de Jonge was on his way out. He looked away when I said hello, as if avoiding attention, and disappeared. He wasn't how I remembered him.

Though he was over forty, he had the sideburns, close-cropped goatee, and Caesar haircut of a college student, and the clothes to match: white T-shirt under a baggy flannel shirt and baggy jeans under his parka. It looked almost like a disguise.

"What was his hurry?" I asked Stefan, who gave me a big welcome-to-my-country hug at the door and pulled me inside.

"Who knows? He wasn't here long and didn't say very much."

"Didn't you tell me he was on the staff at Neptune? Counselor or something? Is he dressing like that to connect with the students?"

Stefan shrugged.

"He's good-looking," I said. "I sort of forgot."

"Of course he is—he looks like you."

"Oh, stop it—you think everyone looks like me. He's taller."

"Not much."

"And his hair's lighter."

"Not very."

"He's got sideburns and a beard!"

"They're light."

"And he looks *Dutch*."

Stefan held up his hands. "You win." Stefan moved to the open door and peered out into the crowded dark hall. "I still think he's got a real problem he wants to tell me about, tell somebody about."

"So ask him."

Stefan turned back to me. "Not my style."

"Thanks."

"I didn't mean anything critical—you know that."

I nodded. "Just kidding." And we exchanged what I'd read once some psychologists call "extended mutual facial gazing." It was very nice.

"You know, when I couldn't get a hold of you, Nick, it made me think about that time you got lost driving from the airport. . . ."

Our first semester at SUM, I'd been heading home from a conference in San Diego, but Northwest's last flight from Detroit to Michiganapolis had been canceled, and I rented a car rather than stay overnight at an airport hotel. The hour-and-a-half drive took four hours because I got lost several times, first in Detroit, having never driven the route before. I had no cell phone back then, and every time I stopped somewhere to get directions and to tell Stefan where I was, the nearby pay phones were either busy or out of order. Assuming I'd been the victim of a carjacking or in an accident, Stefan had panicked and was only a few minutes away from calling the state police when I finally drove up to our house, totally frustrated and crazed myself.

Stefan had grabbed me and whirled me around that night as if we'd been separated by years, not hours, and by a war rather than misdirection.

"That was a nightmare," I said, thinking, And only the beginning.

I smelled Juno's perfume before I saw her. "Jesus H. Christ, it's the *Night of the Living Dead* out there," she growled, standing in the doorway of Stefan's office. "Bring your wooden stakes and a mallet. Unless you have a flamethrower?"

Stefan locked up, and he and I followed Juno as she cut through the stream of faculty members heading to the departmental conference room, a dismal, claustrophobic former classroom that had been remodeled by a sadist. As if the hideous beige venetian blinds and painted-over wainscoting weren't ugly and depressing enough, someone had installed too many buzzing neon lights in a lowered ceiling and added some fifty butt-tormenting small chair-desks that were unmovable because they were bolted to the floor. Sitting in one of them for more than a few moments was like being in an outtake from *Clockwork Orange*, and they were only easy to extricate yourself from if you were a double-jointed expert at the lambada.

Stefan and I sat in the far corner near the back. I wasn't used to going to a meeting with him because he avoided them and got away with it as writer-in-residence. Juno sat nearby, but in the last row, as if she wanted to have her back to a wall so she could survey everyone who walked in. I watched her and realized it was true—she was scanning the room as if expecting to unmask her persecutor. Her small shoulder bag sat in her lap, and looked over-stuffed; I assumed she had brought her gun.

As the room filled up, I felt both comforted by Stefan's great relief that I was okay, and troubled by what his reaction might be to my discovery in the Campus Center. He'd asked me not to go detecting with Juno, and that's exactly what I'd done, risking my career in the department and at SUM, a career whose end result I saw all around me in the faces of the older faculty. Tenure and decades at the university had done nothing to sweeten their dispositions; they looked sour, bitter, or sneeringly contemptuous. The ghost of Nick Hoffman future.

Serena arrived right at 4:00, with as much ceremonial stiffness in her walk as if she'd been borne in on a palanquin. Her dense geisha-black hair was rolled into Princess Leia buns, and with pounds of silver bracelets at each wrist and a dark blue, wide-shouldered, double-breasted suit that looked like a uniform, she had a weirdly hieratic chic.

She stood at the front of the room and clapped her hands together like a magician. It worked. People rushed to fill the remaining seats, and she smiled knowingly at her success. "Thank you," she said softly, and it felt rather snide. I expected Juno to make one of her typical undercutting stage-whispered asides, but she was oddly silent.

"Thank you for coming at such short notice. And I owe a special thanks to the department's secretaries for contacting everyone so expeditiously. I'm sure we all appreciate the hard work they do."

I wondered if that was meant for me, since I'd had a run-in with Dulcie Halligan before.

"Now, there are a number of issues we need to address immediately."

My day had been so strange that I'd never thought much about why the meeting was being called. After all, as Juno had noted, we were addicted to meetings at SUM, to the appearance of movement, activity, and progress. It seemed just standard operating procedure, but I was wrong about that afternoon's gathering of the clans, because Serena had a surprise for us.

"In my discussions with the provost," she began confidingly to the packed room—and there was a rustle she clearly enjoyed as people registered that she'd been communing with SUM's Kubla

Khan—"it has become clear that we need better lines of communication between the faculty and the administration. To further that significant goal, the provost has appointed ambassadors to each college who will liaise and create and promote a deeper level of understanding." She sounded like a memo, not a person, and there was something Alice in Wonderland-like about not mentioning the recent riot.

"This program will be named LOCK: Lines that are Open Create Knowledge. And there will be mission statements in your boxes soon. The highlight is that the provost intends to be regularly in touch with our needs and concerns. Right now I'd just like to briefly introduce the new ambassador to our college."

Serena waved a lordly hand, and a man stood up in the front row. It was one of the thugs who'd been at the reception riot, defending the plaque table—either the shorter one or the taller one, I couldn't tell which. He bowed his head modestly as if about to say grace, and Serena introduced him: "Tyler Mooney-Mauser."

"I'm looking forward to working together," Tyler said, smiling unctuously, and he sat down to a profound silence. He was much milder than he'd been at the reception.

Serena went on in the mildly rhapsodic accents of a decades-old World's Fair documentary about the glories of future living. "Tyler will be attending all department meetings and regularly consulting with the provost to keep lines of communication open and free. This is a wonderful opportunity to increase understanding across the university, and I hope you'll all make him feel welcome." And then, in another tonal change, she asked, "Are there any questions?" with the bored chirpiness of a waitress asking if you'd made your beverage selection.

People shifted as much as they could in the torturous chairs, shuffled their feet, cleared their throats, scratched—everyone apparently waiting for someone else to take the lead.

Stefan looked at me quizzically and then bugged out his eyes. With difficulty I kept myself from laughing, hoping that we weren't being noticed at the back of the room, which was already too hot.

"LOCK?" Stefan whispered. "Can you believe it?" I shushed

him with a shake of my head. I wasn't surprised by SUM's latest purchase from Acronyms R Us, but it did seem ridiculous just the same.

Byron Summerscale raised his hand in a parody of a good little schoolboy. Serena nodded reluctantly at him, and he asked, "Since open communication is so important, does someone from EAR get to sit in on all of the provost's meetings?"

Serena frowned, patently disappointed that EAR's new rabble-rouser had asked the first question, but probably relieved he wasn't shouting. "Of course not."

"Then the knowledge flows only one way. Which means these ambassadors are nothing more than spies." Summerscale's reasonable tone paradoxically made the charge even more outrageous—and more believable.

The word *spies* triggered muttered conversations across the room, but no one else's voice rose enough to be distinguished. But maybe they were also commenting on the fact that his fires were banked; the raging bull of the faculty reception was curiously subdued.

"This, shall we say, ambassadorial oversight seems an unwarranted intrusion into academic affairs," Summerscale went on, almost as if talking to himself. I thought his formality sounded loony but appropriate. I mean, whose idea was it to call the provost's flunkies "ambassadors" anyway? How pretentious!

Serena looked torn between wanting to disembowel Summerscale and wanting to impress Mooney-Mauser with how well and patiently she ran things at EAR. Looking as frozen and tense as Gene Wilder when he stabs himself with the scalpel in *Young Frankenstein*, she said, "Thank you for your opinion, Professor Summerscale. Are there other comments?"

"We don't need better communication, and we don't need the Gestapo watching what we do and say at meetings. We need higher salaries," said Cash Jurevicius.

Professors turned and stared at him or leaned in to one another, everyone muttering like actors backstage saying "Peas and carrots, peas and carrots" to simulate crowd noise. People's faces were wide open, and I could read agreement with Cash's complaints wrestling with anger that he had spoken up. After all, he was only an adjunct professor despite his connection through his grandmother to EAR's grand past, and if he got more money, it could mean less for other people.

"My grandmother would never have agreed to such a totalitarian step," Cash insisted, his pretty, pouty head held high.

I watched Juno fumble with her purse, and for a moment I thought she was going to whip out her gun and plug Serena (or even the ambassador), but she dug out a black-and-gold sequined compact, set it down on her desk, opened it, and unostentatiously proceeded to touch up her makeup. It was a magnificently quiet gesture of contempt for the whole discussion. Her gestures were so soft and elaborate she might have been a mime. She was certainly richly costumed enough.

But why was she ignoring Cash, too? Shouldn't she have been seconding his remarks? Perhaps I was misreading her, and she was trying to hide her relationship with him.

"Your grandmother isn't chair of this department anymore," Serena pointed out to Cash with a sickly sweet smile. Making nice must have been killing her. "I am."

"Not for long," Juno murmured, putting her makeup away. The stone-faced remark spread plenty of ripples through the room, and Serena bristled. I doubted whether she'd heard exactly what Juno had said, but like a substitute teacher facing a class dotted with troublemakers, she could tell where the disturbance was emanating from. She glared at Juno, whose shoulders rippled as if she were limbering up for an attack.

"Are there any other comments or questions?" Serena asked, her voice severe.

The answering silence made me realize not just how cowed and beaten down EAR faculty were, but how angry the provost must be about the reception-gone-bad, and how determined she was to rule SUM with an iron fist, gloved in velvet or not. No wonder the EAR faculty looked shocked and confused now. LOCK was more than just a stupid acronym; this new initiative completely broke with academic tradition at SUM. I could mock the name, but the reality was bitter. I glanced at Stefan and read the same question in his eyes: Should I say something?

Was it wiser to wait and see if this initiative actually flew, if it survived any possible challenges from the faculty senate or the board of trustees? Did it make any sense to stick our necks out so early?

Stefan shrugged, looking somewhat embarrassed. I felt ashamed myself to see the department roll over and play dead, but there wasn't much I could do facing the administrative juggernaut. As writer-in-residence, Stefan had far more clout than I did, but that was all relative, and if he wasn't going to say anything public yet, I sure was keeping mum.

Then Juno spoke up, with the silky deference of Lucretia Borgia inviting a guest to have more wine. "Isn't it somewhat irregular to discuss the presence of an administrative observer in the presence of the administrative observer? How can you expect an open forum?"

Serena rolled her eyes, but Tyler Mooney-Mauser answered, turning around in his chair: "I've been instructed to observe *all* proceedings."

"What else have you been instructed to do?" Juno inquired calmly. Everyone was so used to her high-volume presence that these subdued comments were electrifying, far more so than even Summerscale's reasonableness.

"That's confidential," Mooney-Mauser said, turning his back to her and making some kind of signal to Serena, who took over. "Juno," she said spitefully, "I can't imagine you holding back anything. Even if you tried."

"I'm speaking for other faculty whose positions aren't as secure."

"Why not speak for yourself?" Serena said through clenched teeth.

I expected one of the department's old boys to hiss, "Catfight!"

"Juno's right," Cash said, amid a chorus of approbation. There were calls for Tyler to leave, and the loudest came from an unlikely source. Rusty Dominguez–St. John stood and said, "Dudes, we need to create a safe space." Then he blew his limited credibility by adding, "We should find a retreat center where we can all unwind and get to know each other in an uncompetitive, nurturing environment. Trust walks, guided imagery, drumming—"

A few faculty members laughed, and Juno raised her voice to be heard as Rusty sat back down: "There's no need to go anywhere. This is our fucking conference room, and no one invited that bloody intruder."

"I did," Serena shot, and then shook her head quickly as if to deny any association with Juno's insult. "He's here at my invitation and—"

"Send him home!" Rusty warned. "He's got bad karma."

Serena turned red. "Will you—"

Juno cut her off. "How can you expect to run a department when you can barely control a meeting?"

"Why don't you ladies ease up?" Summerscale rumbled. "Scratch each other's eyes out someplace else. This is a serious crisis." Les Peterman, Martin Wardell, and Larry Rich guffawed at Summerscale's sally. Unrepentantly boorish, they were EAR's answer to the Weird Sisters. Grizzled boozers and jocks, the three of them had been so rude for so long, they took pride in being members of what H. L. Mencken called The Booboisie. I suppose they adopted this manner to show they were just regular guys even though they had Ph.D.s. They were the kind of men you could find at The Club, harassing teenagers on the court in pickup games of basketball, sooner or later blowing out a knee or collapsing with a heart attack, having forgotten they were no longer young.

As EAR had become more cliquish and embattled, the three had seemed to band together as a sort of old guard, snarling about the way things should be and cackling over dirty jokes. I rarely saw them except in the decrepit coffee room or at meetings, where one of them was bound to say something ridiculous. Until now, though, they'd been pretty quiet.

But they were outnumbered. After a shocked pause, the room erupted with boos from women and men, repeating the taboo word *Ladies*. Summerscale didn't seem at all bothered—he basked in the attention.

Serena cut off the noise with a karate-like hand chop. "There is no question about the provost's observer leaving. That is not an option."

"Then why bother with a discussion at all?" Stefan whispered to me, clearly not wanting to get drawn into the conflict. I shrugged.

"Let's move on," Serena said briskly, as if there had been no flaring tempers, no controversy, nothing—not even Summerscale's sexism. For all its surface amiability, her response had the off-putting feel of "Take a hike!" Would anyone vote for her as chair when the elections were held over break? Or would the animus most faculty had for Juno be enough to secure her a win as the lesser of two evils?

Before she could deliver her next pronouncement, Summerscale asked, "Given your access to the halls of power, can you tell us whether the rumors about Comerica are true?"

Serena looked sharply at Mooney-Mauser, who spread his hands out in a quick dismissive gesture. "We're not here to talk about rumors," she said briskly.

"Is it true now that Comerica's name is on the stadium in Detroit, they're in negotiations with SUM? That they've offered SUM *half a billion dollars?*"

The room was hushed in that academic mix of outrage, envy, and alarm at the mention of serious money.

"Half a billion for what?" Juno guffawed. "To rename the university? What will they call it? Comerica University of Michigan? C-U-M? CUM?"

Nobody laughed.

Very stiffly, Serena said, "I will not comment on gossip. Let's move on." There was a visible easing of tension at that point, since I'm sure nobody—except perhaps Juno—relished the idea of becoming a national joke.

"The provost and President Littleterry are dedicated to seeing the Whiteness Studies Task Force take shape—and to that end, they have asked department chairs to solicit self-nominations for representatives from each college."

It took me a second or two to untangle the last bit of bureaucratese, but I wasn't sure I completely got it. How was someone self-nominated, and if he or she was, did it mean anything? But before those questions could get sorted out, Cash Jurevicius erupted. "I can't believe you're bringing up that bogus bullshit! There's no such thing as Whiteness Studies—it's without any merit whatsoever."

An illogical position, but that didn't matter much. I studied the room and could make out some clenched fists—the people who disagreed—and gleaming eyes—those who supported him.

He held out a hand and ticked off his points, finger by finger. "Where are the respected journals?" he asked. "The conferences? The departments or programs at major universities? The endowed chairs?" That phrase produced some gasps, since EAR had recently seen trouble with an endowed chair. But Cash didn't relent. "SUM cannot possibly foist this idea on its students or faculty when there's absolutely no legitimate scholarly foundation."

Serena kept her cool and replied, "Similar complaints have been made in the past across the country about women's studies. And black studies. And gay studies. And Jewish studies."

"But those are established fields," Cash argued.

Serena grinned. "They are now. At one time they weren't."

Both Kinderhoeks spoke at once, saying, "Count me in!" Then turned to each other and laughed gently at having been on the same wavelength. It was heartwarming in a putrescent kind of way.

"Thank you," Serena said to them. "I'll pass both your names along to the provost and the president."

"That's it?" Cash said. "No vote? No discussion?"

Serena dutifully asked, "What else would you like to say?"

Cash looked around the room as frantically as a revolutionary in *Les Mis.* "Are you all going to give your approval to this racist garbage?"

Juno sighed melodramatically. "I wouldn't worry about it. The whole fucking thing is a joke, and it'll never happen even if there is an actual task force—which I doubt."

She had everyone's attention, especially Mooney-Mauser.

"It's a fucking public relations disaster. There's already been several demonstrations on campus. There'll be dozens. Hundreds.

Every minority group in the state will have something to say. They'll be busing in supporters from all over the country. Leaflets. Pickets. Strikes. A boycott. SUM officials will be heckled at speeches. SUM teams will be harassed when they travel, and the away games will be disrupted. Nike may even want to remove the swoosh from SUM uniforms." The room was utterly still. Juno continued in the rapt silence like an oracle: "And anyone associated with the idea will damage their career beyond hope."

The Kinderhoeks glared at Juno; then their eyes dropped, as if they were calculating the chances of Juno being correct.

At the front of the room, Serena had moved to Mooney-Mauser's chair and was bent over it, listening to his harsh whispering. She nodded and regained the floor. "There have always been naysayers any time this university has sought to move forward, to claim a bold new vision. This is a chance for our department to have a say in what could become a stellar program that brings SUM honor and national attention." The Kinderhoeks sat a bit taller.

I felt like a coward. Stefan and I both thought whiteness studies was a terrible concept, shallow and divisive; it could convince white students that they were a historically oppressed minority. Yet neither of us had the courage to speak up at a department meeting, now that the provost's spy was here. I suppose that was the point of Tyler Mooney-Mauser's presence—to quash dissent and identify troublemakers in advance. It was an insidious policy, and already damnably effective. I felt as paranoid as if I alone were the target of the provost's surveillance. No doubt most of the faculty felt the same, which explained the general torpor in the room despite the rumblings of dissent.

Serena was explaining something to the Kinderhoeks about how the task force was to be constituted and when, but I tuned out as Stefan tapped my arm. "If this is what Glinka wants, it's going to happen," Stefan whispered to me. "There's nothing we can do."

"But why would it be a priority?" I asked, sotto voce. "What's in it for her?"

"Something new? Something with her stamp on it?"

"Stamp" was right. Merry Glinka was determined to stamp on the faculty that had attacked her with brownies, humiliating her as much as themselves. The whole episode was ludicrous. Faculty

Food Fight. And the EAR department was already giving way under Glinka's pressure, I thought. That wasn't surprising. Too many lost causes over the years—too much dissension—too little respect from the university and for itself. I pictured people sulking in bars after the meeting, or drinking quietly at home, cursing their powerlessness.

Avis and Auburn Kinderhoek were thanking Serena and the department for the honor of being chosen. But Avis hadn't even received an appointment to the task force. "I'm so grateful for your trust," she burbled.

"And confidence," Auburn chimed in.

"Absolutely."

"We're thrilled."

"It's an honor."

It was pathetic. Avis and Auburn Kinderhoek were published authors with decent enough reputations in the small world of writers who made the circuit teaching summer writing workshops, yet they were groveling to Serena and the provost's emissary. But would Stefan have felt as grateful for similarly dubious recognition if he hadn't felt his career rescued by the chance of seeing one of his books made into a movie? Would I, if I hadn't been lucky enough to wind up with not one but two Wharton projects in press that could flesh out my meager tenure application portfolio? Probably.

God, EAR turned people into bootlickers—even after they'd been kicked by those boots. Quoth the craven, "Give us more!"

But I was wrong to think there wasn't any fight at all left in EAR. Just because EAR wouldn't stand up to its administrative tormentors didn't mean it couldn't turn on itself like jackals. Like the witch's chorus in *Dido and Aeneas*, they could easily have joined hands and sung, "Destruction's our delight/delight our greatest sorrow."

7

SERENA clasped her hands together as if about to launch into a fervent curtain call and said, "We need to speak about the Diversity Tree." That's when I realized that I hadn't even seen the source of controversy, I'd been so rushed. It would have been rude to ask for an adjournment, I suppose, even though the tree must be the main reason for the meeting. The most important agenda item was always saved for last. Still, it was bizarre to be right across the hall from the tree and not have any idea what it looked like. Should I just slip out as if I were going to the john? But then I'd miss EAR's own theater of the absurd.

Before Serena could continue, Avis Kinderhoek said, "I think it's shameful, a disgrace!" She seemed emboldened by the attention she'd received from Serena. Auburn nodded vigorously and clucked his tongue.

Treading carefully, Serena asked her what she meant.

"Well, it's just an itty-bitty tree. Who's it gonna hurt?"

"But it's a Christmas tree," Cash said.

"Nonsense! Didn't you bother to read the e-mail from Dulcie? It's a Diversity Tree. It's celebrating the diversity of our department." Avis grimaced even as she said these words, unable to hide her distaste for the concept, and I looked around the room. It was an amazingly undiverse department—mostly white, male, and WASP. Lucille Mochtar was the only black female, and whatever credibility she gave the department was painfully absent now that she was visiting at Duke.

"The provost and the president are always talking about diversity," Avis said. "Everybody at this university is always talking about diversity until you'd think they didn't know any other words, and now, suddenly, you've got something against diversity? What is your problem?"

"My problem is that it's a *Christmas* tree!" Cash insisted.

"Did the e-mail mention Christmas in any way? No! Can't you let someone do something nice without ripping it apart? Leave the poor woman alone."

Stefan and I glanced at each other. Dulcie Halligan was anything but a weakling deserving pity.

Auburn raised a new point. "Shouldn't Dulcie be here if we're talking about her?"

"This doesn't have anything to do with Dulcie," Cash countered.

Serena informed us that secretaries never attend faculty meetings. "After all, someone has to mind the store." It was clearly an attempt to make people laugh, or at least smile. It failed.

"They have eyes and do not see," Avis intoned mournfully at Cash, "and ears but do not hear. This is a time to feel good and share the holiday spirit, to let the things that make us different bring us together."

"What the fuck does that mean?" Stefan muttered to me.

"Who cares? She doesn't value diversity, she just wants a tree no matter what it's called."

Auburn put a hand on Avis's shoulder to quiet her down. "Now, let's face facts, everybody. Christianity is the major religion in the United States, right? Just like Islam is in the Arab countries. And you have to respect the majority. Would anybody here who was a citizen of one of those lands want to be telling those folks how to observe their holidays? That would be just plain rude, and ignorant, and dumb, and bigoted."

If I were Cash, I would have wanted to deck Auburn for his condescension.

"How many Arab states are democracies where people get to choose?" Juno asked him.

"That's beside the point."

Juno snorted. "Not when they chop off your hand for stealing."

"Then what about Israel?" Auburn said. "Don't they have that Star of David on their flag?"

Juno looked incredulous. "And England has several crosses on its flag—what does that have to do with anything?"

"It—is—a—Christmas—tree," Cash said slowly, as if counting to ten. "And you've just said it's connected to Christianity."

Les Peterson piped up. "But everybody knows that the Christmas tree started as a pagan symbol. You could look it up."

Avis and Auburn seemed split about how to take this—was Les on their side or against them? And the very word *pagan* seemed to have alarmed them. I imagined they had visions of writhing voluptuaries wreathed in incense and not much more.

Martin Wardell cleared his throat as if he were about to spit and said, "Why are we wasting all this time about a tree? Inclusion, outclusion—who cares? It's just a tree that makes people smile, makes them feel good. I'm sure that's all Dulcie was talking about. That's no reason to call her a monster or anything."

Cash was furious. "Who used the word *monster*?"

Wardell shrugged dramatically, as if Cash's vehemence proved the charge.

Juno launched another salvo. "If everybody's smiling, then why is the suicide rate so high this time of year?"

Larry Rich quipped, "It's all those damned fruitcakes. They wear you down."

Cash smacked his desk. "Having a tree in the office is terrible—it's a complete reversal of department policy. We haven't had trees in EAR for years."

Larry Rich said, "We had one when Grace Jurevicius was chair. She loved it."

Cash softened a bit. "That's true. But times have changed, and she would understand how divisive it is."

Avis whirled around, or as close to it as you could get in that straitjacketing chair, and said, "Who asked you! Who cares what you think! You've been riding your grandma's coattails forever. How do you know what she would say anyway—she's dead! And if you're such a hot shot, how come you can't get a full-time position babbling about those French construction workers or whatever the hell they are?"

"Deconstructionists," Auburn murmured, along with several people sitting around them, but Avis forged ahead: "I don't care what the hell you call them—it's all bunk and a waste of print. But the heck with that mess. You're an adjunct—you have no right to be mouthing off about what we do or don't do."

Serena stopped her in mid rant. "Actually, adjuncts have historically attended EAR meetings with the full understanding that they can participate but not vote—if there is a vote. We like to feel that everyone can be heard."

Unfazed and unimpressed, Avis tossed her head in an unflatteringly girlish way, given that she didn't have much of a neck. It actually looked as if she were practicing some self-chiropractic move.

Serena added, "And to be totally fair, I should remind everyone that we all have more or less private offices we can decorate or not in whatever way we want, but Dulcie and the other secretaries have only the main office, which they're obliged to share with everyone else."

We all mulled that over. Was Serena saying she was in favor of the tree? Or was she giving herself a way out and reminding us that Dulcie had a union and this controversy might embroil the department in larger trouble?

Cash had subsided for a moment, apparently embarrassed by Avis's attack. Yes, the academic job market wasn't very good, but still, how could he not feel on the spot and exposed to be rebuked for not having a tenure-track position? His grandmother had been so important a figure in the life of EAR and the College of Arts and Letters, and here he was, her epigone.

Avis wasn't done. "This country is becoming more and more godless every minute, and so is this department!" She glared around the room as if ready to denounce the devil worshipers (and humanists) among us.

Perhaps trying to palliate her rage, Auburn tried a different approach, sounding as jovial as if he were buying us all a round.

"Let's remember that a tree isn't a religious symbol anyway. It's a cultural thing, it's just part of our Western culture."

"Then why did Dulcie ask people to bring signs of their faith?" Cash fired back. "It's a damned Christmas tree, no matter what you call it."

"Don't you defame a symbol of Our Lord!" Avis shouted, cheeks as puffed out as a Renaissance cherub.

That dished Auburn's defense, and Cash crossed his arms with a QED smirk, unfortunately looking as smug as Martin Wardell had just looked, though a lot more decorative.

Everyone seemed to be waiting for Serena to fully declare herself, but with scrupulous neutrality, she said, "Other opinions?" I had to admire her for keeping cool, and wondered if it was real, if she had no opinion on this issue.

"I think we need a bigger tree," Les Peterman joked.

"And a better Christmas party," Martin Wardell chortled, never looking more like a Toby mug than at that moment.

"Holiday party," Serena corrected.

Larry Rich piled on, shouting, "With a keg!" Given his hippie-dippie clothes and hair, I'm surprised he didn't suggest hash pipes and body painting. God, in another minute the three of them were going to become as repulsive as Beavis and Butthead. Their jokes did break the tension, though, and even Serena smiled. I leaned forward and could see that Tyler Mooney-Mauser was making notes on his PalmPilot.

"I happen to support the Diversity Tree as a symbol of hope," Rusty opined. "But no matter what you feel about it, I think we all need to slow down here and contact our Higher Power." In response to jeers and puking noises from several quarters, he held out his hands palm upward as if about to invoke a blessing on us and said, "See? There's so much hostility here when there should be love. It's all about love."

"Give it a fucking rest," Larry groused, "Sell your psycho-tapes someplace else." And Martin said, "Go hug a tree. A live tree."

"Please," Serena said. "Let's maintain a dignified exchange of ideas."

In an undertone, Stefan said to me, "Right. In the middle of a war zone."

But I was furiously debating the costs of speaking out myself. My parents were emigrants who got out of Europe well before the Nazi death factories, but for all their sophistication, they were marked by having escaped, and they had always counseled caution, not standing out in a crowd when it was unnecessary: "*Sois sage, sois chic,*" as someone in a James Baldwin novel expressed it. As for debating Jewish subjects in a potentially hostile environment—that was always dangerous. So I felt their years of advice holding me back, but I knew that if silence didn't quite equal death at this meeting, it was certainly suffocation. I felt compelled to tell people how much I disliked the idea of a departmental tree, but didn't know how or where to begin.

Avis wouldn't let go berating Cash, and she had another weapon, given what he'd said in e-mail about a grandparent of his. "Are you planning to bring in some ugly Jew lawyer from the ACLU to drag our department's name through the mud?"

"You're the last one to use the word *ugly*." Juno laughed.

Avis practically spat out her reply: "Whore!"

I noted pleasure at seeing Juno abused flit across Serena's face before she said, "Let's not lose our tempers, please." Was she on Prozac?

Stefan rose from his seat, his hands clenched, his eyes tight. "Avis! Most of my family was murdered in the Holocaust. How dare you say what you did?"

Auburn was ineffectually trying to quiet his wife, who looked as cocky and belligerent as if she were ten feet tall. "Poor suffering Jews," she mock-moaned. "That's all we ever hear. Well, *you* don't seem to be suffering very much as far as I can tell, with a fancy office and a Hollywood film deal!"

Stefan looked so stunned by her making light of the Holocaust that he sat back down as if he'd been sucker punched. Cries of outrage and disgust echoed in the room while Serena tried to restore order. She didn't have a gavel, though, and her voice was drowned out by the confusion.

In a sudden lull, I jumped to my feet. "You're a hateful bigot," I said to Avis, feeling shocked but not silenced. "And like most bigots, you're stupid and smug, too. You're so blinded by Christian privilege you think everyone sees the world the way you do, and if they don't, there's something wrong with them." I told myself to slow down, to speak distinctly, to not yell. "That tree is offensive because it makes people feel left out and inferior. I'm Jewish, and it disturbs me. And I'm not bringing in any Jewish symbols to hang on it, because I'm not going to trivialize my religion by ornamenting a Christmas tree."

"It's not a Christmas tree!" several people snarled.

I kept going, amazed at my own verbosity but feeling as reckless and exhilarated as if I were heading down a water slide at an amusement park. "The tree isn't half as offensive as the kinds of things you've said on e-mail and in this meeting. And the worst part is that you're probably not that bad a person, just shallow and vindictive and resentful, and you can't stand to see anyone doing better than you. So you're mouthing slogans you don't even believe, at least not completely. You probably think Stefan got the writer-in-residence position here because of some Jewish conspiracy, but he got it because his writing has something to say, and it's been noted and admired. You'll never have Stefan's reputation or talent, no matter what you write or how long you live."

Juno applauded. Les, Martin, and Larry did a football-game chant, "Hit her again—hit her again—Har-der, har-der!"

Serena called out, "Decorum, please!" but she might as well have tried covering an open manhole with a dime.

Avis goggled at me, and so did most of the faculty in the room. I was only the lowliest of assistant professors, and I did not have tenure. I had never spoken that long on any point at any meeting, and never openly criticized another professor. Serena's offended silence had something lethal about it.

Breathing hard, Avis said, "You're nothing but a—"

Auburn slapped a hand across her mouth, and the two of them wrestled.

"Can we stay on track and not insult one another?" Serena

said, as out of touch with reality as the Red Queen calling out "Sentence first—and verdict afterward!"

Stefan pulled me back into my seat, where I knew that after this outburst, with a representative of the provost in the room, I was sure not to get tenure no matter who was on the committee and who became EAR chair. The university was full of rumors about public files and not-so-public ones, and if there wasn't a secret upper administrators' file on me yet, there would be one soon. Tyler was studying me as if I were Alger Hiss and he Joe McCarthy.

"We've let things move too far from the topic," Summerscale said magisterially, as if judging the entire roomful of people. "Dulcie Halligan is the office manager. She is not a faculty member and not bound by our decisions or traditions."

Nods flitted around the room like a line of falling dominoes.

"Let her have her tree and call it whatever she likes. She works hard, she should have some joy in her life." More approbation, especially since Dulcie was such a grouse. "And let's have some order returned to our department." Summerscale quickly lost his audience, since he'd never been a part of EAR until recently, and people resented his presence. "Judging from their behavior today, I don't think either Juno or Serena would make a good chairman. I'm throwing my hat into the ring."

Juno and Serena looked at each other in shared outrage, and Serena blew her cool. "You can't run for chair," she hissed at Summerscale. "You're a hooligan!"

"Better a hooligan than a harridan."

The jocks whooped at that retort and started another chant, "Summer-*scale!* Summer-*scale!*" Could they have been out drinking before the meeting?

With nothing really decided, nothing resolved, Serena yelled that the meeting was over, as a crescendo of shouting squeezed the remaining air from the room. She practically flew out into the hallway, sweeping up the provost's snitch in her wake. It wasn't quite as ignominious a display as the faculty reception (there was no food, for one thing), but it was close.

People crowded around Stefan and me, alternating expressions of outrage and approval, but none of that mattered. Stefan and I retreated to his office, where he packed his briefcase so angrily I thought he'd rip off its handles. I felt slightly queasy watching his violent movements. "Sit down," I counseled, but he kept moving. Then he stopped. "You were great," he said. "Terrific. I felt like an idiot—like I couldn't talk. I was paralyzed."

I didn't feel proud of my speech but ashamed for having lost my temper, and worse, for having called attention to myself, for having committed that Jewish sin: making a fuss about being Jewish among non-Jews.

"Let's get out of here," he said.

"Of course." I pictured building a fire at home, opening a bottle of wine, putting on some soothing CD on endless repeat—a Chopin piano concerto, Mel Tormé, or even David Bowie's tranced-out *Low*.

But Stefan was thinking big. "Let's quit," he said, chin up. "I don't want to teach here anymore. These people make me sick."

"*What?*"

"You're always complaining about this place, how it's crazy. How it's full of half-wits and creeps. You're right. Didn't that meeting prove it? So why stay here after this semester?" He looked serious.

"Stefan, we have jobs, we have commitments, we have classes to teach, we have a house."

"They'll hire half a dozen temporaries to fill our spots and have money left over."

"But the house!"

"We can sell it. The market's terrific, and the house is a gem."

"We have health benefits!"

"We'll get them someplace else."

"Where? Who's going to hire us if we leave and it's a scandal? We'll be damaged goods."

"So I'll do something else. I'll write full-time. I've never done that. Maybe that's what I need. Time."

I didn't point out that he had plenty of time to write: three months off in the summer, a month at winter break, and a week at spring break.

Stefan was still planning. "If we needed it, my father and Minnie would help while I figured out what I'm doing. Your folks would do the same."

"Stefan, I'm not becoming dependent on my parents at my age! I'll end up arguing about how much time I spend on the phone."

"We can live up north. There's a great artists' community in Leland and Northport and Traverse City."

"The cabin's not big enough to be a home. And everybody up there has two or three jobs to keep it together. Besides, neither one of us is into cross-country skiing or ice-fishing or complaining about tourists or gambling at Indian casinos. What the hell would we do there?"

He sank into his desk chair. "You're right. I'm just furious at Avis, and at myself."

"God, you'd think with a name like hers, she'd try a little harder."

He didn't acknowledge the attempted joke. But despite having argued against leaving, suddenly I thought, Well, why not? If we sold the house and even the place up north, that cash plus the money we had in savings would carry us for a few years until we found another way of life, whether the movie got made or not. Except there was one problem: I'd been teaching for years, and I loved it. I didn't want to do anything else as much as I didn't feel certain I *could* do anything else. The first person at NYU to observe me in a class I was TA'ing for said I was a born teacher. That might have been a disappointment to my parents, who wanted me to go into publishing, but it was the benison I had hoped for. Give that up? I'd been teaching since before I met Stefan; it was part of my identity.

As we got ready to leave for home, I noticed a fat Penguin paperback on Stefan's desk—Alessandro Manzoni's *The Betrothed*, a book I'd heard of but never read. I asked Stefan about it.

"It's a great story, all about tyranny."

"The setting is Italy, right? Sixteenth century?"

"Seventeenth. It's dark, it's funny, it's moving. It has one of those cultivated omniscient narrators who makes you feel like you're a great friend while he's telling you the story, like he thinks the world of you. I wish I could write a book like that."

Curious, I picked it up and leafed through it. I found many passages underlined: "a secret league of atrocious counsels and wicked deeds"; "his power was exercised on behalf of evil intentions, atrocious revenges, or tyrannical caprice."

I read them aloud. "Sounds like academe to me."

Stefan nodded. "Except for the stabbings and the cholera."

When we got home, Stefan said, "You know, I didn't when I started, but I love teaching now, I do. If only there wasn't everything else—the politics, the mania. But I think I can stick it out."

Of course he could. He was a writer-in-residence, with a great salary and a fat travel budget, a plush office, small classes, and a light teaching load. He was at the top of this insignificant heap. And I was down in the basement, in every sense of the word.

I defrosted some ground venison for chili, and while he got the fire going, I cooked minced garlic, onion, and green pepper in olive oil in a cast iron casserole for five minutes. Then I browned the venison, stirred in chili powder, cumin, salt, pepper, Worcestershire sauce, cayenne pepper, and red-wine vinegar.

"What do you think Avis was going to call you?" Stefan asked when the fire had caught and he didn't have to tend it. He had opened a bottle of Santa Cristina sangiovese, and we were sitting at the island. The chili was simmering, and I'd added red kidney beans and some cornmeal.

"The usual. Fag, probably. She doesn't seem literate enough to call me a catamite. Unless she was going to accuse me of being a New Yorker."

We both shook our heads. Neither one of us had faced *direct* homophobia or anti-Semitism in the department, and whatever had been indirect, we'd ignored. Avis's outburst seemed hard to slough off, and yet all I wanted was for it to go away, for no one to mention it to us. Even after we lit the Shabbat candles and said the blessing, I felt oppressed.

"I wish she and Auburn hadn't come back from their leave,"

Stefan said. "Students hate them, and they hate the students. It was a mess with temporaries teaching the other writing workshops, but at least they were dedicated."

Of course they were. "Gypsy scholars" are some of the best teachers in the profession; nothing else but innate talent and passion for their work can compensate for the terrible insecurity they live with, moving from job to job, cobbling together an unsteady and uncertain income, so painfully close to the privileges and comforts of a tenure-track position—the academic version of the kid with his nose pressed to the window of the chocolate shop.

"Avis and Auburn must have amazing connections," Stefan mused. "And they must write good grant proposals, because look how they travel and get excused from teaching here."

SUM was full of academic freeloaders like the Kinderhoeks. "From the way they were sucking up to Serena and dying to get on that task force, I bet they're angling for administrative posts. They're probably just what Glinka wants—they're from Grand Rapids, too, and as conservative as Pat Buchanan."

"He's not conservative—he's rabid."

The chili was terrific, perfect comfort food to take our minds off the meeting, for a while at least. We talked about books and the weather and Stefan's workouts at the gym and my swimming. We opened a second bottle of the sangiovese.

When the phone rang, Stefan said, "I bet it's Juno, for you."

He was right.

"Nick, you'll never guess who I've been spending the evening with. Detective Valley!"

"On a date?"

"Don't make me gag. Of course not on a date. I worked in my office after the circus, and when I tried to go home, I couldn't drive away. Someone slashed my tires. It's like a bad movie. All four of them. I called the campus police, and I swear that moron thinks *I* did it. He asked me if I had any sharp instruments with me, and I'm sure he wanted to check my purse."

Where he would have found her gun, no doubt. That would have made quite a scene. "Why would you slash your own tires?"

Stefan looked alarmed as he handed me a mug of coffee. "Is she all right?" he asked softly. I nodded.

"Why would I send myself threatening notes? Why not? After all, I'm a hysterical woman. Excuse me, that's a tautology. I'm a woman. It must be my time of the month."

"Valley isn't very sympathetic."

"He's the fucking Grand Inquisitor!"

"But did he examine the car? Did he make a report?"

"Yes. So what?"

"Who do you think—"

"It was someone at that meeting, I'm sure of it. Someone who doesn't like me. Serena, Avis, maybe even that creature Summerscale. If he runs for chair it will be a disaster."

Out of some fifty people in the room, the number who didn't like Juno was surely larger than three.

"Those were new tires!" Juno wailed. "It's a new car! I'll kill the asshole who did it."

I held the phone away from my ear while Juno ranted on in a similar vein, threatening death and destruction, but of course she was powerless to wreak vengeance, and she knew it.

Calming down some, she said, "This destroyed my entire evening. After that so-called detective, I had to deal with a smelly fat man from the AAA who dropped my car off and then took me to my house. He was a nightmare, telling me how he'd timed every single traffic light in Michiganapolis, and then he proved it. I had to hold his stopwatch."

I tried not to laugh, which was easier when Juno said, "And I think someone followed me home, followed me from campus to the garage and then home. It was dark, but the same pair of lights seemed to be behind us all the way. I couldn't make it out for sure."

"You have to call the Michiganapolis police, since it happened off campus."

"They'll believe me even less than Valley did!"

She was probably right there, since faculty had a poor reputation in town for arrogance and airheadedness masked by a large vocabulary.

"Nick, don't worry about me, I have my Glock and I'm going to use it."

I was worried about her safety *and* about her using her gun.

"Nick, we have to get right to work and find whoever is doing this to me. I'll hire you!"

"Juno, that's ridiculous."

"No, it's not. If you track this sonafabitch down and prove it, you'll deserve a reward." Then she gave a lurid chuckle. "Of some kind." And she hung up as abruptly as she'd launched the conversation.

"Okay, Nick, let's go through everything you know about what's happening with Juno," Stefan said with no trace of skepticism, so I took him at his word. After my summary, he said, "So what can you do that Valley can't? He's a trained investigator—he's a cop."

"But he doesn't believe Juno. He thinks she's just spouting hormones."

"That's an image," Stefan said. "I'd love to hear what you bibliographers sound like when you're all together."

"We're very quiet. We've all been through library hell and understand what it's like. We drink lots of seven and sevens."

"Okay. You believe Juno. Then what?"

"I guess I could stake out her house. . . ."

"You're going to sit there with cold coffee for hours? Are you kidding? You'd probably end up getting arrested for loitering."

"Well, I should interview her to get more facts and then start asking questions."

"But who else do you interview? It's not like she's Mother Theresa and widely loved. You'll have a hundred suspects."

"Stefan, crank phone calls, threatening mail, lurking outside her house, slashing her tires, following her car, doesn't that sound like—"

"A jealous lover? Like I said, you'll have a hundred suspects." Then he switched direction. "No, that's the obvious way to go. Too obvious. It's got to be professional jealousy. She storms into the department last year, is supposed to be here just as a visitor, then she gets a permanent position? And now she's running for chair?

Think how pissed off people must be. And she didn't make any new friends at the meeting. What the hell was that about anyway, putting on makeup?"

"I thought it was great! It was mockery. It was performance art."

"It was dumb."

"If I wore makeup, I would have done the same thing."

"If you wore makeup, you wouldn't be teaching in EAR, that's for sure."

"Who knows if I'll be teaching there much longer, after what I said."

"You did the right thing. Avis had to be confronted." He pushed his plate away. "That meeting—"

"Avis isn't the only one like that in the department—she's just the most vocal, at least right now. I don't understand why Serena didn't stop her. Isn't she afraid of a harassment lawsuit or something?"

"Serena's hard to figure out. She's always been hard to figure out. Opaque and prickly. Why did she even help you with the Wharton conference? What did she get out of it?"

"She bossed people around. That's something."

"But she should have taken control of the meeting today and kept things in order."

"Stefan, trying to control our department is like running with the bulls at Pamplona—you'll get gored or trampled. I guess Serena decided to get out of the way."

"Unless she's got her own agenda and doesn't want to come off as a heavy."

"Like what?"

"Well, the last chair moved up to provost. Why not Serena?"

"That was Moral Coral—everyone thought she was blameless. Even though Serena's trying to be subdued and normal, there's something rebarbative about her."

Stefan frowned. "Rebarbative? The only person I've ever seen use that word is Anita Brookner. Why couldn't you just say 'repellent'? And how do you have time to read her novels when you're supposed to be reading mysteries?"

"Guilty as charged. I have to read Brookner now and then— the reviewers always say she's the novelist Henry James would be reading if he were alive, so I figure Wharton would, too."

Stefan laughed. That kind of review was one of his pet peeves.

"But if Serena was up to something, what about Byron? Have you ever seen Summerscale that subdued and rational? First he's a one-man rave, then he's an easy-listening station."

"Why does he have to be up to something?" Stefan wanted to know.

"Of course he is! These people can't be at the university for decades without soaking up all that scheming and treachery."

8

All the next day I wondered about the future, and mulled over more immediate concerns, though they connected with our future, of course. I was worried about Juno's gun. She was so combustible, and if she was attacked or felt under attack, wouldn't she use it? While I wanted whoever was harassing her to stop, I didn't think the person's being wounded or murdered was the right answer. I didn't want to see Juno plunged into scandal *or* danger. Yet she was facing some sort of threat, unless she and I were both delusional. Stefan called it a folie à deux. If that were true, we'd be the last two people to recognize it.

And what was going to happen next in EAR? With Juno, Serena, and Summerscale all planning to run for chair, could anyone win except a write-in candidate? The three of them could not have been more unpopular, each in deep and abiding ways, despite some clusters of fans. And why was the provost spying on all the departments—or was that even happening university-wide? Perhaps Merry Glinka suspected that EAR alone was rife with subversion. As for the Whiteness Studies Task Force, last month I'd hoped it was dead, cremated, and the ashes scattered over open water. But it was back, flourishing, and recruiting. What the hell could be going on in the minds of the upper administrators to even countenance such a plan? As the new provost, Merry Glinka could have canned it, giving any number of respectable-sounding reasons, or simply acted arbitrarily and given none at all. I couldn't believe that our lunkhead president Littleterry had that much influence at the university; he was just a jovial fund-raiser, glad-handing and getting drunk and replaying old games, someone who would never intimidate a potential donor to SUM because he simply wasn't swift enough to be intimidating. I'm sure he made even alumni who'd graduated with borderline grades feel superior. Could something so implausible have sprung from his imagination alone?

After dinner that evening I found an e-mail from a student asking if I'd gotten the paper he'd left for me at Parker, and since he must have dropped it off after Stefan and I had gone home, I decided to drop by Parker Hall, pick it up, and check my mail. Stefan came with me, after we did Havdalah, the lovely short set of blessings that bids farewell to Shabbat.

At night, and in the winter, with the leaves gone from the de- ciduous trees, the SUM campus is eerily beautiful—almost a stage set with the gleaming security lights strung along its winding paths, reflecting off the ranks of evergreens and on the stone, brick, and concrete buildings with slate tile roofs and mullioned windows that all seemed more dramatic than by day, framed by the darkness. With few students around, the bare tree branches seemed to create a hush of privacy and privilege.

There were a few cars behind Parker Hall, but they could have been anyone's, since the lot was open all weekend, though we did see some lights on across the building. Stefan got out his key, and we entered the hulking silent building that some people say looks like that cake left out in the rain in "MacArthur Park" thanks to its crumbling sandstone and Romanesque ornamentation, which I'll admit in certain lights does look like a kind of architectural icing.

As we entered through the back door, Parker's inimitable stench hit us: equal parts crumbling file folders, roach spray, and stifled teeth-grinding resentment. Stefan headed up the wide stairs lit by light streaming in from a nearby lamppost, and I headed down into the basement with a casual, "Can you get my mail? Let's meet back at the car."

"Five minutes, tops," Stefan called down to me, and once again, as his steps receded, I was reminded of the immense status difference between us at EAR.

Someone had left the lights on in the basement hallway,

which made it look less like a crypt than usual. Still, I moved along to my office quickly, as if one step ahead of grave robbers afraid of being discovered. Parker may not have been gothic in style, but it certainly provoked gothic thoughts. Who knows what works of genius Mary Shelley could have written there if she'd lived long enough?

With the building creaking like a pile of logs about to tumble over, I unlocked my office and flicked on a few lights, trying not to dwell on its innate grunginess (it had only a half-window, for instance). I rounded up several sets of papers and stuffed them into a large manila envelope, checking around to make sure there wasn't anything else I needed, and also, shamefacedly even though I was alone, to make sure nothing had been tampered with. My office had been broken into before, and I was always preparing myself for the shock of discovering mute violence: a battered-open door, shattered lamps, rifled files, torn-apart books, graffiti-smeared walls. What had actually happened wasn't quite as bad as any of that but had quickly blended with my fears, and I almost felt as if it had—just as the dangers Sharon had faced with her surgery, though they were over, had somehow been subsumed by what actually did happen to her.

I shut off the lights and locked the door carefully, aware as I did so that if someone wanted to get in, a lock made no difference, even though the solid-core door looked sturdy. Shaking off the paranoia, or trying to, I headed for the stairs to go out and meet Stefan at the car, but realized as I opened the door to the stairwell that the contentious Diversity Tree was just two flights up in the main office, to which I had a key, like every other faculty member.

I hurried up the echoing stairs, which were probably metal under the worn brown linoleum. On the second floor, I could see that Stefan's office door was closed, so he had to be waiting back outside already. Talking to myself, I said, "Just a quick look."

There was enough light streaming in from windows facing the parking lot for me to see my way to the main door, and I unlocked it, flicked on the line of switches, and the office jumped into life—or rather, was revealed in all its deathly dullness. It had the worn, gritty, crowded, sloppy feel of a police office in some very poor urban precinct. Files teetered on aging file cabinets, and desks were boiling over with folders, flyers, memos.

And there on the high counter that separated the secretaries from supplicants was the tree. Or shrub, really, since it was only three feet tall. You could call it darling if it was Be Kind to a Plant Day, but it was actually pathetic, especially since it was festooned with the unlikeliest bunch of ornaments you could imagine. Amid the angels and reindeers I made out an ankh, several wooden Buddhas, a plastic cow, a little piece of what I think was kente cloth or an imitation, a Maltese cross, and other ornaments whose significance perhaps only a magpie or shoplifter could guess.

Studying it, I felt almost embarrassed to have said anything at the meeting. The tree was so pitiful, so unredeemably stupid looking, how could anyone take it seriously enough to be insulted? But then, was I supposed to apologize to the department, or slink through the hallways with a penitent look on my face? That didn't make sense either.

I closed the lights and left, locking this door carefully, too, and decided to make a quick stop in the men's room down the hall.

I was holding open the heavy door with my left hand, reaching for the light switch on the wall to my right, when I went flying across the room; only as I fell and started to gasp for breath did I realize I'd been shoved hard in the center of my back. In the dark the room seemed cavernous and cold, and I recoiled from where my face and hands touched the floor, but someone incredibly strong was straddling me, shoving my shoulders down, holding a hand over my mouth. My arms hurt, and my left cheek hurt, even while my body seemed very far away and I wondered why I felt unable to shout or speak even through the stifling hand that smelled of some kind of aftershave. The word *shock* drifted across my mind like a pennant flying behind a plane at a football game.

I tried to get up, but whoever was atop me wasn't going to let that happen.

"*Leave it alone.*" The voice was a man's, as heavy as the hands pinning me to the floor. And then he was gone. The men's room door yanked open, then glided closed, its susurration oddly fascinating and slow. I lay in the damp dark room, waiting for the pain that was surely about to burst inside me as exigent and crazed as a July 4 sale crowd pressing against a department store's glass doors. Would they shatter? Would I?

I must have passed out or slept, because when I heard Stefan shouting my name from somewhere, it seemed from a very great distance. Was I awake? Was that me calling, "Here?"

Light exploded along with Stefan rushing to my side. I squinted at him as he scooped me up.

"Nick, you're bleeding! What happened? Why didn't you come to the car? Are you okay? Did you pass out? I looked for you downstairs! Why were you up here?" Stefan examined me, feeling around for broken bones, I suppose. I watched him with amused affection, as if I were in a hospital bed and he were a brand-new orderly gamely trying to arrange too many flowers in too small a vase.

"Someone attacked me," I said, the words sounding so outrageous and melodramatic I felt ashamed to have spoken them.

Stefan almost dropped me, he was so surprised. "*What?*"

If my head didn't hurt, it would have been funny. Or was it even my head?

"Let me sit up," I said, and Stefan moved me back against the wall. He rose and turned on the sink, cupped some water in his hands, and held it out for me to drink. It tasted metallic, but good. He took out a handkerchief, squatted down, and started to dab at my bloody cheek, which felt very hot. Maybe that was what hurt.

"Don't you think you should call 911?" I asked.

Stefan grimaced, rifled his pockets for the cell phone, and dialed. "Someone's been mugged," he said, sounding amazingly calm. "Parker Hall, second floor. Yes, he's conscious, bleeding a little, no broken bones, but I think— Okay." Stefan sat down next to me. "Tell me what happened."

I tried to, but it sounded fuzzy. He worked at my cheek with the handkerchief, gently. "It's a tiny cut," he said under his breath. "I can't believe it looked so bad. Does it hurt?"

I felt exhausted and spaced out, not least because the men's room looked even larger and more cavernous from the floor. What was I doing there?

That's when I started to shiver and pulled my coat tightly around me. Stefan held me and rocked me. "Last year," I said, trying to block out what had happened right there in Parker Hall.

"I know."

We heard a siren, and right after that, someone was stomping up the stairs, the noise echoing through the building like the T-Rex's crushing steps in *Jurassic Park*. Stefan rose, and I might have giggled, because he seemed as expectant as a party host waiting for the first guest.

The door was flung open—it was Detective Valley, of course, since all 911 calls went to SUM's campus police, unfortunately, and Parker Hall seemed to be his beat.

"Are you hurt?" he said. "Do we need an ambulance?"

I shook my head. "Stunned." I sat up straighter, as if practicing my posture.

Valley walked over to the window and sat on the wide ledge, but he still seemed very high above me. I stood up, Stefan helping me, and leaned back against a sink, not half as dizzy as I would have expected to feel. Valley eyed me up and down, inspecting my face.

"What were you doing here on a Saturday night?" His very flatness made the question sound leading and obscene.

"I came to take a leak—"

"We were checking our mail and picking up student papers," Stefan interrupted.

"Why tonight?"

"Why not?"

"Are you missing anything? Wallet? Keys?"

I searched my pockets slowly, shook my head.

"Okay. When did it happen?"

I looked at Stefan because I wasn't sure. He checked his watch and said, "Fifteen minutes ago." He explained again that we were supposed to meet outside at the car, but I'd come up to the main office and then stopped at the john.

"Did you see the assailant?"

I bristled. "I told you, it was dark, and—"

"I meant him." He pointed at Stefan with his pen. "No?

There's only one staircase here, right? You came up the stairs, but nobody came down them?"

Stefan thought about it, shook his head. "There's another floor above this one."

"I know that," Valley snapped. "Were you meeting someone?"

"In the john?" Stefan asked, and I started to chuckle, remembering a Poirot episode on A&E where Captain Hastings had used the same tone of alarm when saying, "Kidnapped? In *England*?"

Now Valley was really suspicious. "You think this is funny?"

I sighed. "Can we finish this? I want to go to the clinic. Isn't the KwikKare open Saturday nights?"

"Okay. Was the assailant male? Female?"

I gave him as much detail as I could muster: big, male, rough voice, very strong. "He told me to leave it alone."

"What did you think he meant?"

I shrugged, eyeing the floor. It might be very nice to just curl up there and go to sleep. "Wait. Maybe he said, 'Leave her alone.' "

"Which is it?"

"I'm not sure."

Valley looked disgusted, and I answered his next few questions mechanically, thinking about what a lousy witness I would be in a criminal case. I could barely summon the details of what had happened to me less than—what?—twenty minutes ago now. How could I have been suspicious of Juno when she couldn't replay what happened to her at the reception?

"Juno," I said, and from Valley's and Stefan's expressions, I realized I must have been unexpectedly loud. "Juno was attacked at the reception, now me."

"What's the connection?" Valley asked, but neither Stefan nor I could think of one, and Stefan ended the interview by saying we had to go to the clinic to make sure I was all right.

Valley nodded grimly. "I'll want to talk to you again." He left, and we trailed after him. I was surprised that walking and even handling stairs was so easy, but of course, Stefan was by my side, ready to catch me if I stumbled.

When we were outside, I said, "I can walk to the clinic."

"Bullshit. Get in the car, and we'll drive over."

We did. The clinic was only a few city blocks away, but light years in other ways because the building was so modern. The red-brick-and-glass box had replaced a crumbling neo-Gothic structure that had never recovered from being sacked in the 1960s by Ohio State fans after they lost a major football game against SUM. KwikKare was a new service, funded by alumni grants, obviously alums who knew how heavy the weekend drinking was, and how many students hurt themselves or others.

The small waiting room was like any other doctor's office, decorated in chairs that matched the lampshades that matched the wallpaper that matched the rugs, everything aqua, beige, and gray. Even the silk plants matched, in colors that I suppose were meant to be calming. Stefan checked me in with the efficient-looking nurse, showed them my faculty ID and insurance card, and I joined the half-dozen students who were watching or ignoring a movie playing on the wide-screen TV. It seemed to be about talking dogs.

I sunk into a haze, but popped out of it when I said, "Where are my papers?" Stefan assured me he'd brought the envelope down to the car. I studied the students, counting their piercings to keep myself focused. When I hit twenty, my name was called, which made me wonder if these kids were just waiting for friends, not patients themselves.

Another young nurse led us down to a surprisingly cheerful room, despite all the medical equipment, thanks to framed posters of campus views. She took notes while Stefan helped me out of my coat and hung it on the wall. She left, and we waited for a while in silence, with conversations in the hallway drifting into the room.

The sixtyish doctor who appeared was as fat as Orson Welles, but far more jovial. He reeked of cigarette smoke, and when he examined me, I felt like I was in a bar at three in the morning. He needed a shave, and bristly hair poked out of his ears and nostrils at crazy angles. I told him everything in the kind of stop-and-start way you always seem to have with a doctor, feeling apologetic and stupid for having left something out. He nodded as if faculty getting attacked on campus was nothing new. I was fascinated by his name tag: "Damon Tiplady."

Stefan got me out of my sweater, and the doctor felt my arms, chest, and back, listened to me breathe through his stethoscope, took my pulse. It all seemed disarmingly normal, though my pulse was quite high. "No surprise," he said, turning to my cheek. He cleaned that off with an antiseptic, went "Huh" as he applied a butterfly-shaped bandage. "It'll be a great bruise, but you don't need stitches." Eyeing Stefan, who hovered over me, he said, "Fight with an ex?"

"Ex-what?" Stefan snarled.

"Touchy, huh?" He shrugged. "I'll give you a prescription for Tylenol with codeine you can get filled at the pharmacy. You may need it to sleep. You'll be sore, but you'll live." He waddled off after that was done, his parting words, "Stay home Saturday night. That's *my* advice. It's always safer."

Stefan put me to bed, tucked the sheets around me as if I were an invalid, and got me a large glass of Seagram's. I drank greedily, aware that I hadn't yet looked at myself in a mirror. I was afraid to see the face of someone who had been attacked so ignominiously.

Stefan stayed dressed, as if he might have to rush out any minute for some emergency.

"Is this hard for you?" I asked.

"Of course it is."

"No, I mean, because of high school, when you were beat up?"

"Oh." He nodded heavily. "I wasn't thinking about it, but things like that don't go away, no matter how old you are."

"How long before I forget all the crap that's gone on at SUM?"

He shrugged. "Maybe never."

I was beginning to feel like Ethan Frome, whose "plate was heaped up with trouble."

"How's your headache?"

"I'm angry more than anything else. Look at all the shit we have to put up with, and now somebody beats me up, too? God, if Sharon weren't sick, I'd call her, but—"

"She'd just quote *Monty Python and the Holy Grail* at you," Stefan said with a sly smile.

"Which line?"

" 'Run away—run away!' "

I slept dreamlessly and very late, and Stefan brought me breakfast in bed Sunday morning: buttermilk blueberry pancakes with turkey sausages. I could smell a fire going, and Stefan had brought up a pad for the coffeepot, which he set on the nightstand on my side of the bed.

"Good," I said, "I'll need it."

He set the tray down across my legs. "I've been thinking about last night," he said. "About who attacked you. It wasn't random."

"No shit."

"It's connected to the Diversity Tree."

"Why do you say that?"

"You were the most outspoken critic. Well, you and Cash. And didn't you say you went into the main office to look at it? And whoever it was said, 'Leave it alone'?"

I reminded him that the phantom could have said "her." "But if you're right, do you think someone's mounting guard on it? Where would he have been hiding?"

"I don't know. But doesn't it stand to reason it was someone at the meeting?"

"Great—that's fifty suspects."

"You could probably take me and Juno off the list. Juno may be a whirling dervish, but she likes you. She wouldn't do that or hire someone to do that."

"You actually said something nice about her."

Before he could answer, my phone rang. Stefan got it, smiled, and handed me the receiver.

"Nick!" Juno shouted. "Have you found the assailant?"

"Yours or mine?" I asked, and when she demanded an explanation, I gave it to her. She punctuated my account with howls of outrage: "Those fuckers!" That made it sound as if a whole team of assassins was on our tail.

Then she summed it all up for me, neat and tidy: "Nick, you know what you need to do." When she hung up, I didn't repeat that admonition to Stefan, who would have scoffed at my plans.

I snoozed on and off through the day, Stefan plying me with hot soup and an occasional brandy, which was much tastier than Tylenol with codeine would have been, and probably as effective.

We watched TV, played some cards. It was just like being ten years old and home sick from school—except for the brandy, that is.

Even when I finally showered, I was reluctant to look at myself in the full-length mirror, but I peeked. There were bruises scattered across my body, but nothing especially noteworthy, nothing you couldn't get by yourself at the gym or at home. The one on my cheek, though, was starting to look like a George Lucas special effect, and it seemed ridiculous, given that I hadn't even needed any stitches.

Monday morning I ate breakfast quickly, told Stefan that I had some errands to run, and drove ten minutes away to the closest gun shop, one that I'd found in the yellow pages on Sunday without having let Stefan know I was looking it up. The weather was unusually mild for December in Michiganapolis, hovering near fifty, and so I only felt besieged inside, aching far more from the shock and humiliation of having been jumped, roughed up, and threatened than from any actual pain.

The gun shop was in a fairly new stereotypically bland strip mall along with a branch of Old Kent Bank, a hobby and crafts store, a nail salon, something called the Divine Tabernacle of the Lord, and a pizza place whose pizza we'd never tried, even though it wasn't part of a chain. Improbably, the gun shop was called "Aux Armes."

An old-fashioned bell over the door rang as I stepped inside, and from behind a low glass counter, an elderly short woman tossed me a cheerful "Good morning!" with as much energy as if it were a lifesaver and I were drowning. She was not at all what I expected. Pixyish, with permed silver hair, glasses on a chain, and a pale blue linen suit, she wore huge faux pearl earrings, necklace, and bracelet. I had expected the shop to be filled with grizzled, obese Bubba types in overalls who would take one look at me and pull out tire irons to beat against their open palms.

"Is the name of your store a reference to the Marseillaise?" I blurted out.

She smiled grandly and held out her arms as if welcoming a long-lost cousin. "Why, of course, young man. What else could it be? My husband and I wanted to appeal to a better class of customer, though of course we'd never turn away anyone who pronounced it Ox Arms. I'm Jasmine Fennebresque." She spelled it for me. "I know, it's a name better suited to someone's nanny or a heroine in a book with Fabio on the cover, but what can you do?" She pointed to a small bulletin board where envelopes were tacked up. I approached the counter filled with guns in open cases and leaned closer to read. "You can't imagine how people mangle my name." The envelopes from various sources all had imaginative spellings of her first and last names, my favorite being "Fanny-brisk."

I looked around me. The low-ceilinged space was perhaps twenty by thirty feet and looked like a very clean and well-run hardware store, except the shelves were packed with ammunition and cans and boxes whose purpose I couldn't begin to guess. Along the far wall rifles and shotguns were displayed as reverently as golf clubs. It seemed almost pleasant. It helped that the store was so brightly lit and clean, and that there wasn't anyone in it beside her, and that there were pots of potpourri out of sight. I sniffed. Freesia.

"Now then, how can I help you today?"

I wanted to joke and say, "I'm looking for something for a Christmas gift," but it probably would have sounded serious to her. I settled for, "I don't know anything about guns. Not much, anyway. Can you help a beginner?"

"Of course I can," she all but warbled. "I'd be delighted!" I could have been her grandson asking her to bake another batch of oatmeal cookies. "What were you looking for exactly?"

"A gun."

"Yes, of course. For target practice? Personal safety?" She glanced discreetly at the bandage on my cheek and the bruise that seemed to leak out from under it.

"Both, I guess."

"Semiautomatic or revolver?"

I felt like I was in grade school, being hounded by a teacher armed with flash cards. "Uh . . ."

"Semiautomatics have more fire power. And of course they're safer." She slipped a smallish, blunt, gray gun out from under the counter like a jeweler showing off a necklace.

"Safer?"

"Revolvers don't have safeties on them, though the bullets are cheaper, and of course that's always a consideration." She went on to give me a perky mini-lecture, some of the details of which I knew from my reading of mysteries or from movies, but most of it started to wheel and blur in my head like a flock of starlings. As her sweet voice poured forth details about calibers and stopping power and gun weight and recoil and racking and the local gun laws, I felt almost paralyzed to be in a gun shop at all. I couldn't imagine what my parents or Sharon or Stefan would say. Off to her left was a small poster labeled "Ten Commandments of Gun Ownership." The first one read, "Treat every gun as if it's loaded."

"Now, if you're learning how to use a gun for the first time," she said, "I'd recommend this." She pulled out what looked like a cannon compared to the others. "It's a .357 magnum."

"Dirty Harry," I said.

"Indeed. People make fun of it, but look at the barrel." She held it out for me, and when I took it from her, I was amazed at how heavy it was, but also at how strangely natural it felt in my hand. Had I expected it to sear my flesh the way holy water was supposed to scar a vampire?

"With a longer barrel," she said, "there's more to sight down, and you might find it easier to learn how to aim and fire." Then she went on about the bullets, though she stopped when she could sense I had reached information overload. "There's a lot to absorb," she said kindly. "Let me give you some lovely reading material to study." She reached behind her to a rack that held thick, glossy brochures like the kind you'd find at a car dealership, but these all had names like Smith & Wesson, Beretta, Walther, Ruger. "And here's information about local firing ranges, gun safety courses." She added several fliers and mimeographed brochures to the pile.

"I'll have to come back," I said, thinking I'd need a tutor to wade through all that stuff.

"Of course." She studied me , but not because of the bruise. "I've seen your photo in the *Tribune*. You're that professor," she concluded. "The one at the college who keeps getting mixed up with criminals."

I nodded.

"It sounds very exciting! And dangerous. You'll be much better off with a gun."

"That's what a friend tells me. She owns a Glock."

Mrs. Fennebresque nodded sagely, as if I were a novice sailor talking about an acquaintance's yacht. When I thanked her and started to leave, she said, "Thank you for stopping by, and remember, there are no evil guns, only evil people."

The bell dinged behind me as I stumbled out into the parking lot.

9

Luckily, I had classes to teach that day. I threw myself into them, all the while feeling like an impostor. I wasn't a teacher anymore, a decent citizen. Despite all the blather about a right to bear arms, I felt grubby and criminal for having contemplated buying a gun, for having had the urge burst out of me and force me to hide where I was going and what I was doing.

Wasn't I panicking, turning myself inside out, abandoning lifetime values just because I'd been the victim of violence again? Wasn't this all an overreaction to my shame?

These recriminations were obviously the result of having grown up in New York with European-born parents who derided the American love of guns. Yet they hadn't kept cowboy outfits and pistols and holsters away from me, or banned any violent movies. So of course the gun I'd held at Mrs. Fennnebresque's shop had felt somewhat natural to me. I'd probably held a toy one in my hands when I was four or five, if not younger, chasing other little boys with it, shouting, "Bang-bang-bang!"

Maybe that's why Americans were gun-crazy. We worshiped youth, and hadn't outgrown our own as individuals, and as a country. Is that what being attacked had done to me—first sent me to bed, then turned me into a simulacrum of a cowboy seeking revenge on cattle rustlers?

Questions like that roiled at the back of my mind while I was teaching. Hell, they were at the front of my mind, too, and even in the middle. It's a wonder my head didn't implode with all the mental pressure. But despite having a cramped, peeling classroom in nasty Uplegger Hall, one of the least prestigious venues for EAR professors, I taught energetic, exciting classes, and the glowing eyes and active participation in each room proved it, plus the instant explosion of conversation when I let the classes go. People were actually excited about putting the finishing touches on their research papers, due at semester's end in a few weeks.

It was a fun topic to deal with that day, as always when I was helping them explode myths about writing. Even after almost a full semester with me, my freshmen were still under the spell of bad high school teaching that turned writing mechanical, so that almost every one of them thought conclusions had to "wrap up the paper" (and of course, you could never write without an outline).

"In other words," I said in each class, "you've told your readers what you had to say, then you tell the readers again in case they weren't paying attention. Is that right?"

There were the inevitable snickers.

"Sounds really exciting, doesn't it?"

More laughter, and then questions about what I thought could provide a good conclusion, which I always tried to turn back to the class: What did *they* think might make a good conclusion, one that wasn't boring and dull? They always came up with ideas, which was heartening, but sometimes it seemed that half of my work in freshman composition was deprogramming. Like dealing with students who wondered how they could write a personal narrative, since they weren't "allowed" to use "I."

As each class ended, a couple of the guys sidled past me in their best gang-banger imitations, checking out my bruise and nodding what I suppose they thought was homeboy-style approval, or saying things like, "Rockin' class, Dr. Hoffman." I felt like I was in a sitcom, and I felt like a fraud, but I basked in the attention anyway. Who said I had to explain what had really happened? Tell them that it wasn't even the first time I'd been beaten up at SUM? I was no hero, but given the fictions that had sprouted up about my SUM career as a crime solver, in a year's time students would be swearing I'd come into class with a cast on my leg after a kick-boxing finale with some "perp" I'd chased across town in a stolen Jag.

My enrollments would quadruple.

But Juno wanted to know the truth. She found me in my office that afternoon as I was getting ready to leave.

Looking devastating as usual in a very *Dynasty* black leather pantsuit and a leopard-print headband, she shuddered with distaste as she sat at my desk. "Your office—it's chilling."

"It used to be a meat locker."

"No, seriously, you could open up a wax museum here."

"The wax museum's upstairs. It's where we work."

"Too true. Nick, when I'm chair, I'll get you a better office, I promise."

"Where? There's no room in Parker—you'd have to pitch a tent on the lawn outside, or build a shack on the roof."

"We can put you in with someone else." She made it sound like bunking with a buddy at summer camp.

"Who? They all hate me or think I'm cursed—or both."

She clapped her hands together sternly. "Please don't act like a victim—it's very tiresome."

"You think I'm acting like a victim? I went to a gun shop this morning!"

Juno's face was as bright as a sunflower, though I realized my second statement would for some people have proved an affirmative answer to my rhetorical question.

"Did you really? How marvelous—which one? Aux Armes?"

"Is that where you got your Glock?"

She shook her head very firmly, and I took it as a warning not to probe further. "Are you buying a gun, then?"

"I'm not sure."

"Nick—what are you afraid of? You're an American, for Christ's sake—guns should be like Rice Krispies to you!"

"A breakfast cereal?"

"Don't be obtuse. I meant *ordinary*."

"Well, they're not, but I can see it happening."

"Not ten years from now, I hope."

"Are you kidding? I'm getting one as soon as I decide what I want." I couldn't believe how banal the words were to describe buying a weapon. Maybe I should have tried Sears.

"What's wrong with a Glock?"

I fumbled for an answer. What was really wrong was that Juno had one, and I couldn't see myself with the same gun. It would have felt like I was a tagalong or something. A member of the Glock Gang.

"I have to sense it's the right gun for me." Was that even it? Was I actually going through with this? Is that what five years at SUM had done to me? My parents would be appalled, and I could never tell them or Sharon.

Juno nodded. "I understand. It's like a woman finding the right scent."

"I'm not planning on wearing it."

"You never know. This time last year, did you think you'd want to own a gun? Of course not. Things change, people change. Now fill me in on what happened to you Saturday night. In *detail*."

I did, and she seemed puzzled, stroking one cheek as if it were a crystal ball that would reveal the true nature of what was threatening us, or as if she wanted to comfort me by stroking my bruised cheek.

"I was shot at, you were beaten up," she said. "It doesn't make sense. Why such different methods of intimidation?"

"Different people?"

"Do you mean you and I—or them?"

I shrugged. "Both, maybe." Despite the uncertainty hovering over us, and the threat of further violence, I was enjoying myself with Juno. The sight and smell of her, the intimacy, real or imagined. There was an old-fashioned phrase that described our present situation: we were closeted together. I liked the coziness of that image, even though the setting was more dismal than inviting.

She crossed her legs decisively and tightly, as if that could help her think. It didn't do the trick for me, but sent my thoughts lurching in the wrong direction. I looked away.

"Why us, though?" she asked ruminatively. "What's the connection?"

I'd been so dazed Sunday, so sleepy, I hadn't considered that, and neither had Stefan.

"Someone's clearly trying to scare us, but why? What do we know, what have we seen, what did we say or do?"

"We both think the Diversity Tree is a terrible idea," I offered. "There's no other connection."

"Could that be enough?" She looked around. "Jesus, Nick, don't you have anything to drink?" I'm not sure what she expected in my dismal hideaway—a fully stocked wet bar?

"There's a pop machine down the hall, or I could make some coffee. . . ."

"When I say drink, I mean a *drink*, not a beverage."

"Sorry."

She sighed.

"You could always send me a case of your favorite," I suggested. "For when you drop by."

She grinned, and I had a flash of many such companionable times ahead of us, but it didn't last; someone pounded on the half-open door, and we whirled around in our chairs.

"So you're here, too!" Avis Kinderhoek said, glaring at Juno and looming in the doorway as ominously as someone five feet tall could. Imagine the Seven Dwarves' mother annoyed at finding all their little beds unmade.

"I heard about your so-called attack," she went on to me, not moving into the room as if afraid some maleficent influence might cloud her judgment. "I don't believe a word! You made it up to get attention, to get sympathy, and so that EAR would look bad."

As if our department needed my help. "You're nuts," I said, wanting to jump up and slam the door in her face, but Juno restrained me as confidently as Stefan would have done.

"Am I? You came to your office Saturday night? Oh, aren't you the dedicated teacher! Well, your office is in the basement—what were you doing in the bathroom on the second floor?"

I felt cornered in the witness box by a hostile prosecutor. I shot back, "I stopped there after getting my mail."

She nodded cynically. "Great excuse, but I'll bet you were there to sabotage that tree—and somebody stopped you."

Juno waded in. "What is it you're trying to say, Mavis?"

"Avis. I changed my name! It's Avis, not Mavis. You don't respect anything. You people don't respect anything."

"Canadians?" Juno asked demurely.

"You perverts, that's who I mean, and don't pretend you didn't understand me the first time. But I'll tell you something. This university may have let people like you in, but it's going to vomit you forth one day. There's a change coming."

I thought a moment and recalled a wonderful line from *Topsy-Turvy*, which I delivered with quiet joy: "I'm sure that we shall reap the benefit of your remonstrations in the fullness of time."

Avis scowled as if I'd spoken gibberish, but Juno laughed hard. Avis beetled off down the hall, and Juno and I looked at each other as if checking our eyes—had we really witnessed this buffoonish incursion? I was too embarrassed by and for Avis to laugh.

Juno grimaced. "People like that make me admire countries where they have purges."

"You don't mean that."

"Probably not. But I *would* like to use her for target practice. How can she be a writer? She seems impervious to irony and human feeling. What does she write about?"

"She's a memoirist."

"That explains it. I'm so sick of your American confessions. Nobody is interested—can't you get the message? You meet someone at a party, and within five minutes you hear about his gruesome divorce or her child's birth defect or some other equally intimate horror. I suppose Avis writes about being overweight and underloved?"

"Sometimes. But she's never gotten the attention she thinks she deserves."

"She deserves to be bitch-slapped, is what she deserves. What a little commissar!"

"You were the one who was talking about purges."

"After being around her, I need a *purgative*. She's disgusting. What makes her such a termagant?"

"Her first book was published by Knopf, all the others by smaller and smaller presses. She's gone nowhere big."

Juno was musing now as if we'd actually had a civil exchange with Avis and not been the target of raving. "What do you think she meant about us being vomited forth? It's from the Bible, I know, but what's she getting at? She couldn't be the one who's after us, could she? It seems too obvious. And while I could picture her shooting at me, she's a bit small to take you down, unless she's the kind of woman who breeds giants and she had her son run some errands and then beat you up on his way to the bars."

" 'Leave her alone.' 'Leave it alone.' Either way, it could be about Avis. She's the one who defended the tree at the meeting."

"So we're being threatened because someone thinks we're picking on that muskrat?"

Right then, it all seemed so confusing that I did need a drink—whether to clarify my thoughts or to drown them didn't matter. Juno had a better idea.

"How about a swim?" she said. "I've got my gym bag. How about you?"

"It's in the car. Let me call home."

"I'll meet you over at The Club, in the pool." Juno patted my hand and left. I sat back in my chair, closing my eyes and enjoying her perfume.

"Nick. You are called!" Byron Summerscale boomed at me, stomping into my office like a bounty hunter about to drag me off to jail. I definitely needed a doorman.

"What's going on?"

"A crusade! Cleaning out the Augean stables! The cleansing fire!" If he got any louder, he would unsettle Parker's foundation. I didn't bother pointing out that Hercules used water to clean those stables, not flame.

"Byron, I'm not following you."

"But you must! You must follow me—join my campaign—help me become chair of EAR. It's time to end the gynocracy. Only a man can do this job."

"Juno's pretty tough," I said provocatively.

His voice dropped a few decibels, but his generally mobile face looked very Mount Rushmore. "She's dangerous. She's malicious. You should stay away from her. She's trouble."

Suddenly he was sounding like a father warning his teenage son about a date. Could he tell I was attracted to Juno? I wasn't sure what to say, but Summerscale didn't seem to need a reply and surged back out into the hall and down to his office. The door slammed, then opened again, and he bellowed, "Think about it hard, Nicholas!"

French farce meets *Scream*.

Of course part of my problem with Juno was thinking about it hard, but now wasn't the time to mention that. I called Stefan to say I was swimming with Juno, that I needed a quick swim to relax. I felt a twinge when I hung up but shifted gear as I was getting ready to close up my office. I thought about Summerscale. He was big enough and broad enough to have been the one to hold me down on the men's-room floor, and the kind of guy who might use an Old Spice or Yardley-style aftershave. How could I get to smell his hands?

I headed up to check my mailbox in the EAR office, feeling as giddy about having a rendezvous with Juno as if there were much more involved than sharing a lane at the pool. Rusty Dominguez-St. John was striding down the stairs as if he owned them—in a sensitive, life-affirming-we're-all-in-this-together kind of way, of course—and he stopped. The Ego Has Landed, I thought.

"That was pretty courageous what you said at the meeting. You took a lot of risks."

"Thanks."

"Oh, I'm not complimenting you," he said, voice warm and broad and helpful. "I think you made a big mistake. And you're going to have to pay for it."

"Can I put that on my VISA card?"

He gave me a Jack Nicholson grin. "Remember, you did it to yourself, dude." And he strutted down the stairs, as cocky as Brad Pitt in *Fight Club* mocking Ed Norton on the plane. "Nasty-looking bruise," he said from down below, and I touched it as if to shield myself from his quiet contempt. Jeez, he was *two* unpleasant people, nasty one-on-one, smarmy in public.

I made it to the office without being accosted by anyone else, but along with the other usual mail found a bizarre memo in my box from Les Peterman, Martin Wardell, and Larry Rich, declaring their intention to vote for and lobby for Byron Summerscale as the savior of EAR because he was the only person disinterested enough to be a good chair. Great—were we going to be seeing commercials and campaign buttons, too?

As I read it, I felt an unpleasant sensation and turned to see if I was being stared at. I was. Dulcie Halligan had come to the front counter from her desk as if to defend the miserable little Diversity Tree from my depredations—or just plain scorn. Her watchful, hostile attitude told me that she must have been informed of my stand at the meeting. That was great—I could expect her from now on to be even less helpful to me, and even obstructive. She seemed to be staring at my bruise, and I couldn't tell if she were offended somehow, or if she was glad.

"Have a nice day," I said, departing, noting the thickening of objects on the tree since I'd seen it Saturday night. I saw a little white-and-gold teddy bear that definitely looked new—what faith tradition did that represent? Disney?

Dulcie Halligan made some sort of dismissive noise through her nose.

It was late afternoon, and the parking lot at The Club was starting to fill up when I got there a few minutes later, but as always, I looked for a space close to the door, as if the walk from my car was particularly enervating. I tried to think of a Seinfeld-like witticism to explain it but drew a big blank.

Between the eastern edge of campus and exclusive (and flat) Michigan Hills, The Club was Michiganapolis's premier place to work out, or pretend to. It was a lavish, gigantic concrete-and-glass multiwinged structure that looked more like a biotech research center than a health club. Spreading across many acres and built on different levels connected by wide staircases, it teemed with possibilities for physical self-improvement or torment, depending on your perspective: an indoor and outdoor track, dozens of tennis and racquetball courts, three basketball courts, indoor and outdoor pools, and so many aerobic studios and cardiovascular equipment rooms that it was easy to get lost. The weight rooms were so big they looked like warehouses for storing the equipment.

When I checked in, a grinning, chirpy teenage girl ran my card through the slot and wished me a great workout. Her name tag read "Treycee."

Down in the brightly lit, massive, echoing locker room there was a shift change going on: high school students were leaving, and men my age and older were drifting in, having left work early.

As I began to change at my locker, I heard a cheerful "Nick!" and turned to see Cash Jurevicius a few aisles over. He bounded over, a towel rather exiguously draped over his shoulder. His smooth, muscular body was amazingly lean, and he had tremendous vascularity, his veins visible all over. All over. I'd never seen him in the locker room before, and I was impressed—he had the kind of body you don't believe exists on a real human being but you see in advertisements, or your dreams. You couldn't get that way just through the right diet and the right workout; it was a genetic gift.

Cash slapped my shoulder with one hand and shook my hand with the other. "That was a great speech you gave at the meeting!"

"It wasn't really a speech. It wasn't planned."

"That's why it was great. You were carried away by the moment."

Frankly, I found the current moment had more to be said for it. I tried keeping my eyes on Cash's, but it wasn't easy, since his glowing nudity seemed even more effulgent, set off as it was by the grim steel lockers around us. Imagine Botticelli having painted Apollo on that shell rather than Venus, and you get the picture.

There was a discordant note, though. He was probably sleeping with Juno, wasn't he? I felt jealous of his youth, his slimness, his good looks—and his access.

"People are such cowards and quislings in EAR. We've got the fascists marching in, spying on us, shoving Christmas trees down our throat, and most people could care less."

He was on my side, so I didn't tell him that the correct phrase was, *couldn't* care less. Nor did I object to his hyperbolic reference to the Nazis, a maddening rhetorical tic that was culturewide. I refrained because I enjoyed his presence, and the spectacle of him unconsciously grabbing at his balls while he spoke, as only straight men seem to do at the gym, dressed or undressed. To me, that was always the dead giveaway when I was speculating about some guy at the gym—if he grabbed himself, adjusted himself, or scratched, he had to be straight. Otherwise, those gestures were too loaded. So to speak.

"Forget Summerscale," he said, giving himself a tentative shake, making anything else eminently forgettable. "He's a buffoon. Nobody takes him seriously, even though he was right. You should run for chair."

"*Me*? I'm untenured."

"My grandmother wanted the department to be open and democratic, and she instituted a change in the department's by-laws. It's never happened so far, but in EAR, if an assistant professor runs for chair and wins, he's automatically granted tenure. She thought an election like that would be a good sign the person was respected by his colleagues."

"You're not making this up?"

"You can check it out yourself. She had vision, though I don't think she could imagine the department becoming what it is now. We desperately need a fresh voice."

"That's me," I said, "Funky, phat, and fresh. It must be time for me to do a music video."

Cash crossed his arms. "See what I mean? We need a sense of humor in EAR. I don't know what's happened to Serena, but she's a zombie now, and Juno and Summerscale are too unpredictable."

I waited for Cash to say something nicer about Juno to palliate his criticism, but he didn't. That was curious.

"And Whiteness Studies! Do we really want someone like Mavis, I mean Avis, making curricular decisions? That program has to be fought department by department. If we can't do it head-on, then we have to think of other ways."

What was he suggesting? Guerrilla warfare? Between him and Summerscale, I was likely to wind up *hors de combat*.

"We need someone who isn't mired in the past," Cash said, peering at me so eagerly that I said, "Chair? Me?" I knew that would drag the conversation out some more, since I had never been one to not look a gift nude in the mouth.

Now Cash leaned in to me and grabbed my shoulders as if to shake sense into me. He shook something else a lot more, and it wasn't mine. "Really, Nick, think about it. Why should the chair always go to full professors who've turned stale? Why not someone young and vigorous?"

If he touched me anymore, he'd see how vigorous I could be, but thankfully, he gave me a firm man-to-man nod and walked away, heading for the showers, I supposed, or the bathroom. He looked as good in retreat as while advancing, his hairless butt as round and firm as a basketball. If Stefan were there, he surely wouldn't be able to say Cash and I looked alike, not with this much evidence to the contrary. No one could mistake us with all this bright light.

The beauty of Cash's departure didn't stop me from speculating about why he would want me to run for chair when Juno was doing the same thing. Wouldn't my running hurt her chances, if even by a few votes? Unless it was some elaborate ploy to guarantee that she wouldn't win, because he wanted to keep her out of the line of fire. She was criticized enough as just a professor; as chair she would be the object of contumely; if he cared about her, he might not want that to happen.

But what if he was playing me; what if all this was his attempt to turn the tables on EAR? How else could an adjunct achieve success in the department unless he had a friend who could make crucial decisions like hiring? He could be trying to become my Svengali, using flattery (young and vigorous, coming from him!) backed up by his good looks and his amazing body to sway me. Maybe he thought if by some fluke I won, I'd be so grateful to him that I'd ensure he got a tenure-stream appointment and make him an associate chair. Backing two candidates—Juno and me—how could he lose? Either way, he'd have the EAR chair's ear.

The worst possibility was that he thought I was stupid enough to run, stupid enough to make myself even more unpopular in the department, and that for some unfathomable reason, he wanted to bring me down like the dogs savaging Actaeon. But I'd been good to him before, when I didn't have to be, so that was paranoid.

Maybe it was more entertaining: he was a closet case and enjoyed teasing himself and me, and had said the first thing that came to mind just to keep a conversation going. Now that was something I could live with. And at least he hadn't mentioned or seemed to look at my bruise.

I finished changing into my swim trunks, dug out my goggles, closed my locker, and headed to the showers to rinse off before getting into the pool, nodding at all the familiar faces on the way. Chair. Me? I might be able to keep on top of the administrative part because I'd managed the bibliography, but ride herd on EAR faculty? Even if I were completely out of my mind on coke or Ecstasy, I would know that was impossible. It would end up like Charles Laughton being attacked and cut to pieces by the army of half-men in *Island of Lost Souls*.

Before going to the pool, I switched the bandage on my cheek to one that was supposed to be waterproof. The cut was healing well, but the bruise was larger and brighter, like one of those pictures from space of a nebula eating a galaxy—or the reverse.

Juno and I had chosen a good time; the lanes of the Olympic-size pool weren't crowded. She waved at me from the far lane, where she was standing in the shallow end, wearing a black bathing cap and a leopard-print one-piece that wiped the image of Cash's nudity from my mind. He might have been handsome and hung, but the territory was familiar, whereas Juno was the undiscovered country, Shangri-la.

I walked over, bent over to dip my goggles in the water, shook them off, and slid down into the pool. Even dressed as she was, Juno had a kind of breezy bravado that must have made her a terror as a child, or perhaps I was just swayed at the moment by the echoing splashes from other lanes and the way the light shattered in the water.

"Shall we swim traffic pattern?" she said. "I'll follow you, and observe your form. Let's do a few laps and see where we are."

I felt confident taking off down the lane, not at all embarrassed by being observed. It was sexy and thrilling to be swimming with Juno behind me, watching my legs, my arms, the way I turned my head to breathe. I was both in the moment and very much in the pool, but also outside it, enjoying the spectacle. I didn't think of guns or attacks or violence or anything but the movement of myself through water, though my bruise stung a little at first from the chlorinated water.

Back at the shallow end, Juno gave me her director's notes. I was reaching more with my right arm and not pulling through enough, which seemed to throw my breathing off. And my feet were out of the water too much, making my kick less efficient than it could be.

"Is that right?" she asked, brisk, efficient, but not critical.

I closed my eyes and tried to picture it all. "I'm not sure."

"Okay, why don't you swim out to the middle of the lane, and I'll hold you in place, and we'll watch it together to make sure."

I dove under and reached the middle; Juno followed, stood up, and slipped an arm around me. "Go," she said.

She was very strong, and very close, and as I pulled through and kicked in place, I was glad I wasn't doing the backstroke because I would have been very embarrassed by my response to being in her arms. Well, arm.

"I was right," she said, not sounding remotely critical or superior, but encouraging.

"I'll swim down and back and meet you," I said, taking off and hoping that by the time I returned, water rushing past me would have calmed me down. We swam twenty more laps together, Juno reminding me to slow down and not rush through each stroke, since I wasn't exactly escaping sharks and trying to reach shore.

She could say that. She hadn't had my afternoon.

We met upstairs at The Club's restaurant for a quick drink after our swim.

"Do you need help with your gun?" she asked. "Choosing it. I'd be happy to help."

There didn't seem to be any hidden agenda here, so I thanked her and said I might. "I've just glanced at the brochures, and it's hard to keep things clear. Like Smith & Wesson—they make so many different guns."

I didn't tell her that when I'd seen the first description of a .38, I had flushed with embarrassment. Was I going to get a Saturday night special? It seemed so cheesy and vulgar.

Juno sipped her martini and asked if I were free tomorrow morning. I was, and I welcomed the chance to return to Aux Armes early, since I assumed that it would be as empty then as it was on my first visit, and I wouldn't have to face any grizzled survivalists, or anyone who knew me.

"I want to ask you a personal question."

I braced myself. "Go ahead."

"What does Stefan think about your wanting a gun—or haven't you told him?"

"He doesn't know. He'll probably think I'm crazy."

"Do you think you're crazy?"

"Well, I have wondered about it. If I'm overreacting."

"You've been beaten up how many times now at SUM? Twice? And threatened? And been the victim of arson and an office break-in? And discovered a body? If I were you, I'd be looking for a fucking Uzi, not just a pistol."

I drank some more of my seven and seven. It was indeed unreal, the things that had happened to me since moving to Michiganapolis. They were episodes out of a book or a movie—or the kind of disasters that were supposed to happen to somebody else. I was an assistant professor of English. I was a bibliographer. I was just trying to live my life and get tenure.

"You know, I've never wanted to ski or go white-water rafting or rock climbing or snowboarding or bungee jumping or skydiving. I've never been a thrill-seeker."

Juno leaned forward, her perfume wafting over me. "Nick, I can promise you that having a gun is much more exciting than any of those."

"But that's my point. I don't *want* excitement, I'm not looking for danger."

"It seems to be looking for you, and you need to be ready." She finished her martini. "Shall we order some potato skins or something equally disgusting?"

It sounded good to me, and we ordered another round of drinks to wash them down.

"Now, you do know what you need to do?" Juno asked.

"About what?"

"Getting the permit and all that."

I felt like an idiot. I had never bothered thinking through what might be required, and Juno could tell I was unprepared, but she didn't hassle me about it. "You'll have to go to the Michiganapolis Police Department. Before they can issue the permit, they make a background check."

"Wait. What for? I haven't done anything."

"They need more than your word," she said wryly.

I had no criminal past of any kind, but the thought of being checked out by the police disturbed me. What if there were some computer glitch somewhere, and I was falsely identified with some mobster and dragged off to jail, my life turning into a bad imitation of Kafka?

"Nick, buying a gun is more serious than picking up a sink at Home Depot—at least, in theory."

"How long does it take?"

"The background check? They say it can take three to five days. You also have to fill out a form to purchase a gun and take a quiz."

"Citizenship?" I had images of being asked to explain the significance of *Marbury vs. Madison*.

"No, gun safety."

"But I don't know anything about gun safety."

"Then you have a lot to learn, don't you?" She raised her glass, and we toasted. I felt more of a sense of collusion than challenge at that moment.

When I got home, Stefan had a fire going, and he was putting the finishing touches on a venison and shiitake ragout that already smelled wonderful. The venison had marinated overnight in chopped onion, garlic, carrots, coriander seeds, marjoram, and zinfandel. Venison, I thought. Someone shot it. Not with a pistol, perhaps, but it had hardly died of old age or committed suicide.

"Hey—I started dinner late in case you got carried away in the pool. I've already simmered the marinade with the beef broth."

I sat at the island, where he'd laid out a plate of homemade pesto and flatbread. "What?"

"That's how we did it last time."

"No—I mean what were you saying about the pool?" I tried not to look guilty.

He turned from the stove, brushing hair off his forehead. "I figured you might decide to learn a new stroke or something." He put the egg noodles into the waiting pot of boiling water, set a timer, and carefully started browning the venison, which could not get overdone thanks to the new well-calibrated cooktop. "How was Juno?" He seemed surprisingly cheerful about her now.

"She's a good teacher," I said. "I think she can help me."

"That's great."

Stefan peppered me with questions about the swimming lesson as assiduously as a parent worried about a child's potential drug use but trying to stay cheerful and cool. Was he suspicious of my spending time with Juno and trying to cover that up, or was he so happy his antipathy to her was subdued? His questions about my time in the pool continued after the ragout was spooned into large blue bowls and garnished with chopped, toasted hazelnuts. We ate on the floor by the fire, laying placemats on the hearth. I wasn't very thirsty for the Côtes-du-Rhône Villages he'd opened, but Stefan seemed too upbeat to notice.

"How come you're so cheerful?" I finally asked midway through the meal, feeling that I didn't deserve his zest.

"Because all the crap about Whiteness Studies and the Diversity Tree and who's running for chair of EAR just doesn't matter. You and I have a great life despite all of that. How were your classes?" he asked.

"Terrific." I raved about how well they'd gone, feeling mired in dishonesty. What I was saying wasn't the problem; it was what I kept back. Not only was I attracted to Juno, she and I were going to a gun shop for my second visit—how murky was that? And would I end up feeling about myself the way Lillian Hellman had been described by Mary McCarthy: Every word she said was a lie, including the prepositions?

If Stefan noticed that I was mildly distracted, he said nothing, and we finished dinner and got the dishwasher going with every appearance of harmony and ease. We checked the digital cable menu, and Stefan was surprised when I said I wanted to see Ar-

nold Schwarzenegger's *Commando* again, but he was happy to join
me. It was a taut mix of thrills and comedy, mostly in the interac-
tions between Arnold and Rae Dawn Chong, but every scene with
a weapon in it had tremendous resonance for me as I tried
matching it against guns I'd read about. When Arnold crashed into
the gun shop, I felt a sense of glee and greed I knew I hadn't experienced before.

Stefan went to bed early, and I stayed up for an hour or two in
my study, going through the brochures that Mrs. Fennebresque
had given me.

I met Juno at Aux Armes Tuesday morning while Stefan was at
the gym. When I got there, she was leaning comfortably on the
counter, chatting as easily but seriously with Mrs. Fennebresque as if they were at a Clinique counter assessing a new
beauty regimen. Juno looked gorgeous as ever in a black coat-
dress with large leopard-print buttons. Mrs. Fennebresque was
wearing a pink lace-collared blouse, red skirt, and several neck-
laces of amber beads. She grinned. "Well, hello! I wasn't sure
you'd be back."

"Did you think you scared him off?" Juno asked in an intimate
tone that made it clear she knew me well. If that wasn't enough,
when I walked up to the counter, she slipped an arm in mine, and
now Mrs. Fennebresque eyed us both with as much friendliness as
if we were neighbors who had brought her a housewarming gift.

"I like seeing a couple share interests," she said. "It keeps you
together. How long's it been for you two?"

Juno laughed and squeezed my arm harder. "Not long
enough!" If I didn't blush, I should have, because I enjoyed feeling
Juno's breasts rub against me.

"That's the right sentiment."

"I'm not letting this one go," Juno said. "He's too good a
catch."

"My husband and I were together for forty-five years before he
passed. Say—I just made myself some tea, would you like a cup?"

We said yes, and soon Mrs. Fennebresque was serving us tea

in ivory-colored cups with tiny shamrocks across them, a pattern that Juno recognized as Beleek, from Northern Ireland. Juno and Mrs. Fennebresque spent a few cozy minutes comparing Irish origins.

"Before you got here, Mrs. F. was telling me she used to teach at SUM," Juno said, bringing me back into the conversation which had seemed bizarre, surrounded as we were by ranks and ranks of weapons and surveillance cameras, which I noted for the first time.

"Really?"

Mrs. Fennebresque nodded. "In the School of Nursing. I left before they closed it down. I could feel the disaster coming. And my husband had always been a gun aficionado, so this was the natural choice. Speaking of choice, have you thought any more about what you need in a gun?"

Juno and Mrs. Fennebresque eyed me expectantly, and I tried to concentrate hard. It felt like an oral exam in which I had to draw on a night of cramming.

"I don't think I'm ready for anything as heavy-duty as a .357. If I'm just getting started, I think accuracy is more important now than stopping power. I'm thinking I should start with a .22 and perfect my aim in target practice."

Juno and Mrs. Fennebresque glanced at each other and nodded, eyebrows up.

"That's very sensible," Mrs. Fennebresque said approvingly. "Did you have something particular in mind?"

"Show me what you've got."

We spent half an hour looking at Rugers, Smith & Wessons, and Brownings. I held them as she did while she showed me the safeties, talked about bullets, explained why they were called long rifles, discussed pressure in the barrel and accuracy. Every sentence made the situation more and more normal.

"You keep going back to the 22A," Juno noted, and she was right. For some reason I was drawn to that Smith & Wesson. "Does it feel good in your hand?"

I nodded. But it also looked good, plain and black with not too long a barrel. A basic, solid gun, nothing flashy. It wouldn't blow someone away across the street, but if someone threatened me closer than that, it would be enough. And even though the Ruger was supposedly the world's best .22, it looked too much like a toy gun to me.

"You know, these guns aren't concealable," Mrs. Fennebresque said confidingly. Then she pointed to some tiny-looking .22s farther along the counter. "But with these, they say you can take the nipple off a baby's bottle and use it practically as a silencer. It's supposed to be an old Mafia trick. They do call this kind of .22 an assassin's gun. It's just so easy to hide."

I met Juno's eyes. We were both thinking the same thing: that's what had happened at the reception, and why nobody else seemed to have heard a gun.

"The price is right for your Smith & Wesson," Mrs. Fennebresque said. "To start out. I'm sure you'll move up, though." And she eyed Juno fondly. "You're certainly big enough to handle more gun."

Juno did not say anything raunchy. I was buzzing with the information about the other .22s, and filled with a sense of calm wonder that I was moving closer to purchasing a gun.

"Tell me about the safety quiz," I said, setting the Smith & Wesson down on the counter carefully.

"You're already exercising safety! Treat every gun as if it's loaded. That's first and foremost." She handed me a pamphlet about firearms safety and explained in detail the process of applying for a permit. It was more complicated than I thought.

"Why does it take three to five days for the background check?"

"They tell you that, but if your name isn't something ordinary like John Smith, it can be instant. They just check with FBI records. I suppose they want to give people a cooling-off period." She shrugged. "Where do you live?"

"North of campus."

"Then you'll have to go to the North Precinct to start the process, and I'm sure they may try to slow things down." She explained that Michiganapolis was divided into four police precincts, north, south, east, and west, and the northern one included SUM.

"But it's not a high-crime neighborhood."

"True. There are a lot of professors, though, and they can be bad tempered."

Juno and I nodded. I reached across the counter to shake Mrs. Fennebresque's hand and thanked her.

"No," she said. "Thank *you*. You're exactly the kind of people I like to see shopping here, and it's lovely to think of the two of you buying your first gun together. Who knows where it'll lead!"

10

OUT in the sunny parking lot, I confronted Juno.

"What was all that couple stuff?"

"Wasn't it *fun?*"

"She's a nice woman, and now she thinks we're a couple—that's dishonest."

"Give it a rest, Nick. It's not deception, it's entertainment. She thinks we're sweet. To her, we're at the beginning of our lives."

"You make it sound like we were picking out a silver pattern, not a gun."

"And *you* make it sound like we're grifters. Nick, we gave her a little gift. It made her happy. She's a widow, she undoubtedly misses her husband, we made her smile. What's so fucking terrible about that? We're not cheating her out of anything."

I had never thought of Juno as a psychological Lady Bountiful before, but I felt somewhat mollified, even as I knew I wasn't addressing the real question—how disturbing it was to be taken for a straight man. Disturbing because it was so profoundly pleasing.

Juno was right—it had been fun pretending to be something I wasn't. Easy fun. And there was a strange relief to momentarily being one of the pack. Did that mean my self-esteem tank was running low? It was flattering to be thought of as Juno's boyfriend or husband, since she was the kind of woman who would make a man "feel—mighty real," if quoting Sylvester wasn't completely inappropriate in this circumstance.

"You enjoyed it, too," Juno asserted, head cocked to the left, studying me as if she were reading my mind. She was doing a good job. "You didn't pull away. You didn't correct me."

"That would have been rude."

"Oh, really?" She leaned forward and stage-whispered, "It's not that big a deal, Nick." Then she strode to her Lexus and waved as she got in. "See you at Parker," she called, peeling out of the lot like a spoiled teenager who'd already totaled a BMW and a Mercedes and was about to rack up a third disaster.

When she had merged with the light traffic, I realized we hadn't even touched on what we'd learned from Mrs. Fennebresque about the possibility of silencing a .22 with a nipple. It seemed vaguely ludicrous, but no more so than anything else that had been transpiring in EAR.

As I drove home, I calmed down more. I thought that Juno might be right about our brief imposture. It wasn't a big deal. We *hadn't* cheated Mrs. Fennebresque out of anything, just played to her fantasy about us. And so what if for forty-five minutes of my life I had been less than totally authentic? Did somebody behind the counter at a gun shop need to know my whole life story? And what if she didn't even believe it herself—what if she were playing a game with *us*? Anything was possible when a retired nurse sold firearms.

But me passing? I had lived so many years of my life on the outside, as the son of immigrants, as a Jew, and as a gay man. If that wasn't enough, having been born and bred a New Yorker left me open to suspicion and preemptive hostility, since everyone outside the city seemed to expect New Yorkers to feel like exiled royalty longing for home and trapped in some provincial backwater, ready to lash out at their inferiors. New Yorkers I'd met in Michigan tended to reinforce that stereotype by complaining about the lack of culture, the lack of sophistication, the lack of anything and everything they associated with civilized life. Of course, these same people would have been miserable anywhere, but Michiganders tend to be more sensitive to this criticism than Californians or Chicagoans might be.

I drove more slowly the closer I got to home, thinking now about EAR, about who might want to shoot at Juno and was savvy enough to have ingeniously silenced a .22. Did the baby's-bottle nipple point to someone with kids?

Stefan was waiting for me in the kitchen when I walked in, his gym bag over by the laundry room door, and coffee smelling like it had just been brewed; I thought it might be our strongest blend, Vienna roast. He looked flushed and pumped up from his workout, and he was finishing a bottle of Evian. "Sharon called," he said, stretching his shoulders and neck inside his SUM sweatshirt.

"On your line? How is she?"

"No, on yours. She's tired. I heard her leaving a message, and I went into your study to say hi. She hasn't been calling, so I wanted to hear her voice. She asked you not to call her back." He didn't add anything more, but I'd known him long enough to hear the wingbeat of things he wasn't saying. He broke his silence with, "I thought you were going to do the grocery shopping this morning."

"Oh, shit, you're right. I forgot. How was your workout?"

Stefan nodded as if my nervous, deflecting question had confirmed him in some resolution. "After I hung up your phone, I saw some catalogs on the file cabinet."

Too hurriedly, I said, "That's research for my mystery class."

"You need that many gun catalogs for research? What, four, five?" He went to the coffee maker and poured himself a mug of coffee, as if he were giving me time to get my act together and tell the truth. But I resisted.

"Why shouldn't I be informed about firearms? It's part of reading mysteries and thrillers. I have to know the reality." It was lame, but all I could come up with.

Stefan turned, leaning back against the sink with such a casual air I knew he was furious. "You were reading that *Writer's Digest* book called *Armed and Dangerous*. Wasn't that enough?"

"It didn't have pictures."

"Have you bought a gun?"

"No!"

"But you want to." He crossed his arms combatively. "After you had dinner with Juno, you said you thought there was nothing wrong with having a gun, and your face— You didn't look surprised, or grossed out. You were into it. You were fascinated."

"Okay. So. What if I *am* into it? I've been beaten up, I've been threatened, I've seen people killed!" I sat at the granite island, facing him squarely, thinking it was a very civilized room for what threatened to be a very uncivilized confrontation, looking after its remodeling like the kind of glowing large kitchen you see in advertisements, and envy. I had an almost Proustian sense of the summer's maddening chaos, and the dust from drywall rising around us, and the confusion that preceded it as we'd made endless small decisions about countertop edging and cupboard handles and the like. "Stefan, what's wrong with getting a gun after all that? Look at the Jews in the Warsaw ghetto—the Poles refused to sell them guns. If they'd had guns—"

"Nick! Those Jews could have had a hundred times more guns in the Warsaw ghetto, and the Nazis still would have wiped them out—they had *tanks* and *planes*. And the whole German army. That's a bullshit argument, it's beneath you."

I flushed because he was right, but I wouldn't back down. "If your parents had had guns—"

"My parents? If they'd been armed, they wouldn't have survived a minute. They would have been killed right away, even if they'd been able to take some Nazis with them. They were civilians! How can you even bring them into your craziness? That's sick."

"It's not sick."

"It is—it's hysteria." The word sounded more damning given that Stefan's voice was so calm. "If everybody who was in your shoes went out to buy a gun, this country would turn into the Sudan. You got beaten up? Take a kick-boxing class, take tae kwan do—"

"That's the typical over-intellectual response. Is something wrong? Read a book, write a letter, take a class. Do therapy!"

"And buying a gun is better than any of those? That's a solution? It's a whole new problem."

"Stefan, I don't feel safe anymore."

"This is Juno's fault. She's got you hypnotized with her Annie Oakley, funky Amazon routine."

It stung to hear him come that close to how I felt about

Juno—hypnotized—but I was relieved that he was wrong about the direction. "You don't know what you're talking about. Juno has a 9-millimeter, I'm only looking at a .22. People use those for target shooting." I rushed into my study, grabbed the Smith & Wesson brochure, and stormed back into the kitchen, shoved it at him, opened to the page with the gun I was interested in. He took it from me with contempt in every movement.

"See?" I pointed. "Look at the symbols. It's not a police gun, it's not for home defense, it's for target shooting—plinking—small game."

"That's great. You'll be fine if you're attacked by tin cans or rabbits."

"Don't make fun of me."

"How is this gun going to make you feel safer?"

"I feel safer already just looking at it, touching it, reading about it."

His mouth twisted with disgust.

"There's nothing wrong with wanting a gun. Millions of people in America own guns. Tens of millions!"

"That's very convincing. What's next, a pickup with a gun rack and a Confederate flag decal?"

Now I felt disgusted at his stereotyping.

"Listen, Nick, am I supposed to like having a gun in the house? It's my house, too."

"I didn't say it wasn't."

"How would you feel if I started doing drugs and keeping them here?"

"Now it's my turn to say that's a crappy argument. It's a phony analogy. You're not making sense."

"And you are? Nick, you're not acting like the person I've lived with for fifteen years. This is an aberration. You've never wanted a gun, never wanted to talk about guns. You won't watch a John Wayne movie, even that stupid Genghis Khan movie with Susan Hayward when it's on AMC."

"And people don't change? I'm not allowed to change my opinions—I have to stay stuck where I've always been?"

Now he frowned. "You feel *stuck*?" And then he made a leap

that really scared me. "With *me*? Is this all part of some midlife crisis? Are you going to dye your hair, buy a little red sports car, and start running around with some hustler?"

"Hey! I've never looked at another guy like that, and you know it. You're the one who invited Perry Cross to SUM, got him a fucking job in your own department because you weren't sure if you still loved him or not." We had not mentioned the terrible episode involving Stefan's ex-lover in more than a year, and I felt flushed with a sense of reckless bravado.

"You said you were over that." His face was getting red, and he set down the coffee mug so sharply I was surprised it didn't crack. I felt on the edge of a conflagration without even knowing how hot it might burn, and I quickly tried to mollify Stefan.

"I *am* over it," I said reassuringly. "It's just that—"

"You wouldn't bring it up if you were over it. You said you forgave me."

"I did. That doesn't mean I don't think about it sometimes, still."

He whirled away from me and stared out the window. "That's wonderful," he said. "That's just wonderful. I'm going to have to put up with your complaining about Perry Cross for the rest of my life."

I don't know why, but instead of trying to contradict him, I switched gears entirely, as if all my defensiveness were suddenly water draining into sand. "If his name had been Mark Cross, people overhearing us would think we were arguing about luggage."

"What?" He turned around, hands on his thighs, scowling.

"That was a joke."

"A joke," he repeated flatly.

"You know, a remark made to induce jocularity. Sound familiar?"

I could see the corners of his mouth starting to rise and his eyes softening, but he fought it. "Am I supposed to laugh now?"

"Well, it is customary."

I watched him silently debate whether to stay hostile or melt. "Come here." He held his arms open to me, and after a brief hesitation, I stood and walked over, fell into them. We hugged and stayed quiet for a few minutes. "It scares me to think of you having a gun," he said after a while.

"It scares me now to think of *not* having one."

He pushed me away enough to see my eyes. "This is Michiganapolis, this isn't Afghanistan."

"If it were, I'd be in the market for a rocket launcher. But I'd have trouble wearing those funny pants."

"You wouldn't have to shave, though."

"Pray continue, I find your narrative strangely fascinating."

His mood had changed as much as mine; we were clearly both committed to backing down from a rhetorical dogfight. I already felt ashamed of throwing Perry Cross at him, since I had promised myself never to turn into a fishwife harping over the past. I apologized for that, and Stefan seemed to hear it and accept it. But he looked exhausted, as if he'd had two workouts at the gym. His shoulders drooped, and there was a sheen of sweat at his hairline, which he ineffectually brushed at with the back of one hand. I was tired, too, but hopeful that we were done with the fireworks.

We sat at the counter, and I calmly took him through my visits to the gun shop. I omitted Juno's involvement, but his first question was about her. "What does she think of the .22?" Given that he thought she was too volatile, I was surprised he was granting her any authority about guns, but perhaps that was simply because she was the only person we knew who owned a gun, and he was trying to ground himself in this new reality.

"It's not her style, but she understands why I'd want a .22." I didn't say that a .22 was a good place to start, since I hadn't ruled out moving on to a more powerful gun when I was ready.

"Her style? Do they make leopard-print semiautomatics?"

I waited for him to ask me if she'd been at the gun shop with me, but he didn't. He leafed through the Smith & Wesson catalog with as much discomfort as if he'd been looking at a magazine for aficionados of gross-out exotic body piercing. "This is really disorienting."

"I know what you mean. Crate and Barrel's catalog has better illustrations."

He shook his head. "I feel like we've gone Through the Looking Glass."

"Actually, we've been there ever since we started teaching at SUM."

"You'd get a gun lock?"

"Of course."

"And keep the gun in the safe in our closet?"

"Sure. You know, you can't transport it loaded. The ammunition has to be in the glove compartment, say, and the gun in your trunk."

"Good." He nodded. "But wait a minute, you really don't know anything about guns besides what you've read, do you? So how can you buy a gun? What's the point?"

"There's a firing range in town, and I can have private lessons or do them with a group."

He smiled. "Isn't that too intellectual—taking a class?"

"Touché."

Stefan seemed much calmer now, and he asked if I wanted some coffee. He poured it, took some lemon shortbread from the treat cupboard, and laid it out on a plate for me like a peace offering. I indulged.

With my mouth full, I said, "Shit—I never told you about my swim—I mean before my swim yesterday! Cash was in the locker room—"

"Cash? What's he look like?"

That inevitable question (whose unspoken second half was "in the nude") stopped my narrative flow, and I had to take a quick detour: "Ripped, mostly hairless, hung."

Stefan nodded and waved his hand in a "Thanks, go on" gesture.

"So Cash complimented me on going berserk at the meeting, thanked me for it, sort of. I guess he was glad somebody else spoke up. But you're not going to believe what he did next."

"Made a pass at you?"

"Nothing that clichéd. He said I should run for chair."

"*Chair?*"

"Yes, chair. Of EAR?"

"You?" Stefan cracked up, his rare laugh filling the room like a party. "You run for chair? You don't have tenure."

I explained the loophole Cash's grandmother had created, but Stefan didn't seem impressed. "It's still pretty bizarre to think of you running for chair."

"It's mildly appealing to think of doing an end run around the tenure committee. But running wouldn't be bizarre—quixotic is a better way to put it."

"Nick, try suicidal. Why would he even suggest it? Unless he's got some kind of plan. . . ." Stefan squinted as if trying to make out shadowy figures at some distance.

"Exactly. Maybe he's afraid Juno could win and wants me in the race because he thinks I'd siphon off votes."

"That's pretty perverse, but Summerscale's already going to do that anyway. And be serious, Nick—who would vote for you? Don't even pretend to look wounded. Even if *I* did, that would just make two votes. What did he say?"

"Wait a minute. *If* you voted for me?"

"Stop right there and tell me what he said."

I shared Cash's reasoning for why I should run.

"And you listened?"

"He was nude—he was hot. Why should I tell him to shut up?"

Stefan nodded and had some more coffee. "Nick, he may have been around SUM for a while, but he doesn't know it well. Sure, you have a sense of humor, but that's actually a minus in an administrator. So is being young, relatively."

"Relatively young, or relatively a minus?"

"Both. Maybe Cash was stoned. Did he look high?"

"I wasn't paying attention to that. But if he was high, what's he wasting his drugged state on me for? Why wasn't he out getting laid or just enjoying it?"

"And why are we being so cynical? Maybe he feels he owes you something, since you saved his ass, or maybe he really does admire you now, after what you said at the meeting. He was pretty isolated there, and some people would say you defended him. He may think it's time for the Young Turks to stage a coup in EAR, but neither one of you has any kind of power base. You'd be the Young

Turkeys. The department would eat you for dinner and make turkey salad afterward."

"Thanks."

"Nick, you didn't take him seriously, did you? You didn't think he could be your James Carville?"

"Of course I did. I was already planning how to redecorate the inner EAR suite."

"The idea of you running for chair makes having a gun in the house seem a lot less scary. You'd *need* a gun if you ran for chair."

Because harmony and good humor were restored between us, I debated telling him about Mrs. Fennebresque's assassination recipe, but his face was so open and receptive, I couldn't hold it back.

"A nipple from a baby bottle? That's the dumbest thing I've ever heard of."

"Maybe so, maybe not. I haven't tried it. But I'm sure somebody fired a gun at the reception and was trying to hit or scare Juno."

"Are you going to start that again?"

I put my hand on his arm and stopped him. "Listen to this." Then I explained about finding what looked like a bullet hole at the Campus Center.

He didn't criticize me for going there or even try to pin down when I'd made my investigation or why. He sighed when I was done arguing my case, letting acceptance of the reality spread through him. "If that gun woman told you about silencing a .22, who else has she told?" It was an inevitable question, but he said it reluctantly, like a soldier reporting a battlefield defeat to his general.

"Bingo. If we find out who in EAR she's sold guns to or might have talked to, then we'll know who's been harassing Juno and—"

"We? Nick, you're not a PI or a vigilante. This is Valley's job, whether you like him or not." Even though his tone was still warm and his face open, I could feel him drawing away inside, becoming anxious and critical. "And why would this Mrs.—what's her name? Fennel—"

"Fennebresque." I spelled it for him.

"Why would Mrs. Fennebresque tell you anything? Wouldn't that be some kind of privacy violation?"

"I don't think a gun dealer is like a psychiatrist exactly. Anyway, she likes me." That was true enough, but without explaining that Juno had been there on my second visit and our being taken for a couple, it sounded weak and unconvincing.

"I like you, too," Stefan said, eyebrows waggling in a bad imitation of Groucho Marx.

We spent the next hour or so violating each other's privacy.

Stefan had some reading to do, so I drove to campus to pick up his mail and mine when it was getting on to dusk. The traffic heading away from campus was dense and annoying, but you could drive onto campus at that time of day with dreamlike ease. I realize that anyone living in a city would consider our traffic nothing substantial, but when you're used to getting someplace in five minutes and it takes ten or even fifteen, you can feel as trapped and enraged as anyone being cut off at ninety miles per hour on a California freeway. At least it was still unseasonably mild for December; people were wearing light jackets or open coats, and students had no trouble biking around campus.

As I walked into Parker's second-floor hallway, I saw a startling trio leave the conference room and bustle over to the main office: Tyler Mooney-Mauser, Avis Kinderhoek, and Dulcie Halligan. They looked excited, and somehow mean—like high school kids who've just egged the class reject's locker and torn up his homework.

What could they possibly have in common—unless there had been some meeting I didn't know about? I hung back as they entered the EAR office, then hurried down to the meeting room to look inside. It was empty. Puzzled, I trailed to the department office warily.

Inside, Avis and Tyler were nowhere to be seen, but Dulcie was confiding in the other secretaries. When she saw me, she grinned defiantly, looking like a lost Poe story: "The Rictus of Revenge."

"I've just won an award!" she announced, drawing closer to the counter, and the other two secretaries rose symmetrically behind her, like backup singers in a sixties girl group. They even had matching wilted bouffants.

"Really?" Maybe that explained why she'd been hanging out with the provost's bully-boy. But where did Avis fit in?

"It comes with a *medal*. It's called the President's Medal for Service. I'm going to be the very first person at SUM to get it. There's a dinner at the Faculty Club, and President Littleterry is going to make a speech and award it to me, and my picture will be in the campus newspaper and the *Michiganapolis Tribune* and on the university website for a full year!"

"That's impressive." I sidled to the mailboxes to remove my mail and Stefan's.

"It's for the Diversity Tree! Because it's so innovative and because it's done so much for the university." She was as spitefully triumphant as Tim Curry in *The Shadow* bragging, "I bet you never thought I'd grow up to have an atomic device!" The tree shone there on the counter, even more heavily bedecked now with objects so miscellaneous it was hard to imagine they represented anyone's faith. Added to the previous ornaments, I saw a Rubik's cube, a fancy scissors, and a troll doll. I guess no one was vetting these offerings, or pantheism had taken some strange turns at SUM.

"That's great, Dulcie." What had she done for the university? Created more enmity? I tried to exit the office as if I weren't desperate to leave her sneering voice behind me. As the door closed, I heard mocking applause.

Wonderful. Dulcie hated me, and so did the other secretaries.

I headed down the empty, echoing hallway to Juno's office in the hope that she was in; her open door was like a benison. She was at her desk holding what looked like a Waterford tumbler with about a finger of scotch. I assumed she wasn't having office hours.

"Dulcie's getting an award," I said, closing the door quietly behind me though I wanted to slam it shut.

Juno grimaced. "Are you sure you don't mean there's a warrant out for her?"

"No. Littleterry's giving her a medal. For the Diversity Tree. It's called the President's Medal for Service."

Juno's eyes widened, then she squinted. "The PMS? Brilliant."

Despite my outrage, I laughed.

"For that fucking tree?" Juno asked. "Are you sure?"

"That's what she told me."

"Christ, I need another drink as soon as I finish this one." Juno opened up the file drawer on her desk and pulled out a cut-glass decanter. "How about you?"

"It's kind of early."

"Nick, if this university is honoring Dulcie *Harridan*, it's actually too fucking late."

I took a glass, and we toasted each other, then she poured herself more.

Juno was brooding. "The only problem with being chair is you can't fire the secretaries. They have a bloody union."

If she thought that was the only problem with being chair, she would be in for many disappointments in the unlikely eventuality that she won. Though given the field, it seemed just as unlikely that any of them would win.

"How would you like to be associate chair for graduate studies?" she asked. " You're good to the grad students, you treat them with respect. It would be a change to put someone like you in the position."

"I don't have tenure." If Cash was right about his grand-mother's rule, I didn't think it applied to associate chair positions.

"I'd get you tenure," she said dismissively, as if we were talking about nothing more complicated than filling up a car at the gas station.

I downed the rest of my scotch.

"I suppose there's to be some kind of ceremony," Juno said gloomily. "For Dulwit."

I nodded.

"Will they dare invite faculty, though?" Juno seemed to perk up at the thought of more possibilities for academic mayhem. This time she could wear a Kevlar vest.

"They may have us watch it on closed-circuit TV—or on the Web."

Without any transition, Juno said, "You know Nick, I've been wondering if we've gone too far."

She's going to dump me, I thought, and was so shocked at the unbidden words that I wanted to slap myself for even thinking of her in those extravagant terms.

"Everything's quiet—no calls, no more letters, my car's okay. Perhaps it was a fluke or a stupid bloody joke. It could have simply been an accident that I was pushed down at the reception, and even roughed up. There was a mob scene, after all. I suppose I'm lucky there wasn't more of a panic, and I wasn't trampled."

"But what about the bullet hole?"

"Are you a forensics expert? Am I? No. That hole could have a perfectly innocent explanation—several, perhaps. We just don't know what they are."

I felt so disappointed at her backing down from the assertion that she was being stalked or at least harassed that I instantly suspected my own intensity. Shit—did this mean I was committed to the idea of someone being after her? Why? To play savior, or at least sidekick?

Channeling Stefan, I said, "Well, in that case, why not at least tell Valley about the bullet hole—or whatever it was?"

"Nick, Nick, Nick. The man has a foreskin for a neck!"

"What?"

She scowled. "He's a *prick*."

I changed subjects to distract her. "When I came up to this floor, I saw Dulcie leaving the meeting room with Tyler Mooney-Mauser and Avis. What do you think they were doing?"

"Casting spells, I bet. Sticking pins in dolls."

"Be serious."

"Avis is seriously deranged—what kind of person changes her name from Mavis to Avis?"

"Maybe she got some kind of deal on the Internet, I don't know. But why were the three of them together?"

Juno shook her head, exhausted. "Honestly, I can't even imagine. Details about the fucking medal?"

"But Mooney-Mauser works for the provost. And Avis, she doesn't have any connection to Littleterry."

"Perhaps she nominated Dulcie."

"But when? Where? I've never heard of this medal before. Have you? There haven't been any memos about it, and nothing in the *Faculty Bulletin*."

"Ah yes, that landfill of print."

"Secret medal? Secret nominations? What the hell else is going on at SUM?"

"Nick, you're starting to sound just like one of those con- spiracy-theory nuts. It's just business as usual."

I apologized. "You're right, it's probably no big deal. It's prob- ably just another piece of PR. 'Look how wonderful the university is—honoring an office manager.' "

"Exactly."

"You'd think they'd want to make more of a fuss, though, and have it well publicized."

"I don't know. This way, it's a surprise."

"Shock. Why would they give Dulcie a medal? It's crazy."

"Perhaps—" Juno licked her glossy lips, pondering. "Perhaps it's a sign. That the administration approves of the Diversity Tree. That would explain Mooney Mouseboy being here."

I suddenly had an image of Juno and me seen from the out- side, sitting there griping about a stupid medal going to a secre- tary. We were worse than snobs, we were pathetic, begrudging Dulcie some petty recognition. That's what EAR did, made anyone else's smallest success seem like a theft, like it not only robbed you of whatever might come your way, but of what you already had. Stay there long enough, and anyone could become infinitely mean-spirited about what seemed like finite rewards.

"Let's get the hell out of here," I said.

"Amen." Juno slipped on a black sweater-jacket, grabbed her Chanel bag, and followed me out of Parker, which was already as- suming its marmoreal early-evening hush. At a time like this it could seem an intriguing stage set, waiting for its play.

Out in the almost-empty parking lot, Juno said we should have dinner again soon, and she headed off to her Lexus. Traffic on

Michigan Avenue parallel to campus was lighter now. Across the street was what students called "The Mile," a stretch of mostly student-oriented stores and restaurants running for almost twenty blocks across the northern edge of SUM's mammoth campus. Stefan and I lived north of that, well beyond the band of frat houses that huddled near The Mile.

I was parked closer to the lot exit onto Michigan Avenue, and I turned to see Juno approaching her car, feeling a slight pricking of anxiety. Was it for her, or for myself? That faded as I watched her confident, sexy stride and imagined, briefly, that I was slipping into the front seat next to her and that we were driving off madly in all directions, our life suddenly transformed into a road trip—but with a happy ending.

I could just hear Sharon listening to this fantasy and saying in her wry Claudette Colbert voice, "That's lovely. What would Stefan do? Wait at home for postcards?"

I started my car and set the heater, since it felt a bit chilly. As I was taking the right turn onto Michigan Avenue slowly, I heard what sounded like a roaring engine. I looked back over my shoulder and watched, helpless and transfixed, as a black SUV rocketed from the far end of the parking lot and slammed into the side of Juno's Lexus, which catapulted up and over, landing right side up twenty feet away on the grass close to Parker Hall, some of its windows shattered.

Paralyzed, freaked out, I stared at Juno's car as if it hadn't been hit but had somehow magically transported itself from one spot to another, with the fan of my car heater and my own ragged breath suddenly filling my ears. I half expected her car to execute another leap into space. And then I unfroze and frantically reached for my cell phone to call 911, but couldn't find it. Somebody honked at me to speed up. In my rearview mirror I could see the SUV tear out of the other lot exit onto campus while people started running to Juno's car from all directions. The honking behind me intensified, and whoever it was pulled around me, shouting abuse. I sped down Michigan to the first campus entrance two blocks away, the bare, spotlighted trees and bricks whirling past.

But I couldn't make the turn back onto campus right away because of a gaggle of bicyclists. When I finally was able to turn, with the image of Juno's car rolling up and over and bouncing on its tires stuck in my head, I couldn't speed up. In fact, I had to crawl. SUM's roads are almost all narrow and winding to discourage hot-rodders. My throat dry, I kept saying to myself, "No—no— no." It was unbelievable. Her car had flipped over so quickly, so quietly, it was as if it had happened in a silent film.

Before I even returned to the parking lot behind Parker, I heard sirens, and I pulled into the lot just after an SUM paramedics van and an SUM police car. Their flashing red lights were a beacon for anyone who hadn't heard the crash, lashing out at the growing darkness.

I tore open my door and raced toward Juno's car but was stopped by an enormous blue-uniformed SUM officer, who was gesturing people back from the car where two young-looking paramedics in light blue uniforms were simultaneously opening the driver's side door and the back of their van, which was parked just a few feet away, half on and half off the grass. One was male, one female, but they looked identical, with short hair and blank faces.

"You need to stand back," the officer said to me, while I watched the paramedics reach past the airbag into Juno's car and fix a large flesh-colored plastic-looking collar around her neck and chin, first the front half, then the back, Velcro-ing the two parts together.

"What are they doing?" I asked, feeling like a dog straining on a leash. I was utterly helpless, wanting to hold Juno in my arms but knowing that even if I did, it wouldn't matter and might even be a mistake. The officer, as tall and rangy as a basketball player, gazed down at me. The radio at his black gun belt crackled, and he turned his head sideways and said something into the microphone attached to his left epaulet. That's when I noticed the red-bordered shield-shaped badge on his shoulder with an SUM seal and "SUM Public Safety" in big red letters.

My anxiety must have sent the wrong message; he asked, "Girlfriend?"

But I didn't even hesitate. "Yes." Anything else, and he might not have talked to me.

He nodded. "They're immobilizing her neck."

"Why? Is she hurt?"

Before answering, he surveyed the crowd that hung back respectfully. "First thing you do—in case of spinal cord injuries." His cool tone and his height made it all sound theoretical, and in fact the actions just ten feet away were playing out like some well-rehearsed performance.

"Why is there a hole in the front of the collar?"

"In case they have to do a tracheotomy."

"Hey—is she dead?" someone asked in the small crowd, and I wanted to punch whoever had even used the word.

The paramedics had opened a large orange suitcase, and one seemed to be talking to Juno while listening to her lungs through a stethoscope. So she couldn't be too badly hurt, could she?

I asked the officer if that were true, but he shrugged, mumbled something about how they always checked three things first: airways, breathing, circulation.

"ABC," he explained. "Did you see what happened?" he asked casually.

"Yes! I was pulling out of the lot, and some maniac in a black SUV broadsided her and shot off onto campus."

"Did you catch the make? Plate number? Did you see the driver? Which way did they go?"

"It was big—it was black—I think the windows were tinted . . . ." I squeezed my eyes shut to recapture the scene, but the flashing lights penetrated my eyelids and washed everything in red, bloodying my images of Juno's car being rammed, turning over, and bouncing down on its wheels. I thought of Lady Macbeth rubbing and washing her hands, unable to erase the stain. Would I ever be able to separate the crash from these moments? It already seemed blurred and impossible.

"I think it headed back onto campus." I pointed behind me. "That way."

The officer turned to his microphone, and I heard him say something about the SUV and "tricounty." I assumed some kind of call was going out to all the local police forces, and I had a flash of the SUV tearing down a highway in a high-speed chase, hitting a guard rail, flipping over, and bursting into flames. I hoped it would burn slowly.

"They're taking her blood pressure," the officer said, studying me. A faint note of pity had crept into his voice. "You'll be able to talk to her before they take her to the emergency room."

"Thanks."

"Don't worry. Michiganapolis has some of the best response times and best-trained emergency medicine practitioners in the country." Now he sounded like he was reading from some kind of training brochure: "How to Calm Down Bystanders at an Accident Scene."

The paramedics had a long, narrow, plastic-looking board with hand grips all along it, and they were turning Juno carefully out of the car as if she were a fragile old woman being transferred to a wheelchair, lifting her onto the board, strapping her down. I heard her curse but couldn't make out what she had said.

"Can I get your name, address, and phone?" the officer asked me, taking out a small pad and pen. I complied, and then he moved casually through the crowd of some twenty student gawkers who had all been hanging back respectfully. I glanced over; nobody else seemed to be claiming to have seen what happened. Perhaps other witnesses had left when they saw the ambulance and police car show up.

In the mysteries and thrillers I'd been reading so intensely, people were always throwing up at moments like this, feeling their stomachs churn or heave or roil or clutch, but none of that was happening to me. If anything, I felt disembodied, numb below the neck, cut off from myself. And my head seemed unbearably, painfully light, with each repeated flash of the red emergency lights an assault, beating at me like strobes.

Was it taking forever—or only minutes? I couldn't tell.

The female paramedic was carefully running a hand between the board and Juno's body, head to toe, while her companion seemed to be feeling for wounds, too, on top. When his hand reached below her breasts, Juno shouted, "That hurts!"

"Ribs," the cop said confidently, back at my side.

"Broken?"

"Even bruised ribs hurt like hell. But she looks like she's breathing pretty good."

The paramedics now had what looked like a laptop out and were hooking her up.

"Is that a heart monitor?"

"Good guess."

The paramedics lifted out a wheeled stretcher from the back of the van, grabbed the handles on the board, and lifted her onto it. At the head of the stretcher was an extendable IV pole. One paramedic checked the monitor while the other inserted the IV and hung up the bag. Then they brought out a green tank that read OXYGEN—FLAMMABLE and inserted prongs into her nose that connected to the tank via a long tube. It was all very calm, very practiced, very efficient. Neither paramedic raised a voice or seemed at all rushed, yet they moved quickly. The officer was watching them with admiration. "They're in what they call the golden hour," he said. "When they have the best chance of saving somebody."

The paramedics now started to carefully wheel Juno toward the van. That's when I noticed there was someone uniformed seated in the front of the van, speaking on a radio.

"Okay," the officer said, and he moved forward with me, perhaps to make sure I didn't run amok and throw myself on the stretcher as if it were a coffin being lowered into the ground. Juno couldn't move her head, so she didn't see me until I was standing right next to the stretcher.

"He's cool," the officer told the suddenly wary paramedics, who must have dealt with hysterical relatives in their time. "He's the boyfriend."

Amazingly, Juno seemed unbruised, and there wasn't any sign of blood. Breathing stertorously, she flung out a hand and grabbed at me. "Turandot—she needs to be fed . . . let her out into the yard . . . to run . . . keys . . . in my pocket!" And she jerked her hand down to her right side. The female paramedic hushed her.

"It's her dog," I explained.

The officer nodded that it was all right, and I felt in her sweater pocket and found a key ring.

And then, like waiters simultaneously lifting covers off dishes at a chic restaurant, the paramedics glanced at each other and started hoisting the stretcher into the ambulance. Within seconds and almost without any apparent effort, they were loaded up, and the van was wailing off to the nearest emergency room, which the officer confirmed for me was at SUM's Medical School, at the southern edge of campus.

In the dark, I hadn't been able to make out the name on the officer's badge, but when he told me he'd be back in touch, he introduced himself: Harry Protopopescu.

"Rumanian?"

He seemed surprised by my question. "That's right, originally, but my people are from Hungary." His answer seemed delivered with a silent, "No more questions, you can go now," and I heard him calling for a local wrecker to tow Juno's car—to the campus police station, I assumed, since it had been involved in a hit-and-run.

I walked back to my own car as if after a gap of years, staring at its uncracked windows and undamaged driver's door. They seemed strangely unflawed to me. I got in and told myself to pay attention to the road or I'd get hurt myself, and I drove off to Juno's house to take care of her dog before going to see her at the ER, wishing right then for only two things.

The identity of the driver who rammed Juno's car.

And a gun.

11

THE five-minute drive to Juno's house was agony, full of speculation. What if she had a concussion? What if she had internal bleeding? What if she had a punctured lung? What if—what if? Could she have been talking to me one minute, telling me about her keys, and then have lapsed into a coma while she was in the ambulance? Were those closing ambulance doors final?

Before Sharon's gruesome diagnosis and surgery, I wouldn't have needed Stefan to say such questions were stupidly alarmist, but now even he would agree that anything terrible was possible when it came to the body's vulnerability. Of course, Juno wasn't facing a brain tumor and dangerous surgery as Sharon had done, but once again I felt I was in my own version of a Poe story where celebrants give way before an ominous masked figure—or was I thinking of the masquerade scene in *Phantom*? I knew that people derided its specious musicality, but lines from that dark show often floated through my thoughts. After Sharon's diagnosis, we were all most definitely "past the point of no return."

What if. What if I'd walked Juno to her car and chatted? Or we could have stayed upstairs talking another few minutes. Anything, everything, that might have delayed her enough to have missed being a hit-and-run victim, anything that might have changed the shape of those horrendous few moments. What if her car hadn't even started? Then she would have never been in the path of a reckless driver.

I was doing nothing more constructive than picking at scabs. And each time I stopped at a red light, the round glare of the traffic signal seemed to swell and expand until it filled the windshield, invasive and cruel.

I tried to calm down by imagining the next half hour as if scrolling down a list, breaking it all down into simple steps: I would get to Juno's house; I would let Juno's dog out and feed it; I would call Stefan from there, since I seemed to have unaccountably left my cell phone at home; I would not fall apart on the way to the emergency room to see Juno.

But that last item undid the minimal flicker of serenity. Another hospital. First Sharon, now Juno. Stefan and I had been extremely lucky not to lose many friends to AIDS, so neither of us had been intimate with hospital rooms or halls until Sharon's illness. Now the word *hospital* itself seemed polluting and toxic.

The garish Christmas lights I passed struck me as obscenely gleeful, like laughter at a funeral. I found myself thinking of Auden's devastating "Funeral Blues." But did Juno mean so much to me already that I could imagine wanting to pack up the moon and dismantle the sun—or was the metallic taste of grief in my mouth a response to feeling ever more unsafe?

I drove up the quiet residential Michiganapolis street to Juno's house, picturing myself as an intruder even though she'd given me her keys, and even though the neighborhood was much like ours. Mature trees; large yards; middle-class homes. I parked right out front of the unassuming large brick ranch towered over by arborvitae, and walked up the driveway trying not to look suspicious. I heard rustling in the huge shrub along her driveway, but assumed this time that it was only birds or squirrels.

I fumbled with the unfamiliar locks at the bland brown door, and as soon as I managed to let myself in, I heard whining. Turning on lights as I went, I followed the sound to the bedroom, which I hadn't seen before. Unlike the rest of the white-on-white house, this room was a riot of purple and leopard print, from the tumble of silk pillows of all sizes on the canopied bed to the heavily swagged and festooned drapes. It was a baroque, wild room that seemed pathetic without Juno's animating presence. Not even a stage setting, but a shell.

Near a door to what looked like the master bathroom was a

large rectangular plastic purple crate with a fat black handle, small side vents, and a little gated door. Juno's Westie stared out at me, her black eyes and black nose making her look as unreal and adorable as a teddy bear. She barked once, and I reached down, muttered in what I hoped was a reassuring way, and opened the catch to the door, not knowing if she might try to bite me. Turandot raced from the room, and I followed her to the living room, where she did a tarantella in front of the sliding doors. I figured she knew her own routine, so I undid the catch and slid a door open, but it stuck. I fished out a wooden plank in the runner.

Released, Turandot sped out into the dark yard and apparently did whatever she had to quickly, because she was back and tearing off to the kitchen. I closed up the door and found her sitting in front of a counter, gazing upward. The first door I opened had a bag of dog food and a half-cup measure right at the front. Her water bowl was off in the corner, and what I assumed was her food bowl sat next to it. While she sat patiently at my feet, I thought I'd try her with a half cup of dog food, and give her more if she were hungry. I set it down near her water. She ate quickly, slurped up enough water to be getting ready to hike the Appalachian Trail, and seemed done.

It had been easy thus far. But now she sat looking at me with soulful wise eyes as if I was supposed to know what was next. She couldn't have been much more than ten pounds, I thought, mildly alarmed at the image of her fragility. What if I hadn't been there to get Juno's keys, and no one else had taken her seriously? Or if she hadn't been able to speak?

I crouched down to Turandot and held out a hand. That wasn't interesting. She shook herself, then dashed under the table and emerged with a plush toy shaped like a carrot, dashed to the kitchen door, and stopped, looking at me over her shoulder, the carrot in her mouth like a tango dancer's rose.

I'd never had a dog before, but even I could understand that she wanted to be chased, and so I did, ducking around the furniture with her, reversing directions, and letting her chase me while she chomped on the carrot or stopped to fling it in the air and pounce on it, bite it so it squeaked.

Breathless after a few minutes, and awed by her energy, I sat down on the floor, and she charged into my lap. It wasn't until she moved close enough for me to smell her talcum-y little body that I realized I had actually forgotten about Juno for a few minutes, even while I was in her own home, playing with her dog.

But what was I supposed to do next? Shit! I'd been so focused on Juno's puppy that I'd forgotten to call Stefan—or had I been delaying the moment when I had to launch into recounting what I'd seen?

I scooped Turandot into my arms, carried her to the living-room couch, and sat next to the phone on the lamp table. Whether she was allowed up on the couch or not didn't seem to matter now. I took up the receiver and dialed home.

"Juno was in a car accident," I told Stefan without preamble. I explained what happened, where she was and where I was, feeling numb again.

"Nick, do you want me to come over or meet you at the emergency room on campus?"

"I don't know what to do about her dog. I don't think we can take her with us—and if we did, I don't even know where her collar and leash would be."

"Where was the dog when you got there?"

"Some kind of crate in the bedroom."

"Put it back."

"But for how long? What if Juno has to stay at the emergency room for a day or two? Won't her dog get hungry and need to go out again?"

Stefan mulled that over at the other end.

"I can come over and watch the dog until we know what's happening."

I sighed out a "Thanks" and gave him the address and directions.

After I hung up, I got acquainted with Turandot, looking into her eyes, feeling how surprisingly soft her thick white coat was, letting her sniff my hands, and trying hard to think positively about Juno's condition. Seeing Juno loaded onto a stretcher and hoisted into an ambulance had been a profound shock. She was so vibrant, so dynamic, that being reduced to immobility had been more than bizarre—it had frightened me. Much more so than Sharon, Juno was not a person I'd associate with hospitalization.

Sitting there waiting for Stefan, scratching Turandot's furry neck and ears while she closed her eyes in mute ecstasy, I thought of lines from the opening and closing of *Carmina Burana*, about the wheel of fortune turning and melting both poverty and power as the sun melted ice. When I was younger and studying medieval and Renaissance literature in college, the whole idea of fortune turning on people without any warning had struck me as quaint and mildly superstitious, but now that I was middle-aged, I thought that bleak worldview was as accurate as any other. Hadn't I seen proof of the world's sudden, crazy mutability over and over in my own life, and Stefan's?

Turandot rolled over in my lap, legs up, tongue lolling, and I scratched her belly. I was flattered that Turandot seemed to accept me so readily, though I could imagine my parents, who disliked dogs, deflating my pride by saying that there was no reason for this dog not to like me since I'd satisfied some of her basic needs right away.

And I mused over the murkiness of Stefan coming over to take care of Juno's dog while I went to stand by her hospital bed. It was not quite deception, but it was close enough to unnerve me. Yet how could I change what had happened? The SUV that had bashed into Juno's car had hit me, too, in a way. I was more than just a witness to the accident, I was implicated, connected, involved. Yet the event was already as blurry to me as the red stoplights had become in town—a jumble of impressions more than a clear set of details.

When Stefan arrived in under ten minutes, I realized it had been barely half an hour since the doors had closed on Juno and her ambulance had shrilled off from behind Parker Hall. So half of that so-called "golden hour" was gone.

"Are you okay?" Stefan asked, while Turandot sniffed at his shoes and seemed to wait for the tribute of busy hands. Stefan kneeled down and stroked her back, while glancing up at me with concern.

"I feel stunned. I was right there, almost."

"It could have been you," he said flatly, standing up with Turandot wriggling in his arms. She licked his chin, and he agilely slipped off his dark green corduroy car coat, tossed it onto a chair with his free hand.

"I didn't think of that. I just feel guilty."

"Why? How's it your fault?" Turandot wriggled in response to his raised voice, and he set the dog down; she headed for the kitchen. Stefan waited for my response.

"I know it's not rational. I feel helpless." I expected him to say something cynical about how life was always like that if you took your blinders off, but he didn't. He just nodded, and surprised me by saying, "Give Juno my love, and call me as soon as you know how she is." He handed me my cell phone. "It was in the kitchen," he said, and he gave me a kind of ceremonial hug as if I were heading into a hazardous encounter.

"What will you do while I'm at the ER?"

"Interview the pooch, and read." He fished his copy of *The Betrothed* out from his coat and brandished it at me. "There's a lot more skullduggery left."

I drove recklessly back to campus, not caring if I was stopped, and headed south on Parker Road, one of the main avenues on campus, down to where the Medical School's strangely castle-like building loomed over enormous fields of experimental crops. It was a perfect, eerie setting just right for an *X-Files* episode. Though constructed in the 1980s, the sprawling glass and concrete structure had a weirdly crenellated roof, perhaps to remind people of the ceaseless battle against disease. The recent addition of a high-tech glistening emergency room right out of *Gattaca* did nothing to humanize or soften the building.

I pulled into the side parking lot, lined with scraggly new maples, where a huge red neon sign advertised EMERGENCIES as if luring people into a diner. There were hardly any cars in sight. Immediately to the right of the double electronic doors—framed in polished granite—several of those plastic boards with the hand grips leaned up against the dark gray concrete. One of them looked bloody. High above the doors were twin security cameras pointed at me and the lot behind me. I felt somehow on the defensive, even though I had a totally legitimate reason for being there.

As the automatic doors slid open, I entered a small azure-floored, pale-blue-walled corridor. I was stopped by a uniformed guard standing outside a glass-walled cubicle glutted with security monitors, who moved forward as if ready to take me down should I attempt to go any farther without permission. Jeez, was there that much threat of infiltration on campus?

Ahead of me were more sliding glass doors with a big red STOP: NO ADMITTANCE sign. To the right of the doors was a keypad, and behind them stretched a gleaming corridor lined with wheelchairs and wheeled wire shelving units filled with what looked like medical supplies. The guard looked as big and mean as a bouncer, and seemed unimpressed when I said I was there to check on a patient.

"Name?"

The atmosphere felt more than sterile, it was forbidding and a bit anxiety-provoking—as if there wasn't enough oxygen in the small space, made smaller by the guard's broad shoulders, huge chest, and dead-end blue eyes. Those lungs probably sucked in twice what a normal person breathed. If I stood there too long, would I pass out?

Nervously, I said, "I'm Nick Hoffman, I teach in—"

"Not your name." I could hear him add a silent "*moron.*" "I meant the patient's name."

I told him, and he called inside, apparently disappointed that I wasn't inventing a reason to sneak in and steal gauze for a Mummy party. He pointed to my right, and someone buzzed me into a small square waiting room like any you'd find at a doctor's office, only with even less personality. It was filled with vaguely Scandinavian-style chairs and magazine tables, all of which looked unappealing, unwelcoming in the brutal fluorescent light. The royal blue carpet and blue plaid vinyl wallpaper looked new and as deliberately, expensively unimaginative as the paint-by-numbers seascapes framed in chrome. I suppose it was all meant to reassure you, keep you from panicking. It made me feel hemmed in.

"Juno Dromgoole," I said to the slim redheaded receptionist seated at a teaming desk behind a glass window. "Is she okay?" Behind her stretched a jumble of counters and chairs and shelves. I saw nurses bustling in and out of doorways, but I was alone in the waiting room, which had another door to the right of the window with a keypad for entrance. Why wasn't there a retinal scan? I wondered.

"I don't think they're done with X rays yet. You'll have to wait." Unlike the guard, her voice was warm, but it somehow managed to fend me off as efficiently as the guard's stance or the glass windows she sat behind. It was an official voice that drew clear limits—the voice of someone who had been yelled at, pleaded with, probably threatened. Angular and bland, she held herself back from the desk even as she claimed it.

I sunk into a completely uncomfortable chair and added more nervous energy to a room that must have been soaked with it. Two more security cameras took in my every movement. I couldn't imagine relaxing enough to disappear into any of the *Time* or *Newsweek* magazines around me, so I called Stefan on his cell phone.

"No news yet," I said. "They're still doing X rays."

"Is that good or bad?"

"I don't know."

I could feel Stefan hesitating, and then he said, "I like Juno's dog a lot. It doesn't look like a poodle or like one of those bichon frises. It seems sturdier. More solid."

"A *man's* dog."

"Well—"

"A small man's dog? No, a man's small dog."

"Better."

I smiled and told Stefan I'd call back.

"Why? You have something better to do than talk to me? You need both hands free to chew your fingernails?"

"Not really. But it costs so much." That was the voice of my parents, who had plenty of money for phone calls (and anything else) but cautioned against spending too much anyway. Perhaps it was also some kind of old European aversion to the impersonality of the phone, I sometimes thought.

"It's not expensive with the new plan," he reminded me.

"We're both still inside our hundred free minutes. You can even read me to sleep if you want."

I laughed, and the receptionist coughed as if to remind me this was not a fun house.

"Sorry," I said to her, and explained sotto voce to Stefan what I was apologizing for.

"So you like Turandot?"

"I thought Juno would have a dog with leopard-print booties or something like that, or even dyed with leopard spots. I'm relieved it's just white."

"But it has a nice personality," I said.

"Sure," Stefan teased. "We're guests. She's on her best behavior."

"Seriously."

"Okay, it's a nice dog. Do I want a dog? I don't know." He sounded a bit testy.

"If you wanted a dog, would you want one like Juno's?"

Stefan quoted our favorite play, *The Importance of Being Earnest*: "Well, that is clearly a metaphysical question and as such has no relation to the facts of life as we know them."

"I'll call that a qualified yes."

"You know," he said, his voice suddenly serious. "I love you."

"What? Why now?"

"Because you're so worried about Juno. You're a good friend."

If only it were that simple!

"Call me when you know how she is."

I hung up, and felt instantly transported to the nearby hospital where we had been waiting for Sharon's endless surgery to be over. People always say there are scenes they'll never forget, but I wondered if it wasn't the other way around, if when something horrible happens to you it can take over, and *it* remembers *you*, remembers to haunt and stalk you—when you might expect it to, and when you might not. Maybe that's what ghosts are—the return of our worst memories in a perverse disguise that makes them harder to recognize, but no less frightening.

I didn't know what to do. The room I was in filled me with unease, but I couldn't block it out; I felt like Byron's Manfred: "These eyes but close to look within." If only I knew how to meditate. . . . Why hadn't we quit our jobs and forged new identities for ourselves? None of this would have happened, and we would be free.

Freedom, the great American obsession. I could imagine my parents smiling with kind cynicism at my thoughts. And D. H. Lawrence had seen it with perfect clarity—all this American shouting for freedom was nothing more than "a rattling of chains," he said. And who the hell did I think I was, anyway, to imagine I could change my life? Lawrence had also said that none of us are ever "the marvelous deciders and choosers we think we are."

The door to the right of the secretary swung open, and instantly the whole room shifted. The round-faced, freckled, chunky, red-bearded doctor wearing jeans and T-shirt under his white coat approached me with his hand out. Smiling broadly, he had his eyes slightly hooded and his face up as if taking in glorious music or sunshine. If the receptionist was skilled at keeping people away, this fiftyish man brought them close and loved doing so. His handshake was as hearty and comforting as his soothing tenor voice, and I felt instantly at ease with him.

"Dr. Vinciguerra," he said. I read his chest pocket tag: his first name was Lars-Erik, though he didn't look particularly Scandinavian—or Italian, for that matter. He gestured to a seat, and we sat side by side.

"How is she?"

He crossed his legs and nodded without making me feel he'd heard that same question thousands of times. We could have been sitting in a park, about to discuss some fascinating movie we'd both seen. Looking into his gentle eyes, I thought I would not be embarrassed to cry in front of him, or lose control, which conversely made me certain that I wouldn't. Some steely-eyed robot would have thrown my emotions into higher relief and made them more volatile.

"I'll take you back in a few minutes. She'll be okay—it's not too bad," he said. "Because her breathing was difficult, we had to make sure there were no fractures. She's got some bruised ribs, and she's going to be in pain. We're prescribing Motrin and Vicodin—that's a narcotic to help her sleep." He spoke clearly but conversationally, without making me feel he was dumbing down his assessment of Juno's condition.

"Does she stay here?"

"No—we can release her soon."

"What do we do?"

"It'll be important to observe her for twelve hours for any changes, and a few times a day she'll have to take nice deep breaths to expand her lungs."

"Why?"

"There's always the danger of pneumonia after this kind of injury."

"Is she being wrapped up or something? I mean, her ribs?"

He smiled. "We don't tape ribs anymore—it's too constricting."

I took some nice deep breaths myself, feeling a bit light-headed with relief. Dr. Vinciguerra reached out and put a hand on my shoulder. "All right?"

I nodded.

"She's lucky. Please don't think I'm bragging, but we have some of the best emergency care in the country here."

"At SUM?"

He grinned. "In Michigan. This is the home of emergency medicine as a specialty. This is where it first took off, well, here and Ohio." He seemed honestly proud, and I relaxed even more, suddenly remembering a news report about how people with medical emergencies in smaller cities did better after a 911 call because there was so much less traffic to slow ambulances down.

"Okay?"

I nodded.

"Good—let's go back." He hadn't asked what my relationship was to Juno but seemed to assume it was close—or maybe nowadays no one asked? He rose and tapped out a quick code on the keypad, opened the door, and led me through the corridor-like area behind the receptionist to an enormous high-ceilinged room with operating lights and equipment and supplies bristling in every corner. I felt overwhelmed until I focused on pale-faced Juno lying on a hospital bed, wearing a blue papery-looking gown covered with white and blue cornflowers, oxygen plugs still in her nose, and cords running from under the chest of her hospital gown to a black monitor on the wall above her head. There were numbers and two red lines running across the monitor—one in peaks, the other in waves. As I approached her bed, Juno seemed very frail until she snarled, "These fuckers cut off my clothes!"

"With possible injuries to the chest, we can't waste any time," the doctor explained amicably to me and to her, but they'd clearly had this exchange more than once already. "And we try cutting along the seams so they can be repaired."

"Am I supposed to go home in tatters?" Juno wailed.

I moved to her bed and looked down at her contorted, exhausted face. "Juno," I said softly. "You'll be going home in one piece. You're not badly hurt." I wanted to lean over and stroke her face, something, to calm her down.

"Then why am I in agony!?"

I turned to Dr. Vinciguerra, who assured me she'd be feeling much better soon. "We've given her a shot, and it should be taking effect soon. Demerol and Phenergin. It'll last for about four to six hours, and she'll be woozy. We're just waiting for her reaction to the shot. Did you bring her some clothes?" He must have assumed I lived with her. I shrugged helplessly, and told Juno I needed to go back to her place. "What do you want me to bring back for you?"

"Jesus, never mind," she said wearily. "If you let me wear your coat, that's enough. I want to get myself home and crawl into bed." Juno started to sit up, but the doctor eased her back down.

"Wait until we get you a wheelchair."

"Bullshit," she growled, sounding for a moment better—that is, more like her old self.

The doctor shook his head, but motioned me to keep Juno from hurting herself. An orderly in light blue scrubs came in with a wheelchair; he was slim and dark, Pakistani perhaps, with slicked-back hair and big, sensual eyes. Juno didn't even notice his good looks. I took off my coat and handed it to him, then called Stefan to fill him in and ask him to watch for my car, since I figured I'd need help when we arrived.

The orderly fussed around Juno's bed, getting her ready,

taking out her IV, putting some ointment and then a Band-Aid on her hand, removing what I realized were little round patches that connected to the monitor. I tried taking in the rest of the vast, gleaming room, which had another bed partly curtained off and was lined with the same wheeled wire shelves I'd seen in the hallway. I made out bedpans and IV bags, oxygen tanks, and what I thought might be a defibrillator, but everything else seemed intimidatingly foreign, as if I'd been plunged into another country whose language and customs I had no hope of understanding.

"We're ready," Juno said. The orderly handed me a heavy plastic trash bag with her damaged clothes, and a white prescription slip. He started to wheel the subdued and haggard Juno out into the hallway, and I followed, but we were stopped by Officer Protopopescu, who appeared as sneakily as a process server, with as minatory a look on his face.

"I need to get your statement," he said to Juno. "Is this a good time?" It was a heavily rhetorical question, and Juno was too wiped out to argue. She nodded and told him a quick, clipped story not much different than my own. She was pulling out of her parking space, heard an engine being gunned, and suddenly was broadsided. She hadn't noticed the driver or the make of the SUV either, and Protopopescu looked more than disappointed—he looked annoyed.

"That's it? You don't remember anything else? Not a single detail?"

"Give her a break," I said, curious myself at how offhand Juno's narrative had been. But then why wouldn't she want to get rid of him? I'd probably have done the same thing, tried to keep any interrogation short so I could escape to my own bed.

The officer glared at both of us as if we were hiding something, flipped his pad shut, and practically warned Juno he'd want to talk to her again. He turned and stalked away.

I thanked Doctor Vinciguerra, who was already in consultation with another doctor, examining something on a clipboard. He looked up at us and grinned. It was a real flash of warmth, not at all mechanical.

"Remember!" he said. "Nice, deep breaths! Expand those lungs."

Was he thinking about the image of Juno's sexy chest rising and falling, or was she just an anonymous damaged body to him, stripped of the possibility of attractiveness? As we emerged through the automatic doors with their warning sign near the security post, the orderly said something under his breath to the hulking guard, who chuckled. It sounded as ominous as the beginning of a rock slide. Perhaps they'd been joking about her "lungs" —she certainly had quite a set.

I kept right behind the young orderly on the way out. Given her bursts of feistiness, I was surprised to see Juno double over in pain as she was helped into the passenger side of my car and strapped in. It was as disorienting as watching a champion athlete stumble and clutch herself, the body that has always been a perfect machine unexpectedly breaking down.

"Thanks."

The orderly smiled shyly at me, and hurried back into the building.

Juno gasped again when we drove away and said nothing as the darkened campus slid by us, though whether she was feeling pain or relief to be leaving, I didn't know. I realized it was pain, though, when she clutched her side and said, "I feel as if I've been kicked by someone with metal-toed boots." Was the injury making her think of falling at the reception?

I tried to reassure her. "You're going to be okay." I gave her a rah-rah version of the doctor's report, and she nodded absentmindedly, seeming almost to fall asleep.

"Physically," she said.

"What do you mean?"

She shook her head, wouldn't answer. Her perfume filled the car, and something else, some heavy, medicinal smell I hadn't noticed before. It was as if her skin had absorbed the atmosphere of the ambulance and the room she'd been in.

"Which drugstore should we stop at for your prescription?"

"The Rite Aid near campus."

It was one of their brand-new behemoths, set down on the corner of a major intersection looking as out of place as Dorothy's house in Oz. We were there in a few minutes. I dropped off the prescription for Juno and told the clerk I'd be back, not wanting to leave Juno alone for too long. The bright lights and canned music stunned me, and I thought I'd send Stefan over for the prescription.

When we pulled into Juno's driveway, Stefan was out her door and heading down to the car, and together we helped Juno to her house. In her heels and hospital gown under my coat, she looked as disreputable and tottery as some drunken derelict. I dropped the bag of her clothes inside the front door.

"I have to go to bed," she said with quiet urgency, and we made our unsteady progress to her bedroom, Turandot keeping pace, staring up at Juno. It might have been anthropomorphizing to say her puppy was upset and surprised, but that's how it seemed to me. Without even a flicker of surprise at the visual splendor of her bedroom, Stefan cleared off most of the wealth of pillows and pulled back the sheets. Juno sat down, wheezing a little, on the edge of her opulent, luxuriant bed, as frail and woebegone as a little child who fears her birthday has been forgotten. She groaned and held her injured side.

Together Stefan and I steadied Juno while slipping off my coat. I felt keenly aware of her lush and vulnerable flesh under the thin gown and tried to help her without looking too closely, which made me awkward. Stefan was brisker in his movements, and more efficient. As soon as she was under the heavy covers and leaning her head back, Turandot made a flying leap onto the bed and snuggled into a remaining nest of pillows by her side, and the two of them fell instantly asleep. Stefan turned the light on in Juno's bathroom, and we picked up my coat and closed the bedroom light and door.

In the living room, Stefan looked as shaken as I felt.

"Wow," he said. "And she's not even badly hurt, right?'

"That's right."

"Let's have a drink." I followed him into the kitchen where he had already located a bottle of Bacardi and a lime. He made us hefty rum and Cokes, and we sat at the table where Juno and I had so recently had dinner.

"I bet you never thought you'd be getting Juno in bed," Stefan said in a mock-frat-boy voice.

"*What?*"

He reared back as if I'd thrown acid at him and assured me, "It was a joke."

"A terrible joke." And painful, too.

"I'm really sorry. I was just trying to lighten the atmosphere. Something happened while you were gone," Stefan said in a carefully steady voice, as if trying to keep even a scintilla of drama out of his statement.

"Something happened?"

He nodded, set down his drink, and crossed his muscular arms. "Juno got a phone call. Turandot was chewing on that carrot thing, I was reading, and I heard her answering machine come on. Somebody was threatening her."

"Oh, God. What was the message?"

Stefan rose and went to the kitchen counter, which seemed to function as her home office. There was a small under-the-cabinet memo board to which bills were thumbtacked, and a tape dispenser, pencil sharpener, and other basic equipment. I noticed then that the red light was blinking on the same kind of sleek little AT&T machine we both had at home. Stefan pressed the message button, and a gravelly man's voice that sounded disguised barked out, "We're not done with you, bitch!" Then the machine's microchip gave the date and time: an hour after her accident.

"So she wasn't inventing the phone calls," Stefan admitted.

It was not a moment to say, "I told you so." I shook my head.

Stefan rejoined me at the table. "You know what this means, don't you? It wasn't an accident. It wasn't a hit-and-run."

How do I describe what I felt at that moment? It was a kind of whirlwind of dread and self-recrimination for not having suspected as much myself, for having been so overwhelmed by the accident scene and its sequel that I had not placed the event in any kind of context. I felt disgusted, fearful, and ashamed of my own stupidity.

"Does Juno think that?" I asked.

"You tell me. That phone message also means that whoever tried to kill her in the SUV knows it didn't work, and either hung around Parker Hall to watch what was happening—"

"But the SUV disappeared!"

"—or there's more than one person after her." He repeated: " 'We're not done with you.' Somebody stuck around to see what was happening, or followed the ambulance to the ER."

"Shit."

"It's the second time," Stefan brought out. "First at the reception, now this. She has to go to the police."

"But they're on it already. There's an APB or whatever out for the SUV. What else can they do?"

The doorbell ringing just then couldn't have startled us more if we were in a bank vault trying to blow open a safe and the knocked-out guards had suddenly come to and started firing at us.

Stefan strode to the door, looked through the peephole.

"It's Rusty Dominguez-St. John," he said.

"Juno? Are you all right? Who's in there?"

"Should I open the door?" Stefan hissed at me.

"If you don't, she's going to wake up." Stefan let in Rusty, who was in full Clint Black mode this time, down to—or up to—the hat. I heard scratching from inside Juno's bedroom door, and when I opened it, Turandot rocketed out and started curveting around Rusty, who swept her up for some big sloppy dog kisses. She wagged her tail wildly, and when he set her down, she was up on her hind legs begging for more attention.

She clearly knew who he was, but still I asked, "What are you doing here?"

Rusty joined us in the living room, where Turandot continued to fawn over him. I felt a childish sting of jealousy—she was clearly wild about Rusty. Stefan ducked out to make sure Juno's door was closed, and then returned to stand guard.

Legs planted as firmly as if he expected an assault, Rusty said, "I heard Juno was in an accident, and that somebody took her home."

"That was me. But who told you?"

Rusty gave me a sour look. "Her doctor."

"He did? Why?"

"He's a fan of mine. He took my workshop, has all my tapes and books—"

I cut Rusty off before he started quoting any testimonials. "And he called you?"

"Ye-es," Rusty said slowly, mockingly, as if giving the same set of directions to someone who'd already gotten lost twice before. "What are you, Sam Spade? Or should I say Samantha?"

I ignored that. "What's his name?"

He sneered. "Her doctor? Lars Vinciguerra. Do you want a description? What's it your business? What the hell are you guys doing here anyway? Trying on her clothes?"

"Fuck you!" Stefan snapped, stepping forward menacingly.

Rusty eyed him up and down. "You've got a big mouth for a faggot. I guess you need one, though, sucking all those cocks."

I thought Stefan would go for him right then and I'd have to try to pull them apart, but instead he shocked me by grinning. "You're the one who's been in prison, so you probably know a lot more about it than I do. Maybe you could offer a faculty enrichment seminar."

Good line, I thought, wanting to do an *Arsenio Hall Show* "Woo—woo—woo."

Rusty's features were twisted with contempt. "You're a phony! They should bounce you from writer-in-residence."

Stefan was getting calmer by the minute. "Me, phony? You're the one making a living out of stealing other people's work and repackaging it as yours."

Rusty's face turned blotchy red as if he'd been smacked. "What the fuck are you talking about?"

"Everybody knows your work is bullshit, just a brand-new spin on the self-help wheel. Everything in your books is plagiarized. You'd be tied up in lawsuits if this were England, where writers have a chance. I know half a dozen publishers who decided it wasn't worth it because you'd just get more publicity."

Rusty scowled, though he looked startled by Stefan's reference to those publishers. "You're jealous."

Turandot evidently didn't enjoy conflict; she headed for the bedroom. I followed and quietly opened the door for her, listening for Juno's breathing. It was raspy but steady, and I waited until Turandot was back amid the pillows before shutting the door.

"Okay," Rusty was saying to Stefan. He sat down on the couch as if daring us to evict him. "I don't have time for this. Let's start over. How's Juno?"

"Didn't your doctor fan tell you?" Stefan asked quietly.

"For a writer with shitty sales figures, you've got a major attitude problem," Rusty spat, standing up. "I have a right to be here, a right to find out how Juno's doing. More than you do, more than either of you. She's my wife."

Stunned, Stefan and I didn't say anything. We waited for an explanation.

"We got married in Las Vegas seven years ago. She was gambling, I was doing one of my workshops. We met at a strip club. But it didn't last, and we've been separated most of the last six years. Sometimes we get back together, it works for a while, then we split. Right now, it's not working, hasn't been for a couple of years. When I took the job here, she said she didn't care one way or the other, since she wasn't really interested in seeing me again right now."

I objected. "She's never said anything about it. She never said she was married." But then Juno had also until recently hidden the fact that she'd written a trashy best-seller. Major deception was definitely an arrow in her quiver.

He had a ready answer: "She probably doesn't know anyone here well enough."

"What about Serena?"

Rusty shrugged. "Serena's pretty cagey."

Well, that was true.

"So can I see her now?" he asked with mock obsequiousness. He didn't wait for a reply but walked to her bedroom and went in while Stefan and I exchanged a disbelieving stare. Rusty closed the door.

Was this for real? How could we be sure? I didn't know about Stefan, but I felt like a figure in a farce who's discovered that the clown he's beating is actually a prince.

Whatever the current state of their relationship—no, their marriage—Rusty clearly felt a good deal for Juno; he emerged from her room sobered and standing a little less tall in his black cowboy boots. Or was he the kind of man who had trouble with weakness? Because he said hurriedly, "Are you guys staying the night? Good." And he left.

I followed to the door and looked out the nearest window.

"He's driving a black SUV," I said.

Stefan brought me my drink with some fresh ice. "You think he's stupid enough to crash into Juno's car, then drive over to her house a few hours later?"

I looked at my watch. It felt like the middle of the morning but was barely midnight. "I don't know."

Stefan shook his head. "He's a charlatan, he's a thief. Who knows if he even writes his own books? But someone that tricky would never do anything so obvious."

"Unless he's still a real criminal, and all that reform crap is just a sales pitch and he figures he can get away with anything. Smiling sociopaths can go a long way in this country."

Then I realized I'd forgotten about Juno's prescription. I told Stefan I was going back out, but he insisted I stay with Juno and relax.

"You've had enough driving around."

While he was gone, I mused over the very strange scene with Rusty, and his revelation. Why was he so hostile to us, so homophobic? Had he taken the job at SUM to patch up his marriage with Juno? Could things possibly get any stranger? I checked on Juno, and as soon as I softly opened her bedroom door, she said, "Rusty?"

"It's Nick."

Her voice sounding as tentative as if she were trying out each word for the first time, she said, "Nick—thank you," and fell back asleep. She had sounded as grateful as a refugee taking up her first meal in days, and I felt embarrassed. Her gratitude wasn't justified. I hadn't earned it, I hadn't done enough.

But what was enough? Tracking down the SUV driver myself? How? If I assumed it was someone in EAR, was I supposed to hang around the parking lot all day, day after day? I didn't have the time, and it would be too obvious. I'd have to get really close to see if there was damage, wouldn't I? Or if I followed each black SUV home, what then? It was winter; most people would park inside their garages, not in their driveways. I couldn't break into anybody's home, and even loitering too long would arouse all the little old ladies canning fruit and knitting sweaters for their cats. And even if I did find a damaged black SUV, the damage would probably be minor and unrevealing. I'd seen a segment on 20/20 recently about SUV crash testing. At less than highway speeds, they emerged relatively unscathed when they hit sedans. Was I supposed to take a paint sample or something? And even if I did, so what? That didn't help the French much trying to trace the car that hit Princess Diana's limo.

12

I found linens in a lavishly stocked closet near Juno's bedroom, and used a set to make up the living room couch to spend the night. They were leopard-print, of course. Feeling suddenly dehydrated, I got a bottle of Evian from the kitchen and drank all of it down as if I'd been running a marathon.

I was spending the night at Juno's. On her couch. How bizarre. I kept flashing on disturbing images of Stefan and me helping her slip into bed, her breasts rich and full under her gown. I wasn't perversely turned on by her suffering and sudden debility the way Nate was by Sophie, an Auschwitz survivor, in *Sophie's Choice*, but I did feel a new level of physical intimacy that was inextricably linked with the visions of Juno as a one-woman parade when she strode down a hallway in Parker, and of water dripping from her lush body as she stood chatting with me in the pool at The Club.

This was the first time I would be spending a night even a room away from a woman whom I could imagine making love with. When it came to women as a sexual possibility, I didn't think I was much more advanced than those gawky kids in *American Pie* for whom their female peers were an alien universe. A lesbian friend had once proudly confided that she was "penis pure," but I didn't feel any sense of rectitude or accomplishment in being able to make the analogous claim for myself, mutatis mutandis. While I had never made fun of women's bodies or bodily processes, I hadn't ever ogled or even admired them except as elements of a performance or as evidence of personal chic; seeing Sharon do a fashion show once had been an experience that filled both those categories.

Growing up in New York and going to the Metropolitan Museum of Art with my parents, I had loitered in front of mythological scenes to look at the gods, not the goddesses, who had been just as much decoration as the trees and clouds and whirling draperies. I saw composition, history, line, and color when I looked at those painted women—or sometimes personality. Looking at the male figures, I felt possessed.

It's what Julian Barnes says in *Flaubert's Parrot*: "You do not choose. You are *elected* into love." And Henry James wrote that it was art that makes life. Well, for me it was art that revealed my life to me, a life that had unreeled without a psychosexual hitch until now. Juno had burst out of previously static and unemotional categories for me and was forcing me to consider redefining myself, whether she cared about it or not.

But that wasn't the only blurring going on. Right then, the accident was so present for me that I felt plunged into that weird mix of sex and violence Faye Dunaway negotiates in *The Eyes of Laura Mars* as she photographs models in highly charged erotic tableaux of death around New York City.

Remembering the Metropolitan Museum made me wonder how my parents would see Juno. I pictured the four of us dining together somewhere in New York, after an opera, perhaps. My very comme il faut mother and father would most likely not appreciate Juno, and would be mildly alarmed by her extravagance of voice and clothes, reading it as typically American, even though she was from Canada. Sometimes it amazed me that they could after decades in New York still draw back in discomfort from someone who'd make Madonna seem subtle, when all around them the city shrieked and roared like one of those movie aliens writhing in a pool of its liquefaction after the hero's given it a death blow: cabs, construction sites, airplanes heading into LaGuardia and Kennedy, belching buses, car alarms, the whole extravagant, endless, maddening sound track. And what about the people my father worked with? Editors, publishers, agents, and authors were none of them especially known for their quiet dignity. I'd lived with a writer for a decade and a half—I'd listened to him complain about the denizens of that world, and had met more than enough of them.

Stefan returned with Juno's painkillers, which weren't as expensive as I'd expected them to be, and asked if I wanted him to stay the night, too.

"Your choice," I said. "I saw a couch in Juno's study—maybe it's a foldout, and we could both use that." We checked, and it wasn't. Stefan opted to go home, which was fine with me. It's not that I was planning on insinuating myself into Juno's bed—or giving her a sponge bath! I didn't need a witness for my discomfort.

"We'll have to do a sleepover some other time," I said. "Popcorn and brownies, *Babe*—"

"Knowing Juno," he said, "it would probably be more like a rave. Call me as soon as you get up," he said, and then, as if picking up on the unease I was trying hard not to betray, "You know, Nick, Juno isn't Sharon. It was a car crash, not brain surgery. She's hurt, but she's not in danger of dying." We stood by Juno's front door, and he clamped his hands on my shoulders and fixed me with as serious a look as if he were a pope sending a crusader into battle.

"You think I'm confusing them?"

"I don't know—you could be. It's natural—two crises, two hospitals, it all blurs together."

I was so beat right then that all I could do was make a joke. I half-quoted from *Ghostbusters*: "Thanks, Egon, for that important safety tip." Stefan got it, kissed me, and wished me sweet dreams. But after closing the door, I thought about what he'd said. If he was right, and my concern about Juno was actually displaced from worrying about Sharon, it wasn't surprising. Sharon's diagnosis and surgery had made me think about death and loss far more than the tragic events here at SUM over the previous few years, as if I'd been one of those lovely tourist islands in the Caribbean that had always before been just outside the swath of hurricanes: I felt brutally awakened, sick with the devastation and the loss of placidity.

Disasters. My bond with Sharon was so close, we had often joked about being together in former lives—it was a good way to explain how we clung to each other like passengers fleeing a sinking ship. Perhaps we had even been exactly that, Sharon had often said, "though not on the *Titanic*! I'd never go anywhere with a Celine Dion sound track. Give me the Chemical Brothers any day." Had images of disaster flitted through our conversation—even as jokes—in some kind of psychic foreshadowing?

I stripped down to my shorts, turned off all the lights, and crawled into my makeshift bed, worried that I might not be able to fall asleep, but the very next sounds I heard were Turandot's exigent barking and Juno's voice croaking out, "I know, Turandot—you've never seen a man on my couch before without me on top."

It was Wednesday morning, and she was wearing black silk pajamas that made her face even paler.

"Don't say a word," she warned, suddenly hovering over me, very film star-ish with a black towel wrapped turban-style around her hair. "I know I look like death eating a sandwich, and I feel twice as bad." She gingerly touched her ribs. "I found the pills, but they're working slowly. Now, if I give you instructions, do you think you can do breakfast for us and Turandot? I can let her out into the yard, but that's about my limit for the morning."

I assured her it would be okay. "French toast all around? With a ginger-Cointreau conserve?"

"Hah. This is for you," she said, handing me a man's terry cloth robe. "Sorry there's no logo on the pocket, but if you like it anyway, you can have it added to your bill when you check out. Everything you need is in the master bath."

Juno shuffled painfully to the kitchen. I donned the robe, which I assumed she kept for her male guests. It smelled of just-sprayed Obsession. I headed for her bathroom, which was as well equipped as she had promised: the black marble shower bristled with heads at all heights and was large enough to do a number from *Flashdance* in. There were dozens of soaps, shampoos, scrubs, and brushes; I did feel as if I were in a very exclusive little hotel. It was so delicious in there I wanted to stay longer, but I knew Juno needed help, and the last thing I wanted to do was soap myself up one too many times in Juno's shower, though I doubted mine would be the first personal libation.

"Turandot's breakfast first," Juno said, leaning back in her kitchen chair, eyes closed, when I emerged. I knew where the kibble was from the night before, and Juno directed me to the organic vanilla yogurt and diced chicken in the fridge. She said it was okay that I hadn't known about the mix last night, especially since Turandot ate anyway.

Following Juno's recipe, I mixed half a cup of kibble with two tablespoons of chicken and two of the yogurt. It actually smelled pretty good. Juno had me call Turandot in from the yard. The puppy bounded in, sat as Juno commanded her, and then advanced when given the okay. She ate with more deliberation than I would have expected, since I assumed most dogs gobbled. "Could you wet a paper towel and wipe her mouth and chin? Thanks."

Unlike our dinner, which had been tinged with Eros and danger, this whole scene was pleasantly domestic. I was seeing Juno without makeup, without her typical flash and fire, and instead of being disappointed or dismayed, I felt at ease. There was much more to her than the brass band. I could hear Sharon warning me that this insight made Juno even more dangerous.

Turandot sat through my ministrations without squirming, stretched luxuriantly, and then burped. I chuckled, but Juno was so out of it that she didn't seem to notice, and that helped me feel more comfortable, given that I was barefoot and wearing nothing under the thick robe.

"That is an adorable dog," I said.

"Don't say it too often—she may try to get an agent." Juno moaned as if the joke had pained her. "Sweet Jesus, if I were a smoker, I'd have gone through half a pack by now, and I'd be licking the wrapper. You know, I remember a doctor with an odd name, and I have a vague recollection of some dark and dusky lad wheeling me to your car—was all of that a dream?"

"No."

"Too bad."

"How do you feel?"

"Wretched." She paused. "Miserable." She paused again. "No, wretched was right the first time." Feeling comfortable in her kitchen, I put up a pot of coffee, then set out bowls of granola with blueberries. Juno had soy milk in her Sub-Zero, and I put that out, too, and sprinkled some slivered almonds across the top in each large white bowl. Juno slurped down her cereal, unashamedly noisy. I couldn't tell if she was just hungry, or didn't care what I thought, or was just glad to be awake and alive.

I wondered what effect the accident would have on her. Contrary to departmental expectations, an irascible former chair of EAR had become even more cantankerous after his heart attack, his brush with mortality not reducing his general level of hostility at all. He had almost seemed determined to prove he wasn't weak, diminished. Would Juno be like that, become even more outrageous in an effort to prove that the accident hadn't shaken her? As she groaningly sipped from a French-size coffee cup, I thought it possible.

"You didn't say very much to the officer last night about your accident."

"Of course not! I was nauseous, I'd been connected to all kinds of—all kinds of tubes and whatnot, do you think I had time for a chat? I only wanted him to get the bloody hell away from me so I could go home. And it wasn't an accident, was it?" Juno said after her second cup of coffee, while I rinsed the cereal dishes and set them in her dishwasher.

I poured her another, grateful to be able to tend to her in some concrete way. "That's what Stefan and I think."

"Because whoever it was sped up only after I pulled out of my space. He *intended* to hit me. Or she."

There was no point now in holding back my bad news. "You got a phone message yesterday, when Stefan was here. That it wasn't over yet. Do you want to hear it?"

She shook her head dejectedly. "I can wait. It'll be the same crap as before. It's poison, I don't need to take that in right now."

"It was a man's voice."

"Muffled?"

I nodded, and then went back to what bothered me. "Why didn't you tell the SUM officer you thought it was deliberate?"

"Nick, there is no fucking way anyone would have believed me. Lying there in a hospital bed with all that commotion, right after a crash, I would have just come off as irrational. The only reason you believe me is because you've seen violence yourself."

Was that it, or did I also believe her because I was swayed by my attraction to her, and would it be possible to disentangle all the motives?

"Rusty has a black SUV," I said. "And he's your husband."

"So you think I might be protecting him? The Battered Bitch Syndrome? Please." That was the first time she had smiled since the previous night. "Rusty is just a spoiled little boy," she said fondly. "He's too much in love with himself to risk damaging his car or his hair plugs."

"They look real to me."

"He's got the money for it."

"Why haven't you divorced him?"

Juno didn't seem at all startled that I knew about the marriage, and she wasn't remotely apologetic. She sat up a little straighter, wincing. "You know, Nick, for a gay man you have some very straitlaced ideas about life. Get a clue. Rusty and I are divorced emotionally. Who gives a fuck what the law does or doesn't say? I don't need his permission or anyone else's to do what I want."

"Fine, be Walt Whitman. But it means you can't get married again."

"Why would I want to make the same mistake twice?"

I poured myself more coffee, feeling a Sally Jesse Raphael moment coming on, but unable to stop it. "Are you keeping him in reserve? Are you afraid to move on?"

Juno gave me a rich Tallulah Bankhead laugh. "I've moved on and over and under any man I wanted to. That has nothing to do with Rusty."

"Maybe he thinks it does."

"And so he tried to kill me? Not possible. He's in love with me—well, let me amend that. He's as much in love with me as he can be with anyone. He's an almost total narcissist, so there's not a whole lot of love left over for anyone else."

I suddenly saw myself and my friends back in high school air-guitaring to Led Zeppelin's "Whole Lotta Love," one of the raunchiest songs we knew back in the dark ages before "Me So Horny" and the like.

Juno was still smiling. "Rusty could never commit a crime when he has his career at stake, his reputation. He's too wrapped up in being a guru."

"But committing a crime and going to jail is how his career got started!"

"You don't like him, do you?" She studied me, a little more color in her face than before. Maybe it was the painkiller. "He's not very likable," she admitted. "But all that ego is intensely entertaining—and besides, he's very fuckable." She shrugged. "These days, that's a lot."

I could believe Juno's version of "A hard man is good to find," and wasn't I drawn to her pizzazz? Why shouldn't she find someone else's pyrotechnics intriguing?

Turandot curled up under the table and promptly fell asleep. Juno gazed down at her fondly.

"Juno, somebody is trying to scare you and hurt you—"

"—and doing a good job," she muttered. "Of the second one, at least."

"Right. I don't think you can dismiss Rusty as a suspect."

"Aren't you leaving something out? You were attacked, too. Someone's after the both of us."

It was like that door opening in *Close Encounters* and all the extraterrestrial light flooding in. I had been so overwhelmed by the last twelve hours I'd actually forgotten my attack. It had all faded like brush strokes from one of those public-TV-catalog "Zen boards" where what you write disappears in a few minutes and you supposedly learn lessons about impermanence. None of it seemed real.

"And while you may be able to cook up a motive for Rusty," she observed, crossing her legs as carefully as if they might break, "Why would he want to target you as well?"

"He's homophobic."

"So it's a two-for-one special? What did he say to you?"

I told her how he'd insulted me and Stefan the previous night.

"That's it? He was just trying to score some cheap points. He was simply feeling protective. It's rather sweet. He didn't mean a word. I'd believe he was a homo hater if he were an insecure teenager, but he's every inch a man."

Despite the seriousness of the moment, we both grinned at the pun, recalling our dinnertime conversation.

"Nothing outlandish," Juno added with satisfaction. "Though it does curve as sharply as a hat rack—"

"Are you still sleeping with him?"

Juno hesitated.

"You won't involve the campus police, you ask for my help—"

"I offered to hire you," she interrupted.

"Fine. But you won't tell me who you're sleeping with. How can you expect me to even start trying to figure this mess out if you keep things secret?"

"Everyone has secrets! It's half of what makes people interesting."

"What's the other half?"

"Hiding them, of course."

"That's pretty good, but you're stalling."

"Nick, I don't see the relevance of discussing my love life."

I must have looked pretty disgusted, because she flared up: "Shall I give you an alphabetical listing? Geographical? By specialty? Ethnicity? Perhaps you'd like a flow chart!"

"It's not me you're angry at."

Juno snorted. "You've got that right. I'm angry at the fucking sonofabitch who rammed my car. God—where *is* my car? Is it a disaster?"

"It was towed to the campus police station. It looked pretty bad."

"Shit! I have to call the insurance company! " Her shoulders drooped, and her chin fell. It wasn't a plea to be rescued, but real fatigue.

The phone rang, and we both jumped as if someone had been spying on us and was now going to tell us what he'd heard. Juno nodded at the phone, and I got it.

"Nick—is everything okay?"

I told Juno it was Stefan. Some of the tension left her face.

"I'm sorry I forgot to call," I said. "We were having breakfast, I had to feed the dog, and—"

"Sounds cozy."

I think he was joking, but it made me nervous anyway. I filled him in on Juno's condition while she winced or made faces to match my recital. It wasn't quite mockery of me and Stefan, but it was close.

"We've also been talking about her case," I said.

"Her case. Huh." He paused. "You know what was on last night on the Mystery Channel?"

"*Suspect?*"

He laughed because right after we had signed up for digital cable, it had seemed that the Cher/Dennis Quaid movie appeared almost every night for a month or two on one channel or another except for the Italian Soccer League. "Not *Suspect*, no. *Black Widow*. With Debra Winger? She's tracking the woman whose rich husbands keep dying?"

"Okay, I remember that. And your point is?"

"My point is the private investigator she hires in Hawaii. Remember him—the cranky guy? He ends up dead."

"And?"

"Don't be dense, Nick, you know what I mean. If somebody hates Juno enough to be harassing her and crashing into her car, that person might hate you more if you help her. You've already been warned."

I turned my back to Juno. Though she was absorbed in the newspaper, and had that I'm-not-listening air about her, I needed something between Stefan's advice and her—if only my body. Juno wasn't being helpful enough, and Stefan wanted me to back off completely. The way I added things up, those were two perfect reasons for plunging headlong into my own investigation. The hell with both of them.

"—so you should be careful," Stefan was saying.

"Wait a minute—careful about what?" Was he *still* warning me off?

He didn't sigh, but he didn't exactly not sigh either. "I was telling you about the protest, but I guess you were distracted. What were you doing? Helping Juno pick a new wallpaper pattern?"

"She doesn't have wallpaper."

"I said new, didn't I?"

"Okay, tell me, what protest?"

"You probably haven't seen the *Michiganapolis Tribune* today, right? I can't picture Juno subscribing to it."

I asked Juno if she had the *Tribune* delivered.

"Delivered?" She sounded as outraged as Lady Bracknell discovering that the rich young bachelor who wants to marry her daughter has no family background and was in fact abandoned as an infant at Victoria Station's cloakroom. "Delivered? Deliver me from that dreck! I wouldn't read the *Michiganapolis Spittoon* if it ran an obituary of my worst enemy."

A ringing non-endorsement.

"So they interviewed Avis Kinderhoek," Stefan continued, "because she's the chair of the Whiteness Studies Advisory whatever."

"Avis?"

Juno muttered, "Avis—Mavis—Davis—Save us."

"That's right, Avis. Don't ask me how she went from just being a volunteer to the big cheese. A reporter interviewed her about the whole idea of Whiteness Studies, and she said it was brilliant, that white people had for too long been made to feel ashamed of themselves, and that they were in danger of internalizing demeaning stereotypes and it could seriously damage their self-esteem—"

Stefan stopped because I was laughing in outrage, and Juno demanded that I catch her up with the conversation.

"That's exactly what women and minorities have been saying," she said. "To justify changing the canon. That roly-poly pygmy is co-opting their rhetoric!"

Stefan heard that at his end and agreed.

"But what protest?" I asked.

"Peter de Jonge called me to say that the graduate students in EAR were going to stage some kind of demonstration at Parker. He sounded worried. He wouldn't say why."

"But he's always worried, isn't he? And how come he's a source, and why did he tell you?"

"I would have to say, Yes, Don't know, and Don't know."

"Funny guy."

"Just trying to be efficient."

"So what's the problem if there's, what, picketing?"

"I have no idea. When are you coming home?"

"Soon. We're going to make Singapore slings and watch Martha Stewart's show first."

"Bullshit—you have classes to teach." Stefan air-kissed his receiver, and we hung up. I filled Juno in, and she went from mildly alert to wide awake and ready to rumble. Well, potentially.

"Avis Kinderhoek is a moron," Juno said, holding out her cup for more coffee. I filled her cup and mine, and poured us both some water. "No, that's too benign. She's a virus. No brain, just deadly mindless activity. The only good news is that she's so bloody convinced she's right that she's going to hurt her own cause by blurting out any idiocy that occurs to her. Whiteness Studies as therapy for poor dejected Caucasians! It's sick-making. It's ridiculous. Have you ever felt there's anything inferior about being white?"

"Inferior to whom? If I could be anything, it would be French. Maybe then I'd get the subjunctive right. But I'm the wrong person to ask, because I'm only an honorary white man."

"What the hell does that mean?" She frowned.

"I'm only part of the patriarchy if I keep my mouth shut. As soon as I say anything about being Jewish and gay, I'm doubly demoted."

"Honorarily white? You love quotations so much, well here's a little Hemingway for you: 'Isn't it pretty to think so?' You're white, like it or not, so don't try to score any minority points from me." Then she smiled in a pre-accident way. "As for scoring, however—"

But I wouldn't be deflected. "In the nineteenth century, Germans didn't used to be considered white in America, or Italians, or Poles, or Jews—"

"Spare me the self-pity."

"It's not self-pity, it's history, damn it!"

Juno mockingly rolled her eyes, then winked at me, and even as I was furious, I enjoyed her winding me up. But the image made me think of the connection between sex and clock-winding in *Tristram Shandy* and at that moment, with caffeine and contempt animating her, I wouldn't have minded grinding a few gears with Juno. Tick, tock.

Just then the doorbell rang, and with Turandot darting around our feet and barking, Juno waveringly headed for the door while I followed.

"Wait," she commanded, and the puppy obediently backed up several feet from the door and sat down, tongue lolling, practically vibrating with suppressed excitement.

It was Detective Valley, dressed as shabbily as if he'd chosen his suit in the dark—the very first time. He eyed me with amused surprise, and glanced behind me as if expecting to see some sort of evidence of debauchery or crime.

"I wanted to talk to you about last night," he said, waiting for Juno to invite him in. She bristled and looked as if she wanted to slam the door in his face, but hesitated. Weakness? Or guilt?

"Oh, all right."

Valley marched in, and Juno compromised by shutting the door loudly. It was childish, and I would have done the same. I don't know if I would have stuck my tongue out at him behind his back, though, as Juno did. Turandot followed cautiously, nose down as if following a trail, and hanging back from Valley. Was she picking up on Juno's distaste for the man, or had she made her own canine decision?

"I believe you're withholding evidence," Valley said with his back to us, surveying the living room as if that very evidence were hidden in plain sight, or perhaps waiting for us to produce it before we were face-to-face again.

Juno made it to a chair and settled into it as unsteadily as if she were eighty. "Really?"

I sat on the wide arm of her chair, feeling protective, concerned.

"The officer who interviewed you in the emergency room believed you were holding something back."

"Well, I did think I was going to puke, if that's what you mean."

Valley breathed in with all the impatience of a headmaster used to being subtly taunted by defiant, rude pupils. He sat down on the couch opposite us, looming there with the loony stiffness of a praying mantis.

"You all think you're clever," he said, and I could feel Juno's temperature start to rise as her body gave off waves of heated disapproval.

"Canadians? Oh, no, we're too nice to be clever. We leave that to the Americans. You'd never catch us trying to dazzle anyone with a bon mot."

"Professors," he said, as if Juno hadn't spoken. "You think you're gods just because you have Ph.D.s, just because you write books and know lots of long words. You're just like your students when they get drunk and run amok on campus—only you act that way when you're sober. Reckless and stupid."

It was hard for me to completely disagree with his assessment of professorial lordliness and entitlement, but it was also limited, unfair. In my opinion, the administrators at SUM were the real thugs, the real menace. They were the ones who set the tone on campus in their hypocritical way, acting as if they were each and every one ruler of some petty authoritarian state obsessed with its own rituals and reputation.

Now Valley took me in as if committing every detail to memory for later dissection. I tried not to shift under his hostile scrutiny, but it wasn't easy.

"Why are you two always together?" .

"Friendship," I said. "You should try it sometimes."

Juno took my hand and held it to her cheek, which was as warm as her hand, but softer. "You can tell him the truth, Nick, I don't mind." Her voice was low and provocative, and Valley actually looked shocked for a moment, or equal parts vexed and nonplussed. Me, I tried not to blush, imagining what else Juno could be doing with her hand, and what I could be doing with mine. That is, without Valley watching. I may have been a closet heterosexual or bisexual, but I certainly wasn't into anything kinky like voyeurism. Not yet, anyway.

"Now, did you have a point in coming here?" Juno asked Valley. "What about finding whoever was shooting at me at the Campus Center?"

I teach composition, and couldn't help but notice that her choice of tense—the past progressive—made it sound like she'd been in a gun battle, or under sniper fire.

"Nobody tried to shoot you," Valley said disgustedly.

"But we found—" I couldn't finish because Juno squeezed my hand hard, then let it go.

"Found what?" Valley asked, not missing any of this byplay. "Found what?"

"Nothing," Juno said. I echoed her denial, and sat there trying to make myself expressionless, and more, to blank my mind of any images that would betray me. Like most people, I tend not to believe in psychic communication except when around authority figures I feared could read my thoughts. It's probably a holdover from childhood, when we all grow up in a land of omniscient giants, whose power only starts to fade in our teen years when it's too late to change those searing first impressions.

"It's a crime," Valley said, "to withhold evidence in a criminal investigation."

"What investigation? As far as I can tell," Juno snarled, "the only thing you're doing is harassing me, and I'm the victim!"

Valley raked her with his clinical, contemptuous eyes—as if he were a nineteenth-century physician about to diagnose a woman as hysterical due to a "floating uterus."

"I'm getting out of here," Valley said, eyes doing a Clint Eastwood squint. Turandot followed him to the door a few feet back, but Juno and I didn't move. Valley expertly let himself out, as if he'd worked those exact locks before, and Juno and I both slumped.

"I need a drink," she said. "A triple vodka martini."

"I have to get home and change and get ready for classes. Do you need anything?"

"A howitzer," she grumbled. "And barbed wire and land mines."

I wasn't sure if I should or even if I dared kiss her good-bye, but after what we'd been through that morning and the night before, something was required, wasn't it? Juno rose and haltingly followed me to the hall closet, where I took out my coat. She tried helping me put it on, but groaned when she raised her arms.

"I'll kill him," she gasped.

"Valley?"

"Someone. Someone has to pay for this."

I knelt and ruffled Turandot's sides, surprised at how affectionate I felt toward Juno's puppy—or would a psychologist have called it displacement?

"Thank you doesn't seem like enough," Juno said throatily. "You've been wonderful." She gave me a quick girlish hug, then slapped my butt as if we were football players, and I left, wishing I'd had the nerve to pull her close and feel her silk-covered breasts against my chest. But I was also glad I was a coward; who knew where that moment would have led, and what changes it might ineluctably bring with it?

I didn't go right home. I detoured to the Campus Center, parked, and hurried inside, trying to act inconspicuous as I waded through the shoals of students who looked like fans at a rap concert in their Tommy Hilfiger hats and FuBu attire.

There was no one in the room where Juno had been attacked, and with as much trepidation as some adventure novel hero unmasking a veiled and jeweled idol, I walked over to the curtain and pulled it aside.

But someone had been there before me. The small hole, whether created by a bullet or not, looked as if it had been enlarged by a hammer or chisel. Anyone else would think it was just random property destruction on campus, like the battered NO SMOKING signs or gauged bathroom stall doors. I felt stupid in that large airless room. I could have told Valley sooner what Juno and I suspected. I had let her determine what I said or didn't say, and that was a big mistake.

In novels or movies this was the kind of moment where you hear a sudden noise and dash behind the curtain and then overhear some incriminating or perhaps mystifying exchange, but I wasn't that lucky. Conversations drifted in from the hallway, but they were random, and I headed back to my car dejected and annoyed. As I drove away I marveled, however, at the still-peculiar December weather—no snow yet, and temperatures often in the low fifties like that morning.

"I would have made you breakfast," Stefan said when he opened the door, "but—"

And we hugged there with the cool air seeping into the house, holding each other as if I were a voyager in the tropics who'd been given up for lost. I felt all of that: battered, besieged, exhausted, and restored. And something else—intensely guilty for having imagined Juno in my arms not too long before. What would that be like? Stefan's body was hard and lean and unyielding. Juno's was athletic, too, but bounteous, resplendently fleshy. I thought of Glenda Jackson in *Women in Love* asking the half-naked coal miner bathing outside his grim home, "How are your thighs? I want to drown in flesh." Juno would be a sensual *noyade*.

And Stefan, who could finish my sentences and often said exactly what I was thinking, Stefan moved me inside and closed the door, kissing me now rapaciously. Without a word, we pulled at each other's clothes like love-starved teenagers and did it on the foyer floor. Actually, we did several things, quickly, in increasing orders of complexity. Did I think about Juno while we grappled and groaned?

There wasn't time.

"I have to shower again," I complained, when we were standing again.

"Better lock the bathroom door, or you'll have to shower twice," Stefan leered, and I broke away, put my coat on the rack, and climbed the stairs to clean up.

After my shower, I settled down in the kitchen for a few minutes to read Avis's interview in the *Michiganapolis Tribune* before driving to campus to check my mail and start my day of teaching. It was almost a puff piece that presented the task force as another example of SUM being progressive, forward-thinking, innovative—all the usual bunkum.

Stefan sat opposite me, watching my reactions. Even strong

coffee didn't make Avis's offhanded offensiveness palatable. She was quoted as saying things like, "You don't hear white people whining about their rights when the country is changing and they're going to be in a minority," and, "We need to preserve our embattled culture."

But the short interview didn't provide clues as to what the threat was exactly, and what was threatened. Shakespeare? Dolly Parton?

"This is unbelievable," I said.

Stefan nodded. "But totally in character."

"Isn't she going to get censured for shooting her mouth off like this?"

"By whom? Serena's staying neutral, and I don't think the provost or anyone else really cares if anyone's offended."

"You're probably right—Glinka appointed her to the task force, so she must have official approval to blab."

"Unless she doesn't, and she's trying to drum up publicity for herself. Make some news and make some noise."

"You know, I have this impression," he said, "that Peter de Jonge is more than a graduate student."

"Meaning?" I wondered why he'd brought it up now.

"I don't know. It's not just that he has his own life down in Neptune, that he's older than most of the graduate students. It's something else, something nebulous."

"Nebulous in Neptune—could be a musical."

"Not a very good one."

Though I felt refreshed after my shower and more coffee, the subject of Avis's interview and whatever was or wasn't going to happen in response to it already seemed weary, stale, and unprofitable.

"Oh, shit!" I said. "I forgot to tell you that Valley came to Juno's house this morning."

"Investigating?"

"Accusing. He thinks she's hiding evidence, that she knows more than she's saying."

"He could be smarter than he looks."

"That wouldn't be hard."

"So what happened?"

"Stefan, it was like those two-minute scenes you used to make fun of in *Dynasty*. Someone stalks into a room, makes an accusation, the charges fly, and then he or she marches out. Dramatic, but kind of pointless. Like most things connected to EAR." I didn't add that I'd gone to the Campus Center.

Stefan drove off to do the grocery shopping, and I drove to campus. As I pulled up to Parker Hall, I had the strange sense of being at some kind of historical theme park. The ornate, crumbling red sandstone nineteenth-century building was eerily beautiful in the gray morning light. Rectangular, three-storied, and covered with ornate and fussy stone bands above each line of windows and along the roof line, it looked like a battered antique coin bank.

Dutch elm disease had long since defoliated the area right around Parker, so the saplings at its perimeter made it look even more one-dimensional. Before I entered the parking lot, I could hear chanting from a group of several dozen students at the back of the building facing the lot: "Two, four, six, eight, White Studies Equals Hate."

But I was distracted taking a parking space in the ranks of faculty cars; Juno's accident rushed back at me like a ravenous black bear attacking campers who've been foolish enough to leave food in their tent. I had to sit in the car with my eyes closed for a few minutes, telling myself it was over.

Over? I could hear Sharon's gentle, pitying voice asking "Really? How do you know?" Based on all my previous experiences at SUM, trouble was sure to follow in some new and dispiriting guise.

Hell, as I took up my briefcase and got out of the car, wasn't it there? Some twenty or thirty students in typical SUM motley circulated in an oval in front of the back door to Parker. Since the parking lot was at the back of Parker, this entrance was actually the most used, but from where I stood, I could see a smaller group off at the side door, and assumed another one was around the front as well. There were black, Hispanic, and Asian students primarily, and some gay ones I recognized from previous protests on campus, and with faces pierced like pincushions.

Their sturdy-looking signs demanded Avis's resignation, accused Arts and Letters and EAR of racism, and demanded more minority faculty and administrators—an old and perpetually unsatisfied complaint at SUM. Most of the signs did not seem slapped together that morning, so I wondered if this demonstration had been planned well in advance. The gay students glared at me, and I felt awkward. Stefan and I had resisted becoming representative gays at SUM, called in for any and all panel discussions no matter what the campus venue. While we were completely out, we did not relish becoming "homos on parade," as people used to call them when we were growing up in New York. That job at SUM had been eagerly taken on by boring thirtyish Jurgen Pfefferblit, a diminutive professor in the School of Engineering whose glutinous conversation was swollen by stupefyingly dull statistics. Jurgen managed to reduce all questions about homosexuality to medians and percentiles, and had his own little ardent following on campus.

If the professional touch to the signs was unexpected, I was even more surprised to see Bill and Betty Malatesta join the picketers. They were EAR's star graduate students, blond, handsome, accomplished, but deeply disgruntled because they hadn't found jobs and were stuck at EAR teaching as adjuncts. I would have expected them to stay away from such blatant criticism of the department, but they joined the picket line, unfurling white cardboard signs of their own: "White Studies Is Lite Studies."

Given that Betty was blunter than Bill, and he had the sense of humor, I suspected he'd come up with the very catchy slogan. As soon as they saw me approach, they broke away from the line and rushed up to me.

"You're not going in there, are you?" Betty demanded, looking unusually sweaty and disheveled in her corduroy jacket and jeans —like someone contemplating living up in a redwood to save it from loggers.

"Why not?"

"It's a picket line," Bill said grimly. Usually he greeted me with a pun or a lightbulb joke, but he seemed to have lost his spark. It had to be the strain of living on an adjunct's salary and hopes, though having been kicked out of his office and moved to a cramped one because of me might account for his tone just as much. He had a gold hoop in each ear, sideburns stretching down from under his dark ski cap, and had grown a tiny triangle of beard under his lower lip—all of which seemed like an attempt to achieve student solidarity, at least visually. But the effect on his clean-cut looks was as artificial as the black velvet patches aristocrats used to adorn their faces with in the eighteenth century.

"You can't cross a picket line," Betty explained.

"But you're not auto workers, and this isn't a factory."

Bill shook his head sadly. "Of course it's a factory—we just do cultural production here."

I wanted to tell him to spare me the critspeak, but I didn't. "So you're telling me I can't get my mail, I can't go in to get ready to teach my classes?"

Before he could answer, EAR's shabby Three Amigos, Martin Wardell, Larry Rich, and Les Peterman—all of them looking just this side of homelessness—marched toward the picketers in a wedge formation, blaring "Out of my way!" and "Watch out!" Fat Wardell was on point, and he easily pushed through the startled demonstrators, who started reacting only when the doors shut behind the three professors. They shouted, "Racists!" but who could say what the weird trio had in mind with their act? They might simply resent being barred from their offices. After all, unlike me, they had aboveground offices that would not have been good settings for a Roger Corman film.

Betty and Bill turned to me, eyebrows up, as if daring me to cause a similar disruption, and they rejoined the picket line, starting up the chant that was on their signs, alternating it with "White Studies Is Not-So-Bright Studies."

I stood there hesitating, unwilling to be intimidated by graduate or any other kind of students, feeling I owed my own students loyalty, though I also knew they'd welcome an excuse to have free time. Then a black BMW pulled past me and parked, and Tyler Mooney-Mauser emerged as briskly as if he were making an arrest. He was dressed for the part in a Nuevo Gestapo black leather trench coat, belted as tightly as his little smile of greeting.

"Well, Professor Hoffman." He half sounded like Olly telling Stan, "This is another fine mess you've gotten us in."

"Well, what?" I snapped.

"I hope you're not here to lend support to these—these instigators."

"What are *you* here for?" I asked, trying to turn the attention away from myself. I'd be damned if administration pressure forced me to go into Parker—but I wanted to anyway, and felt caught.

"The provost has asked me to note who respects the picket line and who doesn't. If you have business in Parker Hall, I certainly hope you'll go in. It's one thing to respect student freedoms, another to let students create a disturbance."

"Is this a disturbance?"

His eyes dimmed at my questioning his assessment.

"Are you behind this?" he asked. "Don't lie. If you are, it'll come out."

"Oh, yes," I said recklessly. "I planned the whole thing. And in five minutes a crop duster is going to start spraying the campus with defoliant. We'll have you by the balls."

Just then, Byron Summerscale lumbered out of the building in a shabby-looking raccoon coat he must have worn in college, stopped a few feet away from the demonstrators, threw his arms out wide, and launched into the "Marseillaise."

13

I wished Stefan were there for the performance. Summerscale's voice was hoarse, but his accent was credible, and he threw himself into the bloodier parts of the French anthem as if he were a cheerleader whose team was a field goal behind, with under a minute left in the game.

The picketers hung back, staring at him, clearly not sure if his serenade was mockery, a tribute, or madness. Other students making their way across campus drifted over, drawn by the spectacle, and soon Summerscale had a crowd of fifty or sixty, constantly growing by two's and three's. I heard muttered questions around me, students wondering, Was this a theater department skit of some kind? Was Summerscale a nut like those Bible-waving preachers who hit campus in the spring and thundered about hell? Was he singing in Canadian? And, like, what was with that coat?

But students who had either taken one of his classes or knew about his eccentricities were egging him on with a rhythmic disco-floor chant of "Go, *By*-ron! Go, *By*-ron! Go, *By*-ron!" An interesting musical counterpoint, and so much lighter in tone than the demonstrations I vaguely remembered against Nixon and the Christmas bombing of Cambodia that this could have been performance art rather than a protest.

Tyler Mooney-Mauser was not remotely entertained by the display. If Summerscale were a crab, he'd be boiled by now, and Tyler would be cracking open his legs with grim satisfaction and scooping out the meat.

Summerscale finished to spirited if generally uncomprehending applause and shouted, "Freedom!" before ducking back inside Parker. That was a clarion call that covered a lot of bases—would it be his campaign slogan when he ran for EAR chair? Or was it an ironic reference to Janis Joplin's "freedom's just another word for nothing left to lose"?

As the doors shut, I saw Peter de Jonge sidle around the side of the building and wondered if he were involved in the demonstration. It seemed a risky thing to do for a new graduate student, even if he did have a job in the outside world. Or was he just observing? If that was the case, why? He had to have some kind of connection, or he wouldn't have called Stefan. Our eyes might have met, but I wasn't sure. In any case, he ducked back around Parker Hall and disappeared.

I thought of following, since he was acting so suspiciously, but just then my cell phone rang. I set down my briefcase and turned away from the crowd. It was Stefan, who said, "I tried your office phone but you didn't answer—where are you?"

"Outside Parker." I quietly explained my dilemma, moving farther from the building and gawkers to get some privacy, nudging my briefcase along with one foot. Cars passing on Michigan Avenue were starting to notice the throng of students with signs and some were honking in support—unless it was just to make noise. Even some of the shop owners on the stretch of The Mile right across campus were in their doorways, observing this latest rumble from the SUM volcano.

"Are you going in?" Stefan asked.

"Shit—I don't know—it's not exactly like an afternoon at the beach out here, but—"

"—you grew up in New York just like I did and crossing a picket line makes you uncomfortable."

"Yes. That's it. Exactly." How had I missed it? Standing there facing the demonstrators had triggered scenes from decades ago—and they filled me now with a sense of drama and unease. I didn't want to feel like a scab, a word that had always sounded hideous and polluting to me.

"So don't cross it," Stefan said. "You don't really need to check your mail, do you? You could just go to Uplegger and teach, then check your mail another time."

I squirmed, and it wasn't just at the mention of Uplegger, the cramped and malodorous building nearby where many EAR professors were assigned to teach (another example of their low status vis-à-vis other faculty at SUM). Stefan may have been right about just going with the flow, but I actually did want to cross the line, and not solely because the Malatestas had urged me not to and I disliked being bullied by anyone.

I had some student papers in my office I wanted to return in class, and more inconsequentially, I had a routine of going back and forth between Parker and Uplegger when I taught. I was embarrassed to admit it even to myself, but Stefan seemed to read my silence.

"So today won't be as organized as usual. What can you do?"

He was absolutely right. I laughed and told him I'd keep him posted. "If there are any arrests or fire bombings or whatever."

As I put the phone away, Avis Kinderhoek sallied up to me, her prim little mouth as tight as if I were a store manager and she had a complaint. "What's going on here?"

I gestured to the picket line. "Isn't it obvious?" Why was she even talking to me after our confrontation at the faculty meeting? Wasn't I the Antichrist to her?

Her piggy nostrils quivered with disgust. "They should be thankful we let them in here at all, instead of biting the hand that feeds them!"

"Avis, this is a university, not a zoo."

"Really? Tell that to the animals."

I didn't know if she was targeting the students of color, students in general, or just hated anyone who disagreed with her—including me. Whatever her object, it was a repulsive attitude, and I was appalled she thought she could talk that way to me, as if I somehow approved. Her disdain made me mad, and I said, "SUM wouldn't turn away a brick if it paid tuition."

Avis eyed me up and down as if to intimidate me, but given our respective heights, her stance had all the threat of a dog inspecting a pole before peeing on it. "You're playing a very dangerous game," she said, sounding like a villain in a bad spy movie.

"There she is!" someone called. It might have been Bill Mala-testa, but I wasn't sure. Now cries of "Racist bitch! Racist bitch!" rose from the demonstrators, punctuated by the kind of hand-chopping fans do when their teams have Indian names. Why should SUM be any different from the rest of the country, where politics and entertainment are indistinguishable?

Tyler Mooney-Mauser beetled over and laid a sympathetic hand down on Avis's well-padded shoulder. "Are you all right?" He could have been a mourner at a viewing asking the widow how she was bearing up. Milking his sympathy, she shuddered.

"This isn't the place for you," he said, and she nodded as dain-tily as she could. It was sick-making. Avis headed away from the growing tumult, and Tyler rounded on me as if I had been baiting Avis and had arranged the whole demonstration just to torment her. "Why don't you leave her alone?" He stalked back toward the demonstrators as if the force of his disapproval could somehow si-lence them. Was there something about my personality, some kind of Kick Me aura that made people think they could say any-thing, accuse me of anything?

Suddenly, with a faint cry of "Get him!" Tyler was up in the air as if the crowd had turned to a mosh pit. Did they know who this supernumerary was? How could they? It must have been the Malatestas who had identified him as the provost's stooge and therefore worthy of harassment.

Students gleefully passed Mooney-Mauser back and forth over their heads as he struggled and shouted inarticulate rage, ob-jects falling from his pockets as he traversed the scornful, mocking hands, some of which may have been copping a derisory feel of his lean body or smacking at him.

I should have felt sorry for Tyler; after all, I decried people being "passed up" at a football game. But I was glad to see him re-duced from self-styled magnificence to the poor forked creature King Lear talks about.

Now ancient, shuddering windows were being heaved open at the rear of Parker, and faculty and secretaries were peering out from every floor at the growing commotion. Dulcie Halligan was at one of the EAR main office windows, flanked by the other secretaries, looking censorious and concerned. EAR did not need any more bad press for the next decade or so, and a protest like this was bound to eventually attract cameras, reporters, and the kind of freelance troublemakers who could subvert any campus celebration and turn it into a riot.

"Don't worry!" Dulcie called down from the EAR office, where she had a perfect view of his humiliation. "The campus police are on their way!"

Cheers rose from the mix of demonstrators and spectators, as if a Roman emperor had turned his thumb down in the arena and more glorious bloodshed was coming.

Two years ago I had seen a fracas on campus turn into utter chaos that left one student dead, but I was able to watch this morning's trouble with more than equanimity. I was in full schadenfreude mode, enjoying Tyler Mooney-Mauser's downfall, or upfall, or something. As an agent of the provost, he was intent on making all of us feel powerless, and here he was, experiencing just that himself.

I checked my watch. I still had time to decide about going to my office or not, without being late for my first class. But when I looked up, Tyler was disappearing—he was being dumped in the middle of the demonstrators, and I had a horrible flash of the movie *Suddenly Last Summer* and the scene where Sebastian Venable is torn apart in a crowd of starving Mexicans—and eaten.

I hurried to intervene, trying to push through the crowd of students, which must have numbered well over a hundred by now, but then I heard clanking, and Tyler's shout, "Let me go!"

The demonstration had been planned well by somebody, because Tyler was now handcuffed to one of the metal bars that opened the doors to Parker, and another set of handcuffs acted like a chain by locking the bars together. Tyler looked rumpled, outraged, and dangerous, yanking furiously at the cuffs that would not release him. Students stood in a semicircle facing him, staring, muttering derisively, their signs drooping. This was clearly more satisfying than the task of marching and chanting, only what would they do next? Assault him?

Betty and Bill Malatesta looked abashed enough when they saw me to make me believe this hadn't been their idea. But who was in charge, then? No one seemed to be directing what was happening, which made me nervous and curious.

There was a Jamie Lee Curtis scream from above us that silenced everyone standing outside Parker. We all looked up to see where it had come from.

"It's gone—it's gone—it's gone!" Dulcie was wailing. "My *tree!*"

Puzzled students looked at each other, repeating the word "tree" as if it were code that needed deciphering.

"Someone stole the Diversity Tree!" Dulcie cried, as horrified as if she'd been the victim of an assault.

Around me, confusion didn't just reign, it was creating a dynasty. "What the hell is a Diversity Tree?" came from several people. I didn't bother explaining, not wanting to call more attention to myself, but the idea of anyone caring enough to steal the Diversity Tree was as ridiculous as the tree itself. Why bother?

Sirens now hit us like bombs, and half a dozen campus police cars screeched into the parking lot, policemen pouring from them like Greeks from the Trojan horse, ready for savagery. I expected the crowd to disperse immediately as the police lined up at a distance in two groups of ten each, but no one left. The policemen had the blank, vaguely ominous look of any mass of uniforms, evoking images of power and repression. One of them resembled the officer on the scene of Juno's accident, but I wasn't sure.

I tried squirming away from the crowd, but around me, people had drawn in more closely as if for protection and I started to feel smothered by the clashing smells of cigarette smoke, mothballed winter coats, and CK One. I looked around for the Malatestas but they had somehow slipped off. Wonderful. I was smack in the middle of what could turn into another fabled SUM riot—and would be late for class, if I didn't get arrested.

One of the campus policemen stepped forward and said quietly, "You need to disperse."

No one moved. I sensed an adamantine, sheeplike stubbornness that would have taken more than Babe and a magic formula to melt.

"Officer!" Tyler Mooney-Mauser called. "No violence! Please!"

Was that latent humanitarianism in him, fear, or just the typical administrator's obsession with PR?

Parker Hall's windows were now as stuffed with spectators as an all-you-can-eat buffet. And when I craned my neck I could see that Serena was there, too, at the EAR office window. Could it get any worse? I was the only faculty participant in a student outrage targeted at the administration and sparked by Avis's interview in the *Tribune*. After I had denounced Avis at the faculty meeting, my presence here would be considered intentional—that's how it would be reported and gossiped about, no matter what I said or how I tried to deny it. This was the kind of imbroglio that didn't just torpedo your tenure application, it could lead to being fired.

But surprisingly, at the thought of being dismissed, and despite being pressed against on all sides, I suddenly felt as liberated as if Summerscale's shout of "Freedom!" before really had meant something. Worrying about my security at SUM was a knee-jerk reaction, unworthy of this moment or any other. I surrendered, closed my eyes, and let my mind drift, assuming we were not about to become a byword for gun control. I heard traffic noise, panicky breathing, bare tree branches rubbing against themselves. The crowd was so closely packed that the air on my face and head felt even cooler, as if I were in a hot tub.

"I'm okay!" Mooney-Mauser shouted, sounding far less anxious than before. Perhaps he had been having some quiet inner moments for himself. If that were the case, they didn't last, because there were sharp cries of alarm around me, people jostling and scattering, a shout of "Look out!" and then a weird muffled crash, then another. The Diversity Tree had been flung from Parker Hall, maybe even from the roof, and everyone around me legged it as quickly as if they thought the tree were about to explode. It was a wonder nobody got trampled. Maybe they expected more shrubs to rain down on them from some maddened horticulture student, enraged by genetic engineering.

With its ornaments bent, broken, drooping, the mangled Diversity Tree lying only ten feet away looked even more pathetic than it had on the EAR counter. From up above us, Dulcie leaned out the window wailing, as if she were a mother grieving her son's loss and ready to throw herself into the grave. It was bizarre and excessive—but touching. I felt sorry for her; she had invested much more than I'd realized in the benighted plan. I just hoped there wouldn't be copycat crimes at SUM and further assaults with a deadly sapling.

Then I heard another strange sound, like a low whistle, and something shattered so close to me I thought I'd been shot at. I jumped back, as startled as when you turn a corner and see someone when you thought no one was there. Recovering from the surprise, I could see that around me lay fist-size chunks of sandstone that looked like bits of the ornamental coping around the roof. I stepped back to look at the roof but couldn't see if a piece was missing. Judging from the rubble, what had fallen must have been as large as the head on a marble bust, more than enough to have hurt me after falling from three floors up. Had it come down accidentally following the tree, loosened by the activity up there—or was someone really trying to brain me?

Tyler was shouting, "Get me out of here!" while several campus policemen were attending to the shackled, miserable-looking shnook, who had been forced by the cuffs to squat against the door. Other officers circled round Parker in two groups, evidently heading for the other entrances to trap the tree thief.

They unlocked Mooney-Mauser's handcuffs and helped him to his feet, dusted him off while he imperiously pointed at various scattered personal belongings—a phone, a fountain pen, a Palm-Pilot—that the police dutifully gathered up for him. With the doors also unbarred, he was led inside—to clean up? to make a statement?—and I decided to avoid Parker that day and head straight to class. But Officer Protopopescu approached me, asked if I was okay.

"I thought that was you. Yeah, I'm fine."

He returned to the officers attending Mooney-Mauser, and I phoned Stefan en route and left a message that I was okay, it was all over, and I'd fill him in later. As I closed the phone and put it away, my hand was trembling, and I heard the crashing stonework again, wondering how close it had really come to hitting me. But I couldn't dwell on that; I had students waiting for me. I hurried into the closest men's room at Uplegger and, after taking a leak, noticed some reddish dust across my face. I'd obviously been closer than I realized to that piece of balustrade or whatever had fallen from Parker's crumbling roof, or been hurled.

It was too soon for my first class to have heard about the incident, but everyone in my second class already seemed to know something, which meant that I had a lot of rumors to deflate before we could start.

"No, sorry. No fistfights. No blood. Nobody was kidnapped, not really. Nobody got pushed off the roof. Trust me, I was there." That was a mistake, since my students clamored for details, and then we wasted half the class talking about Avis and Whiteness Studies, which most of my students thought was a joke, and who could blame them?

"So, like, I could do a paper on Nine Inch Nails and suburban white teenage angst?" Todd, one of the livelier students, asked. "If this were a Whiteness Studies class?"

"You can do one now."

"No, that's cool, I'll pass." Everyone laughed.

I called Stefan right after class from an empty classroom in Uplegger where I could feel private. Even he, with all his experience of SUM's surrealism, had trouble believing me. I had to repeat each outrageous statement of fact: Yes, Tyler was picked up and passed along; yes, he was handcuffed to the door; yes, someone stole the Diversity Tree from EAR and tossed it onto the ground.

Stefan wasn't agog, he was Magog. "From a window? From the roof? Did you see who did it? Holy shit! Was it the same person who stole the tree, do you think? Well, you couldn't know, could you? Tyler was really *handcuffed*? I don't believe it!"

He could have been a scandal junkie hungrily switching channels to find out the latest dish from D.C. It was a very repetitious conversation until I told him about the follow-up to the tree.

"You think someone tried to warn you? To hurt you?" he said. "Or was it an accident?"

"It was probably the Hunchback of Parker Hall—he ran out of boiling oil."

"Don't joke about it. Stay away from Parker," Stefan warned me, turning serious. "There could be more trouble. Okay?"

"Okay."

Before he hung up, he said, "How were your classes?"

"Thanks for asking."

I know lots of professors don't like teaching the same class back-to-back with only a twenty-minute break, but I enjoyed the challenge of making the material (when I was lecturing) different the second time around. That day, however, I was exhausted when classes and the phone call with Stefan were over, and I dragged myself back to my car. I would have gone straight there but ran into interference of a sort before I crossed over to Parker. Rusty Dominguez–St. John came striding along with a black leather knapsack slung over the shoulder of his fringed black suede jacket. Head high, chest out, and shoulders back, he could have been walking onto the set of a music video, with that glossy fake look of his, like someone about to lip-synch.

"Nick, my man, are you self-destructive or what? Why didn't you just shoot Tyler instead of chaining him to the doors?"

"That wasn't me! I was just a bystander."

"Right. Not the way I heard it." He shook his head solemnly, then gave me a hideous, triumphant grin. That's when I realized he was mocking me. And threatening me, too, reminding me he could say anything about me he wanted to, and that he probably would, just to blacken my name, which he didn't regard in the slightest.

"That is a sick joke," I said. "Really sick." What made him feel free enough to even say it—was I the scrawniest chicken in the yard, waiting to be pecked to death?

He laughed and jauntily walked on as if nothing could touch him. Students stopped and looked at him, but I didn't know if they were wondering who he was or wondering who he *thought* he was. Stefan's advice to stay away from Parker before the morning's events and even after was good, but something in Rusty's mockery changed my mind about heading right home. Why should I be afraid of going to my office? Wasn't that what he was trying to do with his mind games—make me more paranoid than I was already?

I marched myself to Parker Hall, determined not to be intimidated by anyone. The mob scene hadn't really been violent, so there was no trace of the morning's frenzy, and the tree and stone debris were gone. I wondered if Dulcie had reclaimed the tree, and I pictured her woefully carrying it up the stairs in her arms, a piney pietà. "The calla lilies are in bloom again," I muttered, recalling Katharine Hepburn's tear-jerker line from *Stage Door*.

The basement was utterly quiet. Summerscale hadn't built a *Les Mis*–style barricade across the middle of the hallway, and there weren't any bare-breasted heroines waiting to lead a charge. Too quiet?

Yes, indeed. Stickpinned to my door was a white business envelope of departmental stationery. My name was typed and underlined: *Dr. Nick Hoffman*. There was something derisory about the underlining. Dulcie, I thought. Who else? I pocketed the note, let myself into the office, and had sat down at my desk to read what could only be bad news when the phone rang.

It was Juno. "Nick! What the hell is going on there? I've heard a dozen stories—a *hundred* stories—that you were beaten up, arrested, talked down from the roof when you threatened to jump, assaulted a campus cop—"

"You're kidding, aren't you?"

"Absolutely not."

I glanced around the shabby office, thankful I hadn't been there long enough to feel comfortable despite the grunge that paint and posters couldn't really camouflage. I doubted I'd be sitting there much longer.

"They're going to fire me."

"Why? Did you do any of those things?" She sounded impressed.

"Nothing. I didn't do anything. I was just standing there when it got out of control."

"What did? Tell me what happened."

So once again I was reporting from the scene. I wondered how CNN's Christianne Amanpour could stand it.

Juno kept roaring with hoarse laughter as I told my story, then groaned. "Oh, Christ, it hurts, but it's wonderful. Merry Glinka's little bum boy stripped and chained. It's fucking marvelous."

"Juno, he wasn't stripped."

"Oh, yes he was, that little twat was stripped of his dignity. Every time people look at him, they'll imagine him at the mercy of those students. Too bad it wasn't Glinka herself, then she'd have to resign. It would be too shameful to stay."

"Administrators have no shame."

"Well . . ."

"How are you feeling?" I wondered if she'd taken more pain-killers than prescribed.

"Glorious! One more story like yours, and I'll be dancing a jig." In the background I could hear Turandot barking, perhaps responding to Juno's excitement, but Juno's naked delight made me regret my own earlier enjoyment of Tyler's predicament. Weren't Juno and I both cruel? And shortsighted.

"This is going to piss off Glinka and her gang," I said. "And they'll want revenge."

"Balls! They can steam all they want, but they can't shit on minority students—it would look bad. They'll weasel out of it. You'll see."

"They'll want a fall guy, someone to blame."

"Yes, it's time for a human sacrifice—but perhaps it'll be someone in the provost's office, someone who should have known better."

"It'll be me."

"Never."

I felt drawn to talking to Juno longer, for many reasons, but right then the most seductive one was delay. I didn't want to open the envelope addressed to me because I was sure it had something unpleasant inside. Not the kind of virus terrorists might disperse on a subway train, but something almost as terrifying, and probably as lethal—for me, anyway. I told Juno I had to go, said I'd check in with her later, and hung up. I stared at the envelope, then ripped it open.

On EAR letterhead, and fully addressed to me as "Dear Dr. Hoffman" as if I were a stranger, Serena Fisch had sent a brief message: "I must speak with you immediately." It was signed,

"Cordially." I felt as chilled as a kid whose parents never use his full name when he hears it intoned from a distance, but I didn't loiter in my office trying to convince myself that I needed to reorganize everything in my file cabinet. Face the music, I thought, even if it was going to be a dirge or Chopin's Funeral March. I locked up and ascended to my doom.

But as I climbed the stairs I flashed back to that moment of exhilaration I'd felt outside Parker. Freedom. What was wrong with me? I wasn't remotely doomed. I'd been in an inferior position so long as an untenured assistant professor that it had completely warped my thinking. The worst that would probably happen to me is that I'd be threatened with dismissal, and I could counterthreaten a lawsuit and we could turn the thing into an endless Dickensian wrangle. Or, more satisfyingly, I could come up with the academic version of "Take this job and shove it."

An atmosphere of perfervid grief hung over the main office, with the secretaries seated at their desks in attitudes of barely concealed prostration. You might have thought there had been a national disaster, or that they were the women of Corinth dreading Medea's emergence from the home inside which she wailed about her betrayal by Jason and planned revenge. Clearly, I had underestimated what the tree meant; it was more important and more symbolic than I'd imagined.

"I'm here to see Serena," I announced.

Dulcie gave me a smoldering glare from her mask-of-tragedy face and motioned for me to walk around the counter and enter the inner EAR suite, where Serena had her office. The scarred oak door, which didn't quite fit its frame anymore since the building had settled so much, was closed. I knocked, and Serena told me to wait. Pettiness, or rage?

"Come in, Nick," she called after only half an eternity.

The previous EAR chair had kept this large office drastically bland and bare, so that might be why Serena had gone in the opposite direction. The chair's digs were now a kind of Pier One Casbah, the furniture draped with tasseled velveteen throws and pillows, the walls hidden behind deeply colored Pre-Raphaelite posters, the linoleum floor disguised by an Oriental-style rug, the paisley curtains as heavy as an SUM progress report, the lamps dimmed and softened with silk scarves. Though I couldn't see any potpourri pots, the room had a musky perfumed smell.

But Serena wasn't about to offer me a glass of tea or some Turkish coffee in a tiny copper cup. And her face wasn't just blank, it was cold and inhospitable. Charm wouldn't work on her, only an ice-breaking ship.

"How do you expect me to help you?" she said curtly, after nodding at a chair set well away from her desk, as if I were contagious. I sat down and put the briefcase at my feet, wishing it held a bomb, or at least a poisoned apple.

"Help?" Her question had completely thrown me a curve, even if it was meant to be rhetorical.

Serena breathed in deeply as if she were a dragon preparing to incinerate a knight. "Your tenure committee needs reformulation after last month's—" She struggled for a word to describe EAR's most recent craziness, then gave up. "And I'm the one who makes the appointments. Don't you consider that help?"

"I didn't realize that's what you meant."

"There are a lot of things you don't seem to realize. You can't associate with rowdy students and involve yourself in a campus takeover—"

"Whoa! What takeover? And they weren't rowdy, not at first, anyway. And I wasn't associated with anybody. I was on the way to my office."

She surveyed me with utter contempt, her overly made-up face clearly conveying her disappointment that I couldn't supply a better excuse. I studied her while trying not to stare. Serena still favored a Midwest Mikado look, lacquered black French twist and circles of blush on a pale, almost white foundation, but her stint as acting chair seemed to have alerted her to the fact that rising in the power structure might require some changes. She seemed ever so slightly uncomfortable behind the administrative hauteur and the layers of makeup, which made me think of the stories about Queen Elizabeth I dying with an inch of the stuff on her face, though in her day it was supposedly made with egg yolks.

"Serena, I always go to my office before classes." It was true, but perhaps because it was the truth, it sounded lame. Now Serena folded her hands like a cynical judge listening to a call girl explain what she was doing at 4 A.M. in hot pants at a scummy intersection. Yet I felt strangely aloof from the inquisition. I didn't need her—I didn't need EAR or SUM. "And how can you call it a takeover? They were just demonstrating here at Parker. Don't students have a right to free association?"

"They don't have a right to take hostages! They don't have a right to destroy Dulcie's tree, *our* tree, or tear apart Parker Hall—and that was just today."

Evidently Serena believed in some kind of academic domino theory: today Parker, tomorrow the entire campus would be swarming with vandals and Ohio State football fans ready to sack and burn.

"You're more concerned with that tree or a bit of stonework than with my getting beaten up, or Juno's accident, aren't you? Property over people."

Serena blithely ignored that. "This is a conspiracy to undermine SUM," she said.

"What?"

"And you're telling me that you had no connection with the demonstrators? None at all?"

"That's what I'm telling you, yes. Is somebody giving you a different story? Who?" I would say that her tightened lips looked like an asshole, but that would be a poor reflection on assholes.

"Then why were you there?"

"I told you already. Who's been lying about me? That crazy Avis? Tyler?" It couldn't be the bitter Malatestas, could it? I wasn't going to mention their names, though. I was sure they were in enough trouble.

"Nick, lower your voice. You're in no position to be a bully."

That was it. I stood up, and leaned onto her desk with my fists, and she drew back. One for me. "Serena, even a freshman psychology major would know that calling me a bully isn't just bullshit, it's projection. Try looking it up. And try intimidating somebody else." I grabbed my briefcase and left, not bothering with any of the niceties. She could help me, hinder me, or even fire me. I didn't care, though in typical *esprit de l'escalier*, I wished I'd used Jack Nicholson's line, "Sell crazy somewhere else."

Dulcie and the other secretaries raked me with their eyes as if I were King Kong and they were the airplanes, but their scorn seemed ludicrous. Unwilling to be driven off by their silent screaming, I deliberately slowed down to check my mail, then exited the EAR office feeling "blithe and bonny," as Shakespeare put it, while behind me was a scene of woe worthy of *Titus Andronicus*.

Happy and hungry, I strutted into the cavernous hallway and down the stairs as if I'd just bought Parker and had plans to tear it down. Even running into Valley in the parking lot didn't faze me.

"Wait a minute," he said, as I was setting my briefcase in the backseat of my car.

I turned and smiled. "What for?"

"I want to ask you some questions."

"Call my lawyer—call my accountant. Call anybody you like."

He peered at me as if wanting to smell my breath for alcohol. "Why are you always around when there's trouble? First the faculty reception turning wild, then Juno Dromgoole's accident, now all this: abusing a university official and destroying university property."

I slammed the back door. "That is a stupid question. I've got a question for *you*, and it's not stupid. Why are you always wasting my time? You think I'd want to start a student protest and handcuff some twit administrator to a door? To do what? To sabotage my career even further?"

"Maybe. Maybe you know you're going down in flames so you don't care anymore."

"Let me ask you something. Do you know who started the riot at the Campus Center? Do you know who attacked me? Have you found who slashed Juno's tires or crashed into her car? That wasn't an accident, and she wasn't just pushed at the reception—somebody shot at her, no matter what you think, and somebody's after both of us."

He didn't even touch the shooting question, just said, "Those investigations are ongoing."

"Those investigations are bullshit. You don't know squat, and you're not a real cop. A real cop would have found something out by now. Three crimes, and you don't know shit! A real cop wouldn't bother harassing me when he could be out doing police work."

Valley stood back as if I'd just challenged him to a fight in a bar, but instead of taking offense, he chuckled appreciatively. "I guess porking that babe is making a man out of you. Finally."

It was my turn to laugh. "Yeah, and maybe if you got porked, it would make a man out of you." In the time it took him to register exactly what I meant, I got in, started my car, and pulled away, not bothering to check his face in the rearview mirror. I didn't care if he was angry or shocked or anything. I'd had enough.

I drove home just dying to bitch out somebody else. It was clearly habit-forming. How long would it last? And was it more than just the shock of seeing the plummeting tree, then the sandstone chunk come down off the roof—both of which could have hit me?

Stefan was home, unpacking some groceries from the health food store: soy milk, flaxseed oil, cashew butter. Chet Baker was playing low on the portable CD player.

"Congratulate me!" I said, dropping my briefcase and tossing my coat onto a chair. "I'm going to get fired."

Stefan eyed me warily, waiting for the punch line.

"I'm not kidding. Serena tried to blame me for what happened to Tyler, or implicate me, anyway. So I told her to go fuck herself, and ditto Detective Valley."

"Why him?"

"Because he was nagging me in the parking lot, and I'm sick of it. He's useless. He's an idiot, and I'm his number-one suspect whenever anything happens on this campus. He probably thinks I beat myself up in the john. Shit, he probably thinks I'm behind global warming. He's been working my last nerve, and I just blew up."

"You told him to go fuck himself?"

"Well, basically. Not with those exact words." God, I hated temporizing! Why hadn't I used those exact words? "He got the message, so did Serena. They both knew what I meant. I'm going to get fired for sure."

"How do you know?" He folded up a recycled brown paper bag as neatly as if he were doing origami and slipped it into the appropriate drawer. I looked around the kitchen, wishing we hadn't spent so much money remodeling it: granite countertops, wine refrigerator, all new appliances, custom cabinetry. . . . We'd gone deliriously over budget, then had felt justified not simply by the picture-perfect results, but by the promise of Stefan's advance on the film deal. But who knew where I'd be working next, and when?

"Get me something to drink—no, I'll do it."

"It's the middle of the afternoon."

"Really? I didn't know that."

He frowned.

"Stefan, don't be prissy. You're too buffed to be prissy. I need to celebrate." And I needed to deal with everything else. I took the bottle of Stoli from the freezer, grabbed a shot glass, poured myself a shot, downed it, and sat at the counter with my liquid courage. Stefan sat on the other side of the counter, observing me. "Haven't we talked about leaving, giving this place up?"

"But that was talk. And I want to stay."

"Well, maybe I'm ready. Maybe I need to move on." He looked stricken, and I grabbed his hand. "Not from you, from *the* U."

He smiled weakly at my pun. "But how do you know for sure you're going to get fired?"

"Come on, Stefan. I talked to Juno, and there are rumors that make me sound like the Chicago Seven and Dr. Moriarty combined. Avis was there, and she hates me, and Tyler accused me of setting things up. Somebody's out to get me. Why wouldn't they fire me? It's moral turpitude or whatever they talk about in the faculty handbook as grounds for dismissal."

"You can't be fired because of rumors and a misunderstanding. We'll sue."

"Right, and use up your option money on legal bills in a few months—and then what?"

He took my glass and poured himself a shot, downed it as if he were G. Gordon Liddy holding his hand over that candle flame. "You sound like you *want* to be fired," he said. "I don't understand. You love teaching, you love your students."

"Of course I do, but it's wearing thin," I said, reaching for the bottle to pour myself another shot. "It's wearing pretty fucking thin. It costs too much. What's that line from that spiritual you like? 'I been 'buked and I been scorned.' Well, that's how I feel, and I'm tired of both. Sure, teaching here is better than being stuck in a civil war in Sudan or what have you, but so what? I'm tired of thinking of all the ways my life could be worse than it is. That's no consolation. I don't know if I want to be fired, but if I am, why fight it?"

I half expected Stefan to complain or even freak out, but wise, calm introvert that he is, he simply nodded and chose a different tack altogether.

"Well, it could be wonderful for you to be home. I'm not saying give up the cleaning lady and have you do the housework! I mean, you'd have more time to read, garden, swim, and"—he grinned—"have lunch with the girls."

"Stop it."

"Doesn't Sharon call it the Countess Tolstoy life? You could take long walks, think about deep issues."

"Stop."

"Okay, seriously? Maybe you need the time off. It would be too bad if you didn't get to teach that mystery class, but so it goes. You could do another bibliography or write a book about Wharton. You know more than anyone else about her. You've got to have a book in you somewhere. Or you could write a memoir, 'Confessions of a Bibliographer.' Or you could get a dog."

"You make it sound like retirement."

"Think of it as a long sabbatical until you figure out what to do next. So how about eggplant parmigiana tonight? And that Montevina barbera that's so good with tomato sauce?"

"Terrific. You're on. When do we start?"

"No. I'm cooking. I'm done with all my errands today, and you've had enough to deal with."

Stefan prepared the eggplant dish but didn't put it in the oven, so as to give us time for a salad of mushrooms, green beans, and Vidalia onions with cumin, parsley, and a Dijon/red wine vinaigrette. We had that while I filled him in on my talk with Juno, or at least her part of the conversation. This was so much of life, the reconnections, the reporting, going over what had just happened. Was that to make events more real, to keep them from slipping away? But they did, no matter how you tried to hold on. Wasn't there a Talking Heads song where David Byrne crooned about staying awake because his memories couldn't wait?

"It's on 'Fear of Music,'" Stefan reminded me.

14

G IVEN that the end of the semester was coming and students would have escalating, nervous questions about their final papers, I expected that my Thursday office hours would be crowded, but the noise I heard roiling from the basement as I entered Parker Hall made it sound like a hot new club had opened down there. And in fact the atmosphere was more partylike than apprehensive. Easily fifty students were encamped in the basement, lined up down the grim low-ceilinged hallway as if they were waiting to buy tickets to Smash Mouth or Shania Twain. There were a lot of kids I didn't recognize, and when I saw them, I assumed they were friends of my students who wanted to check me out, now that I was truly infamous.

As soon as I appeared, there was a wave of applause, whistling, and cheers. What could I do? I bowed gratefully and headed to my office while someone took off his headphones and momentarily blasted a Moby song that I was also hearing in TV ads now that techno was so hot, and a few students did some hot rave moves (without the lights, of course). It wasn't the theme from *Rocky*, but it would do just fine.

Perhaps because I felt onstage, I was more aware of how decrepit the basement was, almost as if I were that TV ad party host discovering spots on her glasses just before company came by. The basement floor dipped and rose noticeably under the cracked and blackened shabby linoleum. Given Parker's decay, that chunk of sandstone could easily have been dislodged by someone heaving the tree off the roof if the building was in such disrepair—it *could* have been an accident.

Students waved the student newspaper at me, but I resisted looking at a copy, just as I had not read the *Michiganapolis Tribune* that morning despite Stefan's chuckling at breakfast, and had refused to take any calls from local media the night before, not wanting to feel poisoned by rumors, distortions, and the grab-grab-grab of reporters.

Given my confrontations with Serena and Valley, I couldn't help feeling a sense of nostalgia in that crummy basement as I settled into my office, admiring the enormous pot of silk hydrangeas Sharon had bought me on her last visit to liven up the office. Where would I put them at home? This could well be my last semester working with students at SUM, and I felt a bit mawkish when I was able to help with transitions, illustrations, conclusions.

Almost everyone who had come to see me wanted an override to get into my mystery class next semester, for themselves or for someone else. I didn't have the heart to say I doubted I'd be around, so I just told everyone to check back with the department at the beginning of spring semester. I wasn't sure what the procedure was, anyway.

One of my students, Carter, who dressed in very preppy loafers, chinos, white T-shirt, and V-neck cashmere sweater, said, "You should go on TV, like to sell Mace or something. Or The Club."

I laughed. "I'm not well known enough."

"No way!"

"Way."

Another who was a Sinead O'Connor clone and double-majoring in journalism and criminal justice wondered if I was interested in being interviewed for her thesis on campus crime. "I could write you in somewhere, since you're so out there and everything."

I demurred.

She shook her bald head. "My parents ask me about you all the time, and they live in Cheboygan!"

Several students had screenplay ideas they either wanted my

feedback on or collaboration with; in each case the story involved a serial killer.

As I met with more and more students, many of whom had as much stargazing on their minds as questions about their work, the party atmosphere intensified out in the hallway. I could smell Domino's pizza and Kentucky Fried Chicken (both places were right across Michigan Avenue from Parker). And students shared various food items with me over the course of my meetings, since I had forgotten to bring a lunch.

After an hour and a half, there was a sudden shout in the hallway of "Qui-et!"

Byron Summerscale, Captain of the Stentorian Guard.

"This is a hall of learning, not a bar and grill!" His words resonated in the cavernous silence. Then he appeared at my open door with giggles foaming up in his wake, looking as large and hearty as some Norse sea god.

"Nicky! I'm proud of you! I need you in my administration! A man of courage! A man of conviction! A man who speaks truth to power."

Byron flung his arms wide and waved them as if he were hoping to leave the ground. His tone was as wildly confident as if he'd already won the EAR election, which hadn't even taken place yet; department bylaws required the campaigning to occur over breaks so as not to pollute the supposedly unpolitical semesters. But worse than the timing was Byron's self-congratulation, because his praise of me was really directed at himself.

The academic mind is a terrible thing to taste.

My poor student cowered in her chair. Michiko was a shy and elfin Japanese exchange student (with fashionably dyed red hair) who must have thought the statuesque Summerscale was both hideously rude and essentially crazy.

"Byron, I'm no biblical prophet."

"Ah, but prophets are never recognized in their own land," he intoned with satisfaction, as if checkmating me.

I didn't bother arguing with his misquotation, just smiled, and he headed off to his supply-closet office, having delivered his verdict. My student went on with her questions as if Typhoon Byron had never ravaged our little isle, and I welcomed her tact. As the song almost goes, How do you handle a problem like Summerscale? Perhaps silence was the best solution.

I was equal parts exhausted and exhilarated when my three office hours were done, as if I'd drunk far more coffee than I really had, and it was starting to make me flicker on and off. Perhaps the true cause was all the misplaced admiration from my students. It was one thing to be thought well of for my teaching, for my assistance in helping them find their voices and craft their thoughts, but being admired for my ersatz celebrity seemed disturbing and very personal proof of how our culture was becoming ever more shallow and media-centered. Some students had even suggested I run for state office, under the misapprehension that I was some kind of Rudy Giuliani-type crime buster!

I was packing up to go home as the phone rang. When Juno said hello, I felt vaguely guilty for not having thought about her during the previous few hours, but then realized it was healthy to have been focused on anything but her troubles, and mine.

"Nick, I'm feeling marginally better."

"That's good."

"Could you come by?"

I was tired, but since her home was only five or so minutes away, I didn't see any point in saying no. Still, I did wonder if this demand for attention was going to become oppressive. Then I felt ashamed of my own reaction. Juno had been crashed into by some stalker, and I was being parsimonious with my time? What the hell was wrong with me? Was I nervous about being around her so much, or was I wishing she had been more concerned with my having been beaten up? Here I'd been slamming Summerscale for his egotism, but wasn't I just as guilty?

I thought of a line from one of Linda Pastan's poems about being tired of my own insistent griping, like a mouse running up and down a keyboard.

"Nick! Are you still there?"

"Sorry, I've been seeing students for hours, but sure, I can come over. And you said you were feeling a little better?"

"Somewhat. I'm angry, and I'm disgusted—and sore as hell—but I'm better."

Well, that was certainly an invitation, now, wasn't it?

As I left Parker, I imagined what it would be like to walk out of there and not be returning, carrying, say, a last pathetic box of books and Sharon's wildly colorful silk flowers. Would I cry? Dance? Throw my hat in the air like Mary Tyler Moore? I'd have to get a hat, first, and that might take forever, since there wasn't a hat in existence that didn't make me look depraved.

Driving to Juno's in the traffic that was already heavy for Michiganapolis because of all the Christmas-season shoppers, I thought about how much time I was spending with Juno, how our lives had become entangled. Would it continue, and would Stefan begin to be jealous, even though nothing had happened outside my dreams?

Then I recalled Edith Wharton being overwhelmed by the illnesses of two of her most intimate friends, Henry James and Walter Berry. My parents were in good health, and I hadn't lost anyone really close to AIDS, so being any kind of caregiver was still new to me, and maybe that accounted for my twinge of reluctance when Juno had called. Still, her condition was minor compared to Sharon's and sure to improve more quickly, and it was premature to be worrying about having her on my hands, so to speak.

Juno met me at her door dressed in the kind of hostess gown I had never seen anywhere except on reruns of 1950s TV shows. It was black and lacy, with a very pointed leopard-print collar. As I stepped in and she closed the door, she did a slightly shaky Loretta Young twirl, and I applauded her style and her nerve.

"I know," she said. "It's so outré it's postmodern. I found it in San Diego at a thrift shop and couldn't resist. I put it on—"

"—instead of whistling a happy tune?"

"Yes. Besides, I wouldn't waste my lips on whistling. They do other things much better."

I didn't ask what those were, and Juno led me to the kitchen, where Turandot was sound asleep in a small wicker dog basket, though one of her ears twitched at my approach.

"Coffee? Tea?" Juno was doing her best to act normal (for her, that is), but I could sense the desperation and fatigue behind her Potemkin Village sociability.

"I'm floating in caffeine as it is. You sit down, and I'll just get myself some water."

"Fine." She settled wincingly into a chair, arranging the cantankerous folds of her outfit with slight annoyance. She was probably wishing she'd opted for a simple robe at that point. "Tell me about your day." Juno had only missed one day of classes, but she sounded starved for reports from the teaching front. I dutifully gave her a picture of my office hours, complete with menu, music, and interruption by Summerscale, though eruption was closer to the truth.

"No offense to dogs, but the man's barking mad. Unless it's all an act and he's really the evil genius behind Glinka and all the other stinkers on campus."

"Glinka and the Stinkas. It has possibilities."

"Could he be very canny and putting it on?"

"Sure, why not? Anything is possible. But my guess is that he's as loony and self-obsessed and bursting with grievances as he seems."

"Well, I'm glad to hear that. You obviously won't be supporting him for chair." Juno raised her eyebrows, but the gesture seemed to almost pain her. She checked her watch. "Not time yet," she muttered. For the next painkiller, I assumed.

"Of course I wouldn't support him for chair, or anything else."

"Despite his offer of a position in his—what did he call it?—his administration? Is he planning to issue postage stamps and currency with his portrait? Will there be an anthem?" She grimaced, and in the growing silence between us there loomed the question of Juno vs. Serena and which of them I would choose after the brief campaign that would run during break. I wondered if Juno, having tried to bully me, would try to sway me by milking her accident, but before either of us could say a word, Turandot burst into a wild crescendo of barking and rocketed to the front door. I followed quickly and looked through the peephole, but I couldn't see anyone. Yet Turandot had gone berserk, whining, spinning, clawing at the door as if ready to tear it apart, scoring it with her nails.

Juno hobbled up, trying to silence or at least comfort her dog, but Turandot's frenzy of barking didn't stop.

"Should I open the door and see—"

Juno nodded, and asked me to hand Turandot to her. It wasn't easy. The puppy wriggled and squirmed and tried rolling over to slide out of my arms, but I held on and Juno took her. In Juno's arms, she calmed down a fraction but now started snarling at the door as if it were a beast.

I don't know who or what I expected, but I gingerly turned the handle and pulled the door open just a crack. A suffocating stench hit me like a small sonic boom. On Juno's doorstep lay the car-squashed brown-and-red remains of a raccoon, flattened but still juicy and reeking as heavily as if all the filth from a Dumpster that had been left unemptied for weeks were concentrated in its ruined little body.

I slammed the door as if the corpse might spring up at me and jerked my hand from the doorknob. I was afraid to breathe.

Warily, stepping back with the struggling dog in her arms, Juno asked, "What was that horrible, horrible smell?"

"Roadkill. At the door."

"Oh, God!" Clasping her hands to her face, she dropped Turandot, who yelped and cringed at the unexpected fall. Juno painfully got to her knees to comfort the poor dog, but it ran off to the bedroom.

"Roadkill?"

I nodded. "A raccoon." I felt as grossed out as if I had run over the thing myself.

"Horrible," Juno repeated, and that word made me think of Hamlet's response to the ghost of his father relating how he'd been killed. "Did you see anyone? Or a car?"

"No." Did I look? I was too stunned. "Do we clean it up now—or wait?"

"Wait for what—till the snow starts to fall and it freezes?"

Juno shook herself as if she'd been splashed by something filthy. We did not let our eyes meet. This was as obvious a message as anyone could ask for. Juno hadn't been flattened by the black SUV, but she could have been. She could still be. There was time. There was lots of time.

"I meant, it's evidence, so maybe we shouldn't—" I was going to say "shouldn't touch it," but couldn't get the words out because the image was so revolting.

"Whoever's doing this to me is sick," Juno said, head high, back straight, looking suddenly strong and dangerous despite her outrageous dress. "And I know the cure. A couple of lead aspirin."

I didn't tell her she was overreacting. I nodded.

"Doing this to *us*, I should say." Juno found a seat on the couch and wearily leaned back into the soft cushions as if settling into a bubble bath. "I've been so furious I've forgotten to ask how you are. Your bruise doesn't look so bad."

I sat opposite her and thanked her warily. I remembered a scene years ago on *Bosom Buddies* where a very unflappable woman in a surprising emotional exchange said something like, "I've heard about these moments. How long do they last?" But I needn't have been cynical, because Juno's attention didn't drift off; she was waiting for me to answer the question.

"Well, physically, I'm okay. Some twinges." I shrugged.

"Are you embarrassed to talk about it? Gay man getting beaten up? Has it happened to you before—back in school?"

It was a very perceptive question, but not quite on target. "Not to me, no. In junior high, there was a guy named George that everyone called 'fagfoe'—don't ask me why—and they used to shove him around in the halls, put squashed Ring Dings in his bookbag —nothing like what happens now with hazing and shoot-outs, but it was pretty bad for back then. He got roughed up in the locker room after gym class once. I was paralyzed. I just stared at it, as if it were happening a million miles away. I could have done something—they would have listened to me because I was the class comedian. But I didn't. I was too ashamed for him—he was such a wuss. Skinny, runty, toothpick arms and legs. I don't even think he was gay, they just picked on him because he was so weak."

"I hate bullies," Juno said. "Maybe that's why I'm so loud—it's to sound the alarm."

Juno had spoken intimately about herself before, yet this seemed more personal than anything she'd revealed so far. "But nobody else seems to care around here. There's a culture of cowardice."

I knew exactly what she meant. Cover up, avoid conflict, protect your turf, take no risks. You could describe SUM in Shakespearean terms as "ruthless, dreadful, deaf and dull."

"We have to call the police," I repeated.

"*Again?*"

"Of course. It's got to be reported. There has to be a record." I didn't add, "In case it gets worse." I rose. "The Michiganapolis police and campus police. You can handle that, can't you?"

She agreed. "Going home?"

"No, I'm going back to the gun shop to talk to Mrs. Fennebresque. Maybe I was wrong to think about getting a .22. I may want something bigger. It's time."

"Don't get mad, don't get even—get a gun, eh?"

"Exactly."

"You won't mind if I stay seated, will you? I need the rest."

"No problem." But as I reached the front door, I hesitated, picturing the disgusting mess outside.

"Just breathe through your mouth," Juno called, "and keep clear." Good advice, but as I awkwardly stepped around the roadkill, trying both to avoid looking at it lest I throw up and needing to at least keep it in my peripheral vision, I wondered if I should have taken another route out of the house, to avoid any chance of tampering with the "evidence."

As I started my car, still shuddering, I looked up and down the street to make sure there were no obvious threats. Then I pictured the raccoon being dusted for fingerprints by Detective Valley, and I started to laugh. I hoped Juno wasn't studying me from a window, because I must have seemed totally unhinged.

But laughter wasn't enough, and I decided to drop by the gym for a quick workout, since it probably wouldn't be too crowded. In fact, the parking lot was more than half empty, with far less than its usual amount of SUVs, though the dozen or so black ones seemed more visible to me. I briefly considered inspecting all of them for damage, but it would have been too obvious with people leaving and entering The Club. Someone might mistake me for a car thief or another kind of miscreant.

I grabbed my gym bag and hurried inside. The echoing hallways and locker room were almost empty right now, and even though it was nice to have the place virtually to myself, it was all slightly creepy despite the neon lighting, or maybe because of it. The semicircle of blue-gray armchairs facing a widescreen TV tuned to CNN was unoccupied by the usual retirees, and there was no one behind the counter where the towels were stacked. Good place for a murder, I thought, glancing around the locker room, which was also free of the clang of doors closing and men kibbitzing about their workouts or local real estate deals.

I wished then that I had Stefan's creative talent. I loved mysteries, had read them for years, and now had been studying them intensely, but knew that despite the ideas that came to me intermittently, I didn't have the vision to write a book. Could we write one together? We edited each other's work, but editing wasn't very creative, was it? I could imagine Stefan's jibe, "Sure, what kind of sleuth would we have? An alcoholic divorced ex-cop wisecracking bibliographer?" I would counter that we should bring Sharon into the mix and do a sort of high-fashion *Charlie's Angels* thriller. They both would laugh.

I started to change quickly but slowed down from habit when I saw a redheaded young man walk from the showers to one of the mirrors nearby, pick up the clunky black blowdryer, and start working on his hair. But he was posing for himself as much as anything else—shifting his position, putting weight first on one leg, then the other. Oblivious to anything more than his reflection, he was certainly worth looking at: totally hairless (with shaved pubes), his flawless skin creamy, his body not ripped but taut, with the rounded muscles of a gymnast who's had some time off, and large surprisingly dark nipples.

As he finished drying his short curly hair, he padded off, looking just like the Who album: meaty, beaty, big, and bouncy. I shook my head to clear the vision of his macho stride and then smiled, thinking of the fun I'd have describing him to Sharon, who still liked hearing about cute men at the gym. If that was so, I didn't mind, and feeling invigorated by imagining my next chat with Sharon, I headed upstairs to one of the cardio rooms jammed with rowing machines, stair climbers and the like, which was empty. I ran on a treadmill for fifteen minutes and worked up a good sweat, my mind filled equally with visions of the redheaded guy and Juno. I wondered what she would look like nude, blow-drying her Tina Turner hair. Would she need one in each hand; would she do it upside down wearing grav boots? Now that was kinky.

I moved downstairs to one of the smaller mirrored weight rooms to do chest work and shoulder work, which I knew would leave me well pumped. Swimming would have done the same thing, but I needed to feel the resistance of something heavy, something holding me back that I could conquer. Swimming was too contemplative for my mood that afternoon, though the pool would have been more pleasant; the weight room I picked seemed a bit ghostly with its idle weight machines and ranks of dumbbells. But I started putting together a quick workout anyway. I sat on the pec deck and pyramided up a plate with each set, enjoying the sight in the mirror opposite of my insertions as I did each rep slowly.

I had moved on to some seated shoulder presses with forty-pound dumbbells when I heard a voice so close to me I almost dropped one of the weights.

"You think it'll make a difference?" Rusty Dominguez–St. John loomed up behind my bench, wearing black shorts and a tank top that made his tan seem even deeper. Without street clothes, he had a runner's body, but he was as hairy as an Airedale and smelled a little rank.

I'd been squinting because I was concentrating so hard on my form and hadn't noticed anyone come in. Now I set the weights down carefully and met his eyes in the mirror.

"What are you talking about?"

"Working out, trying to get tough. You think it'll change any-thing?"

"What are you trying to say?"

"You can work out forever, lift all you want, but you still won't be a real man."

"And you are? You're a real man? What the hell are you doing sneaking up on me anyway? Have you been following me?"

"In your dreams, bud." He leaned forward, sneering. "I bet that's how you like it, isn't it—someone up behind you? Grabbing you—doing it rough?"

I should have had a snappy comeback, but I was too astonished by his erotic malevolence. What had I ever done to bother him? And why hadn't I gone into red alert as soon as I'd seen him and diverted all power to my shields?

Rusty strode around the bench, reached down, and snagged my set of forties even though there was another set on the rack. He stood close to the mirror, locked his shoulders, bent his knees a little, stuck his butt out in the perfect athletic posture Stefan had showed me, and started to do by-the-book curls. The veins popped on his long thick biceps.

I recovered my poise somewhat. "Is that supposed to intimidate me?"

He grinned through his slow reps. "You think that hanging around Juno, something's going to rub off?" he asked, showing off that he could talk without distortion even while working really hard.

"She doesn't seem to have rubbed off on you any." It wasn't much of a retort, but I meant it, so I had sincerity on my side if not eloquence.

"What the fuck do you know about me and her?" He sounded rougher, less urbane than usual, no longer the slick media personality but just a thug. "You don't know shit about us."

I'd touched a nerve somehow, but had no idea what it was. "Maybe, maybe not." I tried for my best poker face, but he wasn't playing.

"Everyone in EAR is laughing at you," he said, as unctuous as ever.

"It wouldn't be the first time," I said.

"They are. You're pathetic."

"Are you jealous of me and Juno?" It wasn't a dig—I really

wanted to know what his deal was, and was more curious now than offended.

Rusty had switched to doing hammer curls with his hands held thumbs up, then he stopped, turning to me from the mirror. For a wild moment I thought he might heave a dumbbell at me, but he simply squatted and put them down near my bench.

"You should be careful in The Club," he said. "You could drop a weight on yourself, or slip in the showers. It's easy to get hurt." He ambled off in his typical "I'm ready for my close-up" way.

"It's a lot easier being an asshole," I said to his departing back, loud enough for him—and anyone else who might be lurking—to hear my rejoinder. Of course, I realized someone overhearing us might have thought I was referring to myself.

I didn't go on for a moment, wishing I had been able to face him down, but all I could do was sass my chair and Detective Valley. Rusty seemed more threatening and unpredictable.

I did not want to run into Rusty in the showers, so I added some more sets and was exhausted when I left, though not a whole lot calmer, given our exchange. Showering, I tried not to peg him as the obvious suspect, but it was hard not to. He had a criminal past, was married to Juno even though they were separated, owned a black SUV, and didn't like me at all. He was definitely strong enough to have gone for me at Parker Hall in the bathroom, so if he wasn't harassing and stalking me and Juno, who was?

Mrs. Fennebresque was glad to see me, but she refused to show me any .38s or .45s until I sat down on the stool she brought out from behind the counter and drank a cup of tea.

"Verbena," she said, as I sipped appreciatively. "It has a relaxing effect."

"I'm not relaxed?"

She shook her head daintily. "Now, why don't you tell me about it?" she said in her best nurse-will-calm-you-down voice. If it had been Stefan talking to me like that I would have exploded at the condescension. But Mrs. Fennebresque had age on her side, and the fact that she was a stranger. So, as the Anglo-Saxon poet says, I opened my word hoard and spilled out my narrative. She held her chin in one palm, leaning forward like one of those corny author photos, making *ts-ts-ts* noises at the appropriate points. It all began to sound almost funny, and Mrs. Fennebresque, in her antique-looking garnet jewelry and pink dress splashed with yellow tea roses, seemed like a host of a garden party more than a gun retailer.

"Why did you want to know all that?" I concluded.

"To slow you down, of course. To relax you."

I wasn't sure reviewing the last few days of hugger-mugger was exactly a restorative. "Because you wouldn't sell me a gun otherwise?"

"Of course I'll sell you a gun, but do you think you can walk into a police station as agitated as you are and *register* a gun? You have to go through the registration process first, remember? You'd never make it. They'd pretend there were delays, computer problems, anything to keep you unarmed and undefended. Why, they'd think you were a danger—to yourself at least, if not to others."

Ah, but wasn't that exactly what I wanted to be? Dangerous?

15

THE northern precinct of the Michiganapolis Police Department looked very much like a small branch campus of a hip university. The cluster of five low redwood-sided buildings facing each other around a circle of lawn was set in what looked like several acres of park filled with fairly young evergreens and deciduous trees and lined with beds that had been flowering with purple and orange mums. Connected by winding concrete paths bordered with glazed red brick, the buildings were very appealing and secretive at the same time, mixing warm colors with small windows and deep overhangs.

Under an enormous flagpole that flew the U.S. and Michigan flags, one sign pointed to the Fire Department, another to Service, whatever that meant, and the next to Police. I didn't drive far enough to see who or what was housed in the other buildings, just followed the driveway to the public parking lot. It was set well away from the core of the mini-campus, separated from it by a low, man-made-looking hill, as if to protect against assault. Given the middle- and upper-middle-class neighborhood, I couldn't imagine a reason for upscale rageful crowds hurling Molotov cocktail shakers and exploding cigars. But Michiganapolis did have a long history of sports-related violence, whether SUM teams lost or won, so I suppose the landscaping was a useful precaution.

The lot was uncrowded, and I parked right by a walkway. Getting out of the car, I felt suddenly conspicuous and wondered if there were surveillance cameras monitoring me. It was the vague unease I had always experienced around anything connected to the police. When I was little, along with making me memorize my address and phone number, my parents had adjured me to find the nearest policeman, but the idea of confiding in one of those ominous-looking blue monoliths had seemed more terrifying than the idea of being lost itself.

The residuum of that fear survived and whirled up inside me now as if in some Kafka knockoff I was about to be accused of crimes I didn't know I'd committed. I tried walking from my car as if I had nothing to hide, but then slowed down. If I was being observed, I didn't want to appear cocky or overeager.

The entrance was framed in more of those glazed bricks, but despite the four panels of glass, there was only one door, and when I entered, I was surprised to find myself in just a ten-by-twenty lobby with a bare handful of chairs. Though spotless and obviously new, it looked like a not very imaginatively decorated minor-league bank: shiny and dull, not at all as interesting as the colorful police stations of *Hill Street Blues* or *Silk Stalkings*.

"Can I help you?"

From behind the long security window opposite the door, a slim light-skinned black woman in Michiganapolis's blue police uniform was watching me, her face half past neutral.

"I want to find out about registering a gun?"

There, I'd said it. There weren't any alarm bells, the floor didn't slide open underneath my feet and send me hurtling into a pit of crocodiles or down a James Bond-type roller-coaster shaft.

"Sure." She waved me over. "Is this a gun you own?"

"No, I don't have one yet." I stopped myself from saying more. She did not need to know the story of my life or even the kind of day I'd been having lately.

"Can I have your driver's license." It was not a question.

I fumbled with my wallet, produced the license without too much confusion, and slid it through the kind of small grille you see in pawnshops in dangerous neighborhoods. She checked the license carefully, matching it with my face. "Is this your permanent address?"

I nodded, even though who knew where I'd be living next year; as Oscar Wilde said, this was "not the time for German skepticism." She clipped it to a board, handed me a pamphlet to read, and disappeared behind a high partition. Looking around, I could make out several cameras monitoring the lobby both on my side and on hers. I stole curious glances at the fact sheets pinned to a corkboard for her consultation but couldn't make out exactly what they were about. Mindful of the cameras, I took the pamphlet over to a chair. It was an official publication about gun safety, and as I read through it, I realized it was almost identical to pamphlets I'd gotten from Mrs. Fennebresque, covering safety alone and in crowds, proper targets, gun cleaning, storage, and transportation. But for all the familiarity, my pulse increased so much I could feel veins throbbing in my throat.

"Relax," I thought, imagining Sharon there by my side. It worked, and I was able to focus.

In the next few minutes, the phone rang just once; someone out of sight must have picked it up, because it stopped. The quiet was so intense and the lobby so neutral it could have been a front for some kind of illegal business. The calm seemed as artificial as air spray covering some nasty stench. Was this an afternoon lull? It couldn't always be quiet here, could it? Or maybe it was, and the other precincts saw more action.

"Okay," the officer said when she returned, and motioned me back to the window. She passed my license back to me through the grille. "The pamphlet?" I returned it to her, embarrassed, not having known it wasn't for me to keep.

"Here's a quiz," she said, handing me a white sheet half the size of a notebook page.

Trying not to show my surprise, I took the form back to my chair. I hadn't expected to be quizzed right then and there; I thought the pamphlet was for me to study at home. Was this what Mrs. Fennebresque had said would happen? If not, had the procedure changed?

Fifteen true or false questions covered the identical material I had just read. This was how they checked people's gun safety knowledge? It seemed more like a test of short-term memory, but I thought it wise to keep my opinion to myself.

But as I read the questions, I found them phrased so circuitously that each one felt like a trap. Trying not to grade the person who'd composed these questions, I reread them all as attentively as if I were taking the GRE and my college career depended on it. Despite the subject, and despite having been out of college myself for decades, I was plunged into the disorienting remembrance of tests past: worried that easy ones were really hard, and whether I was being careful enough, and all that other crap that seems to haunt anyone emerging from America's educational swamp.

I brought it back, and she checked the answers on her computer screen. "All right." She didn't congratulate me. "Now, I'm required to ask you these questions." She reached for a pale blue sheet of paper and a pen. "Do you have any criminal convictions?"

"No." I hoped it didn't sound arrogant.

She marked my answer. "Are you the subject of any restraining orders?"

"No."

"Okay, call Records here in five days."

"And then what?"

"We issue you the permit—"

"—I buy the gun and bring it back here to register?"

"That's right."

When I left, I didn't feel like a pariah, I felt liberated. It was as if I'd had psychic liposuction, and my troubles weighed a great deal less. It all seemed so easy. Unless I was a split personality and had committed crimes while thinking I was someone else, I would have a gun in less than a week. I could hear Stefan saying, "No wonder there are so many nuts with guns out there."

Stefan walked down the hall into the kitchen. "I had a very weird day."

"Couldn't be weirder than mine."

"Why?" He set down his briefcase and headed for the coffeepot.

"I went to find out about applying for a gun permit, and they gave me a quiz right there. It's in motion." I gave him a précis.

Stefan nodded. "I guess there's no turning back now."

"I haven't bought a gun yet."

"But you're going to."

"Are you saying you changed your mind?"

"No, I'm just tired. We've had too much happen to us—life has been too crazed. A gun makes it seem even more out of control, that's all."

"I can see that. Maybe once I get the permit, I won't want a gun." I knew that was unlikely, but felt I had to say it to ease Stefan's mind a little.

"So that's it? About the permit? Because unless there's something else, like you were arrested, or deputized as a member of a posse, I have you beat, I think." He settled at the counter and held the cup up to his mouth, blew into it a little to cool it. "Peter de Jonge told me his story."

"He already told you his story. He's Jewish. His parents were ssurvivors."

"No, it's much bigger than that. They were the only ones in both families that weren't found and murdered in the camps. His parents were hidden, and once they left Holland, they stayed hidden. They never told anyone here they were Jewish."

"Oh, my God, like your parents."

"Yes. He's kept it secret, too."

"Did they raise him Catholic? No, they were Dutch—so what is that, Lutheran?"

"They raised him *afraid*. Everything was secret, where they came from, who their family was. Everything."

"I guess with a name like de Jonge, it wasn't obvious. Wow. So that's why he's drawn to your fiction. Maybe that's why he really came up here to take some graduate courses."

"I don't know. There's something else he's not telling me."

"What? What else could there be? Something about the Holocaust?" Most people lionize the Dutch, thinking of them during the war in terms of Anne Frank. But they forget that she and her family were not only hidden, they were betrayed. The death toll for Dutch Jews was very high, and most of the survivors returned to their homes, often living in the same streets as those who had sold them out to the Nazis. Was Peter perhaps on the trail of someone who had betrayed or even murdered members of his family? "Have you suggested he might want to see a counselor?"

"He is a counselor. That's what he does at Neptune College."

"That doesn't exempt him from needing help."

"He's troubled, but he's not disturbed. There's a difference."

"I guess. So his degree must be in psychology or something if he's a counselor. Then why's he interested in American studies and SUM's hate archives?"

Stefan shrugged, and drank some coffee, and murmured his approval. I'd made it very strong.

I asked, "What if he's the one who's been after Juno and me?"

Stefan grimaced. "Peter? What the hell for?"

"Well, he's got something to hide. You feel it, and I've seen it."

"But he's trying to connect with me, and he's even said he'd want me for his adviser if he enters the graduate program."

"That could all be a cover. And if he's after me, getting to know you might be the best approach."

"But why would he be harassing you?"

"After how he grew up, after what happened to his parents, he could be completely fucked up. It wouldn't have to make rational sense." I mused a little. "Like, he could resent you because you've made a career for yourself and you're successful, and he's just a counselor at some backwater college."

"Neptune is one of the best-endowed small conservative colleges in the Midwest. In the country."

"Come on—how long a list is that?"

"Okay, it's possible, but I didn't turn out fucked up."

"You were lucky. You met that girl in college, and you met me. Without the two of us, you might have ended up anything. God, even a Log Cabin Republican! I know Peter's unlikely, but sometimes the unlikeliest person in a mystery is the one who did it."

"I thought you said it was sometimes the person who *couldn't* have done it."

"That depends on the plot."

✦

Juno called me a little while later when I was trying to grade some papers. "How about computer databases?" she said, as if we had been discussing this just minutes before and had been interrupted by a bad connection.

"What are you talking about?"

"Well, I've been wondering, can't we track black SUVs in mid-Michigan that way?"

I lowered my voice because the study door was open. "We're private citizens. How can we get access to that kind of stuff? I can't just do what they do in mysteries and call around to some friends who owe me favors. It doesn't work like that in real life. And even if it did, can you imagine how many black SUVs there are on the road in this city, let alone the whole county?"

"But can't you mount surveillance?" Juno asked.

"I'm just one guy, Juno. I could trail after Rusty or Avis or whoever, but so what? Sooner or later they'd notice. I have no training, and this isn't Toronto or a real city where it's easy to blend in, this is just Michiganapolis. How could I be inconspicuous?"

"Why are you being so negative? You think it's fine for you to get beaten up and me to be sent to the emergency room and then all we do is sit around with our thumbs up our asses while the police are as ineffective as a slobbering blind old collie trying to chase squirrels? You're starting to sound as serious as Stefan."

I didn't like that jab at him. "You'd be serious, too, if the Nazis had put your parents in concentration camps."

It was a cheap shot, but she deserved one right then. It shamed Juno as I knew it would, because she sounded profoundly apologetic. "Were they? Oh, God, I'm so very sorry—"

I let her struggle to find something to say, but she recovered.

"I don't like being helpless," Juno said briskly, and I wondered where she was going. "I want to know who's been after us, and I want *revenge*."

"I just want it to stop," I said—but hadn't I been thinking of revenge, too?

"It amounts to the same thing. Enough temporizing. I have a plan. A little while ago I sent you an e-mail that I know who was driving the SUV, and that I'm going to the police tomorrow morning to lay it all out."

"What?"

Juno cackled. "And I said I'd gone to a hypnotist who put me under and helped me remember all the details of the accident."

"You're making this up."

"Of course I am! I didn't send you the mail. I posted the message to the EAR listserv. 'By mistake.' Then I sent another e-mail apologizing for posting personal mail to the whole department." Things like that happened all the time with our keyboard-happy faculty.

"But why would anyone believe you'd wait?"

"I said in the phony e-mail that I was feeling too woozy and weak from the painkillers to go today or even call. Who would doubt that? Nick, I'm sure someone will be alarmed and want to stop me—I'm bound to have a visitor tonight."

"And you're not afraid?"

"I have a Glock. Remember? When are you coming to join me? I'll need a witness."

Fool that I was, I felt excited by the reckless little plan Juno had cooked up. At least we were doing something, taking action, not passively waiting for the next incident or attack, or for what seemed less likely—the Michiganapolis or campus police to find the culprit. But I wished I had applied for my gun permit sooner, visited Mrs. Fennebresque's gun shop sooner. I wanted to be armed for the coming evening, which I was sure would bear some very strange fruit, but it had to be too soon to call Records. Even though there was no way they'd find out anything about me in a background check that would bar me from owning a gun, if I called this soon, it might get someone thinking I was too eager, and possibly a threat.

Of course I shared nothing about Juno's scheme with Stefan, who would try vetoing the plan, if he didn't have me committed. We ate dinner and watched the news while I calculated what lie would be the easiest to tell. I was relieved when Stefan said he had plans to meet Peter de Jonge for coffee in town, and waited until he was gone a full ten minutes to call Juno and tell her that I was on my way. I left Stefan a note that I'd gone out shopping for some jeans. It wasn't just a lame excuse, it was paraplegic, but I couldn't come up with anything better.

It was after dark when I parked down the street from Juno's house, and she was very keyed up, though she looked elegant in a black velvet warmup suit with a leopard-print headband keeping her wild hair down. As she pulled me inside and slammed the door, her sweet perfume enveloping me, she said, "Can you stay the night?"

"What?" I looked down at her right hand, which held what I assumed was a Glock. It looked larger and more ominous than semiautomatics did in movies, perhaps because I was closer, and perhaps because it wasn't the typical accessory I associated with Juno. The barrel wasn't leopard print, just plain black steel.

"Whoever it is may not make a move until it's very late." We headed into the living room, and I sat on the couch. I decided to deal with the possibility of staying overnight only if it was necessary, but I did have to say, "Juno, are you sure you know what you're doing?"

She put her hands on her hips and looked down her nose at me. "It's a bit late to bring that up, isn't it?"

I nodded reluctantly.

"People think that hypnosis is magic, so whoever's responsible will be terrified and come after me. It's got to work."

"Why wouldn't he—or she—get out of town instead?"

"Really, why are you asking all these fucking questions now?"

"But if it *were* you, wouldn't you just run away?"

"No, because it would make me look guilty. And besides, we're not talking about a bank robbery or murder, it's not that serious."

"It felt serious to me, being beaten up. And you thought having your car smashed was serious."

"Yes, yes, yes, I know all that!" Juno stalked back and forth in front of the couch, and I almost felt we were some couple whose relationship—or marriage—was disintegrating for reasons neither of us completely understood. This anger and frustration felt unfocused, and that much stronger because of its fuzziness. I think an outside observer would have concluded that Juno wasn't playing with a full deck, and that I didn't even know what the game was anymore, if I ever did.

I was starting to feel like I was back in grade school, swayed by a more popular and commanding student to steal candy from a store. Back then my parents had tried to warn me that I was too impressionable and shouldn't follow other kids just because they were magnetic, and I thought I'd learned to avoid that. Apparently not; this was the result. I was in the living room of an armed and slightly hysterical sex bomb, hoping to trap a criminal and suddenly, profoundly distracted from our mission.

As she ranted, I stared at her body in the clinging velvet, imagining peeling it off and sinking down, down, into her flesh. I might have been naive, but I imagined that with Juno we would go almost right to it, that anything other than intercourse would only be a detour. Sex with Stefan, and with the men before him, had never been that predictable or direct. Many things could happen, and did, since nothing was preordained like the basic linkage of a man and a woman. Sex with a woman could be inventive, I thought; with a man, wasn't it that and invention as well?

So, was that what I wanted, then? A simple fuck? Not so simple, though.

"Hey, where's Turandot?"

"She's being groomed and staying there overnight. I wanted to make sure she was safe."

"Good move. Let's check the doors." Juno and I surveyed the house. There was no back door, just the door from the kitchen into the garage, the sliding doors from the living room, and the front door. All of them were secure, so I didn't think we could be easily surprised, but I regretted not being able to set up any booby traps.

Suddenly she seemed uncertain. "Should we turn down the lights?"

We did, and sat in the dim living room waiting. For what, exactly? An armed assault? Scrabbling at the chimney? I was starting to feel almost hysterical myself, so when Juno suggested gin and tonics, I said yes. To my relief, she carried the gun with her into the kitchen. Even though I knew drinking and guns didn't mix, I was desperate to take the edge off.

"Your gun?" I asked when she brought the drinks.

"I'll get it when I make the next round," she said.

"Maybe we could watch some TV," I suggested. We sat there checking the menu on her 32-inch Sony, and even though we weren't sitting next to each other, I remembered some awkward nights in high school with friends who might have been interested in me but weren't about to make a first move. And I hadn't been either, so that years later I'd still wonder about the nuances of what we had said and our body language.

"Wonderful!" Juno applauded when she found *Alien*, which was already under way. She didn't ask if I wanted to see it, and I suppose it was as good a movie as any for that evening. Given her fixed gaze and frequent gasps, I wasn't sure if Juno was rooting for Sigourney Weaver or the creature, and before I could ask her, the doorbell rang.

We shut off the TV, and Juno grabbed my arm and waved at the door. I reluctantly followed her order and went to open it as warily as if some slavering tentacled beast was about to pounce.

"I didn't expect to see *you* here," Cash Jurevicius said, grinning. "Aren't you going to invite me in?"

Startled, I turned to ask Juno what she thought but Cash bulled right by me, and I slammed the door shut and hurried after him. Was he the one? *Cash?* And he'd just come to the front door and rung the bell? How could he be so cocky?

Juno's gun wasn't in sight, and she was looking up at Cash like a graceful hostess pretending to be delighted by a surprise guest. Then she flinched as Cash drew a very small gun from his coat pocket and pointed it at her. I froze.

"Turn up the lights," Cash ordered me. "And then sit down."

I brought the rheostat up to full and edged around where he stood to join Juno on the couch. She cast me a panicky glance and flicked her head ever-so-slightly in the direction of the kitchen. Her gun was still there. I cursed myself. Why hadn't I applied for a permit the day after learning Juno had a gun? Why had I been ambivalent? Why the hell had I waited?

16

CASH sat opposite, keeping the gun aimed at us. From its diminutive size I assumed it was a .22, but it didn't look like any I'd seen at Mrs. Fennebresque's shop.

In the movies one of us would have rushed him at this point or hurled a lamp at him, jumped into the kitchen, grabbed the Glock, and blown him away, but I was too crippled now by fear, and I sensed Juno drawing in on herself. Cash was less than ten feet away from us. He could kill us. This was real. I tried not to gasp for air, but I felt a constriction in my throat, and my ears were starting to ring.

"What do you want?" Juno asked him.

"I want you to stay away from the police. You're not going to let anyone interview you. It's over. Let it go."

"Why?" Juno asked softly, her voice regaining just an edge of its usual steel.

He squinted at her. "You're kidding, aren't you? I have a gun. That's why."

"I can see that. But why have you been harassing me and Nick?"

He snorted. "To scare you into leaving! But you just weren't getting the message. I'm sick of you, sick of people like you. You've turned this department into a joke, the both of you. You, dressing like a cheap whore! And *you*!" He pointed his chin at me as dismissively as if I were a bug smeared on his windshield. "Masquerading as a scholar. Bibliographer? You're just a glorified list maker. You don't know the first thing about real scholarship."

This was not the time for me to make fun of the French criticism he swore by, or to tell him that the hypnosis story was just bait.

Cash glared at Juno. "And you don't know how to behave like a professor. Neither one of you should ever have been hired. It's an absolute disgrace. My grandmother would be revolted to see what you've done to her department. You've turned it into a zoo."

"It's not her department. It never was," Juno retorted, sitting up straighter.

Easy, I thought. Don't make him any angrier.

"Bullshit. EAR owes everything to my grandmother! She fought for more positions, a larger budget, everything. She set an example, she was a genius, everyone loved her, she was a saint."

"So threatening us, attacking us, is how you're honoring her name?" I asked quietly, trying to reason with him. I was astonished at how utterly deranged he was, and more, that he could be so hostile to me after how kind I'd been to him in the past. The recent past, in fact. So all that meant nothing. He probably loathed me even more because I'd done him a favor when he didn't deserve it. Was Cash still enraged because the Grace Jurevicius Memorial Library had been dismantled when the EAR department needed the office space?

"Don't play word games," Cash jeered, his gun wavering. We were all silent, and I was starting to feel numb. Juno took my hand, and I was glad, even though her fingers were cold. Would we die like this? Side by side? Hand in hand? No, surely not. One of us would be able to get to him, but which one? Whom did he hate more, me or Juno?

"Holding hands. That's sweet." Cash sounded as mean-spirited as Rusty Dominguez–St. John.

"Not as sweet as that pussy-ass gun," Juno snapped, her hand tightening around mine. Was she trying to send me some kind of message?

"Bitch! My grandmother left me this gun!"

"That's what you used at the campus center, isn't it?" she said mockingly. "Why? Afraid to hold a real gun?" Juno laughed, and I had a sudden image of Bette Midler in *Ruthless People* turning the tables on her inept kidnappers. But Cash wasn't stupid, he was seething. His face was blotched with red, and I wondered if Juno's tactic was to goad him into some move that she and I could turn against him. I hoped she didn't goad him into shooting us. Was I starting to dissociate? I almost felt I was watching my thoughts appear like subtitles in a film, superimposed over the scene of Cash holding us hostage—or whatever it was he was doing.

"You blame us for your not having tenure," I observed, feeling my pulse slowing down, wondering where the comment had even come from. "You think it's our fault you're on the bottom. It's the system. And what about me? I'm in the basement. And I'll never get tenure."

"You don't deserve tenure! You don't deserve a job!"

His face was so twisted with disgust that I half expected him to rave on and say I didn't deserve to live, either, but I was beginning to suspect the gun was just window dressing, or a gesture. He wanted to intimidate us, and he needed the gun.

"God, I loved going after you. After both of you." He almost laughed. If he'd had a mustache, now would have been the time to twirl one end. I thought of all those times I'd read mysteries where the villain bragged about what he's done; I'd always wondered at some level if people actually behaved like that. Obviously they did. I started to relax—a little. I bet he had no intention of harming us further, now that he'd revealed he was behind the attacks. He was having his vindictive triumph, and that was the payoff. Making us squirm while he watched. A kind of torture.

He grinned. "You're figuring it out, aren't you?" he said, as if he could read my mind. Goddamn, I was sick of people thinking my eyes were so revealing.

I said, "I'm figuring *something* out." Cash seemed bizarrely confident, and I wasn't sure why. It was more than the gun, much more—but what?

"What the hell are you talking about?" Juno asked, eyeing us with confusion, breathing heavily.

"I don't think he's serious," I said. "About the gun, I mean. It may not even be loaded tonight."

Cash shrugged. I had once thought of him as handsome, a

pouty Ryan Phillippe type, but now he struck me as hard, with the kind of brutally untouched face that would make him believable as Dorian Gray.

"There's something else, right?" I said. "You've got an ace in the hole, but I don't know what it is. That's why you're convinced Juno's going to shut up."

"Bravo. You should work as a phone psychic."

Juno was flummoxed by the way the tension had started to drain out of the room. "What the hell is going on here? Is this a practical joke?"

"No joke. I brought the gun to get your attention. To make a point. I want you to shut up about the—about the accident, and everything else that's happened to both of you."

"And tonight, too? Pretend you didn't storm in here and threaten us?"

"I rang the doorbell, you answered and let me in. That's all that happened." Now he leaned back as expansively as a fisherman about to tell the story of his greatest catch. "Let's face it, neither one of you has any credibility in the department. No one will believe you if you start to blab."

He was right. Juno's and my story was so improbable no one would believe it. As the powerful Angelo tells Isabella in *Measure for Measure*, "Say what you will, My false will o'erweigh your true."

Juno bristled. "You're just a gypsy scholar—you're nobody."

His lips twitched as if he were suppressing a grin. "Not for long."

Juno looked as suspicious as I was. I spoke first: "What are you up to? Are you in cahoots with the provost?"

Cash said smugly, "There's a new order at SUM, and I'm not going to be left out."

"Wait—what about your grandmother?" I said. "What would she say?"

I had heard Cash publicly decry EAR's academic deadwood and target Summerscale for his loathing, so how could he approve of Merry Glinka? Was it all about shame? Because he'd been scorned in a department that his grandmother had put her stamp on, had seen her legacy damaged, he was now intriguing to rise above that? I felt slightly nauseous at what he might do if he got any power in his hands; I couldn't imagine he would be a gracious victor.

Cash didn't answer my question—how could he? But he seemed to be boiling over with mischief and contempt. "I've been talking to the provost about a plan to create a special assistant for diversity affairs." He looked delighted.

Juno guffawed. "You? You're a white male!"

"And part Ojibway and part Mexican. A long time ago, and a very small part of each, but it'll look great on paper. And she wants to use my grandmother's name—it still means a lot around here."

"You're making this up," I said, feeling sure that he wasn't.

"So," Cash said, standing. "I'd like you to stay where you are while I let myself out, and remember, there's nothing to connect me to what's been going on—I've made sure of that—and I don't think either of you was smart enough to be hooked up with a tape recorder."

I thought he might back away from us and turn as he left, but he was so confident he strutted to the front door. I glanced at Juno who sat looking slumped and defeated. And I couldn't stand that Cash was getting away with no punishment at all—for shooting at Juno, beating me up, smashing her car—all of it. Feeling that burst of energy I sometimes got in the pool when I pushed myself to take one more lap and suddenly felt unimaginably stronger and did two, then three extra laps, I rushed from the couch and slammed Cash forward against the front door. I grabbed his left arm, yanked it back, and pulled it up between his shoulders, wanting to break him apart. I heard him drop the gun, and Juno shouted, "No!"

His face mashed against the door, he could hardly breathe, but he spit out, "Let me go, faggot."

I ground him into the door, wanted to crush him. I'd never felt such a blast of hatred and power before. I pulled on his arm, and he yelped. Good. He was every bully I'd ever known, and he was in pain. His cologne was mixed with something acrid I took to be fear. I pulled harder, thinking of Avis, Valley, Serena, Rusty.

"Stop it!" Juno cried, surging up behind me, starting to pound on my back. "Are you crazy?"

When I turned to elude her blows, Cash slipped away, scooped up the gun with his good arm and pocketed it, and yanked open the door. His face was bright red, and blood trickled down from each nostril. "You're dead at SUM," he said. "Dead." He hurried down the driveway to—of course—a black SUV.

Juno closed the door and icily asked, "Are you fucking out of your mind? He could have shot you."

"I wasn't thinking about that."

"You should have."

"You're all show," I said, feeling almost betrayed. "You brag about a gun, but you leave it in another room? You plan a trap, but you don't execute it? You talk about revenge, but you wimp out?"

"There was nothing we could do."

"We could have beaten the living shit out of him and taken the consequences. We could have claimed burglary, or attempted rape or assault—or something. A good lawyer would have gotten us off. Now it's too late." My breath was still coming fast, and I could feel heat in my arms and chest as if I had actually been swimming. I was all macho'd, up with no place to go.

Juno said, "I need another drink. I need a million drinks."

"Fine. Drown in them. I'm sick of your games."

Disgusted, I got the hell out of there, but I had no illusion this was the end for me and Juno.

I drove home with the windows cracked open, hoping that the stinging night air would calm me down. But it didn't. Despite my explosion, or maybe because of it, I felt exhilarated by having for a few moments, at least, proved to Cash and myself that I wasn't powerless and weak. I didn't regret attacking him; if anything, I wish I'd had a chance to work him over, to pay him back even more for tormenting Juno and me—and bragging about getting away with it.

I had heard him inveigh against the abuses of power at SUM, and here he was doing exactly the same thing. Selling his name, abandoning his principles, to establish himself higher up on the dung heap—and silencing me and Juno. It was revolting. He claimed to care about people and tradition, and he was ready to throw that all aside to become one of the pseudo-elite.

I kept seeing him helpless against the door, writhing as I twisted his arm. It was an amazing rush. I felt as invulnerable as if I were drunk. Cash had threatened me, said I was finished at SUM, but what could he do now? Have me fired perhaps, but so fucking what? Sue me for assault? I'd tell my wild story in court, and we'd both go down in flames.

Cash was a scab I had picked off, but Juno, she was a deep wound. I felt sundered from her, angry, contemptuous. She had been revving me up with her fulminations, but she was nothing more than a paper tiger.

Paper leopard?

The first thing Stefan said to me when I walked into the kitchen, where he was reading a copy of *Poets and Writers,* was, "Your phone was off. I tried calling you."

I took off my jacket and draped it on a chair, asked if the coffee he had made was decaf, and poured myself a cup when he said it was.

"I guess I forgot to turn it on."

"What did you buy?"

"Uh . . . nothing."

He nodded, and gave me a searching look I couldn't evade. I sat across from him at the island and without a prologue told him everything about the evening. By the end of my narrative, I felt as sweaty and dazed as if I had been puking my guts out in college after a Friday-night binge.

Stefan had heard some wild stories from me in the past, but this was for sure the wildest, and he stiffened several times during my story like a tied-up prisoner anticipating a blow. Then he closed his eyes and rested his hands on his knees, looking as serene and otherworldly as a seated Egyptian tomb effigy.

If I had expected anything from him, it wasn't silence. I waited. He sat. I finished my coffee, hearing the kitchen clock tick and the refrigerator hum, wondering if he had decided to give me the silent treatment or if he were so shocked and appalled he couldn't speak.

"I forgive you," he said, finally, softly. "What you did tonight was stupid, and dangerous, and you could have been killed. But you weren't." He sighed deeply. "You weren't." He shook his head in quiet amazement. "You weren't."

"And how was your evening?" I asked.

He reared back the way you would if a bee had flown at your face. "You really think now's a time to joke? What would have happened if you'd already owned a gun? I bet you would have brought it with you, and you could have shot Cash. You could have killed him."

"Wait—"

"No, *you* wait. You could have killed him. You could have ended up facing a murder trial. Your life would be over even if you got off for self-defense. I'm not talking about the publicity, about being known as a killer, I'm talking about *living* with it, living with having taken his life."

"You're exaggerating. I just roughed him up."

"That's exactly my point. You're not a thug. You didn't used to be. But you attacked him. So what's next?"

"And you're telling me you wouldn't have done the same thing?"

"Well, to start with, I wouldn't have been playing cops and robbers with Juno Dromgoole, so it wouldn't have happened. The woman's a hysteric. No, that doesn't even cover it. It's like calling St. Peter's a church. Juno is the mother of all hysterics, and she's been making you a little crazy, too."

Well, that was true in more ways than Stefan realized and than I was willing to discuss. Even now, here, as angry as I was with Juno, I still thought she was hot, and I wanted to nail her. Being angry might have made me want her more; how screwed up was that?

So it was my turn to be quiet. I went to the fridge, found the bottle of sweet-and-sour mix, bustled around the kitchen assembling the ingredients for sidecars, and poured them into the Deco silver cocktail shaker Sharon had given me. It felt very satisfying to shake it up and down, to make some noise, to be distracted by the quotidian.

"If I'm going to be lectured," I said, pouring out a drink for myself, "I need something better than coffee."

"You think this is a lecture? It's a warning."

I thought of the moment in *Death Becomes Her* when Meryl Streep downs a magic potion, then is informed that there's a catch to it and cries out, "*Now* a warning?" but I wisely kept it to myself. Stefan wasn't in the mood for clever quotations. I sat back at the counter, but pulled my stool a little farther away. I held out the shaker, offering to pour a drink for Stefan, but he declined.

"I don't know why you've gone over the edge," he said. "Maybe it's to compensate for how murky your career's been at SUM, or the Wharton conference turning into *Halloween*, or midlife crisis, or something. But this gun stuff, this playacting with Juno, it's got to stop. It's ludicrous and deadly."

"That's not what you said before, not exactly."

"Because you weren't acting like Agatha Christie in heat before. You weren't making up freaky stories to lure someone into threatening you—and maybe worse. You weren't beating people up."

"I didn't beat Cash up. I knocked him against the door, I twisted his arm." Put that way, it seemed completely unremarkable and uncommendable, a minor tussle at a bar, and I almost wanted to reverse myself and brag a little: "Yeah, dude, I jacked him up—you shoulda seen that bitch squeal."

"Don't mince words."

"You'd rather have me dice them?"

"Stop it!" Stefan slammed his mug down on the granite, and it cracked in several pieces, a tiny bit of coffee spilling out around them. Stefan shook off his hand, grabbed for the paper towel stand, and ripped off several sheets, wiping and sweeping with the angry economy of a losing gambler fiercely throwing his dice. I didn't offer to help.

"Just stop it, okay?" Stefan said when he had pitched the mess into the garbage. He stood with his back against the sink. "You know what makes me sick? It's not your palling around with that fruitcake Juno, or flirting with disaster, it's how much you enjoyed the whole thing. You were trying to sound chastened, but you were smirking like George Bush. You're proud of yourself, aren't you?"

"Why shouldn't I be? I helped expose who's been harassing us, so now Cash is going to stop—he has to."

"But you made another enemy."

"Come on, Stefan, weren't you listening to what I told you? Cash hated me already. I'm a one-man fucking *Decline of the West* to him. Nothing would ever change that. And my future here is so indefinite anyway, who the fuck cares?"

"I do! I care, and I'm not talking about tenure or a job. You want to risk your life? That's what you want? Then go rock climbing or bungee jumping or swim in Australia and dare the sharks to get you!"

I shuddered a little. Stefan knows that *Jaws* is one of my least favorite movies in the world because its horror is so much more real than *Scream* or *The Exorcist* or *Little Women*.

"Nick, I do not want you running around like this anymore."

"Oh, am I getting a curfew, Dad?"

"That is a stupid and insulting thing to say."

"Then don't talk to me like I'm a teenager. You can't forbid me to do something I want to do."

Our voices were growing louder, and I could see the evening turning bitter with all the helpless fascination of watching a train slip from the tracks and plunge off a vertiginous cliff into a gorge far below. And I felt that surge of recklessness when you know you're going to build toward a crescendo of accusations that are hard to take back, maybe even impossible, yet I wasn't ready to retreat. Luckily I didn't have to, because Stefan surprised me again.

"That's right," he said. "I can't make you stop. I think the only thing I *can* do is lie down in the driveway when you try to pull out your car." He smiled, and when I didn't respond similarly, he said, "I was trying to make a joke."

"It did have some vaguely jokelike features," I admitted, and we both shrugged our way out of the tension. It was that simple, but perhaps only because we knew each other so well after fifteen years. We could disengage without shame, without negotiating a truce, without UN observers.

"You're sure you don't want a sidecar?" I asked.

"Why not?"

I made some more, and we moved to the living room, where Stefan had built a small fire while I was gone, since we had a frost warning for overnight. Up till now we'd had a surprisingly mild winter, but the snow was finally on its way from Canada or Minnesota or wherever it had been ravaging the countryside and tormenting the citizenry.

"So what was it like?" Stefan asked after finishing his first sidecar.

"Slamming into Cash?" The images came back, and there was something off-kilter about the memory, but I couldn't identify what bugged me. Maybe I was just wrung out. "It was sweet, as my students would say. I never fought anybody as a kid."

He nodded in anticipation, waiting for me to dilate on that theme, and I did. I told him how, always fast-tongued, I had preferred to wiggle out of tight situations with a joke that would make my opponent either laugh and unhook, or look stupid so that the other kids would laugh and the guy wanting to throttle or hit me would give up. The latter result was riskier, since it could goad someone to more violence, but the strategy had worked until junior high, when a humorless blockhead, new to our neighborhood, had dared me to say something smart, having heard I was a real mouth. I told him I couldn't think of anything, and he punched me, considering my admission enough of a wisecrack to deserve punishment.

Stefan asked almost rhetorically, "Do you think we'll ever get over the past? It's like quicksand, you never know when you'll be sucked under and drown in it. Here you are, over forty, and going ballistic because of something that happened in junior high school."

"It's more complicated than that, and besides, Cash pushed me to it."

Stefan grinned and quoted the bizarre line we'd heard growing up that was supposed to make us avoid peer pressure and turn the other cheek. "Would you jump off the Brooklyn Bridge if he told you to?"

"Of course not, I'd ask him to go first to show me how to do it right. Okay, now. This question is for real: how was your coffee klatch with Peter De Jonge? What did you guys talk about?"

"You, mostly."

"You're kidding."

"No. He was really curious about the way you've been involved with crimes on campus. Sounds like he's read about them, studied the newspapers. He asked a lot of questions. He sounded impressed, and he wants to talk to you sometime."

"Is he writing a book or something?"

Stefan shrugged. "Doubtful. Maybe he's just a crime buff."

"But that has nothing to do with his research. Didn't it strike you as creepy?"

"No. If it had, I wouldn't have talked about you. Hey, it was all complimentary what he said. So what's the problem?"

I probably had no cause for suspicion, but Stefan's calm question somehow made me angry again, at Cash, at Juno, at myself and the whole perverted university system. SUM was as unjust and autocratic as any medieval duchy waging war on its neighbors with foreign mercenaries while torturing its own people for heresy. And look what it turned us all into. Liars, blowhards, criminals—and paranoids.

"People find you fascinating," Stefan said. "It's not just your students."

"The Typhoid Mary syndrome."

"No, it's like Hitchcock, somebody ordinary getting involved in a tangle beyond the world they've always lived in."

"I'm ordinary?"

I wished that were true, but we toasted to it anyway. "What's gotten you so peppy today?"

"I woke up and looked at you and realized you're alive, almost despite yourself."

"I think there's a loving remark in there somewhere," I said.

"Dig deep."

I took the plates to the dishwasher and, loading them in, said,

"It bothers me that after everything I've seen at SUM and in our department, I expect people to behave better."

"Better? I expect worse."

"Well, what would be worse? Cannibalism?"

Soberly, Stefan said, "Cash is worse. He's felt oppressed and victimized so long he doesn't know what he's doing. He's not thinking clearly—"

"That's an understatement."

Stefan nodded. "And he's just grabbing for power, from what you say. He'll end up regretting it."

"Regret isn't enough. I hope he suffers. Remember that Talking Heads song?" I tried singing the first line of "Burning Down the House"—"Watch out, you might get what you're after"—but Stefan stopped me with a mock karate chop aimed at my chest.

"Stick to bibliographies," he said. "And they'll stick to you."

"That's my problem. One of many. I'm a bibliographer. I can't get no respect. I should start a support group."

"So are you and Juno planning any other fun activities this week? You could always join the war on drugs, or fight international terrorism if you have some spare time. I wish I understood your fascination with her," Stefan said lightly, heading off to his study.

No, you don't, I thought. No, you don't.

The next day, I called the Records Department at the station where I'd applied for my permit, and was told it had been approved. Even though I knew I had no criminal record, I was relieved that some computer hacker hadn't turned me into an Interpol-sought terrorist.

I headed over. The Records office was blindingly bright: supernova neon lights blaring down on white walls, floor, and counters, with everything in sight looking as if it had been delivered and unpacked scant hours before. Even the youngish female clerk behind the glass partition looked as flawlessly turned out as if it were her first day at a new job she wanted to keep. She slid me the four-part pea-green permit form, checked my driver's license, explained where to sign and how many days I had to purchase the gun and how to proceed once I bought it. Then she notarized the form, and I was off, wondering again at how easy this all was. No second test, no counseling, no instructional video to watch.

As I drove up to the mini-mall where Mrs. Fennebresque had her gun shop, a 400-pound man in a white T-shirt and mammoth overalls came rolling out of her shop. He was bald and red-faced and looked every square inch a Bubba. I watched him surge toward a pickup truck with—what else?—a stars-and-bars decal and heave himself inside before I ventured from the car.

Mrs. Fennebresque seemed even more out of place than usual in her red-and-green tartan suit and red reindeer-print turtleneck sweater. She should have been gift wrapping presents for charity somewhere, or staffing a holiday bake sale, not selling firearms. Her store was ablaze with Christmas decorations. She'd strung flashing lights along the counters and around the door frames, plopped little plastic trees on every available surface, hung stylized snowflakes and angel mobiles from the ceiling. The sound system was playing Perry Como Christmas songs.

"Well, hello, stranger," she trilled sweetly. "Where's that pretty young lady friend of yours?"

Juno would have snorted at the appellation, enjoying and dismissing it both. When I didn't answer, Mrs. Fennebresque's shiny face softened, and she nodded sympathetically. "Lover's quarrel. It happens to everyone." In the momentary silence I steeled myself for a barrage of romantic advice. But Mrs. Fennebresque was a merchant, after all, and she said "Here to buy that gun?" as if I were about to purchase an engagement ring.

I nodded and handed her the permit, leaned on the counter. She brought out the .22 I'd looked at before, and we discussed ammunition, the best local firing range, private instruction, gun safety, all of it happening with such a sense of unreality I could have been paralyzed in a hospital bed watching myself be attended to. I felt both helpless and remote.

I thought of Stefan's warning. I had never responded to anyone as I had to Cash. Stefan was right to ask what would have happened if I'd had a gun.

"Now, tell me something—are you sure you're ready for this?" Mrs. Fennebresque said, bringing me out of my fog.

"No, I'm not sure."

She patted my hand, and if she were taller, she might have reached over to pinch one of my cheeks. "Your permit's good for ten days," she said. "Why not think about it some more?"

"Okay."

"And have a Merry Christmas!"

I plunged back into the cold, wondering if she were at all concerned about the fight she imagined I'd had with Juno and wanted us to cool off without a gun in the mix. But would that kind of concern even register with her?

As I used the remote door opener, Mrs. Fennebresque came bustling out of the store. "You forgot your permit," she said. "Are you sure you're all right?"

I nodded and took the form from her, and she hurried back into her store, hugging herself against the cold. I drove home, not knowing whether I should feel relieved or annoyed at myself or anything particular. I knew that Stefan would be pleased I hadn't bought a gun the day after roughing up Cash, hadn't bought a gun at all. But did that make him right or me wrong?

Stefan had gone to the gym and left me a message, so I had the house to myself—not exactly a welcome prospect, since I felt somewhat exposed. Was this whole gun thing completely quixotic, or was it realistic and important? And why didn't I know? I drifted through the house as if I were a weekend guest, curiously examining pictures and books and views. I should have been grading papers and preparing for the end of the semester, but my contretemps with Juno and Cash, and my abortive attempt to buy a gun, left me feeling too unsettled. A swim would have helped, but snow was starting to come down heavily, and I didn't feel like venturing out into it.

I made extra-strong hot cocoa, spiked it with rum, and built a fire instead, glad that we had stacked so much wood from out back in the garage. It would catch with no problem.

I sat in the living room, starting to unwind as the logs smoked, crackled, and then glittered with flame. Was there anything more quintessentially human than sitting and watching a fire? The only thing I could picture was staring at waves smacking a shoreline.

A few years before, when I had mistakenly thought my relationship with Stefan was in danger, I had sat up late one night, staring into the fire, recalling how Isabel Archer in *The Portrait of a Lady* stayed up late in her Roman palace, taking stock, reflecting on the ways in which a life and marriage that had seemed open and free had shrunk so horribly that she felt trapped in "the house of dumbness, the house of deafness, the house of suffocation."

It had felt like a turning point, and perhaps it was. I had lost some illusions about Stefan, which was probably a good thing, though at the time I had felt bereft. And where was I now? Our relationship was strong, Sharon had survived her surgery, Stefan had a film deal in the making that might revive his writing career, and what did I have? A job in a department that for the most part loathed me, a department where my friends were either absent (Lucille) or crazed (Juno). And for the first time in my adult life I had used force on someone else—and enjoyed it. I didn't think I'd ever stop enjoying it. Feeling my bruised cheek, I wondered what was next. I couldn't just wait for something to happen, I had to make it happen.

Maybe my parents had been right all along. Maybe I should have gone into publishing. It wasn't too late to get to know my father's business. I might even be able to help Stefan down the road, make useful contacts. But it felt like giving in and giving up.

When the doorbell rang, I was so grateful for the interruption I would have put up with even a pair of Mormons. After the previous night, though, I checked carefully before opening the door—to find Peter De Jonge.

"They said you were at home."

"They were right. Come on in."

He studiously stamped his feet on the welcome mat and shook snow off his FuBu parka. He spotted the fire and smiled, and I took his coat from him, hung it on the rack, and waved him into the living room. He sauntered over as if he were trying for a gang-banger's strut. The oversize clothes, short hair, and sideburns helped, but he would never have been mistaken for Detroit's white rapper Eminem. He was too handsome, for one, and probably too smart.

"Can I get you anything?"

He shook his head and sat down in the chair closest to the fire. "It's a weird time in EAR," he began, puzzling me, since I'd thought he wanted to talk to me about being involved with crime at the university.

"It's always weird."

He hesitated. "Dr. Borowski, Stefan, told me how good you are at figuring things out."

Right.

"And there's something going on back home, down in Neptune."

"What?"

"I can't say. I don't really know."

"But you have suspicions, don't you?"

"Yes."

"And you won't say?"

"If I told you, you wouldn't believe it. I don't want to prejudice you."

"How?"

He evaded that question. "I'm asking you to come down to Neptune and investigate. I'd pay. My wife's family is rich."

"They don't know you're Jewish?"

"No one does."

"Kids?" I asked.

He nodded. "One boy."

"And they don't know either? Is this connected?"

"I want you to investigate."

"Investigate what—investigate whom?"

"You'll know when you get there."

"But why don't you hire a private investigator?"

"Because I don't think I could trust anyone I hired down there, and I think you'd be able to ferret things out without anyone being suspicious. I also know some of what's been happening to you and Juno."

"All that's over."

"No, it's not. I've been following people around, here and in Neptune. There's a lot more going on than you think. The Diversity Tree? Whiteness Studies? The provost's ambassadors? Don't you think all of that is suspicious?" he said with a faint challenge in his tone.

I knew he wouldn't bleat out the specifics even if I squeezed him like a doggy toy, so I just waited.

"I think it's all connected. And I think I know who beat you up at Parker Hall."

"Well, so do I." And as I was about to trump him by blurting out Cash's name, suddenly it hit me that when I was crushing Cash into Juno's door, his cologne had smelled completely unlike what I'd smelled in Parker Hall, something much crisper, fruitier. It must have been someone else.

I could tell from his expression that he'd watched my confidence fade. "You really think you know who did it?" I asked.

He nodded, eyes unblinking. "It's not someone from EAR," was all he would say.

That meant I was still in danger, and it might also mean Juno was, too. Cash might have had an accomplice. Even though I was still pissed off at Juno, I wanted her to be safe. I breathed out. "Okay. You want to hire me to investigate someone or something. You won't say what or who or why—or anything else. And you think there's somebody still out there who's after me? And you'll tell me who it is if I take on this—this job for you?"

He sat there expectantly, not quite a supplicant, but not Joan of Arc urging her king to be crowned at Rheims, either. What he was suggesting was so vague it couldn't even be classed as crazy.

I did the only thing I could do. I said yes.